DEFINITELY DEAD

KATE BENDELOW

BLOODHOUND
— BOOKS —

Print ISBN 978-1-913942-57-1

To Mum,

This one is for you. With thanks for everything, especially the gift of sarcasm and for always finding sun-cream phalluses funny.

I love you

1

D ead body...
      Dead body...
Dead body...

Maya Barton repeated the words like a mantra. Her bowels churned at the thought of the corpse she was about to see. Her clammy hands gripped the steering wheel of the police SOCO van as she manoeuvred her way through the council estate. Normally, the hostile stares from locals would have rankled her, but today she was far too preoccupied to even care.

Maya had arrived for her afternoon shift at 2pm and been asked to make her way over to the crime scene on the Poets Estate. It was notorious for being one of the more dilapidated, deprived areas of the city. Her colleague, Chris Makin, was already in attendance following the report of a sudden death. This was police terminology for an unexpected, unexplained death of someone with no obvious medical issues. In such cases the death would initially be treated as suspicious until the investigation proved otherwise.

The senior crime-scene investigator, Kym Lawson, had assured Maya it would be good experience for her to help with her first body recovery. As much as Maya had been longing for the experience, she was becoming familiar with the adage 'careful what you wish for'. She was normally level-headed and not easily fazed, but the lack of information and not knowing what to expect was unnerving her.

Her heart was racing, her senses heightened. Her tongue stuck to the roof of her dry mouth. Maya's trepidation peaked as the tinny voice of the satnav instructed her to turn next left and then she would reach her destination. The dead man's house.

She arrived at Keats Road, and parked up on a well-worn grass verge. She could see two liveried police vehicles, another SOCO van and two plain cars, which she recognised as belonging to the CID. Maya was aware of being stared at by a pyjama-clad, heavyset woman who lolled over a garden gate, cigarette in hand.

'What's happening then? Is the dirty bastard really dead?' the woman called as Maya stepped out of the van.

'Sorry, not in a position to say. You'll be updated in due course,' Maya replied.

'I told him I'd seen him eyeing our Toyah and her friends in their school uniform.' Maya started to walk away but the woman continued undeterred, 'Toyah saw him playing with himself at the window when they were walking past. Dirty bastard. I reported it, but nothing happened. Waste of time you lot.' Sneering, she hocked a globule of spit on the pavement.

SOCO, Chris Makin, appeared. He was dressed in a full scene suit with a face mask slung around his neck. Beads of sweat gathered like a garland above his thickset eyebrows. He had the physique of a man with a voracious appetite and this made him appear older than his late forties. He was clearly exerted; puffing and blowing in the summer heat and the added discomfort of having his bulk ensconced in a white scene suit and mask.

'Come on, Maya, never mind nattering, it's not a social gathering,' he snapped impatiently. 'Get your arse suited up. The post-mortem has already been scheduled so we need to finish up and get him to the mortuary.' Maya attempted to speak but he cut her off.

'CID are already underway with house-to-house enquiries. DI Mitton is dealing with a shooting from overnight, so she probably isn't going to make it. Instead, I've got DI Redford showing an interest.' He shook his head disparagingly before continuing. 'He's not bothered enough to come down here and get his lovely Italian leather shoes dirty. Oh no, as usual he and Kym are mithering for an update every bleedin' minute.'

He swiped a forearm across his sweating forehead. Maya attempted to speak again, but Chris interjected, 'Do they never stop to think that if I'm all wrapped up in a scene suit, I can't just get my sodding phone out? I'm sweating like a bastard, missed me lunch *and* I've got a ton of statements to write back at the nick. I don't need this shit!'

He stomped off before Maya had a chance to respond. Muttering with indignation, she made her way to the back of the van and began to suit up. She slung a mask over her neck and gathered her thick, corkscrew curls into a topknot before securing it under a hair net. She moved to the driver's window so she could see her reflection and ensure that any loose strands of hair were carefully tucked away.

She heard the watching woman chortle before she shouted to Maya, 'Don't know what you're preening yourself for, love – you look a right state in that get-up.'

'Bit rich coming from someone who should have got changed six hours ago. It's called nightwear for a reason, *love*.' Maya stalked towards the crime-scene tape with as much dignity as she could muster on shaking legs, dressed in a paper suit and matching overshoes which scuffed the floor.

The scene was an end terrace. Piles of detritus littered the semi-paved garden. What little greenery there was, had long since gone to seed and a few half-hearted wildflowers cast an optimistic kaleidoscope of colour amongst split bin bags. A myriad of takeaway cartons, vodka bottles and beer cans lay scorching in the heat. The yellow-and-black crime-scene tape was secured to the crumbling gatepost and was being maintained by a bored-looking police officer.

Maya introduced herself and wrote her details into the crime-scene log which the officer was holding. It diarised the attendance of anyone who entered the crime scene, recording who they were, their reasons for attending and confirmation that their fingerprints and DNA were held on file for elimination purposes. She then waited for Chris to finish his hushed phone call so she could receive further instructions.

'Right, Maya, that was Kym *again*. She's only just decided to tell me that this is your first body. Sorry, love, I didn't know. I thought because you'd come to us from Alder Street you had experience.'

'I was a volume crime-scene investigator there. I've worked on plenty of burglaries and vehicle crime and shadowed at a few cannabis farms, rapes and robberies, but never had a death.'

'Did they not give you any experience at uni?'

'I didn't go. I studied photography and biology for the job. I worked at a car dealership before that, so completely different background.'

'Sorry, I vaguely remember Kym telling me, now you mention it. Well, you never forget your first body. Feeling okay?'

Maya nodded eagerly, despite the trepidation she felt. Chris continued, 'We think he's been in there for a few days and *is* starting to smell, but to be fair, not as bad as the rest of the house. I'll do as much of the hands-on stuff as I can, and you take over the photographs. You okay with that?'

'Yeah, sure.'

'Let me know if you're not. I don't want you puking or fainting. I've put stepping plates down already, so stay on them and don't move anything for now.' Chris swiped at his forehead again.

'Doctor Granger is our pathologist. He's in the back making some notes and wanting everything done yesterday. He's a cantankerous old bastard, but if you mind your Ps and Qs and act interested, he'll tolerate you. Get yourself in. I just need to grab a body sheet and a body bag out of the van.'

The police officer gave Maya an encouraging wink as she adjusted her face mask before ducking under the police tape. As she approached the front door of the property, she understood what Chris meant about the smell. The stench from the heaps of rubbish wasting in the sun were nothing compared to the smell of cigarette smoke, sweat and general grubbiness that engulfed her as she nudged the front door open.

A tatty-looking high-visibility coat was slung over the banister. Years of cigarette smoke had turned the wallpaper into a curious caramel colour and burnished the thickened cobwebs which strung across the cornice. She eyed the dank-looking stairway; the thought of what she would see lying in the bedroom made her shiver, despite the sweltering summer heat. The first door to her right led to what appeared to be some sort of junk room. There was a clapped-out trail bike propped against the door frame, which looked like it was being stripped for parts. As a keen biker, it would normally pique her interest, but today Maya was too preoccupied for it to barely resonate.

Taking deep, calming breaths, she proceeded on trembling legs across the metal stepping plates. She stopped to peer through the second door on the right, which led to a sitting room. It was dimly lit with thick, heavyset curtains pulled across the bay window. Tendrils of sunlight stretched across the ceiling through gaps caused by missing curtain hooks. In the shafts of light dust motes shimmered like glitter. She could make out a maroon couch and a cluttered coffee table with house keys, mobile phone and a wallet nestled against an overflowing ashtray.

The only neat thing in the room was the pile of porn magazines which were proudly stacked on the arm of the couch. There was also an old, boxy-looking TV, which towered on a feeble-looking glass stand, a DVD player and a stash of adult films. Cardboard boxes propped the back wall up; spewing what appeared to be bits of tools and mechanical paraphernalia.

Not wanting to venture further into the room in case she disturbed anything, she continued cautiously up the hall. The door leading to the kitchen was closed. Through the nicotine-stained, mottled glass in the top panel, Maya could vaguely make out the shape of Doctor Granger sitting at the kitchen table. Reluctant to interrupt him, she announced herself with a subtle cough.

'Hello, Doctor Granger, I'm SOCO Maya Barton.' She paused long enough to invite a reply before continuing, 'I've come to help Chris with the body recovery.'

Granger didn't reply and Maya found herself dithering uncertainly at the doorway, wondering whether she was expected to just enter or wait. She was wary of getting on the wrong side of the pathologist after Chris's warning. She certainly didn't want to disturb him and interrupt his train of thought; yet at the same time her nerves were making her impatient.

Maya was reluctant to head upstairs and look at the body on her own. She would rather be with Chris or Doctor Granger, because if truth be known, she wasn't sure *how* she was going to react once she saw it. She wondered how decomposed it would be and how much it would smell. She desperately hoped she wouldn't make a show of herself by being sick or panicking.

She had been dispatched to the scene so quickly she hadn't had time to ask any questions about the body. She didn't know the condition it was in or the nature of any injuries. Nobody had told her who had found him or even how old he was; although judging from what she had seen of the house so far, he wasn't young. She had no idea what to expect and the burgeoning anticipation was making her heart race. Maya tapped on the thick glass door panel.

'Can I come in?' She knew she sounded terse despite her best efforts.

Irritated by the continued lack of response, Maya manoeuvred herself decisively over a stepping plate and pushed the door open. The kitchen was even more dishevelled than the other rooms and the smell hit her like a slap. The bin was overflowing, and it appeared that rather than emptying it, the occupant had just continued to throw rubbish in its general direction.

The stained work surfaces were barely visible due to the filthy crockery, beer cans and crumpled-up super-strength cider bottles. The sink was overflowing and appeared to have been used as a bin judging by the empty milk bottles and tea bags which were piled on top of dirty crockery and glasses. Plump bluebottles ricocheted off the window, imprisoned behind a mouldy net curtain, the colour of earwax.

Maya gagged at the intense smell of rotting food, sour milk and decay. She had never experienced anything like the squalor that surrounded her. The dirt and debris of the place was astonishing. Mouse droppings peppered the torn linoleum and she shuddered at the sight; she had a phobia of rodents. The FFP3 face mask did nothing to minimise the cloying stench. The smell was so thick she could almost taste it. She found it inconceivable that someone could live like this.

She turned to speak to Doctor Granger, wondering how he could sit so calmly in such a rancid environment. The words caught in her throat, strangled by shock, as she realised that the mottled glass panel had disguised the fact it wasn't the pathologist sitting at the table after all.

It was the dead man.

2

M aya took a sharp intake of breath as, wide-eyed, she processed the scene. The dead man was hunched forward, his head resting on the table, half his face lying in a pool of congealed blood. The other half of his face revealed a partially open eye, which was staring vacantly in her general direction. His mouth was slightly open and frozen in a gormless expression. A thick string of jellied mucous hung from his nose.

His arms appeared folded on his lap underneath the table. Lividity had caused his skin to turn a greyish-purple colour. Maya knew this occurred once blood stopped circulating around the body, causing it to gravitate to the lowest point. She was surprised at the almost sinister appearance of the staining. To her untrained eye it looked like heavy bruising. Despite her current lack of experience, she was left in no doubt that this man was definitely dead.

Completely stunned, she managed not to cry out or recoil. Instead, she stood frozen. Fascinated as much as horrified. The sudden sound of footsteps clanging across the stepping plates alerted her to the fact that Chris had returned. Relieved, Maya turned to face him but was distracted by a movement near the back door. Someone was about to walk in. Her nerves were so frayed by now, she let out a small scream as a man emerged through the open back door. He was clad in a full scene suit and carrying an all-weather writer stuffed with handwritten notes.

'Maya, what's wrong?' Chris rushed to her side.

'Nothing. Well, I mean... it's just... I said hello and asked if I could come in... the man at the table... but he wasn't Doctor Granger...' She took a sharp intake of breath. 'I mean... him... the body... I assumed *that* was upstairs... but he's not... he's here. And he's dead. Definitely, *definitely* dead. Jesus Christ!'

'For the love of God, Makin. Is she being deliberately obtuse?' Granger sneered.

'No, she's not. Maya hasn't been with us very long and this is her first body. It would appear she's not known the full circumstances and it seems she's had quite a shock.' Chris placed a protective hand on Maya's shoulder.

'I've neither the time nor the inclination to listen to excuses. Can you just get him shifted onto a body sheet so I can have a proper look at him? I'm just going to my car to make a phone call. Shout me when you're ready and try not to take all bloody day.'

Maya let out a sigh of relief when he left. She had been determined to make a good impression at her first death and had already managed to make a complete fool of herself.

'I am so sorry, Chris. I was convinced for some reason the body was upstairs. It's probably because the last job I heard about was the one Kym dealt with. The overdose found naked on the bedroom floor?' Maya groaned with embarrassment. 'Then when you said Doctor Granger was out the back, I just assumed it was him sat at the table. I couldn't see properly through the glass panel.'

'Don't worry about it. Everyone makes mistakes. Learn from it, get over it and never make assumptions. If you don't know something, then ask. Are you all right?' Maya was grateful for his concern and understanding.

'Yes thanks. I feel like a total idiot, but other than that I'm fine.' She gave a strangled laugh.

'Good. Right. Let's focus. Everything has been photographed up to now and I've taken tape lifts and swabs from exposed areas of his face, neck and hands.' Chris motioned to indicate the areas. 'Help me spread this body sheet out and we can get him laid down.'

'Who is he?' Maya said as they wrestled the plastic sheeting across the floor.

'This is Karl Gorman, sixty-five. A convicted rapist with a penchant for teenage girls. He's also a renowned thief, he'd steal the steam off your piss if he could.'

Maya snorted with disgust. 'He doesn't sound like any great loss to society.'

'Nah. He's a well-known pisshead. I reckon he's spent more time in Beech Field nick than I have. Recently we've had intelligence to suggest he's been the errand boy for one of our local gangsters, Aiden Donnelly.'

Maya nodded. 'I've heard of Donnelly. So, who found him?'

'A fellow barfly. Apparently, he'd not seen Gorman for a few days and called round on the scrounge. Both the front and back door were closed, but not locked. He's not got any medical issues that we know of. Our main area of concern is that last week he was involved in a fight outside the Black Swan.'

'Who with?'

'We don't know yet. CID are still making enquiries. What we need to ascertain is whether his death is a result of that fight, or if anyone's been back here to finish him off. Word has got around recently that he's on the sex offenders' register, which will muddy the motive waters. That *and* his recent dealings with Donnelly means he could have upset someone.'

'And from the conversation I've just had outside, it sounds like there's no love lost between him and the neighbours either.'

'Exactly. There's not gonna be a queue outside the crematorium for this one.' Chris straightened up and patted the corpse on the back.

Maya surveyed the scene of the dishevelled kitchen. Surrounding Gorman on the table was an empty glass, overflowing ashtray, a tea towel, cigarette packet and a vodka bottle, which was nearly full.

'Has Doctor Granger been able to give a time of death?' Maya asked.

'Only an estimation. An exact time isn't something pathologists will commit to. There are so many variables affecting the stages of death, such as rigor mortis, that it's not an exact science.' Chris took another swipe at his sweating brow with his forearm.

'So, what's his estimation?'

'Up to four days, which ties in with when witnesses claim they last saw him. Temperature has a big impact on stages of death. Because it's been so hot lately, rigor has probably worn off quicker than it would have if he'd died in winter. Plus, he's a bit of a skinny runt, so that will also affect the process more than if he was a bit on the cuddly side like me.' Chris winked as he jutted his stomach out.

'Right, enough of the science lesson. I'll lift him from under the arms, you get ready to move the chair out of the way and shift his legs.'

Chris grasped Gorman under the arms, grunting as he heaved him out of the chair and manoeuvred him onto the body sheet. Maya pulled chair out of the way and centred Gorman's legs by reaching for the back of his calves and positioned them on the sheet. The legs felt heavy and unyielding but were moveable and not the rigid stiffness she would otherwise have expected. The body made a gurgling sound as it shifted, and a foul stench hit Maya as she remained crouched over Karl Gorman.

'Eugh, it smells like he's shit himself. Sorry you got the arse end.' Chris took a step back.

Maya surveyed Gorman in his supine position. He looked surreal, the way his mouth remained frozen and the lividity of his skin. She half expected him to sit up and berate them for being in his house. The blood had been coming from a gash above his left eyebrow – the side which had been lying on the kitchen table. His face appeared strangely flattened, and where his skin had pressed on the table, she could make out the heavy grained pattern of the wood on his cheek.

'Do you think that cut is deep enough to have caused a fatal head injury?' Maya asked.

'We'll not know for sure until the post-mortem. It looks a bit nasty but could be relatively superficial. I know there's a fair bit of blood but he's a drinker. Alcohol thins the blood.' Chris pointed towards Gorman's face. 'Head wounds can look worse than they actually are. You'll soon learn that noses and mouths can piss blood, but the injury isn't actually that bad. I'll go and give Granger a shout and we'll strip him off while you carry on with the photographs.'

As Chris stepped out to fetch the pathologist, Maya proceeded to photograph Gorman in his new position. She took a series of close-up pictures of his face and general body shots, including several photos of his hands. As she stood over the body taking the pictures at various angles, she noticed how the smell had grown stronger since he had been moved. The stench of excrement mixed with the smell of death was certainly going to be an unforgettable experience.

Although the odour was undeniably unpleasant, Maya was pleased that she could withstand it. Now she had got used to the sight of the dead body, her initial shock was replaced with intense curiosity. Carefully placing the camera down on the edge of the body sheet, she knelt and cautiously lifted Gorman's right hand. It felt surprisingly cold despite the sweltering temperature of the room.

Like his legs, the hand felt heavy and unyielding, but she could turn it easily enough to inspect the back and palms. The fingers were heavily nicotine-stained, his nails long and dirty. His knuckles appeared bruised and slightly swollen. Old scars were visible on his fingers, consistent with someone who had spent many years labouring and handling tools, but she couldn't see any fresh cuts.

'What are you thinking, Maya?' Chris asked as he returned with the pathologist.

'I was just checking his hands to see if there were any fresh cuts or scrapes. I was thinking that if he'd been attacked the chances are, he would have fought back and maybe sustained some defence wounds, but there's nothing apparent. This is clearly his dominant hand, looking at the nicotine stains,' she added.

Chris nodded at her. 'Good observation. Noticed anything else?'

She looked down at the body and around the dishevelled kitchen. Now that he was laid out on the floor and the two men were in the room with her, it didn't seem as large as it had when she originally entered.

'Actually, yes. If he had been assaulted here, then surely there would be signs of a disturbance. There's certainly enough rubbish in here which could have been knocked over or easily disturbed. Look at the dustbin mountain for a start. Also, if someone *had* been here, then wouldn't they have taken his phone and wallet? They're still on the lounge table. The cigarette packet and vodka bottle are both nearly full. Any self-respecting thief would have taken them, surely?'

Chris nodded. 'Well spotted. That said, the property is still insecure, and we have a dead sixty-five-year-old with an obvious head injury and lots of potential enemies. What are your thoughts, Doctor Granger?'

'No alarm bells ringing up to now. Let's strip him off and see what's what.'

Chris began by easing Gorman's navy T-shirt over his head revealing a skinny, pale frame. Gases had caused his otherwise concave stomach to bloat like a pregnancy. The wall of the abdomen had begun to discolour and had a green hue to it. Had Gorman lain undiscovered much longer, bloating and discolouration would have intensified until the body effectively popped.

The left side of Gorman's ribs appeared slightly bruised, although it was hard to distinguish because of the lividity. Maya leaned over to take more photographs and grimaced as a wave of body odour emanated from the corpse, adding to the noxious bouquet of the kitchen.

'God, he stinks,' she exclaimed, grimacing under her mask.

'Ha, wait for the feet.' Chris chortled to himself as he eased Gorman's trainers and socks off. Maya baulked at the sight of a shower of dry skin, like sawdust, come away as the socks were peeled off.

Chris began to hum *The Stripper* tune as he began to wriggle Gorman's stained jeans down his scrawny legs. Maya's infamous booming laugh filled the room, causing Doctor Granger to wince and Chris to laugh harder. Granger, unamused, shook his head, which brought them both back to their senses. The three of them had cause to take a step back as the smell of defecation became even stronger.

'I think we'll leave his boxer shorts on until we get him in the mortuary. I've not seen anything that's given me any real cause for concern.' Granger squatted down. 'The bruising on his knees and ribs there doesn't look particularly fresh and more than likely relates to the fight he had. Can you just turn him over, Chris? I'll just check his back and then he can be bagged up.'

Maya continued to take a series of photographs as Chris heaved the body onto its side before lowering him face first on the body sheet. Granger grunted his thanks and told them he would see them back at the mortuary. Chris produced a pre-written body tag and attached it to Gorman's wrist and asked Maya to take a close-up photograph.

'I've not seen one of those before, what's it for?' she asked as she carefully zoomed in to ensure all the details of the tag were recorded.

'Think of it as an exhibit label that you'd attach to any evidence, as essentially that's what he is. It helps maintain continuity of the body. Once the duty undertakers come to collect him, they'll take him to the mortuary. A police escort will follow them to ensure continuity is maintained.'

Chris placed clear polythene bags over Gorman's head, hands and feet for further preservation. Then they gathered him in the thick, white polythene body sheet. It rustled like a giant crisp packet as Chris tore at pieces of tape to secure the sheet in place. Next, they opened the body bag and shuffled him in it. The bag was fastened up and the zips secured with a plastic tag bearing a unique police reference number. Maya took one final photograph to record the number and then stood back.

'He's all done. Well, Maya – your first body in the bag, quite literally. How does it feel?'

'It's a relief to have it over and done with. At least I know what to expect in future. I feel okay about it. I think it helps knowing he was a shitbag. What happens now?'

'A baptism of fire, that's what. Might as well get another first out of the way. You can come to the mortuary with me and watch the post-mortem. We've just got enough time to grab some food on the way, I dunno about you but I'm bleedin' starving.' Maya heard his stomach rumble in agreement.

'Nope, couldn't eat a thing. I'll get something later.'

'Well, it's up to you but personally I always find post-mortems make me hungry. It's all those ribs. Let's get out of these scene suits so I can ring DI Redford.' Chris stretched noisily as he straightened himself up. 'He might actually want to meet us at the mortuary. He'll be in the viewing gallery, of course. He'll tell you it's so he can make calls while the PM takes place, but I think it's so he can avoid being in the splash zone.'

Surveying the dishevelled kitchen, Maya took a few final photographs. While focusing the lens she suddenly felt concerned that they had missed something. Nothing she could put her finger on. It was more of a sense that the room was keeping a secret.

'Chris?' she called as he headed down the hallway.

'What?'

'There's... could you just...'

'What's up, Maya? Hurry up, love, I'm starving.'

'Nothing. It's okay. I'm coming.'

She shook her head, ridding herself of the ridiculous notion that something was wrong. Her mother, Dominique, was always accusing her of having an overactive imagination. She'd already made one huge, wrong assumption today and she wasn't going to allow herself to succumb to any more.

Maya took one last look at the body bag and concluded it was probably just the shock of dealing with her first sudden death. After all, there was no sign of a disturbance or that anything untoward had happened. Chris had agreed with her on that, and he had years of experience to fall back on. The post-mortem would help to ascertain the cause of death and would reveal any cause for concern.

If the death *was* deemed to be suspicious then the scene would be examined with a fine-tooth comb, and any latent clues would inevitably be uncovered. Otherwise, the stepping plates would be removed, the scene closed, and the house would be secured until the next of kin or council arranged for the property to be emptied.

Knowing that Gorman had been a rapist and prolific criminal, Maya found she had little sympathy for his untimely death, whatever the circumstances. He was dead, but he was no loss to anyone. Perhaps she would have felt differently if he had been a well-liked family man. Now she was over the initial shock of having dealt with the scene, she was emotionally indifferent. Karl Gorman meant nothing to her other than being her first dead body.

Turning to follow Chris down the hall, she thought of what the mortuary would have in store for her. She shuddered at Chris's comment about being in the splash zone. The earlier trepidation began to resurface, and her stomach lurched unpleasantly. Getting hands-on with her first dead body was one thing, but she couldn't begin to imagine what it was going to be like watching Karl Gorman's body being sliced open and ripped apart.

3

M aya slept restlessly as the images played out in front of her. In the mortuary, Karl Gorman's post-mortem was no longer a challenge to be faced, but a stark reality. Disturbingly, Gorman was still alive as the oblivious pathologist sliced into him. The sound of Gorman's screams mingled with the shriek of the Stryker saw, which was used to remove the top of the skull. The mortician had wielded it effortlessly, as if removing the top of a boiled egg with a teaspoon.

Maya shuddered as each of the organs grew legs and scuttled away, crab-like, from the weighing scales on which they had been placed. As much as she was desperate to, Maya couldn't turn away as the horrific images unfolded. Gorman's unblinking eye remained fixed on her. As unyielding in the mortuary as they had been when she first discovered him in the kitchen. She was about to cry out with shock when thankfully her radio alarm chirruped into life. The dream gradually evaded her, flitting back to the recesses of her subconscious.

The nightmare of Gorman's post-mortem had been far more disturbing than the real thing, which she had found fascinating. It had been a surreal experience. The only real discomfort had caused by standing for over four hours as she watched the post-mortem unfold. Doctor Granger had eventually concluded that Gorman's death was due to sudden arrhythmic cardiac death, caused by chronic alcohol misuse. Toxicology samples had been taken, but it would be several weeks before the results would be analysed and returned.

Satisfied that there was no foul play surrounding Gorman's death, DI Redford had agreed that the crime scene could be released. Doctor Granger had concluded that when Gorman's head hit the kitchen table, it caused the gash above his eye to reopen. He echoed Chris's earlier thoughts, surmising that Gorman's drinking had accelerated the blood loss from the wound due to alcohol thinning the blood. It had been fascinating to watch the pathologist at work, but once the adrenaline rush of her first death had faded, Maya felt utterly drained and fatigued.

Chris had been right about the post-mortem making him hungry. Maya had been ravenous herself when they left the mortuary. They had managed to call at the Chinese takeaway near Beech Field just before it closed and had ordered a ridiculous amount of food between them, which to her surprise, they had managed to eat. As always, the ride home on her motorbike offered its usual cathartic release as the wind whipped past her as she opened up the throttle on the quiet dual carriageway.

It had been late by the time she got back to her apartment. She had been struck with how the familiarity of her home suddenly felt alien. Although everything was the same as it had been when she had left for work, in the aftermath of the day's events she almost felt like she didn't fit in her surroundings. It was a similar feeling to when she had returned from holiday. Although it felt good to be home, it always took her a day to settle back into her own environment.

The anticlimax had made her restless despite her tiredness. She had stood under the shower for an age. The zesty aroma of her shower gel championed the lingering smell of the mortuary and Karl Gorman's festering house. Lying in bed, Maya marvelled at the day's experience.

The relief she felt at having coped with her first body was palpable. After all, it was one thing longing to do a job, but quite another to be able to cope with it. She had come back from training and only been working in her new office for four weeks when the Karl Gorman job had come in. With her first death and post-mortem out of the way, Maya was eager for more experience.

Since being at Beech Field, she had not yet settled in with her new team. She hoped that having this first job under her belt would help her start to build a good working relationship with her new colleagues. While she had been in the shower, Chris had texted her to tell her she'd done well, and to get in touch with him if she ever had a job that she was struggling to cope with. He had extended the hand of friendship which she greatly appreciated, and it left her with a warm glow. Despite his initial grumpiness when she had arrived at the crime scene, Chris had proven to be good company. He swore just as much as Maya and had an inappropriate sense of humour, which she loved.

As Maya began to get ready for work, she found herself reliving the scene and recalled the feeling that they had missed something. She now regretted not saying anything to Chris at the time, but it was too late now. She tried to convince herself that nothing was wrong, and it was all in her mind. Perhaps it was the secret she was keeping which led to her unease. But still the feeling lingered. Was Karl Gorman's untimely death really non-suspicious?

Time.

When I think of time, I think of the hourglass sand timer in The Wizard of Oz. *You know the one the Wicked Witch of the West uses, so that Dorothy knows how long she has left until the witch kills her. I also think of the impatient staccato of the chess clock, and the soporific ticking of my parents' gold carriage clock that used to keep pride of place on the mantelpiece. Isn't it curious that the gold clock is given as a symbol of retirement?*

I always think it's like giving the retiree a sand timer, so they can measure how much longer they have before they die; now they're no longer employed as a functioning member of society. Mind you, old age doesn't bother me anymore, people should be grateful to make it to sixty-five. Not everyone does.

Nobody ever realises how precious time is until it is too late. Until the moment it is about to run out — until there is *no more time. Take youth, for example. The saying goes that it is wasted on the young and how very true that is. Young people don't appreciate the value of education, the beauty of their young bodies or what it is to have a life free of responsibility, until it is too late.*

It's only when you're middle-aged and overweight, carrying a crippling mortgage and fighting to stay at the top of your game that you can look back and appreciate that you once had it all. It's only then you realise how easily you frittered it away due to the ignorance and arrogance of youth.

Not long after Louisa and I first started dating, she bought me a mug which had a picture of a cartoon dog on it, lazing in a hammock. It wore a large, floppy sun hat and had a beer in one paw and a cigar in the other. The caption read 'a moment enjoyed is never wasted'. It's only now, so many years later, that I realise how very true that saying is. It makes me think about all those wasted moments that could have been spent elsewhere. Those precious moments that should have been spent with someone else, anywhere else, doing *anything else.*

This leads to regret and the thing with regret is that it grows like a cancer. It festers and expands until it becomes all encompassing. It weighs heavy like a dirty secret; it is a gnawing, ceaseless, gripe. I think that regret is the cancer of the soul — it's enough to drive you quite mad!

I don't think Karl Gorman realised his time was up. He slipped away quite peacefully. Too peacefully. A huge part of me wished I could have watched him writhing and screaming in agony. I would have loved to have witnessed the terror in his eyes as he realised that it was all over for him. But he didn't die like that. It was quick and painless.

I wonder, if Karl Gorman had known that he was about to die, would he have begged and pleaded to save his pathetic waste of a life? I like to think that he would have done. I love to imagine him doing it.

I would still have killed him anyway.

4

Beech Field police station was a modern building of three storeys. The sandstone-coloured brick and blue window frames and doors were typical of a Carillion police building. The SOCO office was situated at the back on the first floor, adjacent to the CID offices and above the cells. The bubble of conversation and ringing phones accompanied Maya down the corporate blue corridor.

Her footsteps mirrored the rhythmic pounding against metal from an unhappy prisoner in the cells. Her curiosity was piqued as she wondered who had been arrested and what for. One of the things she loved about the job was not knowing what each day had in store for her. Gales of laughter and the sound of a familiar voice stopped Maya in her tracks at the office door.

'Honestly. I shit you not. She'd been talking to him through the kitchen door. The top panel of glass was all speckled, so it obscured the view. When she realised it wasn't Doctor Granger, she was so flustered she just kept saying how he was dead – definitely, definitely dead. I'd have pissed myself laughing there and then if I hadn't felt so sorry for her.' Chris laughed raucously.

There was more laughter as Maya braced herself and walked into the office with a sheepish grin on her face and hands held up in supplication. The laughter turned to mocking cheers as Chris stepped forward and gave her an avuncular pat on the back.

'Ladies and gentlemen! May I present, SOCO Maya Barton, who not only *sees* dead people, but talks to them too.' Chris bowed and waved his hand towards Maya with a flourish which was met with more cheers and laughter.

'Okay, okay – guilty as charged,' Maya grinned sheepishly, 'it's nice to know that what happens at a crime scene doesn't stay there. I'll get you back, Makin, don't you worry.'

'You've got to be able to laugh at yourself in this job.' Amanda, the office administrator gave her a thumbs up.

'Yeah, good job you're black so we can't tell you're blushing.' Andy Carr's caustic remark stung like a slap. A sudden hush fell on the office and the earlier merriment was replaced with a heavy, uncomfortable silence.

'You're a dick at times, Andy, do you know that?' Chris shook his head with disgust.

'Why? What's wrong with saying that? She is black, or half-caste or mixed race or whatever the phrase is today. Does this mean we have to start with all that political correctness bollocks now?' Andy pouted like a petulant child.

He was a good-looking man in his forties, tall and rugged with salt-and-pepper wavy hair.

The click of heels announced another presence in the office. 'Congratulations, Mr Carr, you have just won yourself a place on the next diversity awareness course.' The tone of voice was pure steel. 'If anybody else feels they would benefit from going on it, then let Amanda know so she can email human resources and book you on. If you don't and I hear similar comments in the future, you can look forward to being issued with a formal warning.'

Although she was only short in stature with a trim figure, Kym Lawson, the senior SOCO, had a reputation for being formidable when needed. Her sudden presence in the office caused everyone to sit up and take notice.

She was an attractive woman with large, wide brown eyes. Her dark-brown hair was styled in an elegant pixie cut. She was the kind of woman whose face lit up whenever she smiled, but when she frowned her dark eyes almost looked as if a thundercloud was gathering. That was exactly how she looked now as she glared at Andy, making no effort to disguise the look of sheer contempt on her face.

'Now then, either our local criminals have gone on holiday overnight and not been burgling, or you lot are too busy kicking the arse out of brew time and need to get yourself out to your jobs. So, let's go!' Kym clapped her hands together, a common trait of hers and an exceedingly unpopular one.

'Maya, pop in my office when you've got yourself settled in. I'd like a word, please.' Kym turned on her heel and headed into the side room, leaving a trail of perfume and chastened faces in her wake.

The others gathered their coats, radios, and van keys before scuttling out of the office to their respective crime scenes. Maya gathered her belongings together before logging onto the computer so she could book herself on duty and see what jobs had either come in or been left for her to pick up as part of her mid-morning shift.

'Are you okay, love?' asked Amanda when there were just the two of them left in the office. A retired police officer who had completed her thirty years' service and then, not ready to retire completely, had returned to the force as a civilian in the role of administrator. Amanda was the fount of all knowledge and always ready with an encouraging word and a friendly ear when the job got a bit too much. Tall with greying hair which she still habitually kept tied in a regimented police bun, she had an open and kind face.

'Yeah, I'm fine, thanks,' Maya replied, 'I don't mind a bit of office banter, I know it's all meant in good humour.'

'Do you mean Chris or Andy?' Amanda asked with a raised eyebrow.

'Oh, definitely Chris. I've no time for people like Andy. I've learnt over the years to just ignore ignorant racist bastards like him.' Maya gave a sardonic laugh. 'Being mixed-race means I'm either too white or too dark, depending on who you listen to. Never quite fitting in, you know?'

Amanda smiled. 'I have a feeling you'll fit in here just fine. Go and see what Kym wants and then come and tell me all about the body yesterday.'

Maya made tea then popped her head around Kym's door.

'Okay to come in?' she asked.

'Yes. Let me just finish reading this email but sit yourself down. Just put those drinks down and pull the door shut.'

Maya suddenly felt nervous as she pulled the office door to, worried that she may be in trouble as Kym usually operated an open-door policy. She sat herself opposite Kym and watched anxiously as her supervisor pored over the computer screen in front of her, a slight frown puckering at her brow. She suddenly felt a squeeze of dread in the pit of her stomach. Why was she here? Had she been found out? She began to gnaw at her cuticles; a typical sign that she was beginning to panic.

'Thanks for the brew.' Kym turned to look at Maya. 'So, first things first, tell me about yesterday.'

Maya paused, wondering if she could relax. Surely if Kym had discovered the truth and was going to have it out with her, she wouldn't be asking so casually about yesterday. She dropped her hand back into her lap.

'It went well, despite the really obvious misunderstanding.'

Kym gave a sudden light-hearted laugh which surprised Maya. 'Don't worry. I can see how you came about your assumption. The pressure was on from both Doctor Granger *and* DI Redford to get the body processed as soon as possible. Obviously as a result it meant us having to send you off to a scene half-cock without knowing all the facts. Bit of a learning curve for us all there. Other than that, how was it – any problems?'

'No, none at all. It's a relief to have my first death over and done with. I think I coped okay and feel fine about it.' Maya smiled confidently.

'That's good to hear. You'd be surprised the number of people who do this job thinking they can cope with the dead body side of things, then when it comes to the crunch, they just can't hack it. If you can't, it's nothing to be ashamed of. If you attend a job that causes you issues, you need to speak out. Either to me, one of the others or force welfare.

'*You* are responsible for your own well-being which includes your mental health. We all have that one job that messes us up a bit. If it happens to you, it's essential you let someone know as there is help and support out there. You've come this far into your career; don't risk it for the sake of asking for support if you ever need it.'

Maya was touched by Kym's kindness. Even before moving to Beech Field, she had heard about Kym's notoriety for being a tough boss who didn't suffer fools. She was pleasantly surprised to discover that the senior SOCO had a compassionate side. Perhaps it was this that reminded Maya of that final moment in Gorman's kitchen, when she had a fleeting trepidation that she had missed something.

'There's just one really small thing. Just after we'd bagged the body. I suddenly had a funny sensation. More of a worry really – a concern that we'd missed or overlooked something. Is that normal?'

Kym sat back and looked at Maya, her eyes narrowing slightly as she considered her carefully from over the top of her glasses. Maya thought she looked like a stern, middle-aged librarian rather than a senior SOCO.

'Anything happen to cause this notion?'

'No. Like I said, it was just a... feeling.' Maya was suddenly beginning to regret confiding to Kym's softer side. The atmosphere had suddenly cooled, and Kym's eyes were beginning to brew with that infamous, thunderous look.

'You attended that scene with one of the most experienced SOCOs we have. Not only that but despite being known for being a bit of a bastard, Doctor Granger has been cutting up bodies since you were in nappies. Now you're telling me that something that you can't put your finger on gave you cause for concern. Did you mention this "feeling" to Chris or Doctor Granger at the time?'

'Erm, no. I guess I just dismissed it as being first-body nerves. Probably just looking for something that wasn't there.' Maya back-pedalled frantically, trying to downplay the situation.

'Quite. Just like assuming our dead body was a living, breathing pathologist. In this job, Maya, we stick with the facts. We work methodically and analytically and do *not* allow feelings or assumptions to cloud our judgement. Crime-scene investigation adopts scientific principles which we use to the letter and we don't allow for unconscious bias.'

'I appreciate that, Kym, it's just that...'

Kym raised her hand to silence Maya. 'If you're interested in superstition, conspiracy theories or "feelings", then read the online comments left by the readers of our local rag. Listen to the armchair investigators who constantly criticise us *and* the cops for not doing our jobs properly because their auntie's dog allegedly knows more about the facts than we do. Then decide whether you want to make a success of your career or go along with the mentality of the local gossips and naysayers. Understood?'

To say that Maya was left to feel suitably chastened was an understatement. 'Understood. Sorry, Kym.'

'Right, let's forget about it and move on.' It was like flicking a switch as Kym's terse demeanour suddenly seemed to soften again. 'There's a reason I've asked you in here but I'm afraid it's quite a sensitive issue.' She leaned conspiratorially towards Maya.

'Erm, okay.' Maya's stomach lurched and she struggled to maintain her composure as a surge of panic rose up towards her throat. This was it – Kym must have found out about her.

'I appreciate you're on a rest day tomorrow but I'm a bit short-staffed and wondered if you would be willing to come in on overtime. It means an early start. I'd need you to be on duty and ready to go by 4am. The scene I need you to help examine is part of Operation Chrysalis.'

Maya nearly laughed out loud with relief. She hadn't been found out after all and not only that, she was being offered the chance to work on a major scene. This was one of Beech Field's highest priority operations, which as far as Maya knew, was focusing on a local, serious, organised crime gang ran by nominals, Aiden Donnelly and Piotr Nowak.

The targets of Chrysalis were suspected to be encroaching on smaller drug dealers and using their arsenal of firearms to monopolise the market. More recently a feud had started between Donnelly and Nowak and their rivals: the McCluskey brothers. David and Damian McCluskey were well known for drug dealing and robbery offences. Anything to do with

Chrysalis tended to be highly confidential, hence the need for the closed-door meeting.

'Count me in. Please. Yes. Absolutely. I'd really, really love to,' Maya chattered excitedly, stupid with relief.

Kym eyed her curiously, not used to such an overkeen response. 'Thank you. Right, the team are planning on executing a warrant at an address tomorrow morning. Once the arrest team have been in and the property and occupants are secured, they'll confirm it's safe for you to go in.

'You'll need to photograph and help package any items of interest which might include cash, clothing, drugs and any firearms. You don't need me to remind you that if they *do* find a weapon then wait for the firearms unit to arrive and make it safe before you forensically recover it. We're also going to be looking at proceeds of crime too, so take general photographs to record any items of affluence, such as jewellery, designer clothing, electric items, etc,' she continued.

'It's a high value operation and there is some suggestion that this gang have been given tip-offs in the past, but we don't know who from, so *everything* is being kept under wraps until the very last minute. You won't even be given an address. One of the officers from the Tactical Aid Unit will accompany you in the SOCO van and you'll be at the end of the convoy. Just stay in the van until you're given the all-clear and obviously, ring me on my mobile if you need to ask anything. Does that sound okay?'

'Absolutely.' Maya could barely contain her enthusiasm. 'Thanks so much for the opportunity.'

She stayed in her seat as Kym turned her attention back to the computer and started typing away for a few moments until she turned back to Maya.

'Still here? If there's nothing else I suggest you go and check your van is adequately stocked for tomorrow. Then see if there are any other jobs that need doing today.'

Maya stood to leave, marvelling at the sudden change back to frosty Kym. She appreciated she was only new, but Maya sincerely believed that if she worked with Kym for the next thirty years, she would never figure her out. Maybe Amanda could give her some pointers on how best to work with the boss.

Walking back into the main office, Amanda was waiting for her.

'No time to tell me about yesterday, I'm afraid. You'll have to fill me in later. Sergeant Jeffries has just phoned up. They've discovered a cannabis farm on Copeland Road. He reckons at least 250 plants. The electricity has been abstracted but the supplier has already sent an engineer out to make it safe, so you're good to go.'

'Don't tell me, they want me there yesterday.' Maya picked up the van keys.

'You're learning, kiddo.' Amanda laughed as she handed over the paperwork and bundled Maya out of the office.

Despite the stifling summer heat, Maya shivered as she made her way out of Beech Field police station. The relief of realising that Kym had not discovered her secret was short-lived. The sobering reality hit her. It was only a matter of time before the truth came out. And then what?

5

Maya arrived at Beech Field at 3.30am. As she alighted her motorbike and removed her helmet, she received the usual curious looks from onlookers who had not expected to see a female rider. Her orange-and-black Triumph Bonneville T120 had a retro appeal that caused even non-bikers to stare in admiration.

She was surprised to see the station in the midst of such activity despite the ungodly hour. The few officers she had already met from the robbery unit usually worked in plain clothes, but this morning they were strapped in body armour and boots in preparation for the warrant. The morning briefing had clearly finished, and the unit gathered in the car park preparing their equipment and stocking up the marked police riot vans.

There was also a specialist police search team gathered around a heavily armoured police riot van. Two search officers were leaning on the bonnet attempting to stay cool in the early morning breeze. Despite the early hour, the temperature was still holding out at fifteen degrees and feeling much hotter in full uniform and body armour. Nodding acknowledgement to people as they buzzed to and fro, Maya headed up to the SOCO office.

As she arrived on the first-floor landing, she saw Detective Inspector Alison Mitton walking towards her. Alison was in her late fifties, tall and lithe. Her chin-length dyed blonde hair was smattered with grey roots that belied her age. She was well known at Beech Field, having worked there for most of her career. Alison was renowned for her affable personality and she always had an anecdote to suit every occasion. She had already gone out of her way to introduce herself to Maya on her first day and let her know her door was always open if ever she needed anything.

'Good morning, Maya, you're in early. Everything okay?' Alison held the door ajar for her.

'Yes, ma'am. Kym asked me to come in early and help out with a warrant.'

'Hmm, Operation Chrysalis. Let's hope we get a good result. Donnelly and Nowak are slippery fuckers who have kept us on our toes for far too long. The sooner we make some arrests the better. Good luck with it, I have every confidence in you.'

'Thank you, ma'am.'

DI Mitton strode up the corridor, poker-backed and crisp with efficiency. Maya continued towards the office. The glow from the corridor indicated the lights were on, and the pungent aftershave that lingered like a fog suggested that Andy Carr was in the office. Her heart sank. Not only was she still reeling from his racist comment the previous day, but she generally considered him a repugnant individual. He was a good-mood-hoover, the way he constantly spewed negativity. He was bad enough company when the office was full, so she wasn't relishing the thought of spending any time alone with him.

Bracing herself, she took a deep breath and headed through the office door. She was greeted by the sight of Andy reclining in the office chair, boots up on the desk, as he tapped away on his iPhone. Despite the fact he had three divorces and several ex-girlfriends under his belt, he was still an active womaniser. Rumour had it that Andy's rugged good looks attracted women like flies around shit. Maya could only assume that he made more of an effort with his charm and personality on such occasions than he did when he was in work. She wondered who he could be texting at this time of a morning. Was he on a dating app or worse, sexting someone? She shuddered at the thought.

'Hi, Andy, how are you?' She strained with forced politeness as she placed her belongings on the desk opposite him.

'Bleedin' knackered. Got called out to a stabbing. Been pissing about for the last few hours because of ma'am fuckin' Mitton. I really wish she'd just fuck off and retire. The case isn't going to go anywhere by the time the victim's sobered up, so I really don't know why we've bothered.'

He dropped his feet off the desk and back on the floor and leant forward, not hiding the fact he was staring at her chest.

'I shouldn't even be on call, I've been rubber dicked into covering one of Chris's. It would have been easier if Kym had kept me free for this warrant, whatever it is, rather than paying for you to come in on overtime,' he whined. 'What's the score with it anyway?'

Maya shrugged. 'They haven't told me anything. I was told what time to come on duty and that I'd be escorted to an address. I don't know anything more than that.'

'So, you don't even have an address?' She shook her head and Andy stared levelly at her, weighing up whether she was telling the truth. 'Actually, Maya, I'm glad I've seen you. Just wanted a quick word about yesterday, like.'

'Oh?' Maya raised an eyebrow quizzically as she assessed him. Was he going to apologise?

'Yeah, it's just that sometimes I might stay stuff and that.

Stuff that you lot might not find "PC",' he said, using his fingers as quotation marks. 'I just wanted to make sure we were all right, darlin', and to tell you that there's no need for you to go running to Kym about anything you might get in a huff about. It's just the way I am, so no offence meant or anything.'

Maya was aghast. 'You really are an arrogant bastard, aren't you? Just so you know, any racist, bigoted shite that comes out of your mouth in my direction will be dealt with as *I* see fit, whether that's "running" to Kym or going straight to human resources. If you treat me with respect, I'll do the same to you.

'I appreciate I've not been here that long, but don't for one minute think that I'm a walkover, okay?' She jabbed her finger in his direction, punctuating the words as she spoke. Her mouth curled with disgust as she turned away from him. She was fuming but determined to rise above it. She had dealt with bigger bullies than Andy Carr and she'd be damned if she would let him know he had rattled her.

'Oh, right. Time of the month is it, love?' he sneered as he turned his attention back to his precious phone.

Maya refused to bite at this last comment. Instead, she took deep, calming breaths and turned to the computer. Rather than allowing herself to be riled by a shit like Andy, she was going to focus her thoughts and attention on the warrant ahead. She was determined to make a good job of it and win herself some brownie points from Kym.

Just as she was gathering her keys, police radio and camera kit, there was a knock on the door frame by way of introduction. An officer from the Tactical Aid Unit filled the doorway, his large hand open in a welcoming gesture.

'Good morning, SOCO, who's with me for the warrant?'

'She is,' Andy snarled, not even bothering to look up from his scrolling.

'Hi, good morning, I'm Maya. Maya Barton.'

'Cliff Mitchell,' he replied as they shook hands. Maya turned to Andy. 'See ya then.'

'Yeah, whatever,' he replied, still not bothering to look up.

'Blimey, is he always that warm and fluffy?' Cliff quipped as they made their way down the corridor.

'Mmm, don't ask,' Maya replied with a shake of her head. She followed Cliff as he whistled his way down the stairs. He jaunted ahead of Maya, swinging open the fire doors so she could pass through with her camera kit. Once outside, they settled themselves into the SOCO van and watched as the arrest team clambered into the waiting police carriers.

'It might look a bit over the top, but our suspect, Aiden Donnelly, is known to be a nasty piece of work, so we're not taking any chances. We'll follow the convoy as they set off and keep at the back. When we get to the location, wait at the end of the road in the van until the address and the suspect are secured, okay?'

Maya nodded. She felt exhilarated with the drama of the situation. She had never accompanied officers on a warrant before. Normally, the warrant had already been executed and the property secured before SOCO were requested. Having her in attendance and ready to be deployed showed the severity of the suspect they were dealing with. They needed to get in and secure any evidence as quickly as they could before anything could be compromised.

While they trailed behind the convoy, Cliff told Maya that several other officers were preparing to strike on other addresses on the neighbouring divisions once their suspect was detained. They believed it was possible that his associates might be tipped off about the raid and try to get rid of any items of interest they might be storing in their properties.

She followed the line of police carriers as they snaked down the dual carriageway before eventually turning off one of the A roads which led toward the leafier side of town. Unlike the estates which rooted close to the city centre, here the roads were wider, boasting tree-lined avenues. Grass verges had been neatly cropped and railings were adorned with tubs spilling summer blooms.

Rather than scatterings of litter, loose petals from the floral displays adorned the clean streets like confetti. Instead of the graffiti tags which stained the sides of buildings in town, the library and post office had purpose-built display cases which housed an array of leaflets advertising anything from toddler groups to Tai Chi sessions.

The police vehicles certainly seemed out of place in such a serene setting. The growling of the diesel engines sounded almost offensive as they punctured the sleepy stillness of the early hour. Eventually the convoy slowed to a stop in the middle of an impressive housing estate which backed onto the canal, near the moorings. The area boasted an array of large houses, some with electronic gates and impressive water features, as well as a popular gastropub called The Farmhouse.

Maya was familiar with the pub as she had visited it a few times. It was in a beautiful location and the perfect place to sit outside on a balmy summer's evening while watching the comings and goings on the canal.

'Just pull over here, Maya. I'd rather us stay back a bit until the scene is secured. I'll stay in the van with you unless I'm needed, in which case just you wait here until you're given the all-clear.'

'Is this it, our address. The Farmhouse?' Maya was surprised; she assumed they were going to target one of the palatial houses they had just driven past.

'Yup, this is the place. Take it you've been? Not only is it a nice little business, but we suspect that this place has been used as a front for money laundering as well as for storing various items. Just hope you weren't planning to eat here anytime soon because if we find what we're hoping for, I expect it's going to be shut for quite a while.'

Maya strained toward the windscreen as the entry team quietly exited the carriers and approached the front of The Farmhouse. One of the officers was carrying the large, red, metal Enforcer – nicknamed The Key or wham-ram – which was used to force doors open, allowing entry to the premises. The team remained crouched in a tight-knit unit as they headed toward the front of the pub.

Cliff turned up his police radio and they both concentrated hard until the silence was broken by the urgent request for the entrance team to strike. A flurry of activity ensued as the armoured cops approached with stealth. Maya could hear a couple of quick thuds, which she surmised was the Enforcer being used, and the muffled cries announcing the presence of armed police.

There was a pregnant pause, filled only with the sound of Cliff's heavy breathing. Suddenly the police radio screamed out garbled instructions. The emergency button was activated, filling the air with a shrill bleeping. Amongst screams and swearing, one of the patrols in the address shouted for backup. Chris had already leapt from the van like a scalded cat leaving the door swinging open and Maya dry-mouthed and panicking.

6

Maya sat in silence and waited with bated breath. She chewed at her fingers while she listened to the carnage being played out on the radio. In emergency activation mode, the speech switched between the open mic of the person who had pressed the button and other officers. She could hear guttural screaming and threats to kill, whilst the comms officer issued instructions for urgent welfare checks and an update. It was terrifying to hear such violence and not be able to do anything about it.

Suddenly the threat of a taser was announced which was followed by more swearing and eventually a scream which suggested that the taser had indeed been activated. She recognised Cliff's voice as he shouted up to let comms know the suspect had been detained. The relief was palpable. Maya listened for the request for leg restraints and a spit hood. After what felt like an age, he returned to the van.

'Sorry about that.' He smiled ruefully as he leant in through the passenger door, swiping at his face.

'What the hell happened? Has anyone been hurt?'

Cliff laughed. 'Only Donnelly. Kicked off big time, stupid bastard. He's been Pava sprayed and tasered.'

Maya caught another request over the air. 'Foxtrot Sierra three four, can we have a second van for the other prisoner.'

'Two?' Maya mused.

Cliff nodded. 'Aiden Donnelly and another chap in the property who we assume arrived last night. He must have landed at the address while the observation team were on handover. We certainly weren't expecting him. Just hang fire until we've got Donnelly out and you should be okay to come in.'

Now things had calmed down, Maya was impatient to get out of the van and into the scene. It seemed like an age until Cliff emerged, waving her over. He chatted to her as she gathered her kit out of the van.

'Suspect two is cuffed and compliant and he's not giving us any cause for concern. The arresting officer, Emma Reid, is babysitting him. He's told her he's been out of town for a while and has rolled up here as he's been appointed the position of new bar manager.' Cliff shrugged. 'He reckons he met Donnelly through a friend of a friend but doesn't actually know him. We've currently got him under arrest on suspicion of conspiracy. We'll see what he says in the interview and whether his story checks out. We've got him sat in the bar area, I'm more than happy he'll give you no trouble if you want to come in.'

Maya grabbed her camera equipment and bag containing her scene notes and other paraphernalia and followed Cliff into the bar area of The Farmhouse. It had been refurbished since she'd last been and looked even nicer than she remembered. It felt surreal to be there out of hours. Almost as if she was trespassing. Although the familiar cacophony of chattering customers and staff was absent, the aroma of carvery and coffee lingered alluringly.

The search teams were gathered in the doorway ready to be given their paperwork. Each area or room of the pub, including the residential area upstairs, was allocated a zone number. This allowed each officer to sketch a map of their area and follow a pre-agreed strategy. The strategy was a list detailing all the items of interest that they were hoping to find, including quantities of cash, drugs, firearms, mobile phones and specific items of clothing and footwear.

'There are three bedrooms upstairs. Two are en suites, as well as the lounge, kitchen, bathroom and a loft space. The search teams are going to concentrate up there for now, as well as the kitchen and storage area down here. We'll even work through the toilets and bar area once matey boy is shifted out. Can you just hang fire a moment, Maya, until the teams are allocated and then if you could take photographs for us before we start the search?' Cliff nodded to the seating area.

'That's fine,' she replied. 'Shout me when you're ready.'

Heaving her camera bag onto her shoulder, she walked through to the bar area where she saw Emma, who she already knew from Beech Field. Emma was sat at one of the tables; the suspect seated on a large, brown leather sofa. The two were chatting quite affably. From where she was stood, she could tell he was a similar age to her – mid to late twenties. He was white with a muscular build; his long, toned legs were stretched out in front of him as he lounged back.

He was dressed in khaki-coloured combat shorts and a navy-blue T-shirt. He must have heard her come in as he paused mid-conversation and turned towards her. His brown, unruly hair looked endearingly flattened on one side, suggesting he had been asleep when the search teams entered. Maya was struck by his startling, electric-blue eyes which were framed by long, dark eyelashes, which would be the envy of any woman.

'Another police officer. There's no need – I'll come quietly.

Not like that crazy bastard,' he quipped. Maya's uniform of black police trousers and dark-coloured shirt with epaulettes, meant it was easy to assume she was a police officer as she was dressed so similarly to officers from the search team.

'I'm not a police officer – I'm a SOCO – scenes-of-crime officer – or CSI if you prefer the Americanism,' she explained.

'Wow, really?' Maya caught a flash of dimple as he smiled at her. 'That must be really interesting. I bet you see all sorts doing your job. So, you're a forensic expert then?'

'I wouldn't go that far, no. I prefer to think of myself as a Womble. Someone who collects other people's rubbish; fingerprints, DNA, body parts or whatever.'

'So,' he said, smiling at Maya, 'do you come here often?'

'Do you get arrested often?' she countered. His laugh echoed around the bar. It sounded unnaturally high, suggesting that, despite his apparent bravado, the raid had unnerved him.

'Honestly, no. This is my first and last time. I've done nothing wrong. I promise you. I appear to be a victim of circumstance.'

'Another one.' Emma sighed cynically.

'Innocent until proven guilty,' he replied. 'What do you think?' he said, turning to Maya as he gave her a rictus grin. 'Do I look like a guilty man to you?'

'I wouldn't like to say.'

'Fair enough. Let's talk about you instead. You haven't even told me your name.'

'No, I haven't, have I.'

'Oh, okay. So, I don't have a name, I know what you do for a living and I guess you're local because of your accent. What else?'

Maya had dropped onto a chair and was concentrating on her camera settings. 'That's on a need-to-know basis and you don't need to,' she retorted without even looking up.

'Oh, you're feisty. I like feisty. I reckon you and I would get on well. Don't you think we make a cute couple, Emma?'

'I'm not getting involved,' replied the police officer sensibly.

'Hey, how about, when Emma here realises I'm innocent and releases me from custody, you take me out for a drink and then you can get to know me better?' He feigned a cheeky smile.

'Thanks for the offer, but I'd rather put shit in my hands and clap. Now, how about exercising your right not to say anything?'

He clutched at his chest as he made a mock swoon. 'You are harsh. I think I'm in love.' Maya appraised him with a death stare that would make most people shut up. It had the opposite effect on the suspect as he attempted to talk to her again.

Suddenly, Cliff emerged into the bar area and nodded towards Emma. 'The van's here. The custody suite is ready to accept this one. Can you do the honours and go with them and get him booked in,' he instructed.

'No problem, Cliff. Come on, Romeo.' Emma took the suspect by the elbow and helped heave him up from the couch.

'Bye for now then. Hope to see you around again sometime.' He grinned and tried to give her the best wave he could, despite the handcuffs. Maya couldn't help but smile back. He was quite a character.

'Bloody idiot!' Maya muttered to no one in particular as she followed Cliff through the pub.

'I've met worse,' Cliff commented.

'Oh, so have I, much worse. But not one as annoying as *that* for a long time.'

With a flick of her hair, she dismissed any further thoughts of the arrested man. She concentrated on the task in hand and proceeded to take a series of photographs of the property before the search teams moved in to systematically tear the place apart. Watching the police dog, an eager spaniel called Bailey, sniff around for traces of drugs, cash or firearms, Maya was filled with a renewed sense of exhilaration and a love for her job. Her satisfaction was marred by the underlying knowledge that her dream career was balancing precariously on a lie.

7

W ithin twenty-four hours after his arrest, Spencer James was accompanied out of Beech Field police station. The custody detention officer waved him off as he pressed the exit button to the custody suite. Spence sighed with relief as he pushed his way through the weighted door. The whole experience had left him in a state of shock.

His detention at the police station had been excruciatingly slow and stressful. He had requested a duty solicitor, even though he was quick to point out that he had done nothing wrong. He had been left to stew in a cell until the solicitor arrived. A reedy, exhausted-looking man with bad breath and stale sweat patches under his arms, seemed all that lay between Spence and his freedom. The solicitor advised Spence to provide a no-comment interview, but he had declined. He remained adamant that he had nothing to hide and that by telling the truth, the situation would be resolved. At least as far as he was concerned.

He explained how he had returned home from Spain where he had been living and working for the last seven years. After a failed business venture and a subsequent disastrous romance, he had decided to return home. Before leaving Spain, he had put an appeal out on Facebook for anyone who knew of any jobs going in the bar or restaurant trade. An old school friend, Ryan Johnson, had messaged him about a bar manager's job at The Farmhouse. Spence had jumped at the opportunity and emailed his CV to Ryan, who had then passed it on to the owner, Aiden Donnelly.

Spence had had a brief telephone conversation with Donnelly, who had offered him the live-in position there and then. With hindsight, he should have questioned why he had been offered the job without even asking for references. But Spence had been too grateful for the opportunity to question it. Three days later he had arrived back to England on a late flight. He had hired a taxi to take him straight to The Farmhouse where he had met Donnelly. It had been past midnight, so he had pretty much been shown to his room with the assurance that he would be shown the ropes the following morning.

Spence had only been asleep a few hours when he had been rudely woken by the arrival of armed police. The smashing of doors and sudden arrival of what looked like storm troopers had been nowhere near as scary as Aiden Donnelly's reaction. He had fought against the police who tried to arrest him. Even when the taser officer had red-dotted him, he had continued to lunge at the cops. Swinging out at whoever he could reach.

Fortunately, the taser had subdued him long enough to get him handcuffed. It had taken six police officers to sit on him until leg restraints were applied. They carried him still thrashing and threatening to the police van. Then he had turned his anger towards Spence. He had screamed accusations, blaming Spence for setting him up and threatening to kill him.

Spence had breathed a sigh of relief when Donnelly had

been dragged away to the waiting police van. The heavy police presence had felt like a weak line of defence against Donnelly's wrath. He desperately hoped he wouldn't have to meet him again any time soon. He believed every one of the threats made against him had been genuine. Even in custody, Donnelly had continued to bang around in his cell, screaming Spence's name and promising he was a dead man. He was still shaking now despite being away from the confines of the police station.

Despite the entire surreal and terrifying experience, Spence smiled to himself as he recalled the SOCO he had met. His heart had skipped a beat the moment he laid eyes on her. And it wasn't just because she was beautiful, there was something special about her. He cringed as he recalled their conversation. He knew he had come across as arrogant. It had been a long time since a woman had had such an effect on him. The shock and embarrassment of the raid and arrest had caused him to ramble on cockily and incessantly. Spence would do anything to undo that conversation. To undo the first time they met and be able to start again. To be able to show her the real him.

Now, he was in a quandary. He had no job and no home. He had his savings, of course, but he was astute enough to know that once he started dipping into them, they wouldn't last. Years of conscientious hard work would run like water through his fingers with nothing left to show for it other than an empty bank account. Going back to Spain certainly wasn't an option. He had far too much pride to go scuttling back to his ex with his tail between his legs, begging for scraps.

Plus, the police had pretty much told him not to leave town. Whilst in custody he had phoned his sister who had agreed he could stay with her for as long as he needed. She was married with a young child and he was conscious of outstaying his welcome and intruding on their family life. So much for a fresh start. He was in trouble with the police, had lost his new home and job and received death threats from a renowned criminal. With his future so uncertain, Spence began to wonder if he'd made a mistake coming home.

8

Jim Baron wore his squalid armchair like a shroud. He was watching Terry Brewer warily as the man unpacked his shopping bags. Although they had known each other for decades, there was no trust between the two.

'Change,' grunted Jim as he extended a clammy paw towards Terry. The armchair groaned with exertion as he shifted his expansive bulk forward. Jim was a grotesque man in every sense of the word. His squashed face resembled a toad. He habitually licked and smacked at his lips; a lack of teeth causing him to dribble, so he resembled an oversized baby, but without the cute factor.

His hair was 'styled' in a greasy, greying comb-over. It was longer at the back, giving him an uncharacteristically feminine appearance, which added to his curious bad looks. The only small thing about him was his bloodshot, piggy eyes, which were a dull, watery grey.

'All right, all right. Give me chance,' Terry grumbled as he handed over a black zip-up purse. 'Receipts are in there, so you can check if you want. Which you always bloody do.'

'Nowt personal. Where's me pork scratchings?'

Sighing, Terry sifted through the bags and threw a packet towards the armchair, making oinking sounds as Jim tore at the packet. He shook his head at the repulsive sight, barely able to remember the Jim of his childhood. Back then, Jim had been small for his age; stick-thin with undernourishment. This meant he could easily squeeze his way through the smallest of openings, or scuttle like a rat up drainpipes, so he could enter premises through first-floor windows.

He had started his criminal career at the tender age of nine, when his father had taken Jim out burgling with him. Jim was a natural and infamously evaded prison until nineteen. He was spotted clambering out of a local magistrate's rear bedroom window by an eagle-eyed probationer constable. It wasn't just the burglary that Jim was sentenced for, but also a vicious attack on the constable who was so badly beaten, he was left partially sighted in one eye and with a ruptured spleen.

Jim enjoyed his first stay in prison. Most of the inmates knew the Baron family and Jim's reputation had preceded him. He was notorious for having a criminal career which had lasted long before his first capture. The fact that he had severely beaten a police officer raised his popularity amongst his fellow lags. It was whilst serving this first prison sentence that Jim's criminal education continued, and he left Strangeways with a cast-iron plan to commit armed robbery.

He procured a firearm and began to make plans. Jim was greedy for money and was adamant that his next job would bring him a payday of hundreds and thousands. Jim's lucky streak lasted for years as he meticulously planned and executed several successful robberies at bookies, off-licences, and post offices. He decided that when it came to co-conspirators less was more, so he worked alone other than with the assistance of his old cellmate, Terry.

'Did you get me mag?' asked Jim through a mouthful of

scratchings. His watery eyes pooled as Terry passed him a copy of *Escort*.

'Don't know why you bother. Bet you can't even find it, let alone get it up.'

Jim ignored the retort as he flicked through the magazine, pausing briefly to show a page to Terry. 'Here, look at this one. Reminds me of the tits on that bitch from the travel agents.'

During that previous armed robbery, Jim had taken a fancy to one of the younger female members of staff. After emptying the contents of the safe and ripping watches and jewellery from the cowering hostages, he had made the young girl pull open her blouse so he could ogle her breasts. She had been terrified as he had pawed at them with one meaty hand, while the other pressed the gun against her temple. As she sobbed and trembled in sheer terror, he found himself more and more aroused.

He would have liked to have toyed with the young woman longer, but common sense prevailed, and he knew it was time for him to get away. Before he fled the scene, he had buried his head between the pert young breasts, sucking and biting at them, causing huge ugly red welts to rise angrily on her alabaster skin.

A combination of new and upcoming DNA profiling techniques, as well as the comparison of dental records was all the evidence the police needed to convict Jim Baron to a very long stretch. As the National DNA Database grew from its infancy, those same profiling techniques improved, and old crime-scene stains from other robberies, which had previously been undetectable, now revealed the truth. Jim Baron was found responsible, causing his release date to be extended further. He was eventually released on his seventieth birthday.

Now, five years on, Jim's ulcerated legs caused him mobility issues. He was stuck to the confines of his one-bedroomed, housing association flat. Still, after having served so many years at Her Majesty's pleasure, the flat was a luxury in comparison to his old prison cell. Jim relied heavily on Terry's support. For a regular fee, he brought Jim his shopping and anything else he wanted.

The police strongly suspected that Jim had thousands of pounds of cash still squirrelled away, but had never been able to trace it and, to all intents and purposes, Jim lived like a pauper. If he still had access to the money he had stolen over the decades, he certainly wasn't using it. The only thing that betrayed the fact he liked the finer things in life was his huge bulk. Other than the 'wage' he paid Terry every week to fetch and carry for him, Jim's only indulgence was food and drink.

He had been a heavy smoker most of his life but had been forced to quit due to a crippling diagnosis of COPD, a progressive lung disease, which left him floundering and gasping for breath at the slightest exertion. Jim was reliant on a nebuliser and inhaler to control his condition.

Meanwhile, the community nurses, who had to change the dressings on his legs, were known for drawing straws to choose whose turn it was to visit the despicable character. In the five years since he had been released from prison, Jim barely lifted his arse from his old, yellowing armchair, unless it was to drag himself to the kitchen or toilet. He barely used his walk-in wet-room facilities and had given up on dragging his bulk from the living room to his bedroom, choosing instead to sleep in his chair.

'Right, I'm off. See you next week.'

'Right then.' Jim didn't so much as look up as Terry left. He was too engrossed in his mag, noisily slurping his way through a bottle of super strength cider.

Terry left without locking the front door, something which Jim never bothered about. He preferred to let Terry and the nurses come and go without having the bother of letting them in. He reasoned that nobody would dare try and enter his flat without his permission, and even if they did, they would never find anything worth stealing. His cash was too well hidden.

He never had any other visitors. The neighbours steered well clear and it wasn't the type of area where the local Jehovah's Witnesses would come to call. So, it came as a shock to Jim on that stifling Sunday afternoon, an hour after Terry had left, that there was a persistent knocking at the door.

'Fuck off,' he croaked, angry at the unwanted intrusion. His irritation was soon replaced with intense curiosity as the knocking continued. Eventually, he heaved himself up to see who was there. He'd flatten Terry if it was just him pissing about. His slippers scuffed against the linoleum. He waddled awkwardly, using the wall for support. He swore, vowing it would be the last time he would get up to answer the door.

9

Maya considered the warrant at The Farmhouse to have been a success as well as great experience. Aiden Donnelly had given a no-comment interview and been remanded in custody pending a trial. It was hoped that the prospect of a lengthy prison sentence would be enough to encourage him to start talking. The Operation Chrysalis team needed enough evidence to carry out further arrests and bring the rest of the gang to justice.

Maya had worked the following two weekends after the warrant. Her mid-week rest days allowed her the time to catch up on cleaning and shopping, as well as a couple of trips to the gym and some much-needed time out on her bike with her motorbike group. The weekends had been busy. She had investigated an arson scene and a serious Section 18 assault. She'd also worked with social services on a neglect case and photographed the home of a six-year-old girl who had been diagnosed with gonorrhoea. The implication of sexual assault was horrific enough, but the sheer squalor in which the poor girl lived was heartbreaking.

Maya and the social worker were forced to suit up to protect themselves from fleas. A mixture of human and cat excrement meant the place smelt worse than Karl Gorman's, which was saying something. The fridge and cupboards were empty other than an abundance of alcohol. A handful of Happy Meal collectables were the only toys present. A collapsing flatpack wardrobe housed a pitiful amount of threadbare children's clothes. Typically, the parents' room lacked nothing including a state-of-the-art flat-screen TV with expensive surround sound. Clearly the child benefit had paid for something and the thought caused Maya's blood to boil.

Fortunately, it was now Saturday night. Maya had the promise of a long weekend off ahead of her. She could afford to forget about work, kick back and relax. She was more than ready to have some fun with her two closest friends.

Donned in a floaty summer dress and wedges which accentuated her willowy figure, Maya headed to the pub. The colour of the dress flattered her honeycomb skin. She wore her hair down, her thick corkscrew curls bouncing as she walked. Maya pushed her way through the throngs of drinkers in The Brown Cow. She made her way to the far corner of the pub and the table next to the jukebox, where she and her friends usually sat.

Caitlin and Letitia were already there, shrieking with laughter over something Caitlin had just said. Both girls looked stunning as usual, perched on the tall bar stools, and too absorbed in their conversations to notice the admiring glances from anyone who passed them by. Seeing her two friends, Maya felt a huge rush of affection. Smiling, she headed over and exchanged hugs and kisses with both of them.

'So sorry I'm late. I lost track of time and then Mama called as I was about to set off.' She reached gratefully for the glass of Prosecco Letitia handed her and clinked glasses with her friends.

'How is Dominique?' Caitlin asked.

Taking a large gulp, Maya nodded through a mouthful of bubbles. 'She's fine, thanks. You know Mama, always busy with something or other. If she's not working, she's helping out the neighbours or arranging some kind of charity event. We're overdue a proper catch-up, we only seem to manage snatches of phone calls these days or I see her briefly when I need to borrow the car. She sends you both her love.'

'And, how's work going – have you had any juicy jobs yet?'

Maya began to regale her friends with the story of Karl Gorman. While Caitlin belly laughed at the thought of Maya conversing through a glass door with a dead man, Letitia looked horrified.

'Oh, Maya, how did you manage not to throw up? Eugh, the thought of having to touch it and everything.' She shuddered. 'God, it gives me the creeps.' She was about to give Maya's arm an encouraging squeeze, before suddenly withdrawing her hand as if she'd been burnt.

'Christ, Letitia, you can touch me you know, I've had a wash since. Anyone would think I've just come straight from robbing graves or rolling around with cadavers.' Caitlin burst into fresh peals of laughter as Letitia looked suitably shamefaced. The neighbouring table cast curious glances their way.

'Anyway,' Maya lowered her voice, 'it can't be as bad as doing bikini waxes and stuff. You're not telling me *that's* a pleasant experience.'

'You cannot compare my clients to a dead body, Maya Barton, they're all perfectly lovely, hygienic people.' Letitia sniffed with indignation. She ran her own holistic health and beauty parlour and was fiercely protective of the loyal client base she had built up over the years.

'Well, never mind. Dead bodies or hairy vaginas. They all

pay the bills and cover the cost of Prosecco, so let's not argue and drink up instead.' Caitlin raised her glass to the other two.

Letitia looked thoughtful as she sipped her drink. 'I'm trying to put it into context with me having a bad workday. I guess it would be someone coming in for a vajazzle and leaving with a nose piercing.' They howled with laughter until Maya noticed Caitlin appeared distracted.

'Hey, what's up?' Maya nudged her arm.

'Absolutely nothing.' Caitlin gave a knowing smile. 'I've just been looking over at the bar to see how long it's going to take me to get served, and there's an extremely attractive bloke looking our way.'

'Oh, who? Where?' Letitia strained forward to look towards the bar, not in the least bit subtle.

'Oh no.' Maya's heart sunk as she found herself in full eye contact with the suspect from the warrant at The Farmhouse. He was wearing a black shirt with short sleeves that flashed a hint of tattooed, toned biceps. His wavy hair had been carefully styled and he had a hint of stubble which gave him an edgy look. He was smiling wildly, flashing his dimple and those electric-blue eyes. As soon as he saw her looking he made a frantic drinking motion towards her.

Completely blanking him and turning away so she could avoid further eye contact, Maya gathered her handbag towards herself. The others were looking at her intrigued and bemused as Maya hissed at them urgently, 'He was arrested at a warrant I went to. This is really awkward. Come on, let's go somewhere else.'

The others didn't even have a chance to respond as he suddenly arrived at their table, waving at Maya as if they were old friends.

'Hello again, this is a lovely surprise. How are you?' He leaned towards her to kiss her cheek, but she pulled away.

'Just going actually,' she replied sternly.

'Oh really? That's a shame. Hi, I'm Spencer James, Spence to my friends.' He leaned across the table to shake Caitlin and Letitia's hands.

Letitia seemed reluctant to let go of him, melting as she gazed at him. 'Well, Spence, I'm Letitia and this is Caitlin and I believe you already know Maya?'

He turned to Maya, grinning as he held his hand out to her.

'It's certainly a pleasure to see you again and nice to be properly introduced... Maya.' He said her name slowly, rolling his tongue around the vowels as if he was tasting the word.

She stared fixedly at him, refusing to acknowledge his hand which hung awkwardly. It suddenly felt as if everyone around them was watching the exchange.

'I don't want any trouble, okay?'

'Well, neither do I.' Spence laughed amicably. 'I just wanted to say hello and see if I could have the pleasure of buying you ladies a drink.'

'Like I said, we were just leaving.' Maya glared at Caitlin and Letitia and gestured her head sharply towards the exit.

'Well, there's no rush. I'm sure we can stay for another quick drink. We hadn't actually *said* we were ready for moving on,' Letitia gushed as she grinned at Spence, impervious to the cold, hard stare she was getting from Maya.

'Erm, why don't you two have a quick catch-up while we nip to the bar? We'll only be over there.' Caitlin smiled reassuringly. 'We'll fetch an extra glass if you want to join us Spence. Tish, give me a lift, eh?'

Practically dragging Letitia off her stool, Caitlin gave Maya an encouraging thumbs-up sign behind Spence's back and left the two of them together. Maya was not happy. This was not only an awkward situation to be in but completely inappropriate.

'So how have you been?' He sounded so casual, as if there was nothing the slightest bit strange about catching up with someone he had met briefly having just been arrested. He sat on Caitlin's chair, pulling it closer to Maya so he could lean in as he spoke to her. He was so close she could smell his Tom Ford aftershave.

'Look, I don't think it's a good idea for us to be sat chatting, do you?'

'Hey, they released me without charge.' He raised his hands defensively. 'I told you I hadn't done anything wrong. I was there because I'd been given a job which included accommodation, that's all. I didn't know that Donnelly bloke was a bloody criminal. If I had, I wouldn't have gone within a hair's breadth.' His eyes widened imploringly.

'Fair enough. But I'm sure you can appreciate that the situation is a bit awkward from my point of view.'

'I suppose so. It's okay, I can take the hint.' He sighed heavily. 'I'll leave you in peace. It was nice to see you again though, Maya. Really nice.'

He looked thoroughly dejected as he took exaggerated care to place the stool back under the table. Caitlin and Letitia arrived back at the same time, clutching a fresh bottle and several glasses.

'Ladies,' he said, giving a half bow, 'it was a pleasure to meet you both, I hope you enjoy the rest of the evening.'

'Oh, aren't you joining us for a drink?' Letitia sighed.

'As much as I'd love to, it has been made perfectly clear to me that I'm not wanted,' he inclined his head towards Maya, 'I'm sorry to have interrupted your night out.'

'Just for the record,' he turned back to Maya and fixed his gaze with those impenetrable blue eyes, 'I'm not who you think I am.'

His words resonated deeply with her. *No, none of us are*, she thought to herself. Shaking her head, she gestured towards the stool he had just vacated.

'Oh, for God's sake. I suppose you can join us for one drink. What harm can it do?' If only she had known, she would have followed her instinct and left the pub there and then, taking her friends with her.

10

J im Baron had had the same stupid, shocked look on his face as Karl Gorman when he realised that it was me at the door.

'What are you doing here?' he had blustered as he clung to the wall, gasping with the exertion of having waddled down the hallway. When I told him I just wanted to talk, he'd submitted just as easily as Gorman. Curiosity had obviously got the better of him, and he invited me in, so I didn't need to use the persuasion I had anticipated. Louisa always said I had the gift of the gab, so I knew that convincing a lairy Jim Baron to let me in would be an easy task if I needed to.

I had already decided that after Gorman, I wanted to watch Jim Baron suffer. I wanted him to plead and beg for his life. I had carefully and meticulously planned how I was going to kill him, without arousing too much suspicion and ensuring I didn't leave any forensic evidence behind. I had hardly slept the last few days, as I had gone over the plan time and time again. In the end, I needn't have bothered.

A lifetime of abusing his body with cigarettes, alcohol and processed food finally caught up with Jim, and he conveniently dropped dead right in front of me. Thankfully, I hadn't even needed to *lay a finger on the repulsive bastard. Still, it had been incredibly satisfying watching him suffer as it wasn't a quick death. Not like Gorman's. His disgusting fat face had grown so puce at one point, he reminded me of Violet Beauregarde from* Charlie and the Chocolate Factory.

I knew beforehand that nobody would disturb us, or indeed, arrive in time to potentially save Jim. I had been watching the flat for long enough to know when Terry Brewer and the community nurse called. I was satisfied that he didn't appear to have any other visitors. Hardly surprising, considering what an odious shit he was.

Anyway, when I told Jim why I was there, he had started to get himself into a bit of a state. It was hot in the poky little flat and Baron was perspiring underneath his tatty blue cardigan. He'd begun flapping his podgy arms and squawking like a tantruming toddler. He had heaved himself up from his filthy armchair in an attempt to hit me, but in his haste tripped over his own fat feet. Oh, the indignity!

He had lain on the floor floundering, sweaty, gasping for breath, and becoming more and more agitated at his failed attempts to pull himself up. He had been wheezing heavily, sounding like a dilapidated steam train. He had gesticulated wildly towards the table next to his armchair where his nebuliser and inhaler lay. He actually believed I would pass them to him. After a good twenty minutes watching him become more and more distressed, he had suddenly begun to grasp his left arm and started to grind his jaw.

Every time a fist of pain squeezed his chest, he would grunt like a pig and screw his face up, so he looked as if he was trying to shit. His face grew more and more ashen and fresh beads of sweat appeared on his top lip. As he took his final few breaths, his lips turned a curious blue colour. Once he rattled his last breath, I had a quick root around his grubby little hovel, curious to see if I could find where he had hidden his legendary cash.

Then I had slipped back out through his front door, completely unnoticed by anyone; including the CCTV camera situated in the corner of the car park that had been broken since Easter. Terry Brewer would most likely be the first person to find Jim Baron's dead body in three days' time when he returned to do his bidding. I hoped that the shock would kill him too. That would be a bonus.

11

It was a blisteringly hot Monday afternoon as Maya rode into Beech Field police station ready to start her late shift. She spotted her colleague Connor Dearing loading up the van and wandered over to say hello.

'Hiya. Have we got much on today?'

'Yeah – loads. It's chaos in there. I'm just heading off to a raft of burglaries.' Like Maya when she had worked at Alder Street, Connor only attended volume crime scenes.

'Can I take any breaks off your list?'

'Thanks for the offer, but there's already a job waiting for you.'

'What's come in?'

'Well, to start, Piotr Nowak has been arrested.'

Maya's eyes widened. 'Aiden Donnelly's right-hand man?'

Connor nodded. 'He's the muscle behind most of their nastier jobs. Op Chrysalis have been looking for an opportunity to arrest him for ages.'

'Oh, wow, great result. How did they get him?'

'His name came from a guy called Ryan Johnson. Apparently, in the past both Donnelly and Nowak have put pressure on him to store a firearm for them. Johnson's not been out of prison long. The thought of going back was scarier than crossing Donnelly, so he gave us Nowak's name.'

'What are the chances Nowak has put pressure on Johnson since we raided The Farmhouse?'

'Exactly. Andy is searching though Nowak's house. Johnson seems adamant that there are items of interest in the address and DC Stevenson thinks there's no reason to disbelieve him.'

'Fantastic.'

'Hey, not only that, but there was also a shooting in the early hours. Warning shots were fired at Damian McCluskey's house. Nobody was injured, but on Saturday evening, his brother David was stabbed at his house. It wasn't reported at the time and we only became aware of it when cops gave David a knock to let him know about his brother and saw the injuries and blood. The job's got Nowak's name all over it.' Connor rubbed his hands together, an infectious grin on his face.

'By the way, Connor. Do you know which car belongs to Chris?'

'Yeah, the white Mazda over there. Why?'

'I still haven't got him back for telling you lot about my embarrassing situation with Karl Gorman. Got your fingerprint case handy by any chance.'

Connor gave her a conspiratorial grin. They approached Chris's car like mischievous schoolkids and began to cover the driver's door in black powder. The signature office-banter touch was the white-powdered phallus on the windscreen. Maya's booming laugh filled the air as they high-fived each other before going their separate ways.

She was still chuckling to herself as she took the stairs two at a time. The office was a hive of activity and sobered her up. Amanda was engrossed on the phone, furiously taking notes. Chris was also on the phone, reading from his handwritten crime-scene report and reeling off a list of exhibits. Kym's door was shut, and Maya could see through the side window of her office that there were several people crammed into the small room. The only people she recognised were Kym, DI Alison Mitton and DC Stevenson, who was the detective currently dedicated to Operation Chrysalis.

The hum of office activity was punctuated with the sound of erratic banging emanating from the custody suite downstairs: somebody clearly wasn't happy.

'Hi Maya,' Nicola Warne called out from one of the two small side offices that were used as examination rooms. Maya walked in to see Nicola perched on a stool at one of the examination benches, surrounded by a large amount of property which had been packaged in police exhibit bags.

'Been finding clues?' Maya said, nodding to the bags.

'Just a few! I've just finished a warrant for Operation Chrysalis. It's all happening today.' Nicola grinned. She was slightly older than Maya. Her brown hair was scraped back into a ponytail and she had a smudge of fingerprint powder under her left eye, reminiscent of Adam Ant.

'I've just seen Connor and he's filled me in. Which address have you been too?' Maya asked as she reached out to wipe the smudge of powder from under Nicola's eye. It streaked even further.

'Eugh, black powder? It gets everywhere. Am I covered in it?' Nicola used the camera on her phone to scrutinise her face as she continued. 'I've been to Markita Milani's place. She's Nowak's partner. He was arrested there. The place is packed to the rafters with designer gear,' Nicola continued. 'I've not finished yet. I've just come back for some refs and Kym has said I can have overtime to stay on and finish off. Andy is at Nowak's house, he was pissing and moaning about having to do a bit of work as I'm sure you can imagine.'

Maya rolled her eyes in acknowledgement. At least if Andy was busy there, she might get through her shift without having to see him. Amanda finished on the phone and beckoned Maya over. She looked uncharacteristically flustered.

'Maya, love, step into my office.' She patted the chair next to her. 'Glad you're in. I feel like I'm spinning plates, but at least I can get rid of one action.' Amanda repeated what Maya already knew, before flicking through an array of paperwork and producing a typed-up forensic strategy and handing it to Maya.

'Nowak is in custody waiting to go. DC Stevenson will update you once he's finished in Kym's office.'

'What's with the closed-door meeting?' Maya was curious.

'Sensitive Chrysalis information. We're anticipating a retaliation following the shooting. DC Stevenson seems to think something may happen in the next few days so he's making sure the troops are aware. Obviously, because we suspect there have been leaks in the past, it's all being kept on a need-to-know basis.' Amanda tapped the side of her nose with her forefinger.

'Are they positive that someone from the station has been leaking police information to the gangs?' Maya was horrified. Corruption was a very disturbing thought; one she couldn't countenance.

'It seems the only logical explanation. From what I know, quite a lot of the Chrysalis jobs have proved fruitless. The cops always seem to be one step behind the suspects. In the last few months, we've been tipped off about drugs farms and the locations of firearms, but by the time the warrant has been executed, the scenes have been cleaned. It's too much of a coincidence if you ask me and there's no such thing as a coincidence in the cops.'

Just then Kym's office door opened. DI Mitton headed back to her own office accompanied by the detectives. DC Sean Stevenson gave Maya a nod. 'Give me five minutes to get someone to accompany you to custody,' he called as he left the room.

He was an experienced detective, much to the surprise of anyone who first met him. He was blessed, or cursed, depending how you looked at it, with boyish looks. Visitors to Beech Field CID would catch a glimpse of Stevenson, with his overgrown ginger hair and freckles, and wonder with amusement, which of the exhausted saps in the office had been press-ganged into '*bring your kid to work day*'.

Kym emerged from her office looking hot and bothered. Her face was perfectly made up as always, but a soft sheen suggested she was struggling with the rising temperature.

'Right, Maya. About Piotr Nowak.' Maya nodded eagerly. 'He's a real nasty bastard so make sure you're not left alone with him and watch your back. He'll be taken into the medical room for body mapping with the Medacs nurse, so you can examine him in there. Make sure you hand everything over to the DC when you're done and don't get stuck with booking your exhibits into property. They can do it. We've got enough jobs running at the minute without doing their admin.'

Grabbing a biscuit from the packet next to the office kettle, Kym gave a half-hearted clap and marched back into her office. Maya started to get ready for her trip to custody just as the office phone rang again. She snatched it up quickly so as not to have to bother any of her colleagues with another call. It was the communications officer telling her that they had been shouting for any available SOCO officers over the air but had received no response.

'Everyone's tied up at the minute so probably didn't hear,' Maya explained as she clipped a battery into her own personal radio.

'I know, it's been a crazy day,' said the nasal comms officer. 'I'm sorry to add to your workload, but we've just had a sudden death come in too. Cedar Lane CID are covering it, but they're asking for SOCO to be made aware.'

Taking details of the log number, Maya scribbled a quick note and passed it to Amanda. At times like this, when all staff were tied up on major scenes, assistance would be requested from a neighbouring division such as Alder Street or Cedar Lane. The mention of a sudden death made her think of Karl Gorman and the nagging thought that she had missed something. She shook her head, ridding herself of the notion. It was over and done with and she needed to focus on what was going on today. She pitied whoever picked up a death in this heat. She was glad she was heading down to custody. At least it might be a bit cooler down there.

DC Mike Malone appeared in the corridor and signalled to Maya. Late fifties, grey hair and with a stocky build, Malone had pretty much seen and done it all during his extensive career. Maya was quite glad it was him she was working with. If anyone had the skills to get Piotr Nowak to cooperate, it was Malone.

Clutching the strategy sheet and everything she needed, Maya and Malone headed companionably down to the custody suite. Maya had been before on several occasions, but never felt comfortable there. The airlock passageway between the main police corridor and custody always made her feel claustrophobic. One door had to be closed and locked before the other could be opened. That moment of being locked in limbo seemed to last longer every time she visited.

The suite was painted in the typical corporate blue of the rest of the police station. Opposite the holding cell stood a tall, horseshoe-shaped desk where the prisoners were processed. The custody officers perched on tall chairs as they tapped details into the computer screen, surrounded by posters explaining prisoners' rights and advice for those with drug or alcohol addiction. Closest to the desk was a cell with floor-to-ceiling windows, where any vulnerable prisoners at risk of self-harm could be easily monitored.

Time always seemed to stand still in custody. No matter what mayhem was going on upstairs with requests for urgent forensic examinations and detective actions, the custody suite ticked along at its own steady pace, almost like an airport lounge. Things down here took as long as they took and there was no way of rushing it.

Malone headed behind the horseshoe counter to speak to one of the custody staff and obtain the keys for Nowak's cell. While she waited, Maya watched as a tear-stained, scrawny-looking individual was processed for burglary. He was a pathetic sight, crying and begging to go home. He must have weighed no more than nine stone wet through. He was wheedling and pleading with the custody sergeant to let him phone his mum and girlfriend.

Maya wished that victims of burglary could witness this. She had seen so many people left devastated and terrified after a break-in. Some never got over the fear and violation. It caused them to become prisoners in their own home. Too scared to be there but terrified to leave in case they were broken into again. Most victims pictured a burly, aggressive offender with a sharp criminal mind. They were convinced the offenders had been stalking them and their property for weeks. The reality was this poor excuse for a human. He was either funding a drug habit or just after an easy way to pilfer money. Likely an opportunist who thought it was his God-given right to steal from hard-working, honest individuals. Too arrogant to care about the consequences his actions had on others.

Eventually, the burglar was led away to a cell by a dishevelled custody officer. Malone reappeared at the desk accompanied by a surly-looking man. He was tall with a large build and clearly liked throwing weights around. He was unshaven and his face was fixed in a hard, stony expression. Nowak radiated aggression and contempt. Not one to be easily intimidated, Maya was unnerved by the sight and sheer size of him.

Malone gestured to one of the benches that lined the wall of the custody suite, but Nowak refused to sit, choosing to pace like an angry lion. They waited for the custody sergeant to process another two prisoners painfully slowly before it was Nowak's turn. Malone had attempted to interject and goad the sergeant into dealing with his prisoner first but had been left in no uncertain terms that the custody suite was his domain and there would be no queue-jumping.

When he was eventually summoned forward with a regal wave of the hand, Malone stepped up to the custody desk and explained that Nowak was to be subject to a forensic examination, which would include photographs. He would also have to surrender his clothing and footwear. Nowak was told that he could refuse to consent to be examined, but this decision would be overridden, and the samples needed could be taken by force if necessary. By the time the custody sergeant had finished explaining everything to Nowak, he was visibly seething and posturing in front of the sergeant's desk.

'I know it's a pain in the arse, Piotr, but you've been here before and you know the drill. The sooner we get this bit over with I can sort you out with something to eat and drink and arrange for you to meet with your brief.' Malone talked as if he was coaxing a toddler into doing something he didn't want to do. 'You know me well enough by now. I've always been all right with you, haven't I?' Malone continued.

Nowak responded with a grunt and dropped his shoulders somewhat, giving the appearance of a shrugging silverback gorilla. 'Right, get on with it, but I want a phone call too. I want to check Markita is all right. You've not arrested her, have you?'

'No. She's gone to stay with her sister while we have a quick search of her place. You know it's just procedure, don't you?' Malone sounded apologetic. 'Once this examination is done, I'll arrange for the sergeant to let you ring her before you go back to your cell.'

Malone directed him towards the medical room in an avuncular manner; Maya trailed behind. They stayed outside the room briefly while the Medacs nurse had a quick word with Nowak to establish if he had any injuries or illnesses that she needed to be aware of. The nurse would be present throughout the examination so she could assist with the body mapping of any injuries or scars that might be identified. Once she'd asked the questions, she waved the pair of them in.

Malone took control of the situation and politely asked Nowak to stand to allow Maya to take her first series of photographs. As she took profile shots of the man, she was further astounded by the sheer height and build of him. She was grateful for Malone's appeasing manner as he chatted away. She prayed that Nowak would remain placated and not cause any trouble during the examination. In his presence the small room felt airless, as though the walls could swallow her up.

Fortunately, Nowak appeared to relax, or at least began to respond in a less surly manner. Malone was chatting to him about mutual acquaintances – criminals and cops – as if they were old colleagues, which in a peculiar way, thought Maya, they were. As the lengthy examination progressed, Nowak turned his attention to Maya.

'What's your name?' he said as she swapped her camera lenses over.

'Maya,' she answered without looking up.

'Maya what?'

She paused briefly, reluctant to tell him her surname, but

not wanting to break the fragile acquiescence Malone had worked so hard to encourage, she said, 'Barton, Maya Barton.'

'You local, Maya?' Nowak persisted.

'Fairly,' she replied non-committally, hoping he would stop asking her personal questions. She looked up and caught Malone's eye, hoping he would interject, but he seemed oblivious to her pleading look.

'Brothers and sisters?' Nowak continued.

'Nope, just me.'

'What do your parents do?' He wasn't giving up on his interrogation.

'My mum's a typist.' Maya didn't want to reveal that she was a community nurse as his next question would inevitably be *which surgery*. Maya had worked as a typist for a law firm for eighteen months before she started working at the car dealers and knew from experience that if you told someone you were a typist, they rarely probed further.

'What about your dad?'

'Dead,' Maya said with a finality that appeared to bring Malone to his senses.

'How's your brother doing these days, Piotr? I've not had any dealings with him in years. Is he keeping well?'

Her feeling of relief over the sudden change of subject was palpable.

'He's been straight for years.' Nowak's face contorted with disgust. 'He met a girl who completely pussy-whipped him and he moved to Yorkshire with her. Can't remember the last time I spoke to him, the wanker.'

Distracted by talk of his brother and reminiscing about the scrapes the two siblings had got into when they were younger, Nowak dismissed Maya from any further attention. The rest of the examination proceeded without incident and she was relieved when it was all over. A steady trickle of sweat was snaking between her shoulder blades. It wasn't just due to the temperature, but more the tension of being in the presence of someone so menacing.

Maya nodded towards the nurse and turned to Nowak as she was about to leave. 'Thanks for your time,' she spoke with more cheer than she felt.

'Bye, Maya Barton. I'll see you around.'

Although he spoke pleasantly enough, Maya couldn't help but feel intimidated by the weight of his words. She quickly handed the exhibits over to Malone as if they were a ticking time bomb.

She couldn't get out of the custody suite quick enough. Nowak had unnerved her although she wasn't the faint-hearted type. He reminded her of someone from her past. Someone who caused her to shudder violently. Maya ran back to the office, determined to put as much space between Nowak and her memories as possible. Despite her best efforts, she was sensible enough to know she could never outrun the past. It was going to catch up with her one day. And sooner than she thought.

12

By the time Maya returned to the office from the custody suite, Kym, Amanda and Chris had gone home and Nicola had returned to Markita Milani's address. Chris had texted her a picture of his middle finger, which could only be in response to his powdered car. Smiling, she sent him a kiss emoji back. She decided to update details of Nowak's examination onto Socrates, the scientific support database, and then she would check the police log to see if any other jobs had come through while she'd been downstairs. If not, she would contact Connor and take some of the burglary scenes from his list.

Maya had downloaded the images of Nowak and was checking them on the computer screen when she was suddenly interrupted by a loud exclamation.

'Cor, he's a big bastard, isn't he?'

Maya nearly jumped out of her skin.

'Sorry, love. I didn't mean to startle you.'

Maya hadn't even heard Elaine Hall walk in, which was unusual as she kept all her keys on a carabiner clip on her belt buckle. She usually sounded like Marley's ghost as she rattled around the office. Elaine was the eldest of the SOCOs; she had fading blonde hair, a plump face and rosy complexion. She was known for her mercurial temperament and had a propensity for saying what everyone else was thinking.

'Piotr Nowak. Just had the pleasure of processing him in custody.' Maya turned the computer screen towards Elaine so she could have a closer look.

'Ah, yeah. I recognise him now. He's beefed up since I last saw him. Must have discovered steroids. I met him a few years ago when he was arrested for assault. His solicitor must be fucking good 'cause he never seems to get put away.' Elaine flopped on the chair next to Maya letting an array of exhibit bags drop to her feet.

'I heard you picked the stabbing up. You all done?' Maya nodded towards the exhibits.

'Yeah, thank God. It was a nightmare of a scene. David McCluskey was stabbed on Saturday evening, but didn't take himself to hospital. Instead, he's been administering to his own injuries while slowly pissing blood all over the place. He's not telling us what happened, and if it wasn't for the cops turning up to let him know about his brother, God knows what would have happened to him. He's described as poorly but stable.

'What is it about these criminals, Maya? If that were us, we'd be dead by now. This shower of shites seem to have nine lives. A few hours ago, they were worried his injuries may prove life-threatening. I bet you by this time tomorrow he's back on his feet with barely a scratch. Bastards.

'Did Nowak have any injuries?' Elaine then asked, turning her attention back to the computer screen.

'Nope, a few old scars but no fresh injuries and certainly nothing consistent with him being involved in the stabbing. Did you find the knife?'

'Nah, not in the house. I got the TAU out to do a search. They pulled a couple of the grid covers up, found a rusty old blade and two mouldy-looking cartridge cases, so God knows how long they've been there.' She rubbed her eyes, clearly exhausted. 'Here, you couldn't make us a brew, could you, while I go and stick these clothes in the drying cabinet? His jeans are dripping in claret.' Elaine gave Maya a pleading grin.

The forensic drying cabinet was used to dry out items of clothing recovered from crime scenes. It protected items from cross-contamination because of the thorough cleaning process between uses and helped contain any particulates on clothing. The drying cabinet was situated in the second examination room, towards the back of the office, which also housed a fingerprint powder-booth and photographic copy-stand.

'Go and sort your stuff then, I'll stick the kettle on,' Maya acquiesced.

'I timed that right, didn't I?' said a voice just as the kettle clicked off. Maya grinned at the sight of a short, stocky man with a bald head wearing large round glasses.

'Tony.' She smiled as the two exchanged a hug. 'It's great to see you, what are you doing here?' Maya had worked with Tony Harwood when she was based at Alder Street. He had mentored her the most during her time there. He was an experienced SOCO, a dedicated family man and a genuinely lovely guy.

'Picked up a sudden death for you lot. I believe you've been a bit busy today?' Tony leaned against a desk as he watched Maya make the drinks.

'Yeah, we have. They rang it in as I was on my way to custody to process a prisoner. Bloody hell, Tony,' she glanced at her watch, 'it didn't take you long to do, did it? I've taken longer at burglary scenes!'

Tony laughed. 'By the time I got there, they were happy it wasn't suspicious. Hey, I met your mum there – Dominique?'

'Why was my mum at a crime scene?'

'He was one of her patients. She found him and rang us. She

was giving a statement to the cops when I arrived and asked me if I knew you. Lovely lady. She seemed a bit upset though.'

'She cares a lot about her patients. Who was he?'

Tony laughed scornfully. 'I can't imagine she would have cared too much about this one. He's a bloke called Jim Baron. He was a bit of a nasty bastard back in the day by all accounts, so it's no great loss. He was in bad health, seriously overweight and suffered with COPD. It looks like a heart attack. Cedar Lane took the call and there's a new DI over there. I think he just got a bit overexcited and wanted to call us in before using his common sense. You know what they can be like.'

'I'll ring her later and check she's okay. It's not the first time something like that has happened, but I can imagine it must still have been a shock for her. So, definitely not suspicious then?'

'Nah. He'll go for a coronial PM tomorrow. On the off-chance they do find anything dodgy, which I doubt, they'll stop it and call in a home office pathologist. There's certainly nothing sus at the scene.'

'But how do you *know* there's nothing suspicious. Have you ever been to a job like that and felt that something isn't quite right?' Maya recalled yet again the feeling of apprehension she had experienced at Gorman's house.

'Erm... some jobs have you scratching your head more than others as you piece together what's happened. Usually, we establish relatively quickly whether something's suspicious or not.'

'I know, but have you ever had a feeling that something's not quite right even though everything else points to a non-suspicious death?'

Tony eyed her carefully as he pondered on her question before eventually replying. 'What's happened?'

'Nothing...'

'Maya...'

'I had my first body the other day...'

'And?'

'It seemed really straightforward. Doctor Granger said it was his heart. But... I don't know.'

'Tell me...'

'It was just as we were finishing up at the scene... I got a sense of having missed something obvious. That something didn't quite sit right...'

'Hiya, Tony. Thought I heard voices. Where's that brew, Maya, I'm gasping.' Elaine emerged from the side office wiping sweat from her brow. The moment was lost as Tony and Elaine greeted each other and they all settled down with a brew.

The three of them began to chat amicably, discussing mutual acquaintances and which SOCOs were retiring, pregnant or had applied for promotion. They heard footsteps heading down the corridor and Maya wondered if it was Connor heading back in early, but unfortunately it was Andy.

'Tony,' Andy nodded his acknowledgement, 'good to see you, hope you're well, mate.' He sat down, completely ignoring the fact that Elaine and Maya were also in the room.

'We're fine, Andy, thanks for asking,' Elaine said sarcastically.

While Maya would have chosen to just ignore the rebuff, Elaine was not the type to let it go. Andy grunted incoherently, not even bothering to make eye contact with her. Maya could sense Elaine fizzing with indignation, while Tony sat awkwardly, not knowing how to break the tension.

'How was your warrant, Andy, did you find much at Nowak's house?' Maya attempted to ease the charged moment.

'No,' Andy replied flatly. He didn't look up and his refusal to add anything more caused the tension to build even further.

'Well, I better be getting back...' started Tony, but Elaine cut in.

'You're an ignorant bastard, Andy Carr, what is your problem?' she hissed.

'I haven't got one.' Andy sounded bored. He had resumed his usual position of feet up on the desk. He swept a hand through his hair before tapping away at his phone.

'Will you at least look at me when I'm speaking to you?' Elaine was on her feet now. Her usual ruddy cheeks had deepened to an even darker shade of red and spittle flew from her mouth as she spoke.

'Just leave him to it, Elaine,' Maya said placatingly.

'Yeah, come on, walk me out to my van and we'll have a smoke before I go,' Tony soothed, getting to his feet.

'I don't want a smoke. I want him to apologise for being so bloody rude.' Elaine was shaking now, her fists balled at her sides as she glared balefully at Andy. Maya was surprised Andy didn't drop dead on the spot from the look of pure hatred on Elaine's face.

Andy was still typing away on his phone, refusing to look up. He gave a little sigh and his lip curled in a sardonic manner. 'Bit uptight today, Elaine. You not getting any? Husband still playing away with that sexy little neighbour of yours?'

Time seemed to stand still. Andy had chosen to throw the most hurtful and personal thing he could at Elaine and Maya was shocked that even *he* could be so cruel.

'You *bastard*,' Elaine screamed. 'You complete fucking bastard.' She launched herself across the desk. Andy wheeled back in his chair, openly laughing at her and waving his hands in a mock surrender. Tony had Elaine gripped around the waist and was attempting to pull her back across the desk.

'C'mon, Elaine, he's not worth it.' Tony was panting with exertion. Elaine towered over him and was what Dominique would have called 'big-boned', so trying to restrain her was proving quite difficult. A computer monitor rocked precariously on the desk before crashing to the floor, taking the office phone with it.

'What the hell is going on in here?'

DI Mitton was framed in the doorway glowering reproachfully at the commotion in front of her. Tony still had Elaine in a half-hug across her waist. Maya stood with her hand over her mouth, gobsmacked, the displaced monitor and phone lay at her feet.

Andy was sat back in his chair, a look of pure innocence spread across his smug, angular face. It would have looked quite a comical scene if it hadn't been so serious.

'Alison, good job you showed up. I thought the mad bitch was going to kill me.' Andy puffed out his cheeks in relief.

Maya knew that Alison Mitton was no fool. She'd hazard a guess that the DI had worked with Andy and men like him for long enough to know he was no victim. As for Elaine, she was a respected SOCO known to be a sensible, strong-willed woman who wouldn't react so aggressively to a situation without provocation.

'It's *ma'am* to you.' Alison scowled pointedly. 'Elaine, go and have a cigarette and calm yourself down. Maya, if you wouldn't mind picking those bits off the floor for me, please. Andy, I'd like a full debrief of the scene examination relating to Piotr Nowak. Now please.' She nodded to Tony and stalked out of the office.

Elaine looked close to tears; she grabbed her bag and stormed out of the office, quickly followed by Tony. Maya gathered up the phone and monitor, watching Andy out of the corner of her eye. The smug look had been replaced with an uncharacteristically sheepish expression. Maya noticed his hands were shaking as he gathered up his scene notes and quickly annotated a few lines. Clearly his paperwork wasn't up to date. He hadn't made the contemporaneous notes in his crime-scene report that he should have; something Kym was incredibly strict about.

~

Andy walked into DI Mitton's office and sat himself down without even asking. 'The mad bitch tries to attack *me* and I'm the one who gets the curly finger.' He pouted petulantly, a pathetic look on the face of a man his age.

DI Mitton responded with a raised eyebrow, silently appraising Andy for long enough to make him squirm uncomfortably. She eventually addressed him in an even tone. 'I was coming into your office to ask about the scene at Nowak's. I've reviewed the disc of photographs you left on my desk and have to say they leave a lot to be desired.'

Andy attempted to speak but DI Mitton silenced him with a glare. 'I've been told you left the scene before the search dog was brought in.'

'I didn't know they were using a dog. No one told me,' he replied sulkily.

'Well, fortunately they did as the dog found a quantity of cash and some cocaine stashed in a storage box, which you not only missed, but is in an area of the scene which does not even appear on your photographs.' She tapped the disc as she spoke.

Andy didn't comment. His expression remained fixed; a muscle pulsated near his jaw.

'I'll be discussing your failings with Kym when she's next on duty. You can go.'

DI Mitton concentrated on a raft of paperwork in front of her, not even acknowledging Andy as he left the office. He stormed back up the corridor and began slamming items about as he gathered his paperwork. He could sense Maya watching him and that angered him even more. She'd only been in the place two minutes and was already trying to lord it over him. Playing the race card and pulling her pretty face because she didn't like the way he talked.

Andy raged silently at the injustice that he even had to share breathing space with the likes of Maya and Elaine. Who did these fucking women think they were, treating him like they did? They had no idea who he was and what he was capable of. He should be revered by them, not treated as if he was just a bit of a kid like that Connor. He was a man – a real man's man. He may not be a senior SOCO like Kym, but he had years of experience and that meant he should be afforded the same respect. If not more.

Still, he was patient. He would calm himself down and bide his time until the right opportunity arose so that he could show them all. And as for Kym bloody Lawson, she could stamp her prissy little feet at him as much as she wanted, he wouldn't rise to the bait. He'd been married enough times to know when to say and do the right things to buy himself some peace and quiet. Those women would rue the day that they ever crossed Andy Carr; he would make sure of that.

13

When she opened the door and saw it was me, she had laughed. *Not the reaction I had anticipated. Her eyes had widened fleetingly in surprise before she tossed her head back and barked that hollow laugh of hers. I asked her what the point of expensive electric gates was if she was going to leave them wide open.*

'Anyone could come wandering up that huge driveway of yours,' I had said. 'Anyone did! Come here, you,' she replied. Then she pulled me into the hallway in a huge embrace as if we were old friends. She had wrapped her bony arms around me, smothering me with her sickly scent, oblivious to the fact my arms remained pinned to my side.

She had ushered me into the lounge where unsurprisingly, she already had a bottle of something open. She clumsily forced a glass into my hand, as quick as most people would blink. She pushed me towards the sofa. One of those monstrosities that you sink into and wonder if you can ever get back out. She sat too close. Our knees were touching and as I talked, I noticed she still had that unnerving way of staring. It was as if her eyes were like maggots boring into an apple. She didn't flinch or blink. She just stared, her gaze level and unwavering. I'd forgotten how distracting it could be.

She was dressed to the nines as always. She wore a lightweight designer trouser suit meant for a woman much younger than her. She still had that stick-thin figure and it was obvious that she was no stranger to Botox. Her features were frozen in the recognisable mask of a telltale cat face, and I wondered how many facelifts she had endured. Probably so many that by rights her nipples should be on her forehead.

Her make-up was plastered on. Foundation battled against the warm weather to stop her sweating, and I noticed that her lipstick had bled into the thin smoker's lines around her mouth. Her mascara was so heavily applied it looked like she had a host of errant spider's legs jutting from her eyelids. She was definitely past it but was clearly deluded. She undoubtedly saw the woman of her twenties pout back at her every time she looked in the mirror.

That was probably why she drank. It was like the photographer's trick of rubbing Vaseline on the camera lens to soften the edges. Back in the day she had been beautiful, and she had known it. She used her looks and her body to manipulate people so she could get what she wanted. But our old friend Time had well and truly caught up with her.

As the saying goes, beauty is only ever skin deep. Even in her heyday, on the inside she had always been one hell of an ugly bitch. She was cold and ruthless with a sinister streak that would chill even the most hardened criminals to their core. She had the morality of a sewer rat and the only thing in life that motivated her was money. There was nothing she wouldn't do for the right currency.

Whatever she was up to these days was clearly still financing the lifestyle to which she had always been accustomed. I couldn't help wondering which poor bastard she had pincer-gripped by the bollocks as she squeezed the cash out of them. Her house screamed affluent although the crass furnishings muttered 'woman with no taste'. The place looked like a tart's boudoir. It was all animal print, feather boas and canvases of naked women. There were tits and arses displayed on *every wall; not that I'm complaining about that – I just prefer to think I have a more refined sense of taste.*

And speaking of taste, can you believe she tried it on with me? As if I would ever consider going with a woman like her. At first, I thought I was misreading the signs and that she was just being tactile. But the way she leaned even closer towards me, oblivious to my personal space, pressing herself against me, the flick of her hair, the constant licking of the lips and the hand that persistently wandered above the knee. Oh, and the fact she blatantly announced that she wanted to fuck me.

She had asked me about Louisa. She wanted to know if we were still together. She enquired in that husky voice of hers, her head cocked to one side, I assume to look coquettish. In reality, she looked like she had whiplash. It took me every ounce of self-control not to smash my fist into her ugly, vicious mouth. The juxtapose of Louisa's beautiful name on her cesspit lips was unbearable.

Fortunately, I managed to restrain myself for the sake of the plan and even managed to play along with her. Out of all of them, I knew she'd be the hardest to kill. She was no fool, after all. I knew I would have to tread very carefully to make sure she didn't second-guess my intentions before it was too late. She thought I was an old friend eager for a walk down memory lane, and I was happy to go along with that.

Her constant flirtation made it so much easier to get her where I wanted. She had always liked playing games; she had no idea this would be her last. The champagne was flowing as we chatted. The real deal too, no cheap supermarket version for her. It was also obvious that each time she 'popped to the loo' she was snorting a line of coke as her eyes became glossier and her behaviour even more wild and errant.

She agreed to write the note. She was like an excitable child compiling a Christmas list. It took her a while in her intoxicated state. She knelt at the coffee table, carefully printing each word out, her tongue poking from the corner of her mouth as she concentrated on forming the rounded letters. It was painful to watch, and I swear if I'd had a crayon, I would have asked her to use that. I even had to help her out with the bloody spelling.

As she scribbled away, I steeled myself to respond warmly to her flirtatious touches and even managed to spew a few suggestive comments her way. When she offered me a tour of the place, I was left in no doubt that the pièce-de-résistance would be her bedroom. I also knew it could provide me with an opportunity too good to miss and I was right.

She led me from room to palatial room, the castanet clicks of her Louboutin heels on the expensive tiled floor grated on my nerves. The kitchen made me laugh the most. It boasted a top-of-the-range Aga, huge American-style fridge and a large kitchen island, as well as a host of expensive-looking pots and pans.

My eyes briefly lingered on the knife block which stood alluringly on the kitchen worktop. I made a mental note that they were there. Just in case. It was typical of her to have such an extravagant kitchen. It was all for show. I had no doubt that the only time she came in here was to reach for another bottle of champagne. And as for cooking? No chance. I doubt she could even boil a kettle.

I followed her on the tour across the hallway and up the sweeping staircase. The first-floor landing boasted several en suite guest bedrooms, each as gaudily decorated as the next. There was also a room which she announced was the study. Ironic really, seeing as she was semi-literate. I assumed the computer and DVD equipment in there was where she stored her 'work'. She didn't linger in there. She pretty much dragged me in and then shoved me back out as an afterthought. Maybe common sense had penetrated through the alcohol and drugs, and her natural instinct not to reveal too much had given her a nudge.

She maximised the charm then as she excitedly grabbed me by the hand and dragged me up a smaller, but no less luxurious stairway.

'The penthouse suite,' she had declared with a flourish of the hand, revealing a porn star's paradise.

The huge open-plan room consisted of a circular king-sized bed positioned below a mirrored ceiling. The closet doors were also mirrored so every angle of the body could be captured. There was even more animal print, and the walls were painted a sickening, deep-cerise colour.

'There's an en suite through there,' she had said throatily, pointing towards one of the mirrored doors. She had attempted the coquettish look again as she meandered backwards toward another door which she pulled open with glee. 'And this,' she had purred, 'is my Pandora's box.'

I had to swallow down the bile that rose in my throat as she revealed a walk-in wardrobe which housed countless sex toys. There were dildos of every size, shape and colour, butt plugs, whips, paddles, handcuffs, nipple clamps, and God knows what else. All carefully and proudly arranged.

She had raised an over-plucked eyebrow in my direction. The Botox did its job and no other part of her face followed. 'See anything you'd like to play with?' she had asked teasingly.

I'd forced a smile as I leant towards her, running my hand gently down her frozen face.

'Just you,' I had said, as I stared suggestively into her eyes, before turning and nodding towards the double patio doors. 'What's out there?' I asked and she practically skipped toward them, flinging them open to reveal a rooftop terrace.

We stepped outside and I glanced admiringly at the hot tub and patio furniture. She was leaning against the wall, watching me like a hawk as I sauntered towards her. The view stretched out for miles, from her long, private driveway to the fields and hills of the countryside that surrounded her home. The heavy air smelt so fresh and sweet, a mixture of grass, warm wood and sunshine.

She was smirking as I stood in front of her, so close our hips were touching. Her lower back nestled into the brickwork as she arched forward so she could grind her groin against mine. The bright sunlight accentuated her flaws even more and I was disgusted to see a crusting of white powder in the corner of one of her nostrils. It was as if every detail of her face had been magnified, from her large pores to her overstretched, unnaturally taut skin.

She had wrapped her arms around my neck and began to work her lips over my face and throat. It was all I could do not to retch. I turned her around, so I didn't have to look at that face. Her hips were pressed against the wall, her scrawny arse burrowing into me. I ran my hands along the front of her body, hearing her moan as I skimmed her stomach and breasts. I knew she was aroused at the thought of gaining the one sexual conquest she thought she would never have.

There was a thick piece of trunking which ran along the wall, concealing the wiring for the lights and hot tub. She had giggled childishly as she stepped on it, teetering precariously as she splayed her arms out.

'I'm flying,' she exclaimed, reminiscent of the scene from Titanic. I had gripped her hips firmly as she wobbled precariously, warning her to be careful.

'It's stunning out here. Absolutely beautiful,' I had said as she leant back against me.

'Are you talking about the view or me?' she had murmured hoarsely as she glanced at me over her shoulder.

'I'm talking about the view,' I had said, sweetly. 'It's just perfect. You, however, really are the ugliest, most grotesque woman I have ever met. You always have been. You disgust me.'

She had never been spoken to like that before. Nobody had ever used those words to describe her. She had been adored all her life. A vicious narcissist, who had used her looks to cajole, entice, and destroy others, I loved the irony that these words were the last she would ever hear.

She tried to pull away from me. To step down from the trunking.

She was twisting angrily and spitting profanities. In her inebriated state, she was no match for me as I continued to pin her against me. I had to do it now. I couldn't afford to risk any scratches or other defence marks. My height worked to my advantage as I heaved her upwards from her midriff. She was as light as a feather. Her knees barely scraped the brickwork before she was over the edge of the wall.

For a woman with such a low, husky voice she certainly screamed very shrilly. The thud of her body smashing into the gravel below was encored by a beautiful silence. I glanced over the wall and saw her lying like a shattered marionette. Annoyingly, I had to admit that even broken, her legs still looked good.

14

Andy Carr woke up with a raging hangover. The weekend had passed by in an alcohol-induced blur which he was now seriously regretting. God knows he had needed a blowout after the stress he'd been under lately, but even by his standards, he'd drank a lot. He smiled despite himself, as the memories came trickling back. He recalled the look on her face when he had arrived at her door. He felt himself harden, despite his hangover, at the recollection of everything that had happened afterwards.

Then, as if he'd been slapped across the face, he started, as the gravity of what he had done hit home. He had taken a serious risk; more so than before. He could so easily have been caught out and just because he hadn't, that still didn't mean he had got away with it. And if word got out what he had done, his life wouldn't be worth living. The consequences were too severe to even consider. All his worst nightmares would come true.

Groaning, he sat up, driving the heels of his hands into his eyes as if to rub the pain away. How could he have been so stupid? He had been reckless and impulsive. Again. He frantically tried to recall every detail of last night. He recalled scraps of conversation that made him sigh. Then, leaning over, he pulled his trousers towards him, spilling the contents of the pockets onto the bed. His wallet and phone were there. That was good. As far as he could tell, he'd not left anything incriminating behind. Only she knew he'd been there, and it wasn't as if she could say anything.

He smiled to himself, his usual arrogance like a comfort blanket. The smile quickly faded as he glanced at the alarm clock. He cursed the fact he had either failed to set it the night before or had slept right through it. He was late for work. Very late. That would mean Kym would be on his back too. Although compared to what would happen to him if the truth got out, she was the least of his worries.

Andy reached for his phone. He would palm Kym off with some excuse about a stomach bug. He always knew how to talk women round. It wasn't just his looks that attracted them, but his easy chat and teasing banter. He knew how to charm the ladies and how to keep them wanting more. He practised his poorly voice out loud in his empty bedroom several times, until he was satisfied he had the tone just right. Smiling at his own cunning, he reached for his phone. He had the luck of the devil and could get away with anything.

15

Maya was reading the overnight summary log, which detailed all the incidents which had occurred during the night shift. There had been several assaults, one of which appeared quite serious. The sweltering heat was referred to as Section 18 weather, which was the terminology for grievous bodily harm. Fraying tempers combined with the consumption of too much chilled alcohol resulted in spurts of unpremeditated violence.

Kym marched out of her side office and clapped her hands for attention. 'Ladies and gentlemen, Andy has just phoned in. He won't be in today as he's not well.'

'Nothing trivial, I hope,' Elaine muttered. This caused Chris to howl with laughter and earned her a warning look off Kym.

'In view of the fracas between the two of you the other day I suggest you keep such unhelpful comments to yourself.' Kym scowled. 'We don't want to cause any further animosity, do we?'

Elaine looked suitably chastened and Maya couldn't help pitying her. Kym was now surveying the duties board to see who was working that day, so she knew how many staff she had to allocate to the day's incidents. The phone rang and Maya was about to answer it, but Amanda beat her to it, causing her to flick a playful middle finger in Maya's direction.

'Did Andy say how long he'd be off for?' Chris asked Kym.

'He said he thought it was just a twenty-four-hour thing so hopefully he should be back tomorrow.' She shrugged, still concentrating on the duties board.

'Hangover then.' Nicola smirked. Kym turned to face her, frowning at the comment. She was just about to speak when Amanda raised her hand, indicating the phone call she was having was of some importance. Connor leant over towards the office radio and turned the music down in anticipation. Everyone remained hushed, listening to Amanda's side of the conversation with bated breath. Eventually Amanda ended the call and sat back in her chair, pushing her reading glasses up on top of her head.

'Suicide,' she announced succinctly.

'Anything in it for us?' Kym frowned. It was unusual for them to attend a suicide unless there was something particularly exceptional about the death. Otherwise, a coroner's officer would normally attend if there was no forensic requirement.

'Well, that was comms. They've made CID aware and are letting us know. I guess at the very least we'll have to go and record the scene in view of who it is,' Amanda replied warily.

'Who? Spit it out, Amanda, for Christ's sake,' Kym snapped.

'Celeste Warren.'

It was DI Redford who answered, he had appeared unnoticed in the doorway. He was tall and lean, his buzz-cut hair revealing enough stubble to hint at his auburn colouring. He was dressed immaculately in a tailored suit and highly polished shoes. His face did not reveal anything about the name he had just disclosed, but the stunned silence which followed, indicated to Maya that the person was someone very well known.

Chris broke the silence. Puffing his cheeks, he blew out slowly. 'Celeste Warren? Fuckin' hell. I didn't even realise she was still going. I assumed she died years ago, boss.'

'You're not the only one. We've just had the exact same conversation,' Redford nodded towards Amanda, 'you must remember her surely?'

'Oh yes,' she scowled, 'she was a nasty piece of work. I remember locking her up one day and she ripped a clump of my hair out. Vicious bitch.'

Redford nodded and addressed Kym. 'She was found by the housekeeper. It looks like she's jumped. I've spoken with the first officer on the scene, Greg Owen. He says initially it looks like she'd been pissed and fallen off the roof terrace.

'Paramedics have confirmed life extinct and I've asked everyone to withdraw for now. The housekeeper was quite happy to have the day off. Apparently, there's no love lost between them. Greg's staying near the body until we get there. The property's huge and is gated, so we don't need to worry about prying eyes. He said if we shout up comms when we get there, he'll open the electric gates for us. The housekeeper has left him the keys.'

'No problem.' Kym took one last glance over the duties board before turning to Maya. 'This sounds straightforward enough, are you happy to pick it up? Get a bit more experience under your belt. If there is any cause for concern when you get to the scene, ring me. Otherwise, if you're happy it's suicide, photograph everything and bag her up ready for the mortuary, okay?'

DI Redford turned to Maya. 'We're a bit thin on the ground this morning, but I've got a DS covering who has transferred over from Cedar Lane. I'll ask him to meet you there.' He raised his hand in thanks towards Kym. 'Keep me posted.'

'So, tell me about her,' Maya said, turning to Amanda and Chris, 'what's she known for?'

Connor pulled up his chair eagerly and even Kym perched on the edge of Nicola's desk ready to hear all about the infamous Celeste Warren.

Chris began, 'I first heard of her years ago when we did a raid on a brothel. She was the madam in charge and ran that place with an iron fist. I've done raids on brothels before...'

'I bet, you dirty bastard.' Elaine sniggered, but she was quickly hushed by Nicola.

'But this was different,' Chris continued. 'The women, well, girls that worked there actually seemed relieved to see the cops. It was strongly suspected that Celeste had been people trafficking before it even became a "thing". Anyway, a couple of the girls were underage so obviously they threw the book at her. Don't ask me how, but she managed to wriggle out of most charges and avoided a potentially long prison sentence.'

'It was partly due to the fact none of the victims would testify against her,' Amanda said. 'They were too scared. We also suspected at the time that the prosecutor was a regular punter of hers, so didn't put as much effort into getting her sent down as he should have done.'

Amanda shook her head sadly. 'Of all the people I've dealt with during my career, she's been one of the worst. She used to be a looker back in the day. One of those women who are so beautiful, people just gravitate towards them. Anyway, she used to do the usual pimps' trick. Befriend vulnerable teenagers – girls and boys – who were on the streets or whatever. She'd give them a place to stay and offer to look after them. Next thing you know, she had them hooked on drugs and running tricks to pay her back.

'The money she made off those poor people over the years. She was infamous for her temper and was well known to torture anyone who crossed her, so no one dared to come to us about her. She used to brand people. She had a diamond pendant shaped in the initial C, which she used to heat with a cigarette lighter then press into the face or neck of anyone who worked for her or just pissed her off.

'If anyone tried to get away or refused to work for her, she'd torture them. Really sick stuff you can't even imagine. Any proper beatings she liked to delegate to one of her "bouncers", but she always stayed to watch. The fact she's committed suicide is ironic, because I know of at least five young 'uns who topped themselves in desperation to get away from her.' Amanda shook her head before she continued.

'Not only that, but she also used to blackmail a lot of her clients. Most of the rooms she used had cameras and recording equipment in, so she could threaten the punters with their indiscretion in full Technicolour. It's no wonder she's rolling in it. I guess crime does pay for some people.'

Amanda had been subconsciously touching the back of her head as she spoke, almost as if she could recall the spot where Celeste Warren had once torn a clump of her hair out, back in the day.

'Suicide though?' Chris shrugged. 'Wouldn't have thought that of her.'

'No, me neither,' Amanda said, 'wouldn't have thought it from someone as narcissistic as her.'

'People change though, don't they?' Elaine suggested. 'You said yourself, Chris, you thought she was already dead. If she's been out of the spotlight for the last few years, maybe she's been depressed or whatever. Missed the cut and thrust of her old life and couldn't cope with being a has-been. Maybe age softened her, and she regretted all the bad things she'd done?'

Chris and Amanda nodded in agreement at the suggestion just as something occurred to Maya.

'Bloody hell,' she breathed. 'This year is getting like 2016 was for celebrities.'

'What do you mean?' Amanda tuned to look at her.

'Well, you remember how loads of celebrities died in 2016 and everyone was saying it was like there was a curse or something?'

'Ah, yeah.' Nicola nodded. 'Three of my favourites died; David Bowie, Prince and George Michael. Oh, and Victoria Wood – I always loved her. What's your point?'

'It seems to be the same with our criminals just lately.'

Amanda looked thoughtful. 'Yeah, I get your point. There was Gorman, the guy you and Chris did, Jim Baron, who Tony came over from Alder Street to deal with, and now Celeste Warren.'

'You reckon somebody's bumping off all our criminals then, Maya?' Elaine laughed, 'I hope they'll not put us out of a job. I've got a mortgage to pay.'

Chris was about to make a quip when Kym cut him dead. 'Do you remember the conversation you and I had about conspiracy theories?' She stared icily at Maya, clearly unimpressed with the suggestion regardless of whether it was banter. 'Can I even trust you to attend this crime scene, or are you going to concoct more fairy stories and come back with some magic beans?'

'Yeah... yes... of course you can trust me,' Maya stammered. 'Sorry, Kym.'

'I should think so too. Keep an eye out while you're there for any paperwork or other clues that may suggest that Celeste was in some sort of financial difficulty. Also make a note of any medication that you find, particularly antidepressants, that sort of thing, and anything else that may indicate the state of mind she was in.

'Basically, find me evidence to support the fact that this is the suicide it appears to be, so we can dismiss any ridiculous fantasist notions. In your own time, ladies and gentlemen, can we please get back to doing the job we're paid for?' Giving her usual double clap Kym flounced back to her office leaving the others suitably disgruntled.

Nicola and Chris smiled pityingly at Maya and Elaine reached over to give her a reassuring half-hug. No one liked being on the receiving end of Kym's sharp tongue. They had all been brought to task by her at some point, which is why they empathised with Maya.

'Her bark's worse than her bite.' Amanda smiled reassuringly.

'I feel a right bloody idiot,' Maya mumbled. 'I suppose I was being flippant, but it *is* a coincidence, isn't it?'

'I don't know about coincidence so much. People die, Maya. And the chances are that people like Celeste, Jim Baron and Karl Gorman are all victims of the life they lead, which takes a toll on their health physically or mentally in Celeste's case. You should know by now how logical and systematic Kym is. It's okay to have an opinion, but don't go getting her back up by theorising about events. She doesn't like it.'

'No shit, Sherlock.' Maya grinned, feeling reassured. 'I better go and give this job one hundred per cent then, so she has no excuse to ram those magic beans down my throat.'

Maya hurried out, concerned that CID would arrive before her and she didn't want to keep them waiting. She went over in her mind again and again what she would need to do when she arrived at the scene. This time she really had to prove her competence to Kym. She would find the evidence she needed at the address to prove what state of mind Celeste Warren had been in and that would be that. A straightforward non-suspicious sudden death. What could possibly go wrong?

16

Maya pulled over on the long stretch of country road which led to the driveway of Celeste's palatial home. The property wasn't situated on a typical main road, rather a stretch which cut through the beautiful countryside, past farmers' fields and old stone walls. The property was fronted by large, electric gates. The name Field View was engraved ornately next to a video intercom fixed to a concrete post.

Maya had parked in front of a Vauxhall Astra. The non-liveried vehicles driven by the CID and plain-clothed officers were notoriously either a white Vauxhall Astra or Corsa, all bearing the same sixty-eight registration plate. On seeing her, the driver waved. Maya approached the car, and he released the central locking so she could climb into the passenger seat.

'Maya Barton.' She smiled as she extended her hand.

'Hello, Maya, I'm Dave Wainwright. I've been expecting you. I was just making a few notes while I was waiting.' He tapped the familiar blue hard-backed Banner notebook that detectives used to record their actions in.

Wainwright looked about late fifties, with greying hair and a pockmarked complexion. He was rather rotund, his stomach straining against his shirt and tie. His gold wedding band dug into his sausage fingers. She supposed the typical CID lifestyle of takeaway dinners and McDonald's lunches had taken its toll on the detective's figure.

'So, Maya, what do you know about the job?' He smiled kindly. His avuncular manner and soft tone of voice endeared her to him immediately. Still smarting from the dressing down she had received from Kym, Maya was determined to prove herself at this job and she felt even more confident knowing she was going to be working alongside the seemingly pleasant DC Wainwright.

'I've been told that the infamous Celeste Warren has jumped from her roof terrace in what appears to be a suicide. I take it you've heard of her?'

'Oh, yes.' He held the top of his pen in his mouth as he scribbled some notes down. 'Everyone knew Celeste. I've heard stories about her in my time that'd make your hair even curlier.'

Maya nodded. 'My intention is to record the scene photographically, search for any evidence that may indicate her state of mind prior to her death and then we can scrape her up and ship her to the corpse-cooler.'

'Corpse-cooler?'

'The mortuary.'

He laughed. 'Nice turn of phrase, Maya.'

'At this stage,' she continued, 'there's no suggestion that she will need a home office post-mortem. That may change, of course, if we find anything that arouses our suspicion. The CSM is quite happy from the information we've received up to now, that it's a straightforward suicide.'

'Yeah, fair enough, but suicide? Who would have thought that's how *she* would have chosen to go? I wonder what drove her to it. Have you any idea?'

Maya gave a hollow laugh. 'After the bollocking I've just had, I'm not speculating about anything else today.'

'Oh?' He frowned quizzically.

'Never mind.' She shook her head, still feeling foolish about her flippant theory.

'C'mon,' he goaded lightly. 'You can't say something like that and not tell me. What's happened?'

The fact she was still burning with shame over the recent incident and seeing how understanding and kind Dave Wainwright seemed to be, was all the encouragement Maya needed to unburden herself.

'I made a flippant comment in the office about how this year was becoming the year of criminals dying, in the same way as 2016 became known for losing a lot of celebrities.'

'Okay...' Wainwright said hesitantly as he tried to grasp Maya's understanding.

'Well, it started with Karl Gorman the other week, then Jim Baron and now Celeste. It was just meant as a joke really. But the last few sudden deaths we've dealt with have involved well-known criminals. Anyway, I got a complete roasting off Kym about my "fantasist notions", which is why I said I won't be speculating anymore.'

'These sudden deaths though, have any of them been found to be suspicious?' Wainwright said as he scribbled something down.

'Well, no.' Maya was distracted by a white car that had just driven slowly past them. She could see through the rear-view mirror that it was reversing and heading back towards them and she was curious to see who it was. 'I mean, I only attended Gorman's death, a colleague of mine went to Baron's. There was nothing suspicious about Gorman's in the end and I believe the same was concluded about Baron. I think in both cases, their unhealthy lifestyle had caught up on them, so natural causes really.' She shrugged with little conviction.

'Like you said though, it is bit of a coincidence, isn't it? The death of three known criminals in the space of a few weeks is enough to make you wonder if there *is* something suspicious behind it.'

'Well, they do say there's no such thing as coincidence in the cops. You should know that better than anyone. But that said, we haven't found anything that has given us, or the pathologist, cause for concern.'

Wainwright raised an eyebrow. 'Don't speak too soon; you've not examined *this* crime scene yet.'

The white car that had caught Maya's attention was now parked up alongside Maya's van. Wainwright turned to watch as a man in a suit climbed out of the car. He was clutching a leather holdall and paused briefly to peer through the window of Maya's van.

'Looks like we've got company.' Wainwright nodded towards the man as he spotted them in the car and began striding over.

'It's not the bloody press, is it?' Maya tutted. 'That's the last thing we need.'

Suddenly the passenger door was wrenched open and the man was looming through the doorway.

'Maya Barton?'

'Yes? Who are you and what the hell do you think you're doing?' She reached across to pull the passenger door shut again but he swiftly blocked her with his leg.

'What the hell are *you* doing more like? Get out of the car!' he hissed as he glared at Wainwright. Suddenly a crackle of static from the police radio filled the air, clearly coming from the man's holdall.

Maya was temporarily stunned and confused in equal measures. Despite his padded frame, Dave Wainwright was doing a good job of sinking back into the driver's seat, wearing a sheepish, yet amused look on his face.

'You're not a detective?' Maya stated stupidly.

'He's one of the biggest parasites I've ever met,' the man replied as he pulled the door open even wider and gestured for Maya to get out of the car. 'He's a reporter for the *Evening News*.'

17

Maya leapt out of the driving seat like a scalded cat. 'You bastard. You absolute bastard!' she screamed at the journalist. 'You let me think you were a police officer.'

Wainwright looked completely unabashed. 'Your mistake, darlin' not mine. You were the one who willingly got into *my* car. I haven't done anything wrong.'

He was laughing now, and it was all Maya could do to hold back the angry tears that threatened to spill down her cheeks. She'd be damned if she'd give him the satisfaction of seeing her get upset. She'd fucked up again, and royally this time. That was humiliation enough.

'You've got your pound of flesh, Wainwright, now fuck off,' the man hissed as he pulled Maya away towards her van.

'I'm not breaking any laws by being here and you can't make me move on,' Wainwright shouted after them. 'I told you, I've done nothing wrong!'

Maya climbed numbly into the driving seat and started up the van as the detective settled himself into the passenger seat and shouted up on the police radio, 'DS Dwyer to comms. Please can you show myself and SOCO at the scene at Field View? Can you ask PC Owen to open the gates for us and also update the log that the press are sniffing around on Mile Lane?'

The radio crackled an assent and Maya drove forward in anticipation of the large electric gates beginning to swing open. She was so mortified and humiliated; she could barely bring herself to speak.

'Are you okay?' he asked. She nodded numbly and concentrated on driving through the gates as he exhaled.

'He's a bastard that Wainwright, I've met him before. When I was in uniform. I was guarding the scene of a murder and he pulled up and started chatting to the neighbours. Because of his car and how he approached them, they assumed, like you, that he was a detective and started to tell him all about the family.'

'That's awful.'

He nodded. 'There was no way they would have talked to the press otherwise. He printed every word including the neighbours' names. It was as frustrating as hell because he'd not actually claimed he was a police officer, so I couldn't nick him for that. He just likes playing on people making that assumption and he's very good at it.'

'Well, he had me fooled,' Maya said miserably.

'I know it's easier said than done, but don't beat yourself up about it. You weren't to know. If I'd got here before you it wouldn't have happened. I got delayed on the way out by an urgent phone call, otherwise I would have been here first and you wouldn't have spoken to him.'

'I've only got myself to blame for making stupid assumptions. It's certainly not your fault, but I appreciate the sentiment.' Maya smiled at him.

He smiled back and extended his hand. 'Rude of me to not even properly introduce myself, I'm Jack Dwyer.'

They shook hands as Maya took in his appearance. He was early thirties, tall and lean, with a shaved head and a hint of stubble on his face. He had dark eyes and an easy smile. He was wearing charcoal-coloured suit trousers, a short-sleeved, crisp white shirt and bright-blue tie. He seemed pleasant enough and she appreciated his efforts to reassure her.

They had driven up the driveway and pulled up outside the front door of Field View. Jack let out a low whistle. 'Blimey, it's not often we get to come to nice properties like this. Most of our crime scenes are usually shitholes.' Maya nodded in agreement and was about to switch the engine off when Jack held his hand up to stop her.

'Before we go in, you better just let me know what you said to Wainwright. It might be worth me letting the boss know before we leave as a bit of damage limitation.'

Maya groaned. 'He's going to print what I've just told him, isn't he?' She dropped her head on her hands over the steering wheel and let out a little scream.

'Maybe. What did you say?'

Jack listened in silence as Maya relayed the conversation and admitted she'd shared not only the news of Celeste Warren's apparent suicide, but also their conversation about the coincidental sudden deaths of three known criminals.

'Listen' he said reassuringly, 'this news about Warren is going to be huge. She's been infamous for decades. As for the other deaths, that was just your supposition. I can't see him printing anything so vague that has no basis for fact.'

He squeezed her arm reassuringly. 'What's done is done. Let's check this scene out and I'll have a word with the boss when I ring to debrief him, okay?'

Maya smiled gratefully at him. They made their way round to the back of the van where they busied themselves with selecting the right size scene suits and gathering up masks and gloves. When they were ready, they signed into PC Owen's scene log and Maya took a couple of photographs to record the front of the palatial dwelling.

Jack Dwyer was right, Maya thought. She couldn't take back the conversation she'd had with Wainwright any more than she could take back her sudden death theory in front of Kym. She found herself wondering how Wainwright had heard of Celeste's death so soon. She recalled the conversation she'd had with Amanda about someone in Beech Field leaking information. The word *corruption* hung on her like a dead weight and she wondered whether she should say something to Jack.

Then she thought about how she had already messed up once again and decided to leave it. Now was not the time and certainly not the place to worry about it. Celeste Warren was lying dead on the asphalt at the back of this house and it was Maya's job to record and examine the scene.

'Do we need stepping plates?' Jack hovered uncertainly at the front door.

'There's nothing to suggest anything suspicious, so no, not at this stage,' Maya said. 'Obviously if she'd been found riddled with bullets or with a knife sticking out of her chest, then we'd bring in the stepping plates. Our scene suits and overshoes are a good enough precaution in the meantime.'

Maya entered the front door and photographed her way down the decorative hallway and into the lounge. She was impressed with the size of the house, but not so much with the décor, which was needlessly avaricious. Once she had photographically recorded each side of the room, she began to have a closer look around, starting with the glass coffee table which presented an empty champagne bottle, a champagne glass, two pink Swarovski coasters and a piece of paper.

'Suicide note,' she called to Jack as she took a close-up photograph of it in situ on the coffee table. He quietly appeared at her side and peered over her shoulder as she read aloud.

'*To Whom It May Concern, I would like to say sorry to all the people who have suffered because of me. I am sorry for all the bad things I have done. I am ~~ripent~~ ~~repentunt~~ repentant.*'

The note had been written in a large, looping print. The failed spellings had been scored through heavily as if written by a child. The writing was signed off with Celeste Warren's inimitable signature, the flourish of which was punctuated with a kiss in the form of an 'X'.

Maya placed the note carefully back on the table next to the empty champagne bottle and glass. 'I'll exhibit that and take it back with me,' Maya informed Jack. 'It can always go for chemical treatment to enhance fingerprints if need be.'

'Surely there's no need for that if it's not suspicious though?'

'I'll collect it and if the boss is satisfied there's nothing further to examine, then it can just be booked into property rather than go to the lab. It's quite a succinct suicide note, isn't it?'

'They usually are,' Jack said. 'Usually a line of apology, occasionally a reason why and a final "I love you". Goodbye cruel world, that kind of thing. A lot of people don't even leave them. You have to consider the extreme frame of mind somebody's going to be in before they take their own life. Sad really.' He glanced around the rest of the room, no longer interested in the note, choosing instead to peruse a photograph album of Celeste back when she had been in her prime.

They made their way through to the kitchen where Jack discovered more signs that Celeste had been drinking. Maya photographed another empty champagne bottle and a crystal tumbler that smelt strongly of gin.

She then concentrated on scouring through the contents of a kitchen drawer which contained various bits of paperwork, including an address book and copies of a mobile phone contract and a warranty.

Maya compared Celeste's handwriting and the signature with the kiss, to that from the suicide note. She was happy they were one and the same. She carefully took photographs so the comparison could be shown to the coroner.

'Do you want to come and photograph this too, Maya?' Jack called.

He had disappeared into the downstairs toilet, which was accessed from the utility room, just off the kitchen. He nodded towards the sink where the faint traces of lines of cocaine remained evident on the tiled surface. An empty, clear snap bag and rolled-up fifty-pound note lay next to the telltale lines.

'Champagne, gin *and* charlie. She must've been smacked off her tits,' Jack mused as Maya snapped away. 'Shall we go and have a quick look upstairs and then we can go and see what state Madam's in?'

'Yeah, sure.'

As before, she led the way photographing their route through the house until they arrived in Celeste's bedroom. The patio door was wide open, and Maya took a moment to savour the sweet-scented breeze that drifted across the room. The paper scene suit had become unbearably hot in the warm weather, and Maya could already feel herself begin to dehydrate.

'Jesus, this is the archetypal tart's boudoir if ever I've seen one.' Jack surveyed the room taking in the animal print furnishings and the imposing circular bed.

'Seen many, have you?' Maya said with a smirk.

'That's for me to know and you to wonder,' he replied with a raise of his eyebrows.

It was difficult to photograph the room without Maya capturing her own reflection in one of the many mirrors. When she had finally finished, she made her way out onto the roof terrace and took a few more pictures. Satisfied that she had recorded everything adequately, she looked over the edge of the wall and surveyed Celeste Warren's broken body.

She was joined by Jack, who let out a low whistle at the distance between the roof and the body on the floor.

'She will be known from hereon in as Humpty Dumpty,' Maya quipped as she photographed the body from her advantage viewpoint.

'She'll not be causing any more trouble, that's for sure,' Jack said. 'I'll just have a quick scan round the bedroom while you finish up out here.'

Maya carefully scanned the wall and floor for scuff marks or anything similar. She noticed what appeared to be partial footwear marks on thick uPVC trunking that ran around the wall. The marks were consistent with Celeste having used this as a step-up to the top of the wall before she had jumped. The patio furniture did not appear disturbed, and like the rest of the house so far, there appeared to be nothing untoward. Certainly nothing that would indicate a struggle or foul play had taken place.

'Hey, Maya, come and cop a load of this,' Jack called. Taking one last look at Celeste's body, Maya returned to the bedroom where Jack was stood staring into a walk-in wardrobe. The innocuous-looking space was filled with a huge array of sex toys and other paraphernalia. They had been displayed in a manner that resembled an exhibition.

'Blimey.' Maya let out a snort. 'Humpty Dumpty liked a bit of rumpy-pumpy, didn't she?'

'She certainly did. Rumour has it she's been rogered more times than the police radio.'

'Well, God forbid a woman should be able to enjoy sex too. They'll be giving us the vote next,' Maya said dryly as Jack stepped back so she could include the wardrobe and its contents in her scene photographs.

'All done,' she said. 'Shall we go outside and have a look at her?'

He nodded and the two of them made their way out. As the entrance via the stable door in the kitchen was locked, they walked from the front door to the rear of the property.

Celeste had landed as if she was doing a jumping jack. Her legs and arms were extended; a large pool of blood had settled like treacle underneath her body and around her head area. Celeste's neck lay at an awkward angle and Maya suspected it was broken. Most of her face had been mashed into the concrete. Her left eye had been obliterated causing the eyeball to hang from the socket. It was partially covered with a sweep of hair, which Maya carefully smoothed away before taking a series of photographs.

Maya carefully examined Celeste's exposed hand, wrists and forearms for any obvious injuries that could relate to defence wounds. Once again, she was surprised at how cold the body felt despite the hot weather. Satisfied that there was nothing apparent, she gave Jack the nod and between them, they carefully rolled her over onto her back.

As the body shifted position, a fresh stream of blood pooled from the shattered face. The sudden stream caused Jack to instinctively jump backwards, causing Maya to laugh.

'All right, you,' he said. 'At least I've not struck up a conversation with her.'

Maya rolled her eyes. 'You've heard too, have you?'

'I hate to tell you this, but *everyone's* heard.'

'Well, *everyone* might have to hear about you jumping at the sight of a little bit of blood,' she retorted as she continued to photograph the body. Next, she returned her attention back toward the house so she could record the location of the body in conjunction with the roof terrace.

'So, what do we think?' Jack sank to his haunches and stared at the smashed face. 'Did Humpty jump, fly, or was she pushed?'

'Fly?'

'From the drugs and booze. She might have thought she was flying. It does happen.'

Maya nodded. 'But surely she wouldn't have written that note if she was tripping.' She pondered the position of the body. 'Was the property secure when the housekeeper arrived?'

'Apparently the electric gates were open, but that's not unusual as Celeste didn't drive. She left the gates open for the local taxi firm which she used frequently. Anyway, the housekeeper let herself in the front door with her key. According to her initial account, she knew her employer must still be at home because the entrance panel on the burglar alarm didn't sound when she let herself in.'

'And?'

'She went straight upstairs to her bedroom as, again, it was quite common for her to find Celeste sleeping off the excess from the night before. It's become part of her working routine to rouse her, clean her up and feed her.'

'Sounds like she was extremely high maintenance.'

'It would seem so. Anyway, she spotted the doors to the roof terrace were open and looked out to see if Celeste was in the garden. She spotted the body from up there, which is when she phoned us. As she was clearly dead, she didn't even bother going outside, just sat on the front doorstep smoking a fag while she waited for the cops to arrive. Greg Owen said she was a bit shaken up, understandably, but had seen all sorts over the years she's worked here so wasn't as shocked as you might otherwise expect.'

'It's looking like Humpty jumped then,' Maya said. 'It's a bit strange though,' she mused as she recalled the suicide note.

'What is?'

'The crossing out. On the note. She's attempted to write *repentant* twice before she's got it right. It's as if somebody has corrected her, don't you think?'

'Not really, no,' Jack said bluntly. 'She was never known for being the academic type and she was off her tits.'

Maya thought for a moment. The familiar nagging doubt she had felt at Gorman's had returned. To all intents and purposes, Celeste appeared to have committed suicide, but instinctively, it seemed too... staged.

'It's just... to me it looks like someone has corrected her while she was writing it. She's made two attempts to write it and spelt it wrong, then written it correctly on the third go.'

'Maybe she looked it up?' Jack shrugged.

'Really? There's more chance of finding Viagra in a convent than a dictionary in that house. From what we've seen I reckon the only book she ever read was the *Kama Sutra*. It's just the word *repentant* too. It just seems to me like a strange word for someone like Celeste to use, do you not think?'

'Not particularly. Personally, I reckon you're overthinking things.' Jack sounded terse.

'There were two coasters on the table too. She must have had company.'

'Maybe one was for the gin glass. She'd been mixing her drinks and snorting coke. Her brain must have been fried. She may well have had company earlier and they had the gin. Maybe when they left it caused her mood to drop. Who knows? There are no signs of a disturbance and nothing appears stolen. I'm calling suicide. Do you agree?'

Maya paused. She needed more time to think but Jack's insistence was domineering, bordering on impatience. She was also mindful that Kym would be expecting an update soon. The heat was oppressive, and the glaring sunlight ricocheting off the tiled patio was giving her a headache.

'You're right,' she conceded. 'I suppose I am overthinking it. I just don't want to fuck up any more than I already have done. I'm going to fingerprint and swab that glass before we go anyway, just for my own peace of mind. Can you give me a hand bagging her up? I know the undertakers would normally do it, but it doesn't seem fair leaving it to them the state she's in.'

'If you need me to.' He looked wary at the thought and Maya was beginning to suspect he wasn't comfortable around bodies. It took them a while to carefully package the shattered remains of Celeste Warren into the body sheet and bag, and they were both pouring with sweat by the time they'd finished. Panting with the exertion, Jack and Maya took a moment to sink onto a garden bench, enjoying the welcome relief of the shade.

'I'll ask Greg to contact the duty undertakers and get her shipped off to the morgue.' Jack straightened up. 'I'm going to head back to my car and phone the boss. Are you ready to go?'

'Nearly,' said Maya. 'I'm just going to write my scene notes up and swab and fingerprint the gin glass. I'll recover the suicide note too. I'll come and see you before I go to see what the boss has said about Wainwright.'

Maya headed back into the kitchen alone and proceeded to take a saliva swab from the rim of the gin glass. She wrote the swabs and the exhibit bag out carefully, while considering why she was doing it. Both she and Jack had agreed that Celeste had committed suicide.

And yet... And yet...

Maya still couldn't shake off the peculiarity of the suicide note. She reasoned that swabbing and fingerprinting the glass was a precaution. It was easier to do it now rather than kicking herself later on. If Jack was right that Celeste had company before she killed herself, then maybe evidence from the glass could help identify that person. As the last person to have seen her alive, they could then provide an assessment of her state of mind. She would write up her rationale in her crime-scene report.

After taking the saliva swab, she proceeded to fingerprint the glass, but as she had partly anticipated, the cut-glass pattern caused any ridge detail to become distorted. That, along with the overlapping and smudged marks, meant it was not possible to obtain any clear prints from the glass. 'I've tried,' she said through a sigh as she recovered the note then packed up her kit and left the kitchen, eager to peel off her sticky scene suit.

Maya returned to the van, wishing, not for the first time that it had decent air conditioning. It was not always topped up in the police vehicles as it was not considered essential and therefore a waste of money. She sat sweltering as she wrote up her scene notes. Once she had finished, Maya signed herself out of the scene log and drove away from Field View. She was relieved to notice that Wainwright's car had gone as she pulled out onto Mile Lane. Jack was sat in his car, engrossed in a conversation on his mobile phone. Spotting her, he gestured to Maya to join him in his vehicle.

Maya was locking the van when she heard a familiar voice call her name.

'SOCO Barton, what's the verdict on Celeste Warren's death? Is it suicide or is it suspicious?' Wainwright had appeared out of nowhere and was extending a dictaphone in her direction. Maya was horrified to see he was accompanied by a younger man with a film camera propped on his shoulder, wielding it in her direction.

'No comment. And I don't want to be filmed.' She shielded her face with her hands, willing herself to remain calm as the two men circled her like sharks.

'Have you finished at the crime scene, Maya?' Wainwright persisted. 'Have you scraped her up and shipped her to the corpse-cooler like you said you were going to? Do you have respect for the bodies you deal with, Maya?'

Wainwright was on a roll now, firing questions at Maya. His earlier avuncular manner was now replaced with the callousness of a predator on the hunt, digging for a story at any cost. 'Do you think the last three sudden deaths of known criminals *are* suspicious, Maya? You said there was no such thing as coincidence in the police. Do the public need to be concerned that there could be a serial killer on the loose?'

Maya couldn't speak. She opened and closed her mouth, uncertain what to do or say. The sight of the camera was horrifying. All she could think about was how Kym was going to react. She was overwhelmed with relief to see Jack striding towards them.

He pulled himself up to his full height and directed his comments towards the camera, asserting an air of authority and certainty. 'We are not looking for anybody else following the unfortunate death of Ms Celeste Warren. An official police statement will be released later today,' he stated calmly.

'There have been no suspicious circumstances relating to any other sudden deaths that have recently been investigated. Any suggestion that there has been third-party involvement is pure supposition.' He paused to let his comment sink in, brows creased to accentuate the solemnity of the situation. 'Now, if you'll excuse us, my colleague and I are now leaving the scene. We have no further comments to make to the press.' He flashed a catwalk smile at the camera before giving an imperceptible nod in Wainwright's direction.

Guiding her by the elbow, Jack led Maya to his car where they both sank back into their seats with relief.

'Bastards,' Jack said as he watched Wainwright and the camera man scuttle away. 'I thought he'd gone.'

'Me too.' Maya shook her head. 'I looked for his car as I

pulled out. They must have parked up around the corner and waited for us. This situation is just getting worse. What did the boss say?'

'He wasn't particularly happy but sympathetic none the less. He knows Wainwright of old and doesn't blame you for talking to him. I better let him know what's just happened, though, and the press office can start preparing an official statement. You head back while the coast is clear. Try not to worry, eh?'

Maya smiled weakly. That was certainly easier said than done. Her comments had been shared on camera and were no doubt going to cause a media frenzy. Although DI Redford may be appreciative of Maya's predicament, she knew that there was little hope of Kym reacting in the same way. She had no choice but to head back to Beech Field as soon as she could and fill Kym in on what had happened before she heard it from another source. She was not looking forward to the inevitable bollocking that was headed her way.

18

Piotr Nowak was brooding. He'd been remanded in custody following his recent arrest, which pissed him off enough. What he hadn't seen coming was a request by DI Redford to the prison intelligence unit to have him sent to a separate prison away from Aiden Donnelly. According to his solicitor, Redford had put across a compelling case, stating that if the two men were imprisoned together, it would allow them the opportunity to continue their criminal collusion.

As a result, Nowak had been shipped out of the North West to HM Prison Nottingham. He was away from his best friend, Donnelly, and at a distance too inconvenient for his girlfriend, Markita Milani, to travel to see him. That's what Markita had told him anyway. She had been acting very strange of late and he had decided he could no longer trust a word that came out of her overly lip-glossed mouth. He had sent one of his minions around to her address following his arrest, to make sure she was okay and to see if she needed anything, but the response had apparently been lukewarm at best.

Nowak had access to a mobile phone and had contacted Markita on several occasions, but she remained stand-offish.

When he had challenged her, she claimed it was the upset of him being arrested and that, of course, she still missed him and loved him. He had phoned her last night and made it clear in no uncertain terms that he was expecting her to visit him by the end of the week. Distance or no distance.

Nowak was no fool. He wasn't going to be played by anyone, least of all by Markita. It was time for her to step up and prove that she was his woman; otherwise, he would have to arrange for a little visit to be paid to her. He knew enough people who would be happy to remind her how difficult her life could get if she didn't keep him happy. If Markita wanted to stay healthy and to continue living the life to which she was accustomed, then she needed to make more of an effort to keep him happy while he was inside.

One saving grace was his cellmate, Marcus Naylor, who was decent enough company. He had originally been sentenced for the possession and supply of drugs, and a Section 18 assault. This sentence was further extended after Naylor had battered several inmates while serving his initial sentence at HM Prison Frankland in County Durham. He had also napalmed a prison officer. This is the term given to pouring boiling water and sugar over someone, which intensifies the burns.

Naylor was evil. He had a sick mind and a love of violence. The prison guards had sighed with relief when they realised the two men were going to get on. The thought of the two man-mountains crossing swords would have been too much for the already overstretched staff to cope with. Nowak might be missing Donnelly, but his new cellmate was quickly becoming his new best friend.

Naylor was one of the few people Nowak had ever met who was as big as him. The years he had spent in prison had been whiled away in the gym. As a result, he was a wall of sheer muscle. It wasn't so much his shaved head which added to his appearance as a thug, but the map of old scars which ran across the back of his head and face. Naylor referred to them as his war wounds and had a tale to tell about each one. Each story usually ended with the violent comeuppance of whoever had administered the blows.

The two men were lounging on their bunks, smoking and sharing a companionable silence, waiting for the lunchtime news bulletin to start. Nowak thought Naylor a funny sort, the way he insisted on watching the news, regardless of what else might be on. Still, he didn't mind. Naylor was a decent bloke and if it kept the older man happy to stick to his daily ritual, then he wasn't going to rock the boat. He'd been inside so long with no visitors that Nowak knew of, so the news was clearly his only link with the outside world.

Nowak was only half listening as the television droned on. He was too preoccupied thinking about Markita and what was going on with her, when he became aware of a news bulletin coming from near home. He sat up so he could read the news banner announcing the death of an old madam called Celeste Warren. Nowak knew the name from years back, having had the pleasure of popping his cherry at one of Celeste's brothels at the tender age of fourteen, back when he had first started running around with Donnelly.

The news report quickly switched to an earlier live recording of a local journalist interviewing a crime-scene investigator who had attended the address. Nowak recognised her from being the SOCO who had examined him in the custody suite at Beech Field police station. The journalist was bombarding the startled-looking woman with a barrage of questions and Nowak laughed out loud as he asked her, 'Have you scraped her up and shipped her to the corpse-cooler like you said you were going to?'

'What a quote, stupid bitch.'

'Shhhhh,' hissed Naylor. He was perched like a meerkat, soaking up every detail of the news report.

'All right, keep yer fucking hair on,' Nowak grumbled. God forbid he should interrupt the precious news.

They watched in silence until the report was over and Naylor deflated like a burst balloon. His attention was no longer fixed on the television and he seemed oblivious to the fact that his cigarette had burnt down to his fingers, a long stem of ash dangling precariously over his leg.

'You okay, my friend?' Nowak asked as he leaned over his bunk. His cellmate normally had the typical pale, unhealthy pallor of an inmate, but now, two bright-red pinpricks of colour were glowing on his cheeks. His expression frozen like a death mask.

'Her. On the television. I think I know her.'

'She's a SOCO based near me at Beech Field nick. She's called Maya... something.'

'Maya...' Naylor sighed. 'What else do you know about her?'

'Not much, wasn't with her long and I wasn't in the best of moods at the time. Think she said her mum was a typist or something and her dad was dead.'

'What else?' Naylor was stood up now, face to face with Nowak.

'Fuckin' hell, mate, I dunno. I'd just been nicked, hadn't I? Has she given you a hard on or what? Tell you what, if it means that much to you, I'll find out who she is. It won't take one of my lot too long to find out.'

'Do it. I want to know everything. Trust me, Piotr, I'll owe you big time.'

Naylor turned in his bunk, feigning sleep so he wouldn't have to speak to Nowak again. He was consumed with thoughts of Maya. He lay shaking, feeling the walls close in tighter round him than ever before. He had grown used to being institutionalised, but the sight of her made him want to smash his way out of the prison with his bare hands. He took in a few steady, deliberate, calming breaths. He couldn't afford to lose control. Not now. Not now he'd seen her. The only one consistent thing he had in this shithole was time, and he would bide his for as long as it took Nowak to find out the information he needed to know.

She really was a beautiful young woman. But that wasn't why he was interested. It was more than that. It was uncanny how much she looked like her mother. He would have recognised her anywhere. He was desperate to get to know more about her. And then? And then he would find a way to be in her life, whether she wanted him there or not. It was his opportunity to settle a few scores. Marcus Naylor was looking forward to being reunited with his daughter.

19

K ym was waiting for Maya the moment she returned to
Beech Field. 'My office, NOW!' she exploded before
turning on her heel and storming into her office. Amanda
smiled weakly at Maya, holding up her two crossed fingers and
mouthing 'good luck'.

Maya's face was burning, and she swallowed drily as she
scuttled after Kym.

'Shut the door,' Kym hissed. Her arms were crossed on the
desk in front of her and she didn't speak for a moment as she
watched Maya sink nervously into the chair opposite her.
Eventually, she flung her glasses down on the desk and raked
her hand through her hair.

'For Christ's sake, Maya, one minute you're talking to corpses
the next you're sharing your half-baked conspiracy theories with
the local gutter press. What's next? Are you planning on
conspiring with the local criminals?'

'No! Of course not! I'd never do anything like that. It was a
genuine mistake... I arrived at the scene and the way *he* called
me over and spoke to me made me think it was DS Dwyer.'

'Think,' Kym bellowed. 'THINK? You've made it abundantly

clear, Maya, that the one thing you don't bloody well do at a crime scene is think. Now thanks to you, I've got to go to a meeting at top office and explain to them why the press are circulating rumours that we have a serial killer in our midst.'

Maya cringed. Top office was the term given to the forensic services headquarters. Although all the SOCOs, including Kym, were part of the police force, they were a civilian unit answerable to their own senior leadership team. Knowing her indiscretion was going to be made public knowledge to the powers that be made a bad situation even worse.

'I also have to explain,' Kym continued, 'why a journalist has quoted *you* as saying that you're going to "scrape her up and ship her off to the corpse-cooler". Do you have any idea how crass and unfeeling that sounds to the general public? Do you know how damaging that is going to be to the reputation of this force? The suggestion that we treat people like pieces of meat?'

Maya attempted to interject but Kym raised a hand to silence her.

'I have warned you before about making stupid assumptions, yet you have completely disregarded this and spoken to a journalist – a bloody *journalist* – about your ridiculous conspiracies. This not only reflects badly on you, but all of us as a department, not to mention the force. You have just played into the hands of all the people out there who are quick to discredit and judge us. You've made us *all* look like an unprofessional laughingstock and now *I* have to take the brunt of your actions.'

'But... I...'

'But nothing. Now, bearing in mind you're still under your probationary period, I think you really need to buck your ideas up. Start to think seriously about whether you're cut out for dealing with major crime or whether you should be bounced back to Alder Street and left to fingerprinting stolen mopeds, where you can cause minimal damage.'

'Kym, I am so sorry.' Maya was perched on the edge of her seat now, desperate to make amends, but Kym dismissed her again with a wave of her hand.

'I'm going to top office now and I will try to dilute this situation in the hope that we can both keep our jobs. In the meantime, *you* can go and debrief DI Redford. DI Mitton has also just come on duty and is understandably keen to know what the hell is going on. They're both expecting you. Then I want you to process any exhibits from today and leave a copy of your scene notes on my desk. And woe betide I find you've left anything wanting.'

Maya's heart was in her toes. As much as she was dreading having to go and explain herself to DI Redford and DI Mitton, she was convinced it wouldn't be as bad as the dressing down she had just received from Kym. She was shaking with nerves and embarrassment. The urge to walk out of Beech Field and life as a SOCO was suddenly very tempting.

20

The *Evening News* had a field day with the quotes from Maya. Wainwright had published two stories for maximum publicity. The first piece announced the sudden death of Celeste Warren and the possibility that the recent spate of deaths was more than just coincidental. The second article quoted Maya on the flippant comment she had made about the body recovery and questioned the integrity and compassion of the police.

There were so far over 800 online comments from the public and the general consensus seemed they were horrified that a body had been discussed in such a way. A handful of people had leapt to Maya's defence, stating that gallows humour was a coping mechanism, but the majority of the public were baying for blood.

Wainwright had also released the footage of Maya being questioned outside Field View. It wasn't in the least bit flattering. Maya thought she looked like a floundering fish as her mouth gaped open and closed in response to Wainwright's barrage of questions. She had looked pathetic in comparison to the polished, composed way Jack had responded to the journalist.

Maya had explained herself to DI Redford and DI Mitton, and as predicted, this had been nowhere near as bad as the run-in with Kym. DI Mitton had been empathetic to Maya's situation. She had been reassuring as always, even making light of the incident and sharing her own stories of the times she had messed up.

DI Redford had said very little. He had sat and appraised Maya quietly while she spoke, then reiterated Kym's comments about how assumptions had no place in a police investigation. As far as the meeting with the two senior detectives had gone, Maya thought she had got off lightly. She only hoped that Kym had a similarly lenient response from top office.

For the first time since starting at Beech Field, Maya was glad her shift was over. She wanted to get out of the station and head to the sanctuary of home. She was on rest days for the rest of the week and was grateful for the break away from work. As she walked towards her bike, Maya heard someone call her name. She turned to see Jack striding over towards her, his leather holdall slung casually over his shoulder. He had removed his tie and loosened his top button and looked surprisingly refreshed despite the continuing heat.

'How did it go with Kym?'

'Awful. I got a right bollocking and was reminded that I'm still under my probation period. I'm off the next couple of days and have to say I'm glad. I'm going to go and crawl under a rock until Dave "the bastard" Wainwright's article and footage of me has stopped doing the rounds.'

Jack grinned. 'My mum rang me to say she'd seen it and thought I came across quite well. She felt sorry for you though.'

'Yeah, thanks for that.' She snorted. 'Right, I better get going. See you later.'

'Wait, Maya. I still feel partly responsible for all this. If I hadn't been late meeting you at the scene, I could have sent

Wainwright off with a flea in his ear. I know you've had a shit day and I don't envy you getting a bollocking like that. Why don't you let me take you out for a drink, see if I can't cheer you up a bit? If you're off tomorrow, surely you can afford to let your hair down a bit tonight?'

Maya was taken by surprise. She hadn't expected that. Her initial reaction was to refuse, but then she found herself looking at Jack. He was an attractive man; easy company and he had been supportive. She'd had the day from hell and suddenly the thought of going home to an empty apartment and rattling round on her own all night didn't appeal.

'Do you know what, I'd love too. Where are you thinking? I'd need to call home and grab a quick shower and get changed first.'

'Fantastic.' His face lit up and he positively beamed at her. 'Is there anywhere near your place we could go? I can wait in the pub while you get changed.'

'There's a lovely pub near me called The Eagle. You're welcome to come back and wait at mine. I won't be long, and you can have a drink on the balcony. The view is spectacular.'

'Sounds great. It's a date.' He smiled at her again and they walked across the car park. Maya nodded towards her bike.

'This is Bonnie,' she said with a grin as she patted the seat affectionately. 'She's a Triumph Bonneville 120, hence the name. Ever ridden before?' Jack's eyes widened with shock and admiration. 'I carry a spare helmet which my mum uses. It should fit you okay.'

'There's a first time for everything.' He grinned. Their hands touched as she handed him the helmet. The moment was broken as DI Mitton called her over from further across the car park.

'I won't be a minute,' Maya mumbled as she walked apprehensively towards Alison Mitton.

'Ma'am?'

'Just wanted to see how you were after today's... unfortunate circumstances.'

'I'm still mortified. I'll be glad when today is over to be honest.'

'I can imagine. Just put it behind you and move on. Remember, I'm always here if you need to talk.'

'Thank you, ma'am.'

'I see you're with DS Dwyer. Are you giving him a lift home?'

Maya felt herself blush. 'We're, err, just going for a couple of drinks to take the edge off the day, ma'am.'

'Really?' She raised an eyebrow. 'Well, what you do in your own time is your own concern, but I think it's only fair you should know that Jack Dwyer has a reputation back at Cedar Lane for being a bit of a player. He's known for getting where water can't, if you know what I mean, but don't quote me on that. I hope you don't mind me mentioning it. I'm just looking out for you.' She smiled to show that her comment was well meant.

'I appreciate the sentiment, but it's just a couple of drinks,' she said reassuringly. 'Have a nice evening, ma'am.'

She headed back to her bike where Jack was watching her with interest.

'What did ma'am want?'

'Just seeing how I was after today.'

'That's nice of her. From what I've heard, she's all right. A good boss.'

'She certainly is. Shall we get going?' Maya circled slowly out of the police station as she adjusted to the unusual weight of Jack behind her. Eventually she relaxed as the road stretched out in front of her and Bonnie carried her away from Beech Field police station.

21

Maya sighed, feeling refreshed following a quick shower and change of clothes. 'This was a good idea. What a beautiful evening.' She inhaled deeply, the smell of freshly mowed lawns and summer stocks making her feel euphoric. The stress of earlier events melted away under the lemon-coloured sky.

'Beautiful evening with a beautiful lady,' replied Jack with a wink as he held the door of The Eagle open for her.

The pub was unusually quiet, and Maya guessed it was due to the balmy summer night. People would rather be alfresco than cooped up indoors. Although Maya herself would prefer to be outside, she was grateful for the peace. She was keen to continue getting to know Jack without having to strain to hear him or be heard. She was also conscious of the fact that she may be recognised by members of the public who had seen her interview with that Dave "the bastard" Wainwright.

'What can I get you?' Jack said as they selected a table.

'A large Pinot would be lovely, thanks.'

'Coming up.' Maya watched him walk towards the bar with admiration.

The lone barman was turned away from Jack as he was busily polishing glasses as he removed them from the dishwasher. As he turned at the sound of Jack's subtle cough, Maya was horrified to realise it was Spence working behind the bar. She turned away quickly, burying her head as she fumbled for her phone, so she had an excuse not to look up and be spotted by him.

Although she had to reluctantly admit to enjoying his company in The Brown Cow, it still felt wrong to have spent time with someone she had met during an arrest warrant. She certainly didn't want Jack to know about it. Additionally, she could vaguely recall how Spence had attempted to flirt with her and how she had enjoyed his attention. However, in the cold light of day and the grip of sobriety, she felt exposed and compromised. She decided the best tactic was to either completely avoid him or remain aloof and non-committal.

Because the pub was so quiet, she could vaguely make out the muffled exchange between the two men as Jack placed his order. After what felt like an age, she looked up from her phone so she could steal a glance towards the bar. Her eyes met with Spence's instantly and he gave her a huge beaming smile and a subtle nod of the head. Maya acknowledged him with a wan smile, then turned away quickly.

Jack returned to their table with their drinks and an easy smile. 'Cheers, Maya,' he said as they clinked glasses. The conversation came easily. Jack was good company and they made each other laugh. He asked about how she'd become involved in bikes. She told him about how her grandad used to tinker with them and had got her hooked on riding since she was little. She told him about the group she went riding with and the trips she and Dominique took together. She even forgot about Spence's looming presence as Jack regaled anecdotes that made her laugh out loud. She was surprised to realise that before long, they had both finished their drinks.

'Same again?' Jack nodded towards the glasses. He was just about to stand up and reach for them, when she placed a hand on his arm to stop him.

'Please, let me get these.' She couldn't stand the thought of seeing Jack at the bar with Spence again, but nor was she prepared to leave just so she could avoid him. If working at The Eagle was going to be a permanent arrangement, then she would have to get used to seeing him and would rather get it over and done with. Preferably without Letitia and Caitlin being there too, mooning over how wonderful he seemed.

Maya approached the bar with as much confidence as she could muster, determined not to let the sight of Spence's rictus grin infuriate her. He walked towards her with his now familiar swagger and a pot towel slung over his shoulder. He was wearing a dark, long-sleeved shirt which was tight enough to accentuate his muscular frame. She hated to admit it, but he looked undeniably handsome.

'Good evening, Maya, how are you?' His dimples deepened with his smile.

'Fine thanks, you?'

'All the better for seeing you, obviously.' He laughed as she rolled her eyes with annoyance at his predictable attempt to flirt.

'Just a large Pinot Grigio and pint of Peroni please.'

'Who's your friend?'

'Just a colleague.'

'Looks a bit dodgy to me, police or forensics?'

'He's a DS. Not that it's any of your business.'

'Ha, that explains why he looks so dodgy then. Looks well up himself. You're not on a date, are you?'

'I said, large Pinot Grigio and a pint of Peroni. Please.'

'Oh my God, you are, aren't you?' He laughed as he prepared

the drinks. 'C'mon, Maya, you could do so much better than him. Get rid of him and come out with me instead.'

'You're working.' She handed him the cash. 'Not that it makes any difference.'

'I can get cover and be all yours in half an hour.'

Riled by his persistence, Maya practically snatched the change from his hand. 'Thanks, but I'd rather lick the mortuary floor,' she retorted before returning to Jack with the drinks.

His pealing laughter filled the pub as he called after her, 'That wasn't a "no" though, was it?'

'Friend of yours?' Jack asked, bemused as Maya banged the drinks down on the table and adjusted her chair so her back was to Spence.

'Nope, just somebody I have the misfortune of having bumped into on a couple of occasions. Nobody important. Listen, I don't know about you, but I'm famished. There's a nice Italian around the corner if you fancy it. We might as well make a night of it.'

'That sounds like a great idea. Cheers!' They clinked glasses again and then Jack leant forward, brushing a loose curl from her face as he leant knowingly toward her. For a split second she thought he was going to kiss her, but the moment was broken as a large guffaw from Spence caused Jack to sit back in his chair awkwardly.

Embarrassed, Maya started chatting away about anything and everything, painfully aware that she was rambling on and punctuating the awkwardness with a nervous snorting laugh. With only a quarter of his pint left, Jack excused himself, announcing that he would nip to the toilet before they left for the restaurant. Maya busied herself with her phone again, her back still to the bar, so there was no reason to engage with Spence again. She swallowed the last of her wine as Jack returned to the table, stuffing something into his pocket.

'Are you ready?' He smiled sweetly as he held out his hand.

'Yeah, sure.' She smiled back, feeling more composed. She took his hand and they headed towards the door.

'Hey mate,' called Spence just as they were about to leave. Both Jack and Maya turned to look at him. Jack had a bemused look on his face whereas Maya was fizzing with frustration. What did he want now?

'Yeah?'

'Just checking you got the condom machine working. It's been sticking a bit lately. I wanted to make sure you'd not lost any money.'

'Erm, no. It's fine. Thanks,' Jack mumbled.

'Good luck with – how did you put it – riding her like her motorbike?'

As the door of The Eagle pub banged shut, Maya could hear Spencer James's guffaw following them out on the street.

'Care to explain,' she said tersely. DI Mitton's warning echoed in her mind.

'Hey, you were the one who said we should make a night of it,' he replied defensively.

'I meant this,' she gestured wildly towards the pub, 'a few drinks and a meal. Not bumping uglies with someone I've only known for nine hours.' Maya snatched the packet of fruit-flavoured condoms protruding from his trouser pocket and flung it at him.

'Maya,' he said softly. 'Don't be like that. You can't blame me. You must know how beautiful you are...' He leant towards her and began to run a hand through her hair. She pulled away. She hated it when people touched her hair uninvited. She winced with pain when she realised his watch had caught.

'Ow! Oh, for fuck's sake, Jack.' She pulled at her curls, determined to detach herself from him, ripping out several hairs as she stepped back.

'Oh, shit. I really am genuinely sorry.' He fumbled as he plucked the ripped-out hairs from his watch strap. 'Let me make it up to you. What would you say to going for another drink and starting again?'

'That I'd really rather not. That truth be known, if your penis was as big as your ego then *maybe* you'd have something going for you. As it is, you're not even that good-looking and you've got all the charisma and appeal of a turd that won't flush.'

Turning on her heel, Maya stormed home, leaving him floundering and speechless on the pavement.

22

Days after Maya's television debut courtesy of Dave Wainwright, DI Redford called an urgent meeting with Alison Mitton. As one of the lead officers involved in Operation Chrysalis, DC Stevenson was already seated in Redford's office. It was the first time she had seen him look his age. He was red-eyed and pale. DI Mitton announced her arrival by knocking on Redford's door.

'Alison, come in. Take a seat.'

She acknowledged Stevenson with a smile. 'What's so urgent, Phil? I was due at the morning meeting to discuss the progress of the McCluskey stabbing.' Alison's face was a mask of concern. Not only did Stevenson look like shit, but Redford didn't look his usual composed and immaculate self either. His tie was crooked, and he looked generally flustered.

'It's related to the stabbing. It involves Operation Chrysalis. Things have gone tits up while you've been on rest days.'

'With regards to what?'

'You mean with regards to whom. Aiden Donnelly was released yesterday.'

Alison's mouth dropped open; shaking her head and

blinking quickly, she sat back into the chair. 'How the fuck did that happen?'

'Sean, do you want to explain? I'm still trying to get my head around it.'

'Yes, boss.' Stevenson leant forward on his forearms looking incredibly subdued.

'Remember Ryan Johnson, ma'am? He provided us with information about Nowak and Donnelly, claiming they'd put pressure on him to store firearms for them? Well, not only has he retracted this statement, but he has also admitted that the firearm and ammunition seized from the raid at The Farmhouse belonged to him. He's made a statement claiming that he planted them there deliberately to set Donnelly up.'

'What? No chance. No fucking chance. He's lying,' Alison blustered. 'They've got to him and are pressurising him into saying all this shit.'

'Exactly,' said Redford. 'Carry on, Sean.'

'After the raid, we got authority to fast-track the firearms and the ammunition for examination. Forensically, we have nothing to link that firearm to any other incidents. Not only that, no forensic evidence has come back to Donnelly or Nowak, but Johnson's fingerprints were found all over the packaging.'

'Okay, so the firearm is a new acquisition. Obtaining guns is what they *do*. Donnelly and Nowak are too forensically aware to leave their prints anywhere. Johnson's fingerprints are bound to be on the packaging because he told us they'd made him store it.' She was indignant with frustration.

'We know, Alison, we know. As usual it's out of our hands. Donnelly's brief presented the CPS with this latest evidence. They reviewed it and subsequently issued a Notice of Discontinuance. The CPS contacted us about it while you've been off. I didn't want to bother you at home. I had hoped common sense would prevail at the last minute. The long and short of it is that Donnelly has no case to answer.'

Phil Redford ran his hand over his head as he spoke. The disappointment on his face mirrored that on Alison and Sean Stevenson's.

'So, what now?' Incredulous, she shrugged her shoulders.

'We concentrate on getting Nowak to trial. We prove he was involved in the discharge firearms incident at Damien McCluskey's house. Although he may not actually have pulled the trigger, we all know he ordered it to be done. Next, we need to prove he was involved in the stabbing of David McCluskey. We know that was his own handiwork, we just need the forensics to back it up. Lastly, we need to persuade the McCluskeys to talk to us...'

'There's no chance...' Alison began, but Redford interjected.

'I know it's a long shot but listen. My thinking is we try and get Ma McCluskey on side. Despite the fact they're a pair of big ugly bastards, they're very much still attached to her apron strings. The fact both her baby boys have been so recently targeted might have caused her enough upset to want to bang their heads together and warrant talking to us.'

Alison snorted with disbelief, but Redford was on a roll now and refused to be swayed by her negativity.

'I really believe the violence against the McCluskeys is going to be enough to get Nowak put away for a long time. Who knows, if the "Brothers Grimm" speak out against Nowak and Donnelly, then other people may come forward too. God knows those two have pissed off and hurt a lot of people over the years. As far as I'm concerned, their reign of terror ends now. I'm convinced that if we can get Nowak facing a lengthy sentence, he might be persuaded to dish the dirt on Donnelly, so his time is reduced.'

'No chance. They're far too tight.'

'I appreciate that. But the prospect of fifteen years in a cell, staring at another bloke's bollocks, might just give him a change of heart. Mike Malone said Nowak's arse dropped when he was in. Despite his usual demeanour, he was rattled. Do you remember how much he was kicking off and banging about in his cell? He's never acted like that under arrest before. He's practically living with Markita Milani, who appears to be the love of his life. He's not going to want to be parted from her and his steroids for long.'

Alison pondered for a moment before nodding acquiescence. 'Okay, let's go for it. We've not much choice. In the meantime, what about Donnelly?'

'We keep a very, *very* close eye on him. If he so much as farts I want to know what it smells like. Understood?' This was aimed at Stevenson who nodded emphatically.

'What about Johnson. Has he been remanded?' Alison asked.

'No, he's out on bail. I don't consider him a flight risk. He's too scared of his own shadow at the moment.'

Alison frowned. 'Would he not be safer inside? Away from Donnelly and Nowak?'

Redford paused. His forehead furrowed as he considered the situation. He looked to Stevenson for confirmation before shrugging. 'Let's face it, if Donnelly and Nowak wanted rid of Johnson, they'd get to him whether he was inside or not.'

Stevenson nodded agreement. 'They wouldn't be so stupid as to risk harming Johnson. They must know we're going to be watching them.'

Alison frowned uneasily. 'Let's just hope you're right, gentlemen. For all our sakes.' She nodded to them both before leaving the office. If only they would have known, they would have had Ryan Johnson in solitary confinement. For his own sake.

23

Maya arrived at Dominique's clutching a beautiful bouquet of scented stocks. She let herself in with her key and was quickly enveloped in the familiar smell of home. Dominique met her at the kitchen door and pulled her daughter into a huge embrace, crushing the flowers between them.

Eventually she stood back to take in her daughter's face. She tucked a curl behind Maya's ear and beamed. 'How are you, sweetheart?'

'All the better for being here with you. There you go.' Maya extended the flattened bouquet.

'Thank you, they smell amazing. Come and sit down, dinner won't be too long. The wine's open.'

Maya followed Dominique into the kitchen and settled herself at the table, pouring herself a glass of wine and topping up her mother's.

'Hello, Jet.' She smiled as the cat appeared from nowhere and began to curl herself around Maya's ankles. Maya scooped her up and cuddled her, pressing her nose against her warm head to breathe in her familiar smell. The cat purred happily, burying into Maya.

'She misses you.' Dominique smiled fondly at her daughter.

'I miss her. And you. Sorry it's been so long since we had a proper get-together.'

'No need to apologise. We're both busy and I know how trying your shifts can be. You're here now and that's all that matters.' Dominique sank into a chair opposite Maya and they chinked wine glasses.

'Everything okay at work? Have you recovered from the shock of finding Mr Baron?'

'Absolutely. It's not the first time it's happened, and I dare say it won't be the last. Between us, Maya, he was a horrible man. God knows I took enough racist comments off him over the years. He was warned to cut it out or he'd be struck off from the surgery.'

Maya nodded. 'Tony said he was well known to the police. He also said you seemed quite upset?'

'Not upset. I was fine. It was just more of a shock than anything.'

'Really? Tony said he'd not been in the best of health.'

'No, he hadn't. But no worse than usual.' Dominique took a sip of wine. 'We see some people who, compared to others, always seem on death's door, when in reality, they plod on for years. Jim Baron had various health complications but certainly nothing we were too concerned about. I expected him to be the type that would still be hanging on long after I'd retired.'

'But Tony said there were no suspicious circumstances. Said he'd had some kind of medical episode?'

Dominique nodded thoughtfully. 'It would certainly appear so.'

'You don't agree?' Maya frowned; a niggling sensation caused the hairs on the back of her neck to prickle.

'I'm not saying that. God knows, the police and people like Tony and you know more than me. The flat was insecure, but that's not unusual. Mr Baron had mobility issues, so he kept the door unlocked so we could come and go. He was lying on the floor of his lounge, and like Tony said, had clearly had a heart attack or something. It's just...'

'Mama, what?'

'His medication, including his nebuliser, were still on the table next to his chair. I would have thought that once he started to feel unwell, they would have been the first thing he would have reached for. It seemed strange to me he was on the floor rather than in his chair.'

'Perhaps he tripped on the way back from the toilet or something?'

'Yes, that's what Tony surmised. Honestly, would you listen to me pontificating. Your job has turned me into an armchair detective.' Her contagious laugh filled the room and offered Maya some much needed relief. Time with Dominique was better than therapy. She was good company and radiated an inner calm that was almost hypnotic.

'Are you still enjoying the job?'

'Yeah. Yes, I am. I just keep wondering if I'm good enough. Whether I'm suited to it.'

Dominique sucked her teeth and shook her head.

'Of course you are, girl. What makes you say that?'

'Because I keep fucking up, Mama. I'm trying my best, but I just keep showing myself up. I embarrassed myself at my first death and the situation with the journalist makes me want to cringe. And Kym is furious at me because of my conspiracy theories.'

Dominique let out a low husky laugh. 'Oh, Maya. Stop being so hard on yourself. We all make mistakes. You're just unlucky to make yours so... publicly.'

Maya laughed with her for a while until her face fell again. 'Nicola in my office has a degree in forensics. She's never messed up. Maybe I've been fooling myself thinking I can do such a complicated role with such limited experience.'

Dominique flashed an angry glare at Maya. 'Now you listen to me. You are intelligent, observant, quick-witted and capable. You don't need qualifications to prove how competent you are...'

'But...'

'No buts. There's a new doctor at the surgery who has qualifications coming out of his ears. No doubt medically he knows his stuff, but I've never met anyone who lacks so much common sense. And his people skills leave a lot to be desired. He's so insular he doesn't know how to talk to his patients. You would run rings around him with your personality and compassion. And if you ask her, I'm quite sure Nicola will give you plenty of examples of where she's messed up in the past.'

Maya smiled weakly as Dominique continued. 'I am so very proud of you and everything you have achieved. Not to even mention the wonderful, caring person you have become. God knows life hasn't always been easy for us. We've had our fair share of challenges and upset, and no one would have blamed you if you'd turned out differently. You have more life experience than most people twice your age, and that counts for a lot.'

Maya couldn't meet Dominique's eyes as tears threatened to spill. She buried her face further into Jet's warm black fur while she composed herself.

'Do you ever think about him?' Maya asked tentatively.

'Naylor?' Dominique took a huge glug of wine. 'I have nightmares about him occasionally. Other than that, no. I made a conscious effort years ago not to let him live in my mind. As far as I'm concerned, he's gone. Out of our lives. He may as well be dead.' Despite her bravado Maya noticed the slight tremble of Dominique's lower lip.

'He's not, though, is he?' Maya said quietly. 'As much as we might wish it, he's still very much alive.'

For a while, there was nothing else either of the two women could say. Marcus Naylor was very much the spectre at their feast.

Nowak was grateful to be alone in his cell. He felt he could breathe a little better knowing he didn't have to share the air for a while. Naylor had gone to the exercise yard, leaving Nowak to masturbate while watching *Loose Women*. He was now watching the news and wondering about Naylor's reaction to the SOCO he'd seen on the television. As much as Naylor was good company, it was a luxury to have this time alone to think without having someone else in such stifling proximity.

Donnelly was due in to see him and the thought cheered him nearly as much as if it had been Markita on the visiting order. In fact, one of the many things he was keen to discuss with Aiden was the lady in question. He still felt as if she was giving him the brush-off and he was convinced she had something to hide. He had no doubt that whatever it was, Donnelly would get to the bottom of it and sort it out for him.

The man was like a brother to him. He could trust him with his life and liberty – couldn't he? Although he was pleased that Donnelly was out, he couldn't help feeling a bit resentful. He hated being locked up and it seemed much worse knowing his best mate and girlfriend were carrying on with their lives outside and without him.

He refused to even consider the prospect that he might be sent down for a stretch. There was a reason he and Donnelly paid so much money to their lawyers. It was something they both considered at the start of their criminal career as a good investment. He was hoping it would only be a matter of time before his brief found a loophole sufficient enough to have the case against him dropped.

Either that, or they would find someone who could be persuaded to take the rap for him, just like they had for Donnelly. That was something else he wanted to discuss later. He couldn't countenance being inside any longer than he had to be, and the thought that plans were afoot to get him out would give him the peace of mind he really needed right now. Donnelly was his ticket out of here. Without him pulling strings in the background, he knew he would be going nowhere fast. The thought that his release relied on the actions of one man was overwhelming. He needed to trust Donnelly now more than ever before.

Not getting out wasn't an option. There was no way he could survive a prison sentence. As big as he was, the thought of long-term incarceration absolutely terrified him. It wasn't the constant, underlying threat of the prison atmosphere or even the monotony. Truth be known, he was incredibly claustrophobic – a phobia he knew he had to keep hidden, as showing any sign of weakness would be the end for him inside. Every breath he had taken since being remanded had almost been a conscious one to maintain a level of calm. He needed out and soon. Very soon.

He took a few steadying breaths, ignoring the walls crowding in on him and decided to concentrate on the television instead.

Anything to distract him. The next programme was about to start, but Nowak switched the television off in annoyance, hurling the remote control across the cell. Panic or no panic – he wasn't watching *Judge Rinder* – that was just taking the piss.

25

The rest of Maya and Dominique's evening passed pleasantly, with mother and daughter soon settled back into their usual harmony. Dominique had swept any further mention of Naylor under the table. After a delicious meal and several more glasses of wine, Maya had kissed Dominique goodbye and headed home. Dominique had insisted she call a taxi, but Maya had eaten so much she was keen to walk it off. She had thought about calling Tony on the way to discuss the Jim Baron job but decided against it. She would heed Dominique's advice, and as much as she was curious about the sudden death, she would not allow herself to succumb to any more whimsy.

She was crossing the road near The Eagle, when she noticed a familiar figure collecting discarded glasses from the window ledges outside. She quickened her pace, head down, hoping to slip by unnoticed. Spence, however, had called her name, and with a sheepish look on his face, waved her over. Sighing, she manoeuvred her way around a Mercedes that was parked across the pavement and walked over to him.

'Can I just apologise for the other night? Calling your date out like that. It wasn't my place to interfere.' He smiled apologetically. 'I couldn't help it. He made a couple of derogatory comments when he asked for change for the condom machine. He made my piss boil, but it's no excuse. I should have stayed out of it.'

Maya sighed, she felt too relaxed after a lovely evening with Dominique to be annoyed with Spence. 'Oh, don't worry. You did me a favour. Turns out he was a bit of a prick.' They both grinned.

'Where are you off to?'

'Home. I've just been for dinner with my mum.'

Spence nodded towards the pub. 'Fancy a nightcap. On me? No strings, promise.'

Maya hesitated briefly. 'Thanks, but no. I think I've eaten and drank too much. I'm going to head off home. Have an early night.'

'Just one small wine?' he implored, a huge grin on his face.

Maya was about to concede when she turned to see a group of rowdy couples heading towards the pub. 'I was nearly tempted, but no. I could really just do with some peace and quiet.'

Spence continued to say something, but Maya didn't hear him. Suddenly distracted by the Mercedes she had walked past. She had assumed it was empty, but there was a man craning over the driver's seat with his phone angled towards them.

'Is he filming us?' she said, nodding toward the vehicle.

As Spence looked over, the man turned away and began to start the engine. 'I doubt it. Why would he? I can only see the back of his head. Perhaps he has a kid in the back seat or something. I can't tell from here.'

Maya shook her head. 'Yeah, you're right. I'm seeing things. Told you I was tired.'

'So, what do you think?'

'About what?'

'I was just saying, if ever you're at a loose end pop in one night and keep me company. I'll guarantee you a seat at the bar and faultless waiter service.'

Maya smiled. 'That sounds good. Throw in some bar snacks and I may well take you up on that.'

Nodding goodbye, Spence followed the group into the pub. Maya continued the short distance home; unaware the black Mercedes was following her.

26

Ryan Johnson was like the proverbial rabbit caught in the headlights. He didn't know what to do. Should he run or stay put? The only thing he did know with complete certainty was that he was scared. Really fucking scared. Spencer James had started this. When he'd seen the Facebook post about him looking for bar work, he'd tipped him off about The Farmhouse. It was more of a way to get into Donnelly's good books rather than a favour to Spence.

But it had all backfired. Rather than being in favour with Donnelly, he had found himself in even more hot water. Ryan had recently been visited by Lurch, a giant of a man who Donnelly and Nowak used when they wanted to persuade people to do something without getting their own hands dirty.

Lurch's huge stature and dark-rimmed eyes bore an uncanny resemblance to the character from *The Addams Family*, earning him the nickname. He arrived at Ryan's flat and explained in as much detail as it was possible using words of few syllables, what Donnelly expected him to do to ensure his release. Lurch hadn't laid a finger on him, hadn't even threatened him. His reputation and the almost sinister way he had politely asked, was enough to make Ryan's sphincter twitch with fear. When Lurch told you to do something you did it. No questions asked.

Now, though, he wondered if that meant he was in the clear or whether he was at risk of being surplus to requirements. He'd not left his flat since he'd returned from the police station. Instead, he'd locked himself in with a large supply of weed and booze and was busily smoking and drinking himself into oblivion. It had been the first time he had smoked or drank since leaving prison. His last sentence had terrified him, and he was determined never to get sent down again. Part of his turning over a new leaf included eating clean and getting in shape. He had started running and even bought a fitness tracker so he could monitor his activity.

Now he was annoyed with himself for giving in to temptation and turning to weed and booze, but he needed something to ease his peace of mind so he could think clearly. He was agonising about whether he was safe to stay near his family and carry on with life as normal, or whether he should cut his losses, up sticks and move. But would his family be safe if Donnelly and Nowak were on the warpath?

Maybe it would be better all round if he moved away where they would never find him. He'd always fancied Wales. He'd been on holiday once as a kid and it had been one of the most memorable times of his life. They'd gone to Llandudno and he and his sister had spent days either exploring the beach or the Great Orme. He had happy memories of being sat cross-legged watching the Punch and Judy show, wielding fluffy, pink candyfloss as big as his head, on spindly wooden sticks.

Maybe he could move there. It would be nice to go running by the sea and he could even go swimming. He could imagine falling asleep at night, exhausted from the sea air, listening to the cacophony of seagulls. Then, in a couple of years, when the heat died down, he could get back in touch with his mum and sister and invite them over for a little holiday. His mum would like that.

Yeah, that's what he'd do. He'd throw some stuff in a bag and go. He stubbed his joint out in the overflowing ashtray and bounded from the table with a new-found enthusiasm. He was pleased with his decision. He was just emptying the contents of his wash basket into a holdall when he heard a knock at the door.

If it was his mam, maybe he could persuade her to do some ironing for him. It'd be good to see her before he left. He just hoped she wouldn't start crying, he couldn't cope with that.

He opened the door and baulked at the sight of Lurch filling the door frame. He had a huge grin on his asinine face. An excitable pool of drool brimmed in the corner of his mouth. Tears pricked Ryan's eyes at the sudden realisation he should have ran days ago. It was too late.

Lurch pushed him back gently into the flat with just one finger against his chest. He had a rucksack slung over his shoulder and without saying anything, opened the neck of the bag to show Ryan the contents. There was a pair of overalls, gloves, bed sheet and a hammer.

Lurch held his finger to his lips to indicate silence as he pushed him further back into the flat. Slowly and carefully, he clicked the front door behind them. Ryan thought of his mum and his sister and Wales, as a stream of hot piss trickled down his leg.

27

Nowak was already seated at a table in the visiting room when Donnelly arrived for the afternoon visit. He was dressed in black tracksuit bottoms, grey T-shirt and prison-issue red bib. His casual attire was in sharp contrast to Donnelly, who turned heads in his designer suit and crisp white shirt, casually unbuttoned at the collar. With huge beaming grins, the two men greeted each other with their customary thumb-grab which, for them, passed as a handshake.

'It's so fuckin' good to see you, man, how's it going?' Nowak couldn't keep the grin off his face.

'We're getting there, my friend. I'm just tying up a few loose ends. You know how I like to dot my i's and cross my t's,' said Donnelly with a Machiavellian grin.

'Who have you got taking the rap for the raid at The Farmhouse then?' Nowak laughed nastily.

'That little prick, Ryan Johnson. Let's call it payback. I knew his prints would be on the bag from last time he minded that gun for us. It was one of the reasons I gave it to him. It always pays to have a bit of forensic insurance.' Donnelly tapped the side of his nose with his forefinger. 'Anyway, I sent Lurch round to give him a little wake-up call. You know how persuasive that dumb fucker can be.'

The two men laughed; Nowak leaned across the table to fist-bump Donnelly.

'So, Johnson's currently sat on a bunk in Strangeways that's probably still warm from your arse?'

'Nah, he should be dead by now,' Donnelly said bluntly.

'What?' Nowak leaned across the table again, shoulders hunched, his neck craning towards Donnelly. 'Please tell me you're fucking joking.' His tone was flat, and he was frowning, eyes narrowed as he glared at Aiden.

'No, I'm not joking. Waste disposal innit? What's up with you?'

'What's up with me, Aiden, is that right now I need to shovel as much shit off my back as I can, and *your* way of dealing with things is to cause even more bother?'

Nowak banged the palm of his hands on the table, attracting a warning look from one of the nearby prison officers. Tutting at Donnelly he shook his head with disgust.

'Fuck's sake, chill out man. Look, Ryan Johnson was a loose cannon. Need I remind you he's already done a stretch for us once before and struggled with it? There was no guarantee he'd do the same again. We couldn't be sure he'd continue to keep his mouth shut. He was a fucking contender for Redford and Mitton to pop into witness protection, if ever I saw one.'

'Lurch would have been enough to persuade him to keep his mouth shut.'

'Yeah, probably. But Lurch is as numb as a piss stone and I don't trust him with my freedom. It wasn't a gamble I was prepared to take, okay? I was there, you were in here, so it was *my* call to make.'

'Yeah, cheers mate, don't go rubbing it in.'

'Aw, sorry man, I didn't mean to.' Donnelly looked genuinely contrite. It went against the grain for him to be out while his best friend was still locked up. 'How are you getting on in here?'

'I'm living the dream, bro. The spa can get busy in the afternoon, but the five-star food and cocktail menu more than compensate for the inconvenience.' Nowak sneered sarcastically. 'Seriously, Aiden, I'm glad you're out, mate, but you've got to get the lawyers to get their fingers out of their arses and do the same for me. It's doing my fucking head in, this place. I can't stand the thought of Markita being on her own out there with God knows who sniffing around her. Plus, they're looking at sticking both the McCluskey jobs on me. I'm facing a long stretch and you know there's no way that can happen.'

'I know, I know. Look, just keep your head, okay? I'm already on it and so are the briefs. As we speak, they're making arrangements for you to be transferred to Strangeways, so at least you'll be nearer to home. There's no way the prison intelligence unit should have bought all that bullshit from Redford about us being in separate prisons.' Donnelly snorted with disgust. 'The man's just taking the piss. Everyone knows him and that bitch Mitton have had it in for us for years. It's fucking police harassment is all.'

Nowak nodded in agreement. 'So, what are you planning?'

'I'm going to find someone to take the rap for *you*, of course. They've got no forensics or CCTV to tie you to the shooting or the stabbing. Plus, Markita has provided you with an alibi for both jobs. I've got someone in mind to plant McCluskey's blood on.'

'Who?'

'Spencer James.'

Nowak shook his head. 'Never heard of him. Who is he?'

'New bloke who I'd just appointed the bar manager's position. It's probably my own fault for not checking him out properly, but it's an unhappy coincidence that he arrived at my place the same morning of the raid.'

'Right...'

'Yeah, right. Who put me in touch with him? That little fucking rat, Johnson, remember?'

'You think they both grassed us up? If so, why would this Spencer arrange to be there on the morning it kicked off?'

'I've no idea. It could just be coincidence, but you know I don't buy that. I don't know anything about him, but my instincts are telling me he's trouble. I've had leads put on him. I'll text you a photo of him later. You should at least know what the bloke who's gonna be doing a stretch for you looks like. It's good manners.'

Nowak laughed, allowing the relief to sink in. 'Sounds like you've got it all planned out. I knew you would. I know I can trust you to have my back. Sorry for being a bit arsey, it's just this place. But after this, Aiden, let's just cool things a bit, eh? I want to get out of here and concentrate on sorting things with Markita.'

'Problems?'

'Yeah. No... Oh, I don't know, mate, I really don't.' He sighed, rubbing his hand over his head. 'She just seems different since I got locked up. And she's not even been to see me since I've been in here. Said it was too far to fucking travel. Cheeky bitch seems to have forgotten it was me that bought her that fucking Audi she's so proud of. When I ring her, she can't get off the phone quick enough. I don't know what to think.'

'Leave it with me. I'll go and pay her a visit. Shower her with a few gifts from you. It's probably just all the upset of you being in here. She's most likely in bits but doesn't want you to know, so is saying as little as possible. This place fucks with your head, mate, you've too much time to think and it makes you paranoid.'

'Yeah, you're probably right. I just need to get out and soon.'

'Few more days, mate, okay? Just hold your nerve. What's your cellmate like?'

'Bloke called Naylor. Older fella, but he's okay, a good laugh. In fact, he's after finding out some information about a SOCO who dealt with me when I got nicked. If I text you details, can you ask around?'

''Course, mate. Whatever you need. At least you've not got any bother in here.'

'You know what it's like, Aiden. I'm treated like fucking royalty. The benefits of having a reputation that precedes you is making it go all right. I just can't stand being locked up.'

'I know. Just sit tight because me and you are gonna get over this little glitch and in future, we're going to make sure that whatever we do, we're untouchable.'

'Amen to that.' Once again, the two men fist-bumped, and Nowak smiled. He could practically smell freedom and it was all thanks to his best friend, Aiden Donnelly.

28

Markita Milani was stretched out on her bed wrapped only in a bath towel. She was cooling down after her shower, enjoying the scent of her freshly washed skin. The sudden ring of the doorbell startled her, and she darted up off the bed. She felt a mixture of exhilaration and dismay. He was far too early, and she was nowhere near ready. She wanted to be made up for him and dressed, ready in her new lingerie when he arrived. She knew the corset and suspenders would take his breath away and she grew wet at the thought of how he was going to respond when he saw her all dressed up.

She pushed guilt-ridden thoughts of Piotr to the back of her mind. She knew what she was doing was wrong. Piotr had been the love of her life for a while, but not anymore. She didn't even know at what point she'd stopped loving him. It had just happened. And now? This new fledgling relationship was so wrong, but it felt so right. She knew it was such a cliché and knew the taboo of what she was doing was unthinkable in their world. Unforgivable even. But she couldn't stop herself. God knows she'd tried.

Still wrapped in the bath towel, she dashed to the door like an excited child; her face a mask of sheer exhilaration and pleasure. She pulled back the security chain and swung the door open.

'All right, darlin'?' Donnelly's face was plastered with a huge smile as he stood on the doorstep clutching a bottle of wine, chocolates and a huge bouquet of flowers.

29

Maya had finished her day shift and was crossing the car park when she spotted Chris. She knew he'd been in court all day and was keen to hear the outcome. He had been conversing with DI's Redford and Mitton and had waved the pair off when Maya joined him.

'Hey, how did court go?'

'Not too bad thanks, love. The defence were trying to get me to interpret the blood spatter on my scene photographs. I kept telling them that was a job for a biologist. They tried to lead me a few times, probably hoping I'd trip myself up, but I didn't take their bait.'

'Were you nervous?'

'Shitting meself! I think I was more nervous than the defendant. I always am when I'm in court. Still, talking to the bosses just then, we think it's going to go our way. He's looking at about fifteen years.'

'Nice one, Chris.'

'Can't wait to get home and have a pint and a takeaway. I can't be bothered cooking for myself tonight. Are you off home?'

'Yeah, it's been busy while you've been sipping lattes outside court.'

'Cheeky sod.'

'Hey, can I ask you something? About the Jim Baron job?'

'Tony picked that one up.'

'I know. It's just that I was chatting with my mum about it the other day. She was the community nurse who found him and called us.'

'And?'

'Well, she mentioned that she thought it was strange that Baron was on the floor and his nebuliser and stuff hadn't been touched...'

'Oh, Maya, please stop.' Chris ran his hand across his face, sighing. 'Haven't you learnt anything from the warnings Kym has already given you?'

'Yes... but...'

'No, Maya. You know I like you, but you're even starting to get on my nerves with all this. You've still got the Wainwright business hanging over your head, and now you want to cast fresh aspersions about Jim Baron's death?'

'I'm sorry, Chris. I just can't shake the feeling off that something's wrong. It's like when we were at Gorman's house...'

'You're questioning that now?' Chris laughed, incredulous. 'You were at the scene and the PM. You *know* there was nothing suspicious about that job.'

Maya sighed, exasperated at not being understood. 'I know on the surface it looks that way. But I can't ignore this feeling I got at that scene... and there was something about Celeste Warren's suicide note...'

'Well, I suggest you try ignoring your feelings before you completely alienate yourself from everyone in the office. No offence, love, but I'm off. It's been a long day.'

Maya's heart sank as she watched Chris stride across the car park. She really wished she'd not said anything. She realised she should have spoken to Tony about it rather than Chris. Once again, she cursed herself for her stupidity and lack of thought.

She suspects far too much. She could make things exceedingly difficult for me and I'm not going to let that happen. She needs to learn to mind her own business. If I have to shut her up, I will.

30

G eoffrey Doran sucked in the cool summer air greedily. A breeze tickled his forehead, cooling the perspiration that slathered his face and neck. He had been sat in the hot, cloying living room for three hours. He felt bilious after endless cups of tea and stale custard creams. Still, it had been worth it. The doddering old woman had happily handed him 20,000 pounds in cash. He had taken great care to wash his cup, kissed her papery cheek goodbye and assured her he would be back the following day to take her to the garden centre for lunch.

Bullshit. Being the unscrupulous bastard he was, he laughed as he pictured her clutching her empty handbag on her bony lap. He could imagine her gazing out the window, rheumy-eyed. Her wispy white hair covering her egg-shell skull. He knew the longer she waited, the reality of what she had done would start seeping in. Would she cry when she realised? Hopefully. Undoubtedly. Meanwhile, he would be moving on to the next victim he had lined up. An old boy from Stockport, who he knew had more money than sense.

Geoffrey had been conning the elderly for decades. He had started his criminal career by using many guises such as the bogus builder or 'water board' official, to Jehovah's Witness, Christian Aid or the volunteer from Help the Aged. Many years ago, he had fallen foul of DNA profiling. A saliva swab taken from a drinking glass he'd used while conning a couple out of 25,000 pounds had resulted in him serving a hefty prison sentence. During his time inside, Geoffrey had grown forensically aware, picking up tips from his fellow prisoners. It was quite the education. He learnt so much more than the Open University or Ted Talks could ever offer.

Geoffrey found that since he had reached a certain age, it was easier to con the elderly and minimise the risk of getting caught. They were more trusting of him than they would have been with someone in their twenties or thirties. He was well-groomed and dressed conservatively. The red paisley handkerchief which always protruded neatly from his jacket pocket screamed honest and dependable. He became the older son they'd never had. Or, was the son they had, who was now too busy with his own life to tolerate infirm, needy parents.

Once he had identified his wealthy victims, he spent time checking for nosy neighbours and CCTV. He masked his footwear, wore a trilby hat and carried leather driving gloves as part of his 'older gentleman' disguise. He never, ever left his DNA again, always ensuring he washed any cups he had used and removed any potential fingerprints. He would con his victims so effectively that he was long gone before they realised their life savings had disappeared.

The best part of all was most of them didn't even tell their friends and family, let alone report it. They felt embarrassed for being so naïve. They blamed themselves and as result, believed the insurance would never pay out, so what was the point in calling the police for a crime number? Surely allowing him into their property counted as legitimate access, which meant there would be no case to answer.

Geoffrey chuckled to himself as he thought about the clueless old woman. Even if she did contact the police, her hearing and eyesight were so bad, she'd make a terrible witness. He'd done well selecting her. He was confident his next victim would be just as gullible and easy to manipulate. He loosened his tie and undid his top button. God, he hated smelling of old people's houses. Still, it was nice to be outside now. He breathed in the sweet, fresh air as he strolled along the country road, swinging his briefcase cheerily.

It was a quiet, peaceful stretch. Sparrows darted in and out of the hedgerows whilst up above, swifts twisted and turned, diving for flies. Geoffrey felt relaxed. Rich and relaxed. He'd taken care to park his car at a pub thirty minutes' walk away and was looking forward to rewarding himself with a refreshing, cool pint once he got there. After that he would treat himself to a few glasses of their most expensive Scotch. He could afford it after all.

He could hear a car approaching from behind and moved towards the hedgerow. As the sound grew closer, he became aware that it seemed to be travelling at some speed. He stopped, waiting for it to pass by. Geoffrey's eyes widened with shock as the blue Citroen came into sight. Not only was the car travelling at speed, but it was also heading right towards him. It had veered away from the centre of the road. As it sped towards the verge he realised he had nowhere to go.

He let out a scream as he braced himself for the impact. His legs were flipped up over the bonnet, sending his face smashing into the windscreen. The car pulled sharply to the right and stopped with a squeal of brakes. He was in agony. He had never felt pain like it. Where his forehead and face had so recently felt clammy with sweat, he could now feel the syrupiness of fresh blood stream down his face.

From the crooked angle at which he lay, Geoffrey could see

the vehicle. He watched as the driver climbed out and looked at him. It took every effort for him to raise his hand and signal that he needed help. He couldn't compute what he was seeing, though, as the driver let out a laugh and climbed back in the driver's seat. The engine started up and Geoffrey let out an inaudible sound.

Although the blood streaming down his face was blurring his vision, he could just about make out the lights on the vehicle. He heard a crunching of gears as the reversing lights came on. Tears began to stream down his face as he heard the engine revving threateningly. He tried frantically to move. Tried to roll out of the way. But he couldn't feel his legs and his arms hurt far too much.

His eyes widened with shock as the car reversed at speed back towards him. The engine whined as the rear wheels crushed his skull into the tarmac. Had he not lost consciousness at that point, he would have known that the vehicle then drove forward before reversing back over him a second time. Somebody wanted to make sure he was definitely dead.

Geoffrey's body was eventually discovered by a passing motorist who initially assumed the rags on the floor were a discarded scarecrow. By then, the Citroen had been abandoned on waste ground, doused in petrol and consumed by flames. Any latent forensic evidence which may have led to identifying the driver, had well and truly gone up in smoke.

31

Spence had arrived for his shift at The Eagle earlier than he needed to. Lisa, who he was taking over from, had been effusive at the opportunity to leave an hour early. If truth be known, Spence was the grateful one. As lovely as his sister and her family were, he hated intruding on them.

'Has it been busy?' he asked Lisa.

'Not too bad. The usual stream of regulars, a heavy-petting couple dressed in office clobber who are clearly having an affair and Sloth, who's been nursing the same pint of Guinness for nearly two hours.'

'Sloth?'

'Yeah, you remember from *The Goonies*? He's sat over there by the door.'

Spence glanced discreetly over. He spotted him straight away and understood what Lisa meant; he was an unfortunate-looking man.

'Blimey, he's a big bastard, isn't he?'

'He gives me the creeps. He asked me what my favourite colour is. Weirdo.'

'Ah, did he now? He probably wanted a guess at what colour underwear you're wearing. You might actually be in there.'

'Erm, I don't think there's any chance of that,' Lisa said with a grimace.

'Don't put yourself down, love, you're not that ugly.'

'Cheeky sod.' She swiped at him with the bar towel. 'Right, I'm off. Thanks for the early finish. If you ever get yourself a life and need me to cover a shift for you, I owe you one. See you tomorrow.'

He blew her a kiss as she left with a swing of her hips and a flick of her hair. As he watched her walk out the door, he couldn't help but notice that the man was staring at him unflinchingly. He found it rather unnerving.

'Can I get you the same again, mate?' he called.

The man nodded, swallowing down his dregs. He carried his empty glass over to the bar and watched as Spence pulled another pint. Once again, Spence was aghast at how huge the man was.

He had a large bulging forehead, which was accentuated by his receding, mousy-brown hairline. His protruding eyes were rimmed with dark shadows and his nose looked like it had been broken several times. His mouth hung open causing him to drool slightly.

'What's your favourite colour?' Lurch said.

'Oh, I dunno pal, I've never really thought about it. Orange, I guess. You know that bright orange glow you see during a sunset? The colour of salmon. I love that. Why, what's yours?'

Lurch grinned widely, revealing a mouth of missing teeth. No wonder he was drooling, thought Spence.

'Rainbow. I like the colour, rainbow. That's my favourite. I like all the colours.'

'Good choice, mate. Here's your drink – on the house.'

Lurch smiled bashfully and carried the drink carefully back

to his table with both hands. Spence watched him go. He felt a bit sorry for the bloke. He clearly wasn't the full shilling. He'd pay for the drink out of his own pocket later, to make up for laughing about him with Lisa.

He watched the man as he settled himself at the table. He might be big, but he seemed harmless enough, Spence decided. He hoped so anyway. He certainly wouldn't want to get on the wrong side of him.

32

Nowak listened to the familiar sound of the screws going through the process of preparing for lights out. Sounds of footsteps, jingling of keys and the opening and closing of viewing hatches grew closer. Eventually, it was Nowak and Naylor's hatch which was slid open and the prison officer peered in. Satisfied there was nothing untoward happening in their cell, it was slammed shut and the patrol continued. Nowak listened carefully until he was satisfied the screw had moved far enough away before retrieving his hidden mobile phone.

One thing that he had noticed about the phone since he had been in prison was that it seemed to take an age to turn on. He desperately hoped for a message from Markita. His patience was rewarded as the phone came to life and he was notified of two new picture messages. The first was a sexy selfie of her blowing a kiss and the simple message:

I love you xxx.

The second message was from Donnelly:

Markita's fine, think she's just missing you, mate. I gave her some flowers, wine and chocolate from you. She'll be visiting very soon. Here's a picture of Spencer James, your soon-to-be prison replacement, chatting some bird up outside the pub he works at.

Nowak laughed with surprise at the picture and leaned over his bunk towards the silent bulk of his cellmate below him. 'Oi, Naylor, you awake, mate?'

Naylor mumbled something inaudible, his voice thick with sleep.

'Mate, c'mon, sit up. I've got something to show you and you're gonna love it.'

'Show me tomorrow, I'm tired.'

'It's a picture of your fancy woman.'

Naylor sat up so quickly, he caught his head on the metal edge of Nowak's bunk. Oblivious to the pain he snatched the proffered phone out of Nowak's hand greedily.

'Where did you get this? Have you found anything out about her yet?'

'That bloke she's with? He could soon be your new cellmate. I'm sure he'll be happy to tell you all about her.'

Naylor gazed, open-mouthed at the picture as he zoomed in even closer, so he could drink in every feature of Maya's face.

'All right, you've had a look. Give me the phone back. I need to send a couple of texts.'

Nowak texted Markita back first.

I love you too and I miss you, babe. I've sent you a visiting order xxx

Then he replied to Donnelly, his fingers flying expertly over the keypad as he composed his message.

That's Maya the SOCO from Beech Field I asked you to find out about. My cellmate is very interested to know more about her, think he's got a crush. Find out what you can and let me know.

Nowak was about to play it safe with the phone and turn it off and hide it away when he received a reply from Donnelly.

So, Spencer James must be our grass if he's hanging round with police. Once you're out of there, he's dead.

Nowak turned the phone off and lay back, shaking his head. Typical Aiden – so much for cooling things a bit. Still, he agreed with the logic. If Spencer was involved in tipping the police off about the firearm being held at The Farmhouse, then what else did he know about him and Donnelly? They knew nothing about the man and that worried Nowak a lot. He was a great believer in keeping friends close and enemies even closer.

At the moment they had nothing concrete to suggest that this guy was a threat to them. But there was the coincidence of him suddenly appearing at The Farmhouse on the morning of the raid and *now* they knew he was keeping company with a SOCO, so he clearly had good associations with the police. He had to concede that Donnelly was right. Keeping Spencer James alive in the future was not going to be an option. He was a dead man walking.

33

Lurch sat sipping his drink, smacking his lips against the froth that settled around his mouth. He continued to watch Spence as he served drinks and kept the bar clean. He decided he liked him. Not only had he given him a free drink, he had also asked him what his favourite colour was. Nobody ever bothered to ask him. Spencer James seemed like a nice bloke. Lurch decided that in different circumstances, they would probably become good friends.

Nowak and Donnelly were the only friends he had. Before them, nobody had ever shown any interest in him. Having friends transformed his sad, lonely, and often scary world into something fun and colourful. Having spent his life in care, Lurch had never been socialised. His friendships provided the normality he craved.

For the first time ever, Lurch had full and meaningful conversations. Previously he had only experienced strained small talk with strangers. This limited experience had led to him being educationally disadvantaged. Small talk was the reason he had become so fixated with asking people what their favourite colour was. It was the only conversation point he'd experienced as a child. It was his infantile alternative to discussing the weather.

Lurch felt accepted by Donnelly and Nowak. He shared opinions and in-jokes with them. He had an insight to family life when he was allowed in their houses. He learnt to laugh and play and got up to all kinds of scrapes. He was too naïve to realise that a lot of the time, his friends used him as a scapegoat and laughed about him behind his back. But, even if he had realised, he wouldn't have cared. He would have taken the flack for his friends quite willingly. It was the least he could do to thank them for including him in their friendship and allowing him to be the nearest he had ever been to 'happy'.

As the three of them grew older and the scrapes turned into more serious criminal acts, the dynamics of their friendship didn't change. Donnelly and Nowak were the brains; Lurch was the brawn who contentedly took the rap whenever they were caught out. Now, Donnelly had told him to follow Spence and report back about what he did and who he was with.

He didn't have to hide from Spence, but he did have to take photographs of the people he was in contact with. Lurch had to make sure Spence didn't see him doing that. Lurch was good at the following. Considering his huge stature, he was incredibly good at not being seen. It came from a childhood of being passed in and out of the care system.

In care, Lurch used to hide in the shadows so no one could hurt him. Being in the shadows kept him safe but he didn't like it there. The small spaces made his breath feel snuffly and there was no colour. As he grew, so did his anger and resentment towards all those who had ever hurt him. Soon, he was big enough to make people stop hurting him. That was when he started to notice *all* the colours. He had never looked back.

And as for Spence? Donnelly hadn't said anything about hurting him, which Lurch was pleased about. He didn't want to hurt someone who seemed so nice. Unless Donnelly told him too. Then if need be, nice or not, he would break every bone in his body.

34

Andy Carr was dressed in green hospital scrubs and was now slipping his feet into a pair of mortuary-issue, size ten, white wellington boots, choosing to ignore the sight of a diluted bloodstain on the toe. He had been tasked by Kym to attend Geoffrey Doran's post-mortem and he was not happy about it. Firstly, he hated them. He had been in the job far too long now to find anything remotely interesting about them. They were also a stark reminder of how fragile his own mortality was, something he really didn't need reminding of at the moment.

Secondly, he had enough stuff going on and he could do without this added inconvenience. The last thing he needed was to spend several hours watching some poor fucker get sliced open and be swabbed, weighed and measured.

He was in the company of Anwar Singh, from the collision reconstruction unit. He was part of the investigation team looking into the circumstances surrounding Doran's death. Anwar was joined by Jean Collins, the exhibits officer. Jean was a quiet, unassuming woman who absorbed information through her large owlish glasses while constantly scribbling her way through copious amounts of notes.

While Anwar remained cheerful, keen and enthusiastic, Andy was his usual morose, disinterested self. He continued to be distracted by the chiming from his mobile phone, which he had placed on top of his crime-scene notes.

'Andy, I apologise profusely if we're keeping you from something,' Doctor Granger sneered. He abhorred interruptions whilst holding court and had been continually irritated by Andy's lack of attention as he made his preliminary observations of Doran's naked, broken body. The pathologist expected people to be in awe of his extensive skills and knowledge. Usually, investigators hung on to his every word, desperate to know how their victims had died. He did not appreciate the repetitive bleeping which indicated that Andy Carr had yet another text message.

Andy was either oblivious to the pathologist's sarcasm or in true immutable style, was too arrogant to care. He was just about to reply to Granger when his phone started to ring again. Catching sight of the name of the caller, Andy could feel the blood drain from his face and his sphincter start to twitch.

'If you'll just excuse me, Doctor Granger, I need to take this. It's an important work call. Please, accept my apologies.'

Andy could hear Doctor Granger sighing exasperatedly at Anwar and Jean as he made his first cut into Geoffrey Doran. The scalpel sliced the skin as easily as a hot knife through butter as the Y incision was carved as Andy scuttled away, phone clutched to his ear.

By the time Andy had headed back into the changing room, where he could take the call in private, it rang off. Almost immediately, however, the same number flashed demandingly back up on the display.

'Hello? I was just about to call you back.'

'Really? You've been ignoring my calls and texts.'

'Not intentionally, I'm sorry. I'm at the mortuary, there's a post-mortem just about to start. I shouldn't really be on my phone.'

'Anyone I know?'

'Geoffrey Doran.'

There was a snort. 'No loss there. I hope death wasn't too quick and painless.'

'Doesn't appear to have been, the guy has no face left.'

Another snort. 'I need to speak to you about the forensics from the McCluskey stabbing.'

'Not a problem. I'll ring you once I'm finished up here if that's okay,' said Andy, uncharacteristically subservient.

'Make sure you do. I don't want to have to start chasing you.'

'You won't. I'll call you back as soon as I can.'

'Before you go, there's one other thing. Do you work with someone called Maya Barton?'

'Yes.'

'Good. I want you to find out everything there is to know about her.'

The call was disconnected before Andy could comment further. Sighing heavily, he returned to the mortuary. It wasn't the sight of the pathologist scooping out Geoffrey Doran's insides through a gaping cavity that made Andy want to be sick; it was the conversation he'd just had with Aiden Donnelly.

35

Markita's mouth was dry and her stomach churned as she arrived at the prison. She sat in her car, bracing herself to go and visit Nowak. Donnelly had told her that Piotr was struggling being inside because of how much he missed her. He said she should go and visit and reassure him that things were fine between them. She was to convince him how much she missed him and was looking forward to him coming home. She was also to apologise for not visiting earlier, and explain it was because she found it too upsetting to see him in there.

For Markita, this was going to be easier said than done. She wasn't confident that she could lie successfully to Piotr's face. He knew her too well. She was convinced he would see through her duplicity, and the thought of him finding out what she had done terrified her. He would kill her. He would kill both of them.

With trembling hands, she reached for her phone and read the text message she had just received.

Don't worry about the visit. Just think about us together later.

Despite her anxiousness, she beamed at the thought. Markita texted back that she couldn't wait and included a row of love heart emojis. Her dry mouth moistened at the thought of the evening ahead. Pulling down the sun visor, she slid back the panel to reveal the vanity mirror, and carefully applied a fresh slick of lip gloss. She spritzed perfume over her exposed cleavage and with that, she was ready.

Markita locked the car and steadied herself on her towering heels, before clacking her way towards the prison entrance. Her phone bleeped again with a message from Donnelly:

Make sure you keep Piotr happy.

It wasn't going to be easy, but she would make sure this visit went well. She would tell Piotr everything he wanted to hear and more. She couldn't afford to risk arousing his suspicions, so she had no choice.

The sight and sound of Geoffrey Doran being catapulted from the car keeps playing on a loop in my mind. With hindsight, it was a foolish, reckless plan. Anything could have gone wrong. I could have killed myself. I might not have killed Doran. If he hadn't died, then considering how well he knew me, he would easily have recognised me and that would have been it. Louisa always said I could be too impetuous at times.

The sound of the car slamming into him was unforgettable. The crunching thud and the splintering of the windscreen. The feel of the car mounting his broken body had been a truly cathartic sensation. Each of the deaths had given me a sense of release. I had even managed a full, deep and dreamless sleep after each of them. I like to think if Louisa had been watching, she would have been pleased and felt compensated in some way.

But that was then, and this is now. Yet again, I feel restless and so fucking angry and resentful towards so many people. The only thing I can do to soothe my peace of mind is to think of Louisa. Or decide who I'm going to kill next. And exactly how I'm going to do it.

36

It was another warm day when Maya arrived at work for her afternoon shift. It had rained heavily through the night, leaving a heavy mugginess that threatened to repeat the blistering heat of the last few weeks.

'Good afternoon, team.' Maya was greeted with the smell of fast food as she walked into the office.

'Hi, love.' Amanda gave her usual cheery smile.

Connor, Chris and Elaine acknowledged Maya with a wave; their mouths were full of the fried chicken and chips that they were sat gathered around. Maya guessed it was a quiet day, as it wasn't often that any of the team got to have a proper meal break. It was usually so busy that, at best, they grabbed a quick snack while updating paperwork.

'Where are Nicola and Andy?' Maya mused aloud as she turned to study the duties board.

'Nic's rest day, Andy's at a post-mortem. We've had a fatal road-traffic collision last night. It looks like a hit and run. Or to be more precise, it looks like he's been hit and run over several times.' Amanda grimaced as she spoke.

'God, that sounds nasty. So, has he been hit initially, and then other drivers have just not seen him?'

'The preliminary investigation suggests it's the same car that has driven over him more than once. Whoever was driving, clearly wanted him dead.'

'Oooh, nasty. But interesting.' Maya was startled by the realisation that discussing fatalities had suddenly become normal to her. She was clearly getting used to being a SOCO.

'Yeah, and no sad loss either which is a bonus. Our victim is Geoffrey Doran. The bastard has made a career out of conning pensioners out of their life savings. I don't think anyone will be mourning his unfortunate passing. My guess is he's been finished off by a family member of one of his victims. Who knows?' Amanda shrugged.

'Hey, Maya, he could be another contender for your sudden death conspiracy. D'ya think your mystery killer has struck again?' Elaine laughed raucously.

Maya's eyes darted nervously towards Kym's office door.

'Shh, Elaine. I don't need dropping in the shit again.'

Kym suddenly appeared from her office. 'Who's in the shit?' She frowned, eyeing all the staff suspiciously.

Maya glared at Elaine as Amanda interjected. 'I was just saying, they'll be in the shit if they don't clear all that rubbish away after their lunch.'

'Mm, really,' said Kym dubiously.

'While we're on the subject of food,' Amanda tapped her desk for attention, 'can I just remind you all that the freezer in here is to be used to store exhibits only? I had an officer call in yesterday to collect some blood swabs from one of Nicola's scenes. I was mortified to open it up and find the exhibit nestling next to a box of bloody Cornettos.'

Chris and Elaine exchanged a guilty look, which sent Connor and Maya off in peals of laughter. Kym rolled her eyes and shook her head exasperatedly before turning to Maya. 'Could I have a quick word please.' She spun efficiently on her heel and strode back into her office with Maya following nervously behind, her fingers instinctively in her mouth as she began to chew the skin around her nails.

'I'll not beat about the bush. I just wanted to let you know that top office won't be taking any form of disciplinary action against you following the unfortunate incident with Dave Wainwright. They were sympathetic to the predicament you found yourself in and are satisfied that at no point did you deliberately intend to share information about the investigation.'

Maya slumped back into the chair and sighed with relief. She was about to speak when Kym held up her hand to silence her.

'They have, however, asked me to remind you that you should only ever use respectful language. Our job can be challenging at times and while we accept that gallows humour is a much-needed coping mechanism, there is a time and a place for it. You need to be mindful of that. That applies to whether you are in work or going about your own private business. Do I make myself clear?'

'Crystal.'

'For what it's worth, I have assured them that I think you hold a lot of promise. I think you can go far in this job so long as you stay focused on the task in hand and dismiss any future ridiculous notions and avoid making assumptions. I think you should take this reprieve as an opportunity to reread the code of ethics which were explained to you when you started at Alder Street.'

Maya nodded furiously. She'd do anything to keep her job. 'I will, Kym. Thank you.'

'Good. Familiarise yourself with what is expected of you and ensure you adhere to it. I see this as an opportunity for you to clear the air and start again. Before we do that, is there anything else at all you think I may need to be aware of?'

Maya hesitated. For a moment it was as if time stood still and she was sat in Kym's office at a metaphorical crossroads, deciding whether this was the one and only chance for her to come clean. To share her secret. To unburden herself from the one thing that woke her in a cold sweat most nights.

She chewed her cuticles. If Maya was ever going to admit that she had lied on her initial application form, the time was now. All she had to do was open her mouth and tell Kym that she had not disclosed the fact that the notorious Marcus Naylor was in fact her biological father. But, how could she? How could she admit to other people the one thing that sickened and terrified her to admit to herself? How could she risk her dream job and everything she had achieved by letting people know?

The minute the truth was out there, people would change around her. She would be tainted by association. Not only would she probably lose her job, but she would be judged because of who she shared her DNA with. She had come this far; she had no choice but to carry on keeping quiet.

'Maya?' Kym was staring at her with a mixture of concern and confusion.

'There's absolutely nothing else you need to know about. Everything's fine. Couldn't be better.' Her finger had started to bleed, and she wiped it dismissively on her trousers. With that, Maya excused herself before Kym had the chance to detect the lack of honesty on her face. Either that or have a change of heart and tell her boss the whole, ugly, horrible truth.

37

Nowak was hunched on his bunk, brooding about the visit from Markita. She was definitely hiding something from him. Her faux cheerfulness and disingenuous claims about how much she was missing him were as transparent as the see-through bra straps she wore underneath her scanty top. He couldn't stand that bra. The idea was to make the bra look invisible underneath certain tops, but he always thought the straps looked even more obvious. Cheap and obvious.

And it wasn't just Markita that was winding him up. There was still no mention of a transfer to Strangeways and he felt that both the solicitor and Donnelly were dragging their feet. How much could he really trust these people? He had begun to second-guess everything he saw or heard; poring over every facial tic and word.

He reasoned that if Markita could lie to his face so easily, and he was certain that she was lying, could Donnelly do the same? But why would he lie to him? Rationally, he knew that it didn't make any sense for his friend to want him out of the way. They weren't just business partners; they were practically family. But there was an inkling. The slightest glimmer of doubt that refused to be extinguished. He shook his head to clear the notion from his mind.

All these negative, suspicious thoughts were due to being locked up. Like Donnelly had advised, he just needed to keep his head. He'd be out of here before he knew it. As soon as Spencer James was put in the frame for the McCluskey stabbing he'd be free. Then once he was home, he would find out what Markita was up to. God help her if she was cheating. Woman or not, he would kill her *and* whoever it was she was sleeping with. The thought of such a betrayal hurt him too much to even bear thinking about. He loved her so much and the thought of her being with someone else made him feel sick to the stomach.

It wasn't just the thought of her in bed with someone else, though God knows that was painful enough. He thought of all the money he had spent on her and all the intimate moments they had shared. He remembered how he had opened his heart to her and told her things he had never told another woman. He had not only stupidly shared information about his dealings with Donnelly, but he had declared his undying love to her. The thought that she would now throw all that back in his face made him feel used and humiliated. He hit himself several times on the side of his head, wishing he could stop all the thoughts that were churning around inside his mind. It was unbearable.

'You okay, mate?' Marcus Naylor was sat at the table in their cell, his face a mask of concern. He'd been occupying himself playing solitaire with a pack of well-worn cards but had become aware of Nowak's restlessness. He'd been subdued since he'd returned from his visit with Markita and it didn't take a genius to work out that she was what the problem was.

'Fuckin' women, innit,' Nowak grumbled as he climbed down from the bunk and joined Naylor at the table.

'They're nothing but trouble, mate, trust me.'

'Yeah? Even the lovely Maya?'

'It's not what you think, mate. I'm not interested in her like that. It's complicated.' Naylor shook his head. He avoided eye contact, concentrating instead on shuffling the cards.

'Care to share?' Nowak said flippantly.

'Not really. It's personal, mate. No offence.'

'Jesus, man. I've listened to you snoring, wanking and had to breathe in the smell of your shit for more hours than I care to count. I think we've got past the personal stage, don't you?'

Naylor ran a meaty hand over his head, looking exasperated. 'I don't fancy her. It's not like that. She's the reason I'm in here.'

'What, forensically? She must have been in primary school when you were locked up.'

'She was twelve actually,' Naylor replied bluntly.

'So how did a twelve-year-old end up getting you locked up?' Nowak was looking at Naylor quizzically. He was certainly proving to be a dark horse.

'She rang the police on me. She also knew where I'd hidden evidence and told them everything when they arrived. A fucking kid, can you believe it?'

'How did she even know? Was she a neighbour or something?'

'No.' Naylor sighed disgustedly. 'She's my daughter.'

The silence loomed like an oppressive gas until Nowak eventually let out a rush of air.

'Whoa! You're telling me your daughter is a SOCO. That she's police? Fuckin' police? Jesus, that's really bad, my friend.' Nowak shook his head, eyeing Naylor warily This new dynamic was as unprecedented as it was unexpected.

Naylor hung his head with shame and disgust. 'Now you know why I'm so keen to find out everything I can about her. She and I have a few old scores to settle. I think it's about time she paid for getting me put away, don't you? I want her to suffer. And Dominique, her bitch of a mother.'

Although Nowak appreciated the sentiment, he was shocked that Naylor would go so far. Yes, he deserved some payback, but to wish one of your own dead. It wasn't comparable to his thoughts about Markita – she was his girlfriend. Maya was Naylor's daughter. 'I get it, but she was just a kid. Surely you can't hold her responsible. She's your own flesh and blood, mate.'

'Is that what you think? Maybe when you've spent as much time stewing in here as I have, you'll see things differently. She might only have been a kid, but she knew exactly what the consequences would be once she rang the police.' He snorted with disgust. 'She wanted me to be put away in here and I can never forgive her for that. And now, she's one of them. Talk about taking the piss. Daughter or not, she's dead to me.'

Nowak could tell by the look of sheer anger and contempt on Naylor's face that he meant every word he said. It was obvious that there was no love lost for Maya or the mother. The implications of what would happen to them once Naylor was released from prison were massive. When that day came, Maya and Dominique Barton would be as good as dead. Naylor was hell-bent on revenge. As for Nowak, Maya meant nothing to him. He felt the same contempt for her as he did for all police. If Naylor ever needed any help from him in getting his revenge on Maya, he would be only too happy to help his friend out.

38

There was an unusual lack of jobs. No burglaries had been reported and thankfully there were no serious incidents to deal with. The day staff had finished an hour early with Kym's blessing, leaving Maya alone to cover the late shift. She was grateful for the peace and quiet as it gave her the opportunity to deal with the statement requests that had been emailed to her.

The smell of fried chicken and chips still lingered in the office, championed only by the smell of printer ink and Chris's boots, which he always left festering under his desk at the end of each shift.

Maya hummed along to the radio as she typed up a statement for an assault she had dealt with several weeks ago. She was so preoccupied with transferring details of her scene examination onto the statement that she didn't even hear Andy arrive in the office.

'Hiya, Maya, love. Are you on your own?' His uncharacteristically pleasant demeanour made her instantly wary.

'Erm, yeah. There's nothing doing so Kym let the day shift finish early. How was the PM?'

'Not so bad, long-winded as always. I'm just going to process my photographs before I go. Do you want a brew?'

That was a first. Andy was infamous for making himself a tea or coffee without ever asking anyone else. It was yet another regular bone of contention between him and Elaine.

'No, I'm good, thanks.' She nodded towards the can of Diet Coke on the desk next to her.

Andy fussed about as she concentrated on writing her statement. The boiling kettle soon drowned out the sound of the radio, which Andy was now tunelessly whistling along to. It was starting to grate on her nerves. She hoped he'd hurry up, sort out his photographs and leave her in peace. She groaned inwardly as he finished making coffee, rhythmically tapping the teaspoon against the side of his mug, before clattering it down onto the metal tea tray without even wiping it.

Distracted, Maya observed him out of the corner of her eye as he booted up the computer and removed the memory card from his camera. He prepared two blank DVDs with exhibit labels and proceeded to burn his photographic images onto the discs. The computer wheezed with effort as the process began. The computers were so old and slow that processing images took ages. She was horrified when Andy wheeled his chair over to where she was sat, clearly intent on striking up a conversation.

'So,' he slurped noisily at his coffee, 'how are things?'

'Erm, good thanks. You?'

'Yeah, not so bad, not so bad. You okay after all that business with the journalist? Bloody horrible situation to be in. Could have been any one of us, you know. You shouldn't feel bad.' He leant forward and patted her forearm awkwardly. Maya had to resist the urge not to shiver with revulsion.

'Kym spoke to me about it just before, actually. There aren't going to be any repercussions from top office, thankfully. She's told me to pretty much forget about it and move on.'

'Yeah, good advice. Good advice.' He took another slurp. 'I bet you've got plenty of support at home too.'

'Hmm,' she replied non-committally.

'Who do you live with again?' he asked.

'I live on my own.'

'Moved out of your parents' then? Do your mum and dad live close?' Another slurp.

'My mum is fairly local, yeah.'

Surely her vague answers and the fact she was staring avidly at the computer screen were enough of a hint that she didn't want to talk to him?

'Right. Good, good.' He slurped again. 'Boyfriend planning on moving in with you any time soon, is he?'

Maya had taken a sip of her Diet Coke and the shock of the question caused her to splutter on the drink as she swallowed. 'What? No. He isn't. I mean, I haven't got one. I'm not with anyone.' She resented the fact she was becoming flustered.

'Right. Good, good,' he repeated distractedly as he picked an imaginary piece of lint from his trouser leg. 'So, no boyfriend then. So, what do you like to do when you're not here then? Do you get out much?'

Maya was mortified. What was with the sudden interest and the 'nice Andy' act. God, he wasn't going to ask her out, was he? He was notorious for his reputation with women but, surely, he didn't think she would be interested. He was old enough to be her dad, and even that wasn't a positive comparison given the circumstances.

'I, erm, yes, sometimes. I'm quite a private person actually, Andy.' Surely that was a big enough hint that she wanted to discontinue the conversation.

'Oh, me and you both, Maya, love. Me and you both.' He

took another slurp. 'That's probably why we get on, similar like that, you see. Most of them in here can't keep out of each other's business. That Elaine can't hold her own water. I'm like "too much information, Elaine".' He waved his hand in mock horror.

She was staring at him wide-eyed and open-mouthed now. He was acting so ridiculously out of character; she was even beginning to think he was on something. Why else would he make such a ridiculous claim that they got on. She was feeling decidedly uncomfortable in his presence now and he was making her skin crawl.

'Do you own your own house then or rent? Sorry, I can't even remember where you said you lived?'

'Erm, Miller Court. Near The Eagle pub?'

'Ah, yes. The Eagle. Did a stabbing there a few years back. Nice pub. Do you go in there much?'

'Look, Andy, I don't mean to be rude, but I've really got to get this statement finished. Maybe we could talk another time? Besides, it looks like your disc has finished burning.'

''Course, yeah. No problem. No problem. We'll chat again then. We're very alike me and you. Very alike.' He reached over as if he was about to pat her arm again, then seemed to think better of it. He withdrew his hand and stood up. Gulping the last of his coffee, he banged his cup down on the tea tray and finished preparing his discs.

'Just nipping to the storeroom to get some more paper from the printer,' she called, desperate to be out of the office and away from him. She was cringing with the awkwardness of the conversation and incredibly suspicious of his sudden interest in her. Hopefully he'd be gone when she got back.

Andy watched Maya leave the office, a fake smile plastered on his face. *Bitch*, he thought as he reached for his phone. 'Mr Donnelly, it's me – about Maya Barton? She lives alone. Miller Court near The Eagle pub,' he said hurriedly.

There was a long uncomfortable pause in which he could hear Aiden's rasping breath down the phone. 'Is that it?' he said eventually. 'What the fuck do I pay you for? Get your fucking finger out,' Donnelly snarled before disconnecting the call.

Beads of sweat emerged on Andy's forehead. He didn't mind admitting that Donnelly terrified the shit out of him. Without even thinking of the consequences, he ran into Kym's office and made his way to the filing cabinet in the corner of the room. He had acquired a spare key a long time ago and knew that amongst its contents, this was where Kym stored hard copies of all the staff's personnel files. With a quick glance to double-check he was still on his own, Andy unlocked the cabinet and opened the top drawer. He deftly flicked through the manila folders until he found the one with Maya's name on it.

Hands shaking, he photographed the contents. Not daring to waste time reading anything, he replaced the folder, carefully locking the cabinet back up. He finished processing the final photographic disc, grabbed his jacket and was out of the office by the time Maya returned. Andy sighed with relief as he started his car and drove out of Beech Field police station. He would ring Donnelly again and arrange to meet so he could show him the information on his phone. Donnelly wouldn't thank him for texting the details and risk leaving a digital trail. God, he needed a drink.

39

Wendy Johnson was worried. She had not heard from her son, Ryan, for several days now and it was very unusual. God knows the boy had given her nothing but trouble over the years. He had brought the police to her door more times than she cared to mention, but despite all that, he had always been a good son. His recent stretch in prison had terrified him. He had changed while he'd been inside, so much so, he had vowed to her that from now on he was on the straight and narrow. She had genuinely believed him too, which is why his sudden silence was concerning.

Her worry had intensified further after hearing from her daughter, Chantelle, that Ryan had not been in touch with her either. The two of them had always been close and it was completely out of character for Ryan not to reply to any of Chantelle's text messages. As far as Chantelle was concerned, Ryan had kept to his promise to stay out of trouble and wasn't involved in anything she knew of. That said, Wendy had heard that Aiden Donnelly and Piotr Nowak were still sniffing around her son and trouble clung to that pair like a stray fart in a lift.

Wendy parked her battered old Ford outside Ryan's flat and

reached for the spare key he had given her when he first moved in. She had always kept hold of it in case Ryan was arrested again. That way she could go and check there was nothing incriminating in his flat before the police searched it. Sighing, she heaved herself out of the car and shuffled towards the front door. Her pink T-shirt barely scraped low enough to cover the top of her black leggings. Her greasy hair was scraped up into a large clip and her feet were ensconced in a pair of threadbare beige slippers.

She banged on the door, stuffing a strand of grey hair behind her ear as she waited. 'Ryan, it's Mam!' she shouted through the letter box then stepped back to look for any signs of movement at the window.

Her heart sank a little more at the obvious stillness. He clearly wasn't home. Where was that boy of hers? Sighing again, Wendy let herself into the flat. A pile of post and takeaway leaflets littered the hall. She kicked them to one side, calling Ryan's name as she walked into the lounge. The place was in its usual state of disarray, but there was something different. Something she couldn't quite put her finger on.

As she walked into the kitchen, she automatically went to open the window to let some fresh air in. He was clearly back on the weed, which saddened her. He'd worked so hard to stay clean since coming out of prison. If he was back on the weed, what else was he taking and how was he paying for it? Just then the penny dropped, and Wendy realised with a sinking heart what was wrong.

Despite the overflowing ashtray and reek of stale booze, there was an undercurrent of something else. It had taken her a while to recognise the smell of disinfectant, something which always reminded her of the local pool and the swimming lessons she had dreaded as a child. She could smell it now in Ryan's flat and it surprised her. Ryan normally avoided cleaning like the plague. There was something else, too, another faint odour. It had an underlying metallic tang that she could almost taste but couldn't quite place.

Frantic now, she began to search the flat for clues of Ryan's disappearance. Her heart sank at the sight of his cash card and mobile phone on the kitchen table. He wouldn't have gone anywhere without taking them. Nudging the home key, she could see the list of missed calls from her and Chantelle. The phone was locked with a key code she didn't know.

Her mother's intuition was screaming at her that something was wrong. Very, very wrong. She flung open cupboard doors and drawers, not knowing what she was looking for, but convinced her maternal intuition would know when she found it. She even shifted the mattress off his bed, familiar with his old habit of secreting items there, away from prying eyes.

Moving on to the lounge, she searched the television cabinet and rooted under the cushions. Nothing other than some coins and an empty condom wrapper. Frustrated, she sank down on the arm of the settee and reached for her phone so she could ring Chantelle.

'I'm at the flat,' she said as Chantelle answered. 'He's not here but his phone and bank card are. Something's wrong. I just know it. I don't know what to do.'

She could feel tears pricking her eyes as she listened to her daughter's calm reassurance. 'You know what he's like, Mam. He's probably got involved in some scrape and is lying low until it all blows over.'

As she listened, Wendy Johnson looked down at her feet, suddenly aware of a vague irritation. Her slippers were soaked wet through. How could that be? It had been bone-dry outside when she had walked from the car into Ryan's flat.

She leant forward and pressed her hand against the navy-blue carpet. It was damp. She stood up and moved further across the room, before dropping to her knees and pressing her hands down in various places: the carpet was soaking. She studied her palm, dropping the phone in shock. She pulled out a tissue which she habitually kept tucked inside her bra and began blotting it against the carpet before sitting back on her heels and scrutinising it. The tissue was stained with diluted traces of blood.

'Oh, Ryan,' she groaned. 'Oh, my boy, what's happened to you?' She disconnected the call to Chantelle without any further explanation. With shaking hands, she called the police.

40

As Maya arrived at work for her midday shift, her curiosity was piqued at the presence of more vehicles than usual in the car park. More staff suggested that there may well be an incident ongoing, although she hadn't heard any reports on the news. She reasoned it could be a training course or meeting somewhere which had caused the extra influx of staff.

Maya was met in the corridor by Elaine and Kym who were heading towards her, clutching notebooks.

'Great timing, we've got a job on and the briefing is about to start. I want you to accompany Elaine to the scene so you may as well sit in.' Kym was her usual brusque, efficient self, while Elaine looked flushed and dishevelled in her straining uniform.

Maya hurried along to keep up with the two women as they made their way to the second-floor conference room.

'What's the job?' she asked Elaine.

'A concern for welfare that we're treating as a murder. We've no body yet but a potential scene. The Major Incident Team are covering it along with input from Operation Chrysalis.'

Elaine didn't elaborate any further as they had arrived at the conference room and followed the stream of detectives who hurriedly sat themselves at the large oval table. Some of the faces Maya recognised as being from her own CID. Others she didn't know were clearly from the MIT and had been brought over to Beech Field to deal with the investigation.

A tall lady with brunette hair tied efficiently in a French plait that hung down her back, stood and waited as everyone in the room settled down. Her smart trouser suit commanded attention and her sheer presence caused everyone to quieten down quickly, without the usual banter that such a meeting would instigate.

'Good morning, everyone, thanks for being here. For those of you that don't know me I am DCI Donna Chambers from MIT syndicate three. This is DI Alison Mitton and DI Redford both based here at Beech Field. We also have DC Stevenson and DC Malone who have been investigating Operation Chrysalis. Thanks also to our SOCO colleagues for joining us.'

Kym nodded an acknowledgement as members of the MIT glanced their way.

'Right, most of you are aware of what we're dealing with today but I'm going to briefly summarise for those who don't know. A nominal of Operation Chrysalis, Ryan Johnson, has been reported missing by his mother. The disappearance is out of character and our concerns are that Johnson has had recent dealings with Aiden Donnelly and Piotr Nowak. For my team who may not be aware of these two, they are the two main players involved in Op Chrysalis. You have access to their intelligence, so I suggest you take the time to familiarise yourselves with their backgrounds.'

She took a moment to peruse the room with her steely grey eyes to make sure everyone was paying attention. 'It's rumoured that Johnson could well have pissed off Nowak and Donnelly and, if this is true, from what we know of our suspects, this wouldn't be good for his health. His mother has been to his flat and reported that there is no trace of Johnson having been there, seemingly for several days.'

She paused a moment to allow those who were frantically scribbling notes to finish writing before she continued. 'His phone and bank card are in situ, and the carpet in the lounge appears to have been recently, albeit badly, washed. To quote the mother...' she glanced at the notes in front of her, '"it's pissed wet through and looks bloodstained". In view of this we are treating Ryan Johnson's flat as a potential murder scene. The TAU will be joining us later today to conduct a cursory search of the waterways surrounding Johnson's flat and SOCO are going to start processing the scene.'

DCI Chambers began to relay a list of actions to the team and DI Redford gave a quick briefing on Donnelly and Nowak's criminal history, so the MIT knew the seriousness of the people they were dealing with. Maya had to admit that the fact Ryan Johnson had recent involvement with the pair, and that he was now missing, did not look good at all. She thought fleetingly of Spence. She knew he and Johnson had been very casual acquaintances and she felt relieved for his sake that he was not involved with the likes of Donnelly and Nowak.

The meeting was quickly wrapped up and the scraping of chairs was followed by a hasty exit of the conference room as the detectives filed out, having been issued with their actions. Kym approached DCI Chambers and shook her hand.

'Good to see you again, Kym. It seems ages since my syndicate last picked up a job on your division. The last one we had was the fatal arson, wasn't it?'

'Yes, it was. It's good to see you too. I believe you already know Elaine. This is our newest member of the team, Maya Barton. I've asked her to accompany Elaine to the scene. Although it's only a small, sparse property we'll get things moving quicker with two members of staff down there. Elaine has got a copy of the forensic strategy. I'm holding the rest of my staff back for now as I'm mindful we may soon be dealing with a body and suspects.'

Chambers nodded. 'The chances are that Donnelly and Nowak won't personally have got their hands dirty disposing of Johnson. Nowak's currently remanded and our intelligence suggests that Donnelly delegates his dirty work to Sydney Barber, aka Lurch.'

Elaine snorted at the mention of the nickname earning her a warning look from Kym.

'As we discussed earlier, the forensic strategy is going to initially concentrate on examining the carpet in the lounge. Our own lab is on standby to attend with the luminol. Once that has been done and we can see what we're dealing with, we can devise the rest of the strategy accordingly. A forensic biologist has also been tasked to attend.'

'Which biologist are we using?' said Chambers.

'Derek Billing? Was with the Forensic Science Service, now with Cellmark.'

'Ah, yes, I've worked on a few jobs with him. Surprised he's not retired. Seems deeply knowledgeable and is very accommodating but bloody awful halitosis. At least he'll be wearing a face mask so you two should be spared,' Chambers said to Maya and Elaine.

'He is incredibly good at his job but the man's a menace.' Kym chose not to elaborate any further. 'I'll be in touch, ma'am.' She clapped her hands and lead Maya and Elaine out of the meeting room. Maya noticed Chambers wince at Kym's double clap, whereas Elaine and Maya shared an eye-roll behind her back. Not for the first time, Maya wondered whether Kym could have been a Victorian schoolteacher in a former life.

'We might as well head down in the one van if that's okay with you? I'll recover the exhibits if you scribe. Your handwriting's neater than mine,' Elaine said as they walked back into the office and gathered their belongings.

Maya agreed and grabbed some snacks out of her drawer to take with her in lieu of lunch. She had learnt long ago that a stash of cereal bars and crisps always came in handy when a job came in. It was beginning to look like she and Elaine would be at the scene for a while and would more than likely end up working overtime.

As Elaine drove them to Ryan Johnson's address, Maya regaled her with details of Andy's strange behaviour the night before.

'I don't get it.' Elaine frowned, shaking her head. 'He's never pleasant to anyone. Maybe he fancies his chances with you,' she added with a saucy wink.

'Eugh, a little bit of sick just rose up in my mouth at the thought,' said Maya as Elaine's raucous laugh filled the van.

'Seriously though, just be on your guard. Andy Carr is a slippery fucker. If he's being nice, you can guarantee he's up to something.'

Maya nodded in agreement. Andy had unnerved her last night with his change in attitude and his sudden interest in her. She didn't appreciate or want his attention and sincerely hoped that whatever was going on in Andy's mind, his 'friendliness' wouldn't be repeated. Elaine was right; she would be on her guard as far as he was concerned. She suddenly shivered with trepidation and a sense of foreboding.

41

A ndy pulled up on the derelict pub car park where he usually met Donnelly. The location was perfect – free of CCTV and prying eyes and it wasn't the sort of area that people would normally venture. Even police officers preferred to patrol this particular location in pairs. The only person Andy had spotted as he pulled into the car park was an old drunk who had scuttled away at the sight of Andy's scowling face.

Thirty minutes after arriving, Donnelly's black Mercedes cruised in and parked opposite Andy. Donnelly motioned through the windscreen for Andy to join him and he meekly scuttled towards the car, slipping into the passenger seat.

Donnelly surveyed the man, his lip curling with distaste. 'Well, what have you got? It better be fucking worth it,' he said as he jabbed a forefinger into Andy's temple.

Visibly shaking, Andy pulled his mobile phone out of his pocket.

'I've managed to photograph the contents of her personnel file, Mr Donnelly,' he said as he unlocked his mobile and handed Aiden the phone with the images ready to display.

'Meh, meh, meh, Mr Donnelly,' Aiden mimicked in a girlish

voice as he snatched the phone off Andy. 'You've still got a lot of making up to do for not knowing about the raid that got me arrested the other week. Prick,' he said scathingly. He was silent for several moments as he absorbed the contents, taking in all Maya's personal details including her and Dominique's addresses.

'Anything else?' he sneered as he thrust the phone back at Aiden.

'No, Mr Donnelly. Redford and Mitton have been antsy since you were released, but as far as I'm aware they've nothing to warrant pulling you back in at the moment. I'm keeping my ears to the ground as best as I can.'

'Fuck 'em. The slightest sniff they're looking at doing another search of my pad, I want to know, understood? You will *not* get a second chance after last time.'

'I... I... I told you, Mr Donnelly, they played it close to their chests. There was no way of me finding out what they were up to. If I'd have known, of course I would have told you. Nobody on that warrant knew where they were going until they set off. Even a psychic wouldn't have known what was going on,' stuttered Andy.

'A psychic? A fucking psychic? Are you taking the piss? You're getting very close to needing a psychic to communicate with your family in future, you fucking wanker.'

Aiden leaned in close, his nose practically touching Andy's as he glared at the man, his face flushed with anger.

'Sorry, Mr Donnelly, I didn't mean any disrespect, honestly.' Andy held his shaking hands up in front of him as he shrank towards the door and away from Aiden's glare.

'Whatever. I need to start making arrangements to have Nowak released. The items that you accessed from the McCluskey stabbing need to be placed on a bloke called Spencer James. I'm just waiting for an opportunity to get to his place and then we're good to go. So next time I ring you, make sure you fucking well answer, okay?'

'Yes, Mr Donnelly.' Andy was trembling so much now he could barely keep his knees from shaking.

Aiden surveyed him again with a look of sheer hatred and disgust on his face. Fishing in his pocket, he pulled out a wodge of fifty-pound notes and threw them in Andy's direction.

'Here, it's payday. Now get out of my car and fuck off,' he snarled.

Frantically grabbing at the notes, Andy mumbled something incoherent and flung himself out of the car.

Aiden watched him go. He really did despise the man. Even though he had been useful over the past year, tipping him and Nowak off in advance about the police investigation surrounding them, he despised the fact that a man like that would grass on his own. It went against everything he believed in. He watched as the odious shit circled in the car park before driving off. Even his car appeared to slither. He shook his head again, incredulous as to what a wanker Andy Carr was.

42

L urch was doing the following again. He had followed Spence home from the gym and had been sat outside his address since late morning. Lurch thought the house was pretty. It reminded him of the sort of thing he used to build out of Lego. The housing estate was about twelve years old and the first signs of fatigue had started to show on the flaking paint on the gutters. The shrubs that had been planted in the gardens and flower beds which lined the roads had established well though, giving him plenty of coverage.

He had watched as the lady and the little girl returned home from school. He thought the little girl looked sweet and the lady looked like Spence. Lurch had no opinion on the man. He travelled to and from the address like clockwork. He dressed conservatively and drove a spotless white car. Everything about him seemed nondescript, and the fact that Lurch had taken one look at him and established he was no physical threat meant he dismissed him relatively quickly.

He knew which bedroom Spence's was. He had followed him home enough by now to notice which light at the back of the house switched on not long after he came home. He also knew how easy it was to break into these new houses. The problem was, they were knocked up so quickly, it wasn't unusual for the building contractors to scrimp on certain items.

All the houses had fancy patio doors situated to the rear of the property, which opened out onto the boxy-looking gardens. Lurch knew that a bit of physical manipulation around the door, especially on a hot day, would cause the uPVC to be rocked easily from its frame, allowing the lock to pop open. Not that he would even need to bother with that seeing he had the lock-picking device Aiden had bought for him.

It was time for Lurch to go. Spence would be leaving for work soon, the following had gone well again, and he knew Aiden would be pleased. He had one other job to do and after that he would treat himself to a couple of pints.

He was determined to head back to The Eagle so he would be in his favourite seat before Spence arrived. If he was lucky, he might even get another free drink. He wasn't going to have too many though, as he knew that any day now, Aiden would ask him to break into Spence's house, so he knew he had to be ready.

He grinned as he saw the little girl briefly appear in the lounge window, skipping around the room with a doll in her hand. She stopped at the window, gazing in his direction as he gave her a little wave and pressed his forefinger to his lips to let her know him being there was their secret.

Goodbye little girl, he said in his head to her as he slipped out of his hiding place. He ducked past the neighbour's hydrangea and back onto the road of the estate. Although the following lasted a long time, and made him get cramp in his lower back, sometimes it could be fun.

43

Maya and Elaine had worked quickly and efficiently at Ryan Johnson's flat. On their arrival at the scene, they had donned their scene suits, overshoes, face masks and double-gloved. They signed themselves into the scene log and placed stepping plates throughout the one-bedroomed flat, to preserve any potential evidence on the floor. As Maya placed down a stepping plate, Elaine photographed, then videoed the scene. After this had been completed, Elaine recovered Ryan Johnson's mobile phone from the kitchen table.

The phone was swabbed and fingerprinted before being placed in a rigid container within a tamper-evident bag. An exhibit number was allocated, and descriptions added. Next, it was signed, sealed and handed to the waiting exhibits officer. He had been tasked with submitting the phone to the forensic digital unit at headquarters, so it could be examined as a matter of urgency. Although it was accepted that Ryan Johnson was already dead, it was hoped that information from his phone would provide investigators with much-needed information as to his recent movements.

Maya had already used the Kastle-Meyer presumptive blood

testing kit to screen an area of staining on the lounge carpet. The kit worked by using a folded piece of filter paper to rub against the suspected bloodstain. Drops of the Kastle-Meyer reagent, followed by a drop of hydrogen peroxide were then added to the filter paper. A positive indication of blood caused the filter paper to turn a noticeable startling pink colour.

Elaine had then swabbed some of the blood using a wet and dry cotton swab. This exhibit would be fast-tracked to the forensic service provider for analysis. They would then enter the profile onto the National DNA Database, which in turn would confirm that the profile matched the PACE sample they already had on file for Ryan Johnson.

As they worked, an old, grey Volvo pulled up outside and the forensic biologist, Derek Billing emerged; a tall man with sparse grey hair, donning a ghastly bow tie. He was already visibly sweating as he suited and booted before making his way into the flat where Maya and Elaine met him in the hallway.

'Hello, ladies, how goes it so far?' He spoke in a polished, Pathé newsreader voice. He provided both with a flaccid handshake, barely grazing their fingertips.

'We're progressing nicely, thanks, Derek. We're ready for the lab to come in.' Elaine removed her face mask, gulping gratefully at the fresh air.

'I'm aware from the strategy you've been asked to prioritise the lounge, so I'll not get in your way. I'm just going to do a very quick search in there and mark up any obvious bloodstains.' They watched as he took a series of still photographs on his own pocket-sized Nikon camera before commencing a search of the lounge with his torch.

A short time later, another car engine heralded a new arrival, and Kym's Mini pulled up alongside Derek's Volvo. Maya and Elaine went to greet her at the scene tape, quickly followed by a panting Derek. It became immediately obvious from his reaction that he was a huge admirer of Kym's. What little of his face was showing above his mask and below the hood of his scene suit reddened at the sight of her.

'Oh, look. It's Kym, oh my. I didn't realise I would be having the pleasure of seeing you here, dear lady.'

'It's looking very likely that this will turn out to be a murder enquiry, in which case I, or one of the other senior SOCOs will always turn out,' Kym commented flatly.

'Oh, of course,' blustered Derek. 'I should have clicked when I saw your name on the forensic strategy. Oh my, what a treat. And now you're here, you naughty girl, may I remind you that last time we spoke you promised to join me for drinks while I shared details of my latest paper on ageing bloodstains.'

Kym physically bristled at the phrase 'naughty girl', before replying bluntly, 'Yes, I've been very busy. This can be a twenty-four-seven job at times.'

'You're off this weekend, though, aren't you, Kym?' Elaine asked, all wide-eyed and innocent.

Narrowing her eyes in a disparaging look, Kym glared at Elaine. 'Yes, well, that remains to be seen depending on what happens with this job. Shall we concentrate on the task at hand, people? This is a potential murder investigation after all, there's no time for social niceties.'

Maya and Elaine exchanged a quick, bemused look before Elaine walked Kym through the scene and filled her in on how much they had processed so far.

'As you can see, he hasn't got too much in the way of personal effects.' Elaine gesticulated with her hand and then scrolled through the images she had taken on her Nikon D300 to show Elaine and Derek what items they had already recovered from the flat.

'It's sparsely furnished. His bank card and mobile phone were on the kitchen table. The exhibits officer has already taken that to the digital unit to be examined. The TV in the lounge hasn't been disturbed and there's also a tablet and games console which hasn't been touched, so whatever has gone on in here, robbery certainly isn't a motive.'

Kym nodded as Maya continued.

'There were some beer cans on the floor next to the lounge and some items of post from near the front door which could possibly contain footwear marks. A stain on the carpet next to the couch here has tested positive for blood using the Kastle-Meyer kit. An area has been swabbed for fast-tracking so we can confirm that this is Johnson's blood.

'Great work, ladies. Thank you for your efforts so far and for working so promptly. The lab technicians are on the way, so we'll start the luminol treatment once they get here. I've brought you some cold drinks and ice lollies in a freezer bag outside, so go and get out of your scene suits and have a breather.' Kym nodded her appreciation as she took another walk round the flat with Derek Billing hot on her heels.

Grateful for the refreshments, Maya and Elaine shucked off their scene suits and went and sat in the van.

'She's going to get you back for that "weekend off" comment,' Maya said, causing Elaine to mock shudder in response. They sat and ate their ice lollies in a companionable silence before Maya asked, 'How does the luminol treatment work?'

'Blood is notoriously difficult to clean. Even though the stain might appear to have disappeared to the naked eye, the haemoglobin of the blood is very resilient. We use a brand called Bluestar which is mixed and applied using a spray bottle. Its purpose is to reveal traces of blood which have been cleaned away. When the Bluestar is applied to an area containing traces of haemoglobin, it gives a distinct chemiluminescent result.'

'A what?'

'Sorry, you've got me in geek mode. It basically emits a bright blue light, hence the name. Honestly, Maya, it's amazing to see. It's the sort of stuff they show on those shitty American forensic shows. The lab techs will darken the room to maximise the effect of the treatment and I'll photograph the results. Derek will be able to ascertain from the volume of blood whether Johnson could have survived. It will also enhance any footwear marks in blood.'

'I can't wait to see it.'

They sat and finished their drinks, watching as the neighbours stared in their direction, curious at the presence of police vehicles. Maya felt sorry for the poor officer manning the scene tape. He looked hot and bothered and was being constantly harassed by people wanting to know what was going on and complaining that they had to use the opposite pavement to the one which had been cordoned off outside the flat.

'Hey up, the cavalry's here.' Elaine nodded towards another, larger vehicle which pulled up adjacent to the scene.

The arrival of the laboratory staff caused even more of a stir. The vehicle they were in was a similar size to a large horsebox, marked with the police insignia. It was basically a mobile lab which contained everything they needed to process crime scenes. Maya had only met one of the lab technicians before, a quiet, bespectacled man named Ewan.

Ewan introduced his colleague, a petite, attractive Asian lady called Ushra. Maya and Elaine re-suited at the same time as Ewan and Ushra, and after they'd signed the scene log, gave them a tour of the flat, again commenting on the work they had carried out so far. The lounge quickly became crowded as Kym and Derek joined them in the small room and they all shuffled around to find a suitable position on a stepping plate.

Kym wedged herself between Maya and Elaine, seemingly keen to put a distance between her and Derek, who was gazing at her dreamily from above the confines of his face mask. Maya smirked to herself as she thought this could quite easily turn into a sketch from a 1970s sitcom, with Derek chasing Kym over the stepping plates and throughout the flat.

'Okay.' Ewan surveyed the room carefully. 'Ushra and I will cover the windows with the black roll. Then I just need a few moments to mix the Bluestar while you remove the stepping plates.'

The roll was made of thick, rubbery tarpaulin, which was fixed to the window so the room could become completely blacked out. Once this was done, Maya removed the stepping plates, propping them up in the hall. Elaine made the necessary adjustments to her camera, which she then positioned on a tripod. Satisfied that the room was suitably prepared, Ewan gave the nod to Kym.

'Ready to go?'

'Yes please,' said Kym.

Ewan prepared to methodically spray the Bluestar over the carpet. He started at the far end of the room near the window. There was a moment's hesitation as the water dispenser wheezed, and then Maya was astonished to see a bright blue glow emerge from the carpet. Elaine snapped away, recording the dramatic results. The room remained silent as the luminol reacted and the light intensified.

'Jesus,' Maya breathed as a huge patch of blue staining emerged. The glow was reminiscent of a fibre-optic Christmas decoration. A pattern emerged which resembled the shape of a body, slumped in a prostrate position next to the couch. The heavier blue staining emitted from the head area. Drag marks were evident, leading from the side of the body to the centre of the lounge. Several footwear marks were also visible across the carpet.'

'Very minimal blood spatter with little cast-off,' Derek observed, and Kym murmured in agreement.

Gradually the light faded as Ewan finished spraying the room. Everyone remained silent for a moment. They were gathered at the door now and all equally stunned by the intensity of the staining they had just witnessed.

'Obviously, I will need a copy of the photographs so I can conduct my interpretation, but I think it's safe to conclude that no one could survive that amount of blood loss,' Derek said.

'The lack of blood spatter is leading me to initially conclude that perhaps the body was covered with something during the attack. I'd hazard a guess, having witnessed the extreme chemiluminescence from what appears to be the head area, that the victim has sustained a fatal head injury. The drag marks would suggest whatever he has been wrapped in has then been used to convey him to the dump site.

'Once the rest of the flat has been examined, I suggest we repeat the luminol process throughout, and this will at least give us some indication as to whether the body has been removed via the front or back door.'

Derek tugged at his face mask, breathing heavily in the heat of the small flat. 'Common sense dictates the rear door would have offered the murderer more privacy, but obviously we need that confirmation. It may also provide us with additional footwear marks, so we can interpret the number of people involved.

'I've had a cursory look in the bathroom and noticed some diluted bloodstains in the bathroom sink, which will need marking up later. There's no sign of a towel in there, so I assume our suspect, or suspects, have washed their hands and taken the towel with them. Obviously, I will return tomorrow and examine the rest of the flat further in accordance with your strategy, Kym. I'll bring one of my subordinates to assist and speed up the process.'

'Thank you for your input, Derek, much appreciated as

always,' Kym said. 'Right, I think it's time we call it a day. Ewan, Ushra, thanks for your help. Elaine and Maya, I know it's been a long day for you ladies. Chris is on the late shift this evening and I've asked him to update your exhibits onto the database. So, get yourselves back and straight home. I'm going to amend the forensic strategy based on what we've seen today. We'll look at recommencing at nine in the morning.'

Efficient as ever, Kym left the flat with Derek Billing following her. He made several attempts to engage her in conversation while they wrestled out of their scene suits, but Kym dismissed him with brusque, one-word answers before finally announcing she needed to head back to Beech Field so she could brief the DCI on their findings so far.

Derek watched her go. 'Oh my, what a woman,' he said as he ran his hand across his head, flattening his hair down then wiping his face as if smoothing his whiskers. He watched Kym drive away from the scene with a lecherous grin on his face. Maya and Elaine exchanged a smirk, bid farewell to the lab technicians and after signing out of the scene log, headed back to the station. Both of them wondered when and where Ryan Johnson's body would be found.

44

Arriving at work the next morning, there were even more vehicles in the car park than the previous day. Maya wondered if this meant there had been a development in the Ryan Johnson investigation. This was confirmed by the fact that Chris, who should have been on a midday shift, was already in the office. He looked tired and in need of a shave. A pot of untouched porridge was on the next desk to his elbow.

'Got a job on?' Maya said, as she switched on the kettle.

'Yes, love. Ryan Johnson's body was found last night. The search teams were about to call it a day, but he was spotted in the waterway at the back of his flat. He'd been wrapped in tarpaulin as well as a large bedsheet and weighed down with bricks and covered in shrubbery and whatnot. His PM is scheduled for later on, so I thought I'd stay with it as I recovered him last night.'

'What condition is he in?' Maya asked as she lowered herself into the chair next to Chris.

'He's relatively well preserved, probably due to the fact he's been wrapped up like a Christmas present, so nothing's had a chance to nibble on him. From the neck down, he's barely got a scratch other than a few defence wounds to his hands. His head has been smashed to smithereens, cracked open like an egg, poor bastard.' Chris shook his head sadly and Maya felt for him, he'd certainly had his fair share of bodies in all the years he'd worked as a SOCO.

'You not eating your breakfast?' she asked, nodding at the porridge.

'Nah, can't face it, love. Looks like bloody baby food. I'll pick up a sausage-and-bacon sandwich on the way to the mortuary.' He smiled, brightening up at the thought.

'Here, I'll get the scene photos ready from last night to show you.'

They were soon joined by Amanda, Elaine, Kym and Nicola. They all gathered around to study the photographs of Ryan Johnson.

Looking at the heavy staining on the sheet that had covered him, it appeared that Derek Billing's observation that he had been covered up during the attack was correct. The back of Ryan's skull had been smashed open, revealing part of his brain, which resembled a jellified cauliflower. His face was swollen and protruding as the impact of the head injury had caused his features to engorge.

Everyone remained silent as Chris flicked through the series of images. Even someone with his and Elaine's length of service, were still saddened at the loss of such a healthy young person having had their life snubbed out by an act of sheer, mindless violence.

Maya shuddered at the sight and found herself thinking how glad she was it wasn't Spence that she was looking at. She was glad he wasn't mixed up in the same kind of circles as Ryan Johnson had been. She would have been devastated to think of him ending up like that.

Kym returned to her office and everyone began preparing for

the day. The silence was interrupted by the arrival of DCI Chambers.

'Good morning, is Kym available? I have an update and I also need to take another look at the scene photos of Johnson,' she said, as brusque and efficient as ever.

Kym emerged from her office and gestured towards the door.

'Do you want to come in, ma'am?'

Chambers smiled. 'It's okay thanks, Kym. I have an update I can share with your team. The early phone analysis has come back from the digital forensic unit. Johnson had an app on his phone relating to the fitness tracker we assume he was wearing. The data from that app shows an increase in heart rate at approximately 1900 hours on the twenty-first of July which was five days ago.'

Everyone was silent as they processed the new information, until Elaine tentatively raised a hand like a nervous schoolgirl.

'Forgive me, ma'am, but could you elaborate a bit further? I'm not up to speed with all these apps and technology. You're speaking to someone who is still blown away by the fact you can spell out "boobies" on the upside-down screen of a calculator.'

Chris and Maya howled with laughter as Kym shook her head disparagingly at Elaine.

'In basic terms, we think the fitness tracker may have provided us with a time of death. It's all circumstantial at this stage still, but we think the increase in heart rate occurred during the attack on Johnson. Following this, the app hasn't recorded any other movement or heart-rate data,' Chambers said.

'It's the modern-day equivalent of a stopped-watch scenario from Agatha Christie's day,' Maya suggested.

'Exactly,' Chambers said, smiling at her.

'Here we go, ma'am, I assume this is what you needed to know.' Chris swivelled the computer monitor towards DCI

Chambers and Kym also leant towards the screen. The close-up of Ryan Johnson's right hand displayed a black fitness tracker strapped to his wrist.

'Perfect.' Chambers nodded. 'Thank you, Chris. We're having a briefing in thirty minutes,' she said to Kym before leaving the office.

'I'm going to accompany you to the PM after the briefing,' Kym said to Chris. 'Ladies, ring me on my mobile with any updates from the flat,' she said, addressing Maya and Elaine. 'We've a lot to get through, people, so let's go.'

With a clap, she headed back to her office.

45

Maya worked with Elaine a further three days at Ryan Johnson's flat. The revised forensic strategy saw them painstakingly recover trace evidence, as well as swabbing handles and light switches for DNA. Maya wrote out exhibit bags and updated Elaine's scene notes. This way it took half the time, as the writing-up process took longer than physically recovering each piece of evidence.

They then turned their attention to swabbing and fingerprinting the beer cans in the lounge, as well as recovering cigarette ends from the ashtray in the kitchen. The pair also recovered various items of property, which were to be submitted to the lab for fingerprint treatment. They also considered items such as the post in the hallway, which could be chemically enhanced to reveal any latent footwear marks.

Certain materials were more suitable for chemical treatment to enhance any latent fingerprints, rather than being subject to conventional powdering techniques. The chemical treatment used depended on the nature and porosity of the material, but typically included ninhydrin, superglue or acid black. The lab technicians were as conversant in which type of chemical treatment to use, in the same way as the SOCOs knew which type of fingerprint powders to use on various substrates.

Between them, and with continued assistance from Ewan, Ushra, Derek Billing and his assistant, they combed every inch of the one-bedroom flat in search of evidence. Doctor Granger had concluded that death had been a result of blunt force trauma to the head and suspected a hammer was likely to have been used as a weapon, although they were yet to find it.

Maya had been pleased with how the examination had gone. She and Elaine worked well together, and she had learnt a lot from Derek Billing. Maya also gained invaluable experience into how Ewan and Ushra worked. She watched them use the high intensity light source to search for fingerprints on the walls of the flat and use acid black on various surfaces to further enhance areas of ridge detail.

As they were finishing up on the final day, Maya joined Ewan for a break and the two sat in the van while they shared a flask of lukewarm coffee. They were chatting about how long Ewan had been working in the lab, when she noticed his expression cloud over.

'What's the matter?' Maya asked with concern.

'Isn't that him? The journalist that interviewed you after the Celeste Warren suicide?' Ewan replied.

Maya turned to see the familiar sloping, pear-shaped figure. He was grinning in her direction.

'Yep, that's him. He's been hanging around the last few days. I've been purposefully trying to avoid him, although he had the nerve to wave to me the other day, as if we were old friends. Dave "the bastard" Wainwright.'

Ewan snorted, before looking at Maya sympathetically. 'I really felt for you when I saw that. It was a shit trick and to be fair, any one of us could have been caught out by him.'

'Yeah, well, you live and learn,' Maya said with a shrug.

'According to the grapevine, Kym gave you a real bollocking for your sudden death conspiracy theory too.'

'Ah, yes. Is that doing the rounds as much as my shame of talking to dead people?'

'Afraid so. But the majority aren't judging you unfairly. We're all on the same team after all. You voiced your opinion which you're entitled to do. And for what it's worth, I agree with you. There *is* something strange about the last few sudden deaths we've had. I know none of them have appeared suspicious, but Karl Gorman, Jim Baron, Celeste Warren and more recently Geoffrey Doran, four of the force's most notorious offenders have all died within weeks of each other. And you know what they say...'

'There's no such thing as coincidence in the cops,' they chimed together.

'What about this scene, Ryan Johnson. He was a known offender too. Who do you think killed him?'

'Well, obviously they think he's pissed off some of our local gang members during his time and so far, we've no one arrested, so who knows. And yeah, Ryan had a record but certainly wasn't as notorious as the others and that's really the only link I have between them all. I don't know. I just feel like I'm going around in circles whenever I think about it.'

Maya frowned as she thought once again about the series of sudden deaths. 'This Ryan Johnson job *looks* like a murder whereas the others have just been a classic case of sudden death. But there was something about the scene at Karl Gorman's house which I couldn't quite put my finger on. Just a stupid feeling more than anything. I attended the PM and Doctor Granger, who had also been at the scene, was adamant there was nothing suspicious about his death.

'Tony Harwood from Alder Street attended Jim Baron's death, but they'd pretty much called it non-suspicious by the time he arrived. My own mum, who's a district nurse found him, for goodness' sake. And you know Tony has been in the job nearly as long as Chris and Amanda, so with his experience, he would have picked up on something being wrong. Likewise, with Geoffrey Doran. Although bloody vicious, it would appear to be a random hit and run. But Celeste Warren's death, I dunno. I mean it was *obviously* a suicide, but the note she left still strikes me as strange.'

'How do you mean?' Ewan said.

Maya went on to describe how she thought the crossing out and the wording seemed unusual. She stated she thought it was as if someone was dictating the note to Celeste, rather than it being something she had written spontaneously. She also explained about the glasses and how she had swabbed them for saliva and secured the note for further forensic testing.

'Listen,' Ewan said. 'In view of the fact your DI is happy Celeste Warren's death was suicide, they're never going to agree to have those saliva swabs analysed for DNA. It would be a waste of money in view of the fact there is effectively no crime. And by rights, there's nothing to justify me examining the note in the lab. But, maybe to satisfy our own curiosity, send her suicide note to me and I'll treat it to see if any fingerprints come up.'

'Really? I'd appreciate that, Ewan, but I don't want you to get in any trouble,' said Maya.

'No problem at all. Like I said, I agree with you that these deaths seem suspicious. We're just double-checking we've not missed any obvious clues. We can't be criticised for that. And it's not going to be a time-consuming job, so where's the harm. Anyway, if we do get an ident off the note, it may be from whoever was with her just before she died. They may well provide us with an insight into Celeste's mood and whether they thought she seemed depressed or out of sorts.'

'So, either way we can ascertain whether it was the genuine

suicide it seems to be or whether we are looking at a potential suspicious death. I feel like Scooby Doo on a mission for the truth,' Maya said with a wry grin.

Ewan was about to reply until they both spotted Wainwright making his way along the scene tape towards them. He had his long lens positioned on the camera in the hope he could get a picture of them both in the van. Journalists always loved posting pictures of them in scene suits so they could caption it with exciting headlines such as 'forensic experts combing the scene for evidence'.

'Hoods up and masks back on,' Ewan said, 'let's get back in the scene quick, Dave "the bastard's" coming!'

46

Maya arrived home early Sunday evening feeling restless. Despite the long and exhausting hours she had worked at the scene, she couldn't switch off and relax. The sudden sense of normality was in complete contrast to the intensity and pressure of working on a murder scene. This was one of the things that nobody had told her since she had trained to be a SOCO – how to readjust to her normal life after being exposed to such violence.

The extreme levels of concentration required under highly charged circumstances and tight deadlines was exhausting. On the few occasions she had grown weary and listless during the protracted examination, she recalled the images she had seen of Ryan Johnson's shattered skull. This had been all the motivation she had needed to work with renewed vigour.

Maya had phoned Dominique and a forty-five-minute conversation with her mum had raised her spirits. But once she put the phone down the feeling of restlessness, loneliness even, returned. Normally, she'd relish the prospect of taking the bike for a ride on such a glorious evening, but it was at Dominique's as Maya had borrowed her car and not had the chance to return it. Maya paced the flat, listlessly running her finger across work surfaces, checking for dust that she knew wouldn't be there. Sighing, she flopped on the sofa and flicked through the TV channels, but the words and images bounced off her ineffectively. Muting the TV, she reached for a pad and pen and carefully wrote out each name in her neat, looping handwriting.

Karl Gorman
Jim Baron
Celeste Warren
Geoffrey Doran

She recalled her conversation with Ewan and their plan to have Celeste's suicide note subject to chemical treatment. She circled Celeste's name. Next, she drew a question mark alongside the other three names. She tapped the pen against her teeth as she thought hard. Muttering, she added Ryan Johnson to the list. The pen hovered next to his name as she deliberated over adding a question mark. Sighing, she scribbled lines through the writing before tossing the pad across the sofa. This was futile. Ryan Johnson had been a small-time crook who had been either unlucky or stupid enough to get involved with the nominals from Operation Chrysalis.

It was his involvement with the likes of Nowak and Donnelly that the Murder Investigation Team believed had resulted in his untimely death. But what if that MO was wrong and Maya was right all along about her sudden death theory. Could it be possible that Ryan Johnson was another victim? Would the discovery of his murderer provide a link to the other deaths? Ryan Johnson had been much younger than the others and was certainly no career criminal. Surely there had to be another common denominator that connected them all. But what, and how could she even begin to find out without ruffling feathers.

She was reaching into the fridge for a bottle of wine when a thought occurred to her. Before she even had time to think things through, she was changed, locking up her apartment and heading towards The Eagle. As she made her way through the door of the pub, her stomach lifted at the sight of Spence. He was idling against the bar scrolling on his mobile phone.

'Busy,' she said, causing him to look up, startled.

He gave a huge, beaming grin at the sight of her. 'Hello, you. I shouldn't be using it while I'm at work really but I'm flat hunting. It's really good to see you, how are things?'

'I'm good, thanks. Been working and couldn't face rattling around at home, so I decided to take you up on the offer of waiter service.'

'Madam, please, take a seat,' he said with a bow and a sweep of his arm towards a bar stool. 'You'll have to bear with me though, as you can see, I'm rushed off my feet.'

He gestured towards the bar area where a young couple were sat nestled into each other, oblivious to the rest of the world, and an old bloke who was sat alone with his newspaper, nursing a pint of mild and a whisky chaser.

Maya grinned as she climbed on the bar stool.

'What's your poison?'

'Glass of Pinot, please.'

'Small or large?'

'Large, definitely, definitely large.' Spence gave her a saucy wink as he fetched her drink, setting it carefully down in front of her.

'Been busy then?'

She hesitated, wondering how much to tell him about Ryan. She couldn't divulge any details about the case, and although his name had been released in a press statement by the police, she wondered how much Spence knew about the demise of his old school friend. She wondered if he would know enough to provide any clues as to whether he was involved with the likes of Gorman and Celeste Warren.

'Yeah, it's been busy,' she said hesitantly. She couldn't meet his eye. 'I've been working on a murder.'

He leant towards her and lowered his voice. 'I know you probably can't tell me anything and I wouldn't dream of asking anything too inappropriate, but did it involve Ryan Johnson? I saw something on the news.'

'Yes. I'm sorry. I know he was a friend of yours. It must have been a shock to hear about it.'

'Yeah, it was. It's such a shame.'

'I remember you saying you'd known each other for years. What kind of man was he? Tell me about him.'

'I think I told you before, we'd lost contact years ago other than through Facebook. I didn't know anything about what he was up to these days. We knocked about a bit as kids, but that was it. His family were a bit rough, so Mum didn't encourage me to hang around too much.'

'But he must have posted things on his Facebook account about what he was up to, who his friends were and stuff.'

'I only really paid attention if he posted family stuff. He had a little sister. Ryan adored her; she was a cute, skinny little thing. Always had nits though, another reason Mum didn't encourage the friendship. I caught them once and passed them on to our Tania. You've never known pain until you've had your scalp scarified with a nit comb.'

Maya's husky laugh echoed across the quiet pub, earning her a scowl from the old man with the newspaper. 'Is there anything else you can think of though? Anything at all he may have posted recently that could have indicated who or what he was involved with these days. Particularly in the last few weeks.' Maya was craning towards Spence, eager for some piece of information that would allow all the pieces to fall into place.

'Woah, I thought you were a SOCO, not a detective,' he said, clearly uncomfortable with the sudden intensity of her questions. 'What's with the third degree?'

She laughed nervously. 'Third degree?' She shook her head. 'Not at all. I've been working my arse off at his flat, that's all. Guess I'm just overcurious as well as overtired. Sorry. I'm being tactless.'

He held his phone towards her. 'Feel free to look through his Facebook profile for yourself if you like. If it satisfies your curiosity. Although I'm guessing your colleagues would already have done that. For what it's worth, all you'll see is a load of messages of condolence and banter about MUFC.'

Maya knew she had gone too far grilling Spence. He clearly didn't know enough about Ryan Johnson to support her sudden death theory. It had been a mistake coming here. Not only had she wasted her time, but she had also clearly managed to alienate Spence at the same time. She regretted that, as she had found that despite her initial reservations, she had grown more than fond of him.

'Hey, forget it. Let's talk about something else other than work. I clearly need a break.' She took a large sip of wine. 'How's the flat hunting going then?'

He slipped his phone back into his pocket. 'Not great. Let's just say that my expectations and my budget are currently poles apart. Still, I'm an optimist, something will turn up.' He flashed her one of his wide smiles, which she found nearly as intoxicating as the wine.

'So why the sudden urge to move on? Are things not good at your sister's?'

'I just feel like I'm overstaying my welcome. Bella, my niece, has been acting up a bit. She keeps saying she can see a man watching her through the window and it's been giving her nightmares.'

'Surely that's just a natural childhood phase?' Maya said.

'I dunno. I can't help thinking I've upset her routine. She's only little, it doesn't take much at her age. It's their family home after all and it can't be easy having me dump myself on them. I just need to find something in my price range which is slightly larger than a cornflake box. Another drink?'

Maya was surprised to find her glass empty. The first drink hadn't touched the sides.

'Yes, please. I fancy something a bit different this time. Are you any good at making cocktails?'

He rolled his eyes playfully and gave her a grin. 'I can see you're going to be a high-maintenance customer. I might be able to scrape together a porn star Martini if you don't mind substituting the passion fruit for a glacé cherry?'

'Sounds perfect,' Maya said, smiling at him.

She settled back and watched him as he moved behind the bar. His muscles rippled beneath his shirt. The outline of the tattoo on his bicep peeked out beneath the fabric and she wondered, not for the first time, what the rest of it looked like. What the rest of *him* looked like underneath that shirt, too.

She was glad she'd decided to call in, despite being no further to satisfying her curiosity about Ryan Johnson and his potential connection with the others.

47

A ndy was at home removing some blood-soaked items which he had squirrelled away from Nowak's house when he had attended several weeks ago. He had been instructed by Donnelly that someone would be collecting them from him later. The exhibits were what Donnelly referred to as 'forensic insurance' and were what he paid Andy handsomely for. That and any information he could find in relation to Operation Chrysalis so Donnelly and Nowak could stay one step ahead of the police.

To say that Andy Carr rued the day he had started working for Donnelly was an understatement. At the time, though, Donnelly had been the answer to his financial prayers. Andy had begun collecting ex-wives and partners like most people collected Tesco Clubcard points. With three children and a lot of financially dependent, angry women on his back, Andy was desperate for the means to fund his modest wage. As much as Donnelly was a bastard and terrified Andy, he paid well for his services.

Now however, he felt he was getting in over his head. Donnelly was putting more demands on him and Andy was increasingly nervous that it was only a matter of time before he was found out at work. It was common knowledge that DI Redford and DI Mitton had suspected for a while that someone was leaking information pertaining to Chrysalis. He was also concerned about why Donnelly wanted information on Maya – that didn't bode well. Ideally, he would love to cut all ties with Donnelly, but he knew the man would never let that happen. At the moment he was too valuable to him and he dreaded to even think what would happen once he'd served his purpose.

With the crime-scene samples ready to go, Andy paced the flat, nervously waiting for Donnelly to call him with more instructions. As he paced, he noticed the light flashing on his answering machine. He played the recorded message and listened to the smoky voice of his latest conquest. That voice and accent alone was enough to make him grow hard. His ardour was soon dampened though as, eyes widened with shock, he replayed the message.

'Darling, it's me. Where are you? I've been trying to get hold of you. I really need to see you. We need to talk. I… I know we haven't discussed this, but I love you and want to be with you. I've texted Piotr and have told him it's over. Please call me back so we can talk about us.'

Still stunned, he replayed Markita's message a third time. His bowels had turned to mush. Just when he thought his life couldn't get any more complicated, it sounded like Markita was ready to come clean about their relationship.

What had only ever meant to be a bit of fun had now started to get serious and he was well and truly trapped. Of all the foolish, risky things he had ever done – including working for Donnelly – getting involved with Piotr Nowak's partner had to be the most stupid. And now she was telling him she loved him and had ended things with Nowak. Once he found out Markita had left him for Andy, he was a dead man. What the fuck was she thinking?

He remembered the night their affair had started. He had arrived at her home unexpectedly, with a message from Donnelly. Initially, when she opened the door, she thought he was there to cause trouble for her. She had been drinking and was an emotional bag of nerves. He had quickly reassured her he wasn't going to hurt her but had instructions from Donnelly. Once she calmed down, they had sat and shared several drinks together while she confessed that it had been her who had tipped the police off about the firearm at The Farmhouse.

She had confided in Andy that, at the time, she was concerned about the effect Donnelly had been having on Nowak. She was worried he was going to get her partner in trouble. She thought that if she could get Donnelly sent away for a while, she could persuade Nowak to ease off his criminal lifestyle. Her plan had backfired, though, and now she was terrified that Donnelly would find out. Andy's reassurances and kind words combined with a lot of alcohol had soon resulted in them being entwined in her bed. And so, the affair had begun.

He should have ended it sooner. There had already been one near miss. Andy had been due at Markita's one evening but Donnelly had arrived first. Markita had been white with shock as she told him that Donnelly had appeared unannounced and unwanted, clutching flowers and wine. Donnelly had said the gifts were from Nowak, and that he had come to talk to her about their relationship on his behalf.

Donnelly had told her how much Nowak was struggling being inside because he missed her and didn't feel like the feeling was reciprocated. He had encouraged, no, practically threatened her, to keep his best friend happy. Markita had agreed. She would have agreed to anything at that moment. She had been so desperate for him to leave before Andy arrived, knowing there would be murder if the two of them were caught together.

Whilst Andy didn't doubt for one second that the riskiness of their relationship added to the eroticism, he should have learnt from that night and ended it. Now, in the cold light of day he realised how irresponsible he had been. And not only that, his feelings for Markita were purely sexual. She was high maintenance and had made it quite clear she had a penchant for money, something he had a serious lack of.

Andy was sensible enough to know that if he tried to reject Markita at this point, she would become the epitome of a woman scorned. The thought of her in a rage was nearly as terrifying as the thought of Donnelly baying for his blood. That psycho wouldn't just kill him, he would torture him and enjoy every second.

No, the best way he could control her was to keep her sweet. Then in time, he hoped she would tire of the relationship and find herself someone younger and richer. Maybe he could even persuade her to get back with Nowak. Frantically, he rang her straight back, but her phone tripped straight through to voicemail. Slumping down on his sofa, he cradled his head in his hands and let out a low guttural moan. For the first time in his adult life, he felt like crying.

48

Maya watched Spence through lidded eyes. He had just called last orders and was clearing the tables. Since she had arrived, the pub had only welcomed another four customers. This had given her and Spence time to sit and chat and she had thoroughly enjoyed his company.

'I'll finish this and head home,' she called to him as he collected glasses and torn beer mats from the table nearest to her. Her voice had started to slur, which was hardly surprising as she'd had several drinks and nothing more substantial to eat than three packets of prawn cocktail crisps.

'You'll stay there, love. Wait until I've locked up and I'll walk you home.'

She rolled her eyes. 'I'm perfectly capable of walking myself home, thank you very much.' She realised she sounded like Dominique when she put her posh work voice on, and laughed to herself.

'I don't doubt it, but in your line of work, you of all people should know it would be common sense for me to accompany you. Just to be on the safe side.'

'Are you insinuating I'm drunk,' Maya said with mock outrage.

'Yep, pissed as a fart.' He laughed as she threw a glacé cherry at him.

Maya weaved somewhat unsteadily to the ladies' toilet as Spence wiped the bar down. The old man with the newspaper was the last to leave, his bulbous nose shining like a beacon as it guided him through the pub door, which Spence locked and bolted behind him. Maya gathered her bag and followed Spence through to the back of the pub, watching as he set the alarm panel, they left through the barrel-store exit.

They picked their way through the side streets which led to Maya's apartment. Maya asked Spence about his time working and living in Spain and he regaled her with tales of the cocktails he used to experiment with – the nice ones and the ones that went terribly wrong.

'Who knew Baileys and tomato juice would make such a terrible combination?' He shrugged.

'Erm, anyone with half a brain.' Maya laughed as she elbowed him playfully before linking his arm as they walked.

'I'm glad I popped in. I've had a really nice evening.' She smiled.

'Me too, although I'm going to have to completely restock the cellar tomorrow. Give me advanced warning next time and I'll let the brewery know we need to double our order,' Spence said with a grin.

'Cheeky git,' Maya retorted with a slur as they arrived outside her apartment.

They headed to the lift and rode up to Maya's floor in silence. She wondered whether she should invite him in. Their previous ease was replaced with a weighted embarrassment. The fact they were alone in such a confined space felt loaded with meaning. After what felt like an eternity, the lift jolted to a halt and Spence followed Maya out into the corridor.

She swayed slightly as she wafted her hand at the door. 'This is me. Well, it's not *me*, obviously it's a door, but you know what I mean.' She let out a throaty guffaw, swaying against the wall as she laughed drunkenly to herself.

There was a split second of awkwardness and before either of them knew what was happening, her arms were round his neck and he was pressing her against the door as they shared an urgent, deep kiss. She could feel his taut body as he pressed against her and the feel of him smiling as their lips ground together intensified her need for him. She dropped an arm from around his neck and frantically reached in her bag for her keys.

49

Markita was sat on the sofa clutching onto her mobile phone like it was a lifeline. Andy had left her a frantic voicemail message urging her to say nothing to anyone about their relationship yet and to reconsider ending things with Nowak. He had said he would try to come and see her as soon as he could so they could talk. She hadn't been able to get hold of him since as he wasn't replying to any of her calls or texts.

Well, whatever he had to say it was too late. She had been unable to keep up with the pretence of still loving Piotr a moment longer. She just didn't want to be with him, and the lying was killing her. She had decided to end it once and for all. She knew she had taken the coward's way out by ending things via a text message, but she was too scared of him to do it face to face.

She was falling in love with Andy and despite the fact this new relationship should never have happened, she couldn't deny her feelings a moment longer. Despite not having been together long, she knew they could make a go of things. She just hoped he felt the same. The message Andy left her had been devastating. She could hear the panic in his voice. It had not been the reaction she had expected. She was now deeply concerned that her feelings for Andy weren't reciprocated.

She didn't know what she would do if he told her she should keep up the façade with Nowak, or worse. If he ended things with her, it would break her heart. She stared nervously at the phone as if it was a hand grenade she had just pulled the pin from.

Suddenly there was a frantic knocking on the door.

'Andy?' she gasped to herself as she rushed to open it.

Her eager anticipation was replaced with dismay. Donnelly was stood on her doorstep. Angrily, he barged past her, uninvited.

'No flowers and wine this time, Aiden?' she asked sardonically.

She sank back down onto her sofa and lit a cigarette, conscious of the shaking in her hands as he stood surveying her, a murderous frown on his face. He looked angrier and more threatening than she had ever seen him before.

'You look like shit,' he snarled as he sniffed and pinched at his nose.

'Ah, Aiden, ever the charmer,' she said, sinking back into the cushions. She was dressed in tracksuit bottoms and a vest top and for once her face was clear of her usual heavily contoured make-up. Her hair extensions hung un-styled around her shoulders like a shabby cloak. Her eyes were red and swollen from crying.

'What the fuck is going on, Markita?'

'What do you mean?'

'DON'T TAKE ME FOR A FUCKING MUG!' He leapt towards her, wrenching the cigarette from her lips and grinding it into the plush, oatmeal carpet. 'When I went to visit Piotr, he was in bits over you. I told you to keep him sweet, yet he reckons he's had more warmth from a fucking ice cube.'

He sniffed again and then hocked a globule of spit in her direction. 'You've *dumped* him? By text message! Who the fuck do you think you are? You callous bitch!'

'I've tried! I've fucking tried, okay?' Markita screeched back. She swiped the spit away from her cheek, her body arched towards him defiantly. They glared at each other for a moment, until exhausted, Markita slumped forward, hugging her knees.

Fresh tears sprung into her eyes. 'I just don't love him anymore, okay?' she said wearily. 'God knows I've tried to make it work, but my feelings have changed. There's nothing between us anymore.' She shook her head sadly. 'Anyway, it's between me and Piotr. This has nothing to do with you, Aiden.'

He leant towards her, his face pressed hard against hers, spittle hitting her cheek as he spoke. 'Is there someone else?'

She shook her head numbly.

'Markita,' he said softly in a sing-song voice, accentuating each syllable of her name. 'Tell me the truth. Are you shagging someone else?'

Her eyes widened with fear as he produced a large knife from his waistband. He wielded it in her direction, she shook her head, more emphatically, too terrified to speak.

'You lying fucking bitch,' he said in the same sing-song voice as before. He pulled away from her before suddenly swinging back his fist and smashing it into her face. The momentum sent her sprawling to the floor. She tried to stumble back to her feet to get away from him. He aimed a kick at her head before gathering her hair in his fist.

Markita's head was yanked up roughly from the floor. She felt like her scalp was going to tear and she screamed out in pain. She heard a swoosh before the tension was released, causing her face to smash into the carpet. Donnelly was laughing like a madman as he clutched the large clump of hair he had just sliced from Markita's head. She shook with fear, if the knife could slice through her hair so easily, what would he cut next? She reached a hand to her head, sobbing harder as her fingers brushed against short stumps of hair.

'A little present for Piotr,' he said through a cackle. 'I bet this will go down a treat with all those desperate men inside,' he said, pressing the hair to his nose and inhaling deeply. 'Now what else do you think they'd like? Tits or lips?'

Markita tried desperately to twist and thrash away from Donnelly, but he was too strong for her. She was on her back now as he straddled across her hips, his knees were pinning her arms down so she couldn't move. Menacingly, he traced the knife from her mouth to her cleavage. She felt a sharp sting as the blade sliced into her skin, beads of blood rising to the surface.

Donnelly tipped the blade upward, pressing the edge against her left breast. She was too scared to move. He slowly began to increase the pressure and she prepared herself for the inevitable puncture. He sniffed again. His eyes were bloodshot, and his pupils enlarged, making him look even more deranged. She realised now that he was high on cocaine. Whatever happened this night, she was not going to make it out alive.

'Aiden, please,' she begged, her voice barely a whisper. 'You don't have to do this...'

'Shhhhh...' he hissed soothingly as slowly he began to increase the pressure. The knife began to penetrate her skin and the room began to swim before her eyes. Suddenly, there was a noise from the hallway. Donnelly froze, alerted to the sound.

He and Markita turned simultaneously towards the noise. Andy Carr was framed in the doorway, palms held up towards Aiden. His face was pale, and he was visibly shaking at the sight of Markita, the huge clump of hair and the equally large knife.

'Stop, please,' Andy said pleadingly. 'Don't hurt her, Mr Donnelly. You need to let her go.'

Still holding the knife against Markita's breast, Donnelly surveyed Andy with suspicion and the usual disgust. 'What the fuck are you doing here? And since when did you tell *me* what to do?'

Andy faltered. Time seemed to stand still as seconds stretched into hours. His bowels writhed with fear, as he frantically racked his brains to come up with something plausible. Markita was staring at him, her wide eyes silently pleading.

'Well?' Aiden demanded angrily. He climbed off Markita. She scrambled away from him, across the floor, to the back of the room. Donnelly's attention was on Andy now. The bloodstained knife was now pointing in his direction. Vitriol and aggression exuded out of every pore. 'WELL?' Donnelly repeated.

'I-I... was passing and saw your car. I've just found out that Redford and Mitton are planning on having Markita watched, starting later this evening. I came to warn you. If you mess her up anymore, they're going to start asking questions. You need to leave, Mr Donnelly. Now. Please. For your own sake.'

There was another long, intimidating silence, until eventually Donnelly threw his head back and laughed manically. He approached Andy slowly, a sinister grin on his face. 'Well, well, well, you're not the completely useless piece of shit I thought you were.' He patted Andy sharply several times on his face. Tucking the knife back into his waistband he headed towards the door.

'Sort that out,' he said, gesturing towards Markita without even looking back. Andy and Markita remained rooted to the spot for several moments until certain he was gone. Then Markita began to cry hysterically, like a wailing banshee, and it took all Andy's best efforts not to join in.

50

Maya had fallen asleep in a drunken stupor and was now dead to the world. He lay on the pillow next to her watching her sleep. He grinned widely to himself as she let out a sudden snore. God, she was beautiful. Her long lashes framed her cheeks, her hair a mass of untamed curls spread across the pillow.

He could quite easily lay his head next to hers and succumb to some much-needed sleep, but he knew he had stayed too long already.

Maya let out a little snort as she turned suddenly, rolling onto her side. Her face was now turned towards his and he found himself catching his breath as he gazed at her, thoroughly mesmerised. She was so close. Her breath tickled his face, and he could still smell wine. It had a sharp sour smell, but he didn't mind. He was too captivated by her beauty.

He could lie here all night, just watching her sleep. She looked so peaceful. She looked so perfect. She *was* perfect. Unable to resist any longer, he leant forward and very lightly, very gently, kissed her on her cheek. Unexpectedly, Maya's eyes flew open, wide with shock.

'Hello,' said Lurch. 'What's your favourite colour? Your dad wants to know.'

51

Mark Posner. Drug dealing piece of shit. It's laughable how much of his lengthy prison sentence he actually served. The system is a joke. When I think of the number of lives lost because of the dodgy batches of gear he supplied over the years. It's heartbreaking and an insult to the families. The junkies that survived caused so much misery for themselves and others, they'd have been better off dead. Justice isn't always issued in court though.

To think how he ended up. He'd made a point of never touching the drugs he sold. He knew what a slippery slope it was. He was smarter than that. He'd witnessed the effects of addiction first-hand and would never be so stupid.

But he'd only been inside a fortnight and was hooked. He'd take or do anything to temporarily anaesthetise the harsh reality of prison life. His baby-faced looks had served him well when he was dealing. His sharp suits and swagger had the addicts flocking to him. Inside, that same pretty face made him easy prey. And he was equally sought after. Now he was out, he was homeless and giving head for the price of a bag of smack. Poetic justice really.

With everything that was going on, I'd been unable to sleep that night. I'd been so preoccupied thinking about who to kill next. I hadn't *even intended it to be Posner. He had just presented himself as a glorious opportunity. There was something soothing about strolling around undesirable areas in the dark. I was goading trouble. Tempting fate. The next thing I knew, I found myself in an area frequented by the homeless and drug addicted.*

Bridge Street is a stretch of canal on the edge of town, shrouded by an old railway bridge. The towpath is covered in pools of vomit that glisten in the moonlight. The cover and lack of CCTV footage in that area gives them the perfect place to come and go without being observed. They move like ghosts here. Unseen and unheard. Unclean and unrepentant.

He was alone when I found him. I almost didn't recognise him. He'd aged so much. Toothless and cadaverous. Slumped across the towpath with lungs full of spice. He was a zombie. He didn't react when I nudged him in the ribs. He was already half dead. It didn't take too much effort to roll his skeletal form over a couple of times until he dropped into the moody water.

Splash.

52

Maya was trapped in a living nightmare. She opened her mouth to scream, but no sound came out. She willed her legs to move, but they remained paralysed. The giant's face was so close to hers, she thought he was going to kiss her again. She could smell his foul breath and stale sweat. Slowly he backed away, not once breaking eye contact. Then, surprisingly deft for a man of his considerable size, he swept softly out of the bedroom. Despite the deafening sound of her racing heart, Maya heard him quietly click the door behind him.

She remained frozen on the bed. Frantically listening out for signs that someone else might be in the apartment. She could still smell the man's presence. Still feel the weight and see the indentation on the bed where he had lay. She suddenly became aware of the feel of his wet kiss on her cheek. Retching, she ran to the bathroom, barely making it in time.

Vomit pumped out of her ceaselessly until she was empty, leaving her wobbly-legged and coated in sweat. Still dry heaving, her stomach was wracked with pain. Barely able to stand, she knelt up towards the sink and grabbed her flannel. She scrubbed frantically at her cheek. Scrubbing away the dirtiness of the kiss. What the fuck?

Her limbs were shaking. A combination of fear and the after-effects of having vomited so much. She plucked a pair of nail scissors out of the container on her bathroom ledge. A poor weapon, but better than nothing. She clasped it in her fist as she tiptoed out of the bathroom. Palpitations erupted in her chest as she peered into the lounge. No one there. Still panic-stricken, she continued softly towards the kitchen. Each footstep might as well have been a drumbeat. She arched around the kitchen door; all her senses heightened. Nothing.

Thank God, she was alone. At last, she released a sound. A strangled scream as she hurtled to the door. She checked the lock and could see no damage. She had either left it open or the burglar had used a spare key or some sort of lock-picking device. For what it was worth, she attached the chain. It seemed paltry and ineffective in keeping that monster of a man out, should he choose to return.

Quaking, she pressed her back against the door and slid to the ground. She buried her head in her arms and held herself, rocking slowly. The tears came thick and fast. Sobs wracked her body as snot and tears streamed down her face.

Gradually the tears subsided. Maya gulped occasionally as she rose on unsteady legs. Slowly, she walked toward the bedroom. She stood at the door, afraid to go in. From what she could see, nothing appeared disturbed and nothing had been stolen. Her fear was suddenly replaced with a torrent of rage. She refused to become a victim. She was a grown woman. Strong and resilient. Nobody had the right to fucking scare her like this.

She tore at the bedding, stripping it away. She couldn't stomach the thought of some stranger... some animal lying on her bed. And to kiss her? The paralysing fear returned at the realisation of what else the man could have done to her while she was sleeping. She had to phone the police. She should have done that straight away. What had she been thinking?

But then rationale took over. Other than the kiss, he hadn't touched her. That wasn't his intention. He was there to deliver a message. 'Your dad wants to know.'

She shuddered violently. The thought of Naylor made her feel sick all over again. At the best of times, the thought of him horrified her. And now what? She was receiving messages from him at 4am. Was he even still in prison or had he been released? Surely, she and Dominique would have been informed if he had? The pair had only discussed him recently and there was no way Dominique would hold something so important back from Maya. The possibility that Naylor could be walking the streets was terrifying.

Maya knew she couldn't risk phoning the police. She couldn't afford to expose herself to the fact she was Marcus Naylor's daughter. After all, this was the secret she was so desperate to keep. When Maya had failed to disclose her relationship with Naylor on her application form, she had known at the time that this was contravening the conditions of her application and was effectively fraud.

Maya had willingly taken the risk. She was desperate to be a SOCO and had worked damn hard to get the job. It had never been an option to scupper her chances because of her association with such a violent, deranged man who she was blessedly estranged from. Now she was in it up to her neck. Naylor had been in touch. She knew him well enough to perceive this to be a threat. A warning. And the only people she could turn to for help, were the same people who would probably sack her for submitting a fraudulent application form.

There was nothing she could do. Nobody she could turn to. Not yet anyway. Not until she knew what Naylor was planning.

She thought of Spence. The urge to text him and see him was overwhelming, but she didn't want to get him involved in anything to do with Naylor. She cared about him too much. She was in no doubt that the early morning message was the start of some sick and twisted game of cat and mouse. Well, she wasn't the frightened little girl he used to know. She'd got him put behind bars once before, and if he was out, she would do it again. But could she do it without jeopardising her and Dominique's safety? And could she do it without risking the career she loved?

53

Spence was lying in bed, recalling the previous evening with Maya.

He couldn't stop thinking about the kiss. It had been incredible and mind-blowing. They had ended up in Maya's apartment and things had progressed to the couch until he had become concerned that he could be taking advantage of the fact she'd had quite a lot to drink.

Reluctantly, he had suggested they slow things down a bit. She had resisted at first and told him in no uncertain terms what she wanted. For his own sake, he had insisted they stop. The last thing he would ever want was to see regret in her face the following morning. He also didn't want her to think he had taken advantage. He liked her too much for that. They had both reluctantly kissed each other goodbye after exchanging phone numbers. Maya had swayed unsteadily at the door as she waved him off.

He had already sent her a text message to say good morning and to ask her how she was, but hadn't heard anything back yet, despite checking his phone far too many times. He berated himself for acting like a lovesick teenager. At the same time, the longer the silence continued, the more he knew he had made the right choice to slow things down last night. She had been at a loose end and had quite a lot to drink. She had clearly been letting off steam after working on Ryan Johnson's murder. There was no guarantee that in the cold light of day she would feel the same as she had last night.

He was broken from his reverie by a loud, authoritative knock on the door. He pulled on some jeans and rushed to open it, anticipating the delivery of a parcel for his sister. On opening the door, he saw two men, smartly dressed, wearing police body armour over their shirts. Their white Vauxhall Astra was parked proprietorially on the drive.

'Spencer James?' asked the younger of the two.

He nodded, confused. 'Is everything okay?' He berated himself for the foolishness of the question. Police officers didn't just randomly roll up on somebody's front door just to announce that everything was fine and dandy. He could imagine Maya teasing him for saying it.

The man pulled a lanyard out of his pocket and flashed an ID badge under his nose. 'I'm DS Turner and this is my colleague, DC Malone. Could we come in for a moment?'

'Erm, yes. Please come through to the lounge.' He swung the door open for them and gestured up the hallway.

'After you, sir,' DS Turner said with stern authority.

'What's all this about?' said Spence as he perched on the edge of the sofa. 'Is this something to do with Ryan Johnson? Because if it is, I didn't really know him. He was an old school friend, that's all.'

'We need you to accompany us to the police station so we can speak to you about a serious assault on David McCluskey. We are also going to conduct a search of this address. Do you understand?'

'David who? I don't know who you're talking about. I haven't done anything. And this is my sister's house. She'll go ballistic if you start pulling things apart.'

DS Turner nodded as he fished out a pair of handcuffs from his body armour. Spence was stunned as Turner cuffed him and read out the caution. 'Do you understand?' Turner asked again.

'Yeah.' Spence shook his head, bewildered. 'I mean, I understand the words, but I don't understand why you're here. I've already told you; I haven't done anything.'

'Right, well, we'll discuss it at the station under interview.' Turner sounded bored, as if he'd heard it all before. He gestured towards DC Malone to keep an eye on Spence, while he stepped out into the hall and called up on his police radio.

'DS Turner, comms. With regards to log 897 of today, we've made an arrest at this location. Could you send me a van, please? Also notify SOCO that we might need them for the house search.'

The response from comms was inaudible, but Spence had heard enough. SOCO had been requested, which made him think of Maya. Did she know anything about this, is that why she hadn't replied to his text? She had told him she was off work today on a rest day, so at least there was no chance of running the risk of her turning up. That would be devastating. But what the hell was going on, was it some sort of set-up or sick joke? He didn't even know anyone called David McCluskey and God knows he certainly wasn't the type of person to assault anyone.

He was in turmoil as he tried to gather his thoughts. How had he gone from an evening of sheer bliss with Maya, to living this nightmare and being arrested again for the second time since he had returned to England? He felt sick to his stomach and had to admit, he was scared. Very scared.

54

Naylor was pacing his cell expectantly as he strained to listen to Nowak's side of the telephone conversation. Nowak was grunting encouragingly as he listened to the caller, nodding every now and then. It was the most animated Naylor had seen him since he had been dumped by Markita.

At first Nowak had been enraged, but then once the realisation hit him that there was nothing he could do while he was locked up, he had slumped into a depression. He had barely spoken to Naylor since, choosing instead to lay prostrate on his bunk and feigning sleep.

Nowak's face suddenly erupted in a huge grin. 'Well, cheers for all of that, mate. I'll see you soon, very soon by the sounds of it. In a bit.' He turned the mobile phone off and returned it to its hiding place, oblivious to Naylor's building impatience.

'Well,' Naylor said as he squared up to Nowak, 'what happened?'

Nowak placed his palm on Naylor's chest and firmly pushed him away, a warning look in his eye. 'Attitude, mate, attitude. It's done. Message delivered loud and clear.'

Nowak laughed callously as he sat at the table and concentrated on making a roll-up.

'What did she say?'

'Nothing. My bloke did what he was told and then he left straight away as instructed. The last thing we wanted was her screaming blue murder, him getting locked up and it coming back on us.'

'Yeah...' Naylor nodded carefully, deep in thought. 'I wonder if she'll tell that bitch of a mother of hers. Fucking Dominique. She always thought she was something better than she was. And speaking of which, I think it's time I planned my next little message, don't you?'

His raucous cackle flooded the cell, as he tossed his head back in laughter, revealing an uneven set of yellowing teeth. Cheered, Naylor reached for the tobacco pouch and cigarette papers and began to roll his own smoke. 'So, what else did your mate have to say. Any good news?'

'Yep, looks like you're going to be getting a new cellmate very soon. Your daughter's friend. The one who is going to be taking the rap for me has been arrested. They'll be doing the house search as we speak and will find the bloodstained knife and hopefully other items that we've planted there. Then once I'm out of here, I'm going to be having a very serious fucking conversation with Markita and I'll be finding out exactly what the hell she thinks she's playing at.'

'Fucking women,' Naylor sneered. 'Told you they're more trouble than they're worth. You're not going to get back with her surely?'

'Not now. There was a time I would have considered it, but now she's fucking humiliated me there's no chance. Aiden's already paid her a visit but that's nothing compared to what I've got in mind. Nobody will be able to stomach looking at her by the time I've finished.' He stubbed out his roll-up angrily and returned to his bunk, turning his back on Naylor, making it clear the conversation was over.

Naylor didn't mind. He welcomed the peace and quiet. He had a lot of thinking and planning to do.

55

Being the master of manipulation that he was, Andy had orchestrated events to ensure he was tasked with examining Spence's sister's house. Bloody Elaine had interfered as always and insisted she go. He had argued the toss, fully aware that his sudden insistence of volunteering for a job was out of character. At one point they were both clutching hold of the job sheet in an almost comical tug-of-war until Kym had stormed out of her office and split the pair of them up. Furious, she had ordered Elaine to do a stock check on the vans and told Andy to go straight to the scene, annoyed that the argument meant the detectives had been kept waiting.

As Andy pulled up outside the house, Turner stormed down the driveway towards him, tapping his watch.

'Why's it taken you so bloody long? We're on the custody clock you know?'

'Elaine and I had a misunderstanding and I...'

Turner silenced him with a raised palm. 'The suspect's room is at the back of the house. We started searching and found a knife wrapped in a bloodstained cloth at the back of the wardrobe. Obviously, we've not searched any further until you've forensically recovered it.'

Andy nodded as he wrestled himself into a scene suit. Donnelly had already told him that Lurch had previously entered the address and hidden the knife. That way, on the off-chance that Andy had not been able to ensure he attended the scene, the most crucial evidence would have been discovered anyway. Now he was here, Andy could proceed with planting additional evidence, ensuring Spence was even more culpable.

'How long will you be?' Turner made no effort to keep the impatience from his voice as he and Malone followed Andy up the stairs.

'It shouldn't take too long.' Andy glanced at his camera bag on the landing floor next to Reynold's feet, anxiously aware that it contained dried, bloodstained items which had been passed to him by Donnelly. 'I'll be as quick as I can,' he added, horrified to realise that neither of the detectives were intending on leaving him to it. They appeared to be resolute in remaining on the landing whilst watching him work.

'Crack on then,' Turner said as he nestled against the banister rail.

Sweat snaked down Andy's back, his face growing red as Malone reached down for the camera bag and handed it to Andy. 'Can I do anything to help speed things along?' he said, his fingers twitching at the zip.

'No!' Andy was aware of the high-pitched squeak that emanated from him as he grabbed at the bag. 'No offence, gents, but I work quicker on my own. If you stand and watch me, I'll be all fingers and thumbs. Why don't you two carry on downstairs and I'll let you know when I'm done.'

Turner eyed him suspiciously before grunting something inaudible. He tapped his finger against his watch again before sauntering downstairs with Malone at his heels. Andy's heart was pounding against his chest as he hurriedly opened his camera bag. He took a few frantic photographs before removing the dried, bloodstained items from Nowak, including tissues he had used to wipe his hands on after the attack.

Andy planned to dampen the items using the vial of sterile water he carried, then rub them against Spence's trainers. He could then photograph the bloodstaining and take swabs which would put McCluskey's blood on Spence's footwear. He would do the same with the hem of a pair of jeans.

He would make suggestions on his scene notes that it appeared to him that the jeans had been washed, and he had detected traces of blood in the stitching. Plausible enough if the clothing had been washed at low temperature using non-biological soap powder. Andy would also comment on his scene notes that the trainers appeared to have been wiped. This would explain the lack of blood spatter, which would ordinarily be evident on trainers worn by somebody present during a bloodied assault.

Any self-respecting forensic scientist would be able to ascertain that the location of the staining had not been distributed at the scene of the assault, but Andy hoped the investigation wouldn't be taken that far. He was relying on current financial restraints dictating that it would not be cost effective to submit the trainers and clothing for further forensic analysis. After all, this was a Section 18 assault, which despite being serious, did not carry the same budget as a murder investigation. His observations alone would hopefully satisfy the detectives and the CPS. He was confident he could convince them that it would be futile to submit the items for further analysis.

Hurriedly, Andy began to dampen the tissue and rubbed the bloodstaining against Spence's trainer. Beads of sweat were streaming down his forehead and he cursed under his breath as the fragile tissue began to shred and break up. The blood wasn't spreading as easily as he'd assumed. Fragments of tissue fibre littered the dark-coloured carpet. They were glaringly obvious, like snow on coal. Andy was horrified to hear footsteps ascending the stairs. Wide-eyed, he frantically plucked at the fragments of tissue, the gloves making the process awkward.

'How're you getting on?' Turner called as he reached the top step. Andy kicked the partially bloodstained trainer across the room and sat himself on the floor to cover the carpet.

'What *are* you doing?'

'Just making some notes.'

'Comfy, are we? Why don't you just get on the bed?'

'Not being funny, but I'd be a lot quicker if you gave me some space. I'm sweating like a bastard as it is.'

Turner rolled his eyes before heading back down the stairs. Andy heard him mutter the word 'cock' under his breath but didn't care. Once he was satisfied the detective was out of the way, he carried on with a speed he did not know he was capable of. The relief was immense as he eventually secreted the items belonging to Nowak back into his camera bag. He peeled his scene suit off and gathered his things together. The sweet breeze that carried through the front door was like nectar.

He allowed himself a smile as he took one final glance around the bedroom. His work here was done. He had enough evidence to set Spencer James up for McCluskey's stabbing. There had been no CCTV in the area to capture the assault and none of the witnesses, including McCluskey, were willing to provide a description of the attacker. Nowak was in the clear and Spence had a lot of explaining to do. Donnelly would be happy. At least that would be one less person on his back. For now.

56

Maya arrived at work without her usual enthusiasm. She was a tired, nervous wreck. She had even thought about phoning in sick but couldn't face the thought of staying at home despite the fact she had arranged to have new locks and bolts fitted. Irrationally, she'd changed her bedding twice and cleaned like a woman possessed to remove any traces of the burglar. She had barely eaten; her head was slamming, and the hot weather was making her feel nauseous.

She exchanged pleasantries before hiding herself away in the corner of the office, so she could avoid any further interaction. She didn't feel like talking and was looking forward to the others finishing so she could be alone in the office for her afternoon shift.

'Hey, what's up?' Chris called. 'You've not been talking to dead people and journalists, again, have you?' He laughed, pleased with himself, as Maya flipped him the middle finger.

Amanda scowled at Chris. 'Are you okay, Maya?'

Maya nodded weakly. 'I'm fine thanks. Just a bit hung-over.' It was all she could think to say to deflect any further questioning. Just as the words left her mouth, Kym emerged.

Her lips pursed at Maya's comment and she shook her head disapprovingly. Normally Maya would have been mortified at such a reaction from Kym, but right now she really couldn't care less.

Amanda smiled apologetically. 'Sorry to jump on you, but a job has just come in. There's a body in the canal near Bridge Street. We've been asked to attend. Are you going to be okay with it?'

Maya felt like all eyes were on her, waiting for her response. As much as she had been longing for more experience, the last thing she needed today was to see a cadaver being hauled out of the canal. It took every ounce of her flailing energy to smile convincingly. 'Yes, of course. I'll just read through the log and make my way.'

Maya was desperate not to cry as her nausea grew with every line of the log she read. Surely this day couldn't get any worse. She couldn't think straight, and her mind certainly wasn't on work. But she had no choice other than to focus on the circumstances surrounding the body in the canal. The anxiety was starting to build in her chest, her heart rate quickening as a panic attack threatened to consume her.

She concentrated on taking steady measured breaths in an attempt to stay calm. She closed her eyes and imagined herself anywhere but work. She was so focused that it took a moment to realise that someone had said her name. She opened her eyes and sat up. Amanda and Elaine were looking at her, concerned. Jack Dwyer was stood in the doorway, looking hesitant and decidedly uncomfortable and she realised he must have asked to speak to her.

'Sorry, Jack, I was miles away. Do you want me?'

'Erm, yes please. Could I have a quick word?' He indicated the corridor, making it clear he needed to speak to her in private.

Maya followed him out of the office somewhat impatiently, the last thing she bloody well needed was to listen to any of his flannel.

'Look, Maya, this is a bit awkward, but I thought I should give you the heads-up. We've got a bloke in the traps for a Section 18. Spencer James.'

She felt her face grow hot as she willed herself to remain impassive. 'And?' She managed to shrug non-committally.

'DS Turner has just finished interviewing him. He wants to have a word with you.'

'Why me? A body has just come in. I need to go.' She felt the all too familiar fist-clenching sensation stirring in her stomach. What now?

'He says he has an alibi for the night of the assault on David McCluskey. He's given your name. Says he was drinking in The Brown Cow with you and your friends. Turner is going to want to interview you for confirmation and obviously get a statement. I just thought I'd let you know.' He gave her a wan smile and returned to his office, leaving Maya to slump against the wall in the corridor.

Fuck's sake. She had been wrong. There was still time for this day to get worse. Much worse.

I dreamt of Louisa again last night. She had felt so real, so alive. The craving for her was intense. A physical, gnawing ache. I clung to her. I clung to the feeling of her warm, lithe limbs encircling mine. The intensity of her embrace. The softness of her skin. The tickling sensation of her hair against my cheek as she rested her head on my chest. It was the familiarity of her voice and the easy way we chatted to each other. We talked about nothing – and everything. I wanted the moment to last forever. There was nothing

else in space or time that I needed more than the feeling of her. Of being with her.

As the dream faded, I fought to stay asleep, but consciousness roused. Reluctantly, I conceded she hadn't been real. I took great comfort in the fact that such a realistic memory of her was enough to satiate me. She was my drug. If dreams were all I had left, that would be enough. Something was better than nothing, but why did they have to end? If death meant I could be reunited with her, back with the other half of me, I would happily take it. I found myself choking back tears as I lay awake. The memory of her perfume still lingered in my bed. The pain of the emptiness she had left behind was unbearable. There was only one thing I could do to ease it. There was one other person I needed to kill. And this one was going to feel the same pain I was in. I would make them suffer just as much. If not more...

57

Maya and DI Redford arrived at Bridge Street at the same time as the Underwater Search Team. The railway bridge, which hung over the section of the canal like a frown, gave the area its insalubrious appeal. Here, everything scowled in the shadows, even on the brightest day. Overgrown shrubbery and shallow alcoves provided a level of murky privacy craved by the local smack rats. Discarded needles, used condoms and stolen wallets (long-since emptied) littered the grubby pathway.

The bridge provided a natural shelter for the investigators, so a scene tent wasn't required. The sheer presence of the police kept those who would normally frequent the location well away. As a result, the deceased would have the privacy he deserved. Maya photographed the towpath and took a series of pictures of the floating corpse. He was face down in the water, the top of his head visible. The lightweight waterproof jacket he wore had gathered some air since the body had submerged and puffed out like an ironic sail.

Maya watched as the divers secured the body to the orange plastic scoop and hauled him onto the towpath. The smell of stagnant water made her want to gag. She could hardly even bring herself to look at the sopping body. The shock of the previous evening was still proving too much to handle. The panic attack which had threatened to consume her earlier, was burgeoning again. She took a couple of calming breaths before focusing on the body. If she could just concentrate on the scene and block everything else out, she would be fine.

DI Redford knelt towards the body, scrutinising him carefully. 'Curly, come over here will you, mate?' He called to the bald police officer who was minding the cordon. Curly had worked on section for years and knew all the local criminals and regular missing persons. He was renowned for never forgetting a face. 'D'ya recognise him, pal?' Redford asked as he straightened up, allowing Curly to peruse the corpse. He paused momentarily, studying the face carefully, a slight frown puckering his brow.

'Could be Mark Posner, boss. He looks nothing like he used to when he was dealing. He went into prison looking like the lead from a boy band and came out looking like that.' Curly straightened up. He nodded confirmation of his identification.

Maya frowned. 'What was he inside for?'

'Drug dealing. He was one of the main players years ago, although you wouldn't know it to look at him now. Wanker.' He muttered more disparaging comments towards the corpse as he returned to the cordon, ignoring Redford's tut.

Maya took several more photographs before crouching next to the body. Wordlessly, she and Redford scrutinised the corpse carefully, checking the head and hands before inching items of clothing away so they could examine unexposed areas of skin. As they tugged at his jeans, Redford patted down the pockets before gingerly reaching in and removing a letter. He carefully unfolded it so as not to damage the fragility of the wet paper.

'Bingo!' He held it up towards Maya so she could photograph

it. 'Bail notice in the name of Mark Posner.' He turned to the cordon giving a thumbs up. 'Nice one, Curly,' he shouted, 'I owe you a pint.'

The police officer returned an energetic thumbs up accompanied with his best fake smile.

Identity confirmed, Maya and Reynolds continued their careful search of the body.

'Thoughts?' Redford said as he arched an eyebrow towards Maya.

She shook her head. 'Nothing concerning. He's obviously using, judging by his teeth and general physique.' She nodded towards a pile of belongings stuffed in an alcove which nestled into the wall of the bridge. An array of spice packets littered the floor next to a rolled-up blanket and stuffed duffel bag. Redford searched the bag whilst Maya photographed the contents.

'Well, I think it's going to come down to toxicology,' Redford said. 'It doesn't look like he's been in there long judging by his condition. I'd wager possibly overnight. There's enough foot traffic around here, someone would have noticed him if he'd been in any longer.'

Maya nodded. 'There's no obvious signs of injury. I wonder if he fell in accidentally or was it a suicide?'

'We might never know without witnesses or CCTV. Let's just see what the post-mortem tells us.'

'It's a worry though, isn't it?'

'What is?'

'Well, what if it was neither. What if someone pushed him in?'

'There's no signs of a struggle.'

'But if he was intoxicated, there wouldn't necessarily have *been* a struggle.'

Redford stared at her long enough to make her feel uncomfortable. 'Another conspiracy theory?'

She felt a prickle of annoyance. 'No. I'm just saying, someone could have pushed him in whilst he was intoxicated. Or they could have even killed him first then pushed him in.'

'And,' Redford said pointedly, 'he could have *fallen* in whilst intoxicated. In a situation like this there could be several hypotheses. Not every death is suspicious, Maya.'

'And not every death is accidental. *Sir.*'

There was an awkward stand-off with both of them staring at Posner's body before Redford conceded with a nod. 'Like I said, let's wait and see what the post-mortem says. It'll certainly tell us whether or not he was dead before he entered the water. That will at least answer one of your theories.'

Maya couldn't bring herself to comment, riled by the sardonic tone in his voice. There was another heavy silence as they both stood staring at the corpse.

'Right.' Maya sniffed. 'I'll just ask the divers to collect a water sample for me before they head off and then I'll get him bagged up.'

'Thank you. I'll ask Curly to give you a lift with him.' Never one to get his hands dirtier than he needed to, Redford was keen to get back to Beech Field and his sterile office.

Maya felt detached as she prepared the body bag, placing Mark Posner in it with an automation she would never have imagined possible when dealing with the dead. The stress of the break-in was more than she could endure, and she also had the added pressure of having to speak to DS Turner about Spence's arrest. What the hell was that all about anyway? She almost didn't want to know, she had enough to think about.

Maya yearned to go home. Not home to her apartment, but home to Dominique. There were times when only a mother's hug could make everything better. Plus, Dominique was the only other person on the planet who would appreciate how terrifying the mention of Naylor's name was. She could barely focus on Curly as she left the scene; her eyes brimmed with tears as she drove back to Beech Field. The nightmare of today was far from over. She still had a hell of a lot of awkward hours ahead of her and she was beginning to doubt her ability to cope with much more.

58

Dominique was exhausted. Work had been busy enough, but then there had been the charity sale at the community centre. Her feet were aching after standing for so long and the heat had made her ankles swell. Maya still had the car which meant she had walked home. Although it wasn't far, the hot weather made the journey feel twice as long. Now she was looking forward to sitting in the garden and enjoying a glass of the wine she had just bought to go with her dinner. She turned into her cul-de-sac and noticed a top-of-the-range black Mercedes randomly parked on the grass verge opposite her house. She frowned to herself. None of her neighbours owned such a car and neither did their relatives.

The privacy and seclusion of the cul-de-sac meant it was easy to keep an eye on the comings and goings. Everyone was familiar with their neighbour's activities. Plus, it was an unwritten rule that to preserve the aesthetics of the neighbourhood, *nobody* parked on the verges. This meant the driver of the Mercedes was undoubtedly a stranger to the area. Dominique squinted, the glare of the sun reflecting off the windscreen obscured her vision as she glanced over to see if she recognised whoever was sat in the car.

She hesitated. Debating whether she should go and speak to the driver. Her musings were broken as a flash of black fur hurtled towards her. Jet arched her back and purred as she weaved her way between her legs. Her pink nose perched in anticipation of the fact it was very nearly teatime. Dominique laughed as she stroked her soft coat, muttering platitudes to her fur baby. She was such a social cat and loved her cuddles. Maya often joked she was the ficklest cat in the world, because she didn't care who was stroking her as long as someone was.

Dominique glanced towards the car again. She should really go and investigate but Jet's insistence on being fed decided her. If the car was still there later, she'd go and have a word. But as she placed her key in the lock the Mercedes powered off. The exhaust screamed with a pitch that set her teeth on edge and caused her heart to race. The sudden, unexpected noise was almost violent. Startled, she dropped the bottle of wine and winced as Merlot splashed up her legs. Illuminated by the evening sun, the wine glistened and gleamed like freshly spilled blood.

59

Maya had just finished her interview with DS Turner. It had been excruciatingly awkward as she justified how she had ended up spending several hours in Spence's company on the night in question. She had confirmed the date and times she had been in The Brown Cow with him and her friends. Turner was also arranging to check the pub's CCTV footage. Maya had provided him with Caitlin and Letitia's details so they could also confirm Spence's alibi. Turner had appeared satisfied with Maya's account, but it had left her feeling even more drained. Wearily, she returned to the office. Amanda greeted her with an apologetic smile and nodded towards Kym's office.

'They're waiting for you,' she said kindly.

Maya puffed out her cheeks. '"They?"'

'Ma'am, Mitton is in with Kym.'

'Oh, for fuck's sake,' she hissed as she resisted the urge to slam her stuff down on the desk. She smoothed her uniform down and smiled gratefully at Amanda who gave her a wink and held up crossed fingers.

'Kym. Ma'am,' Maya nodded to the two women, 'I believe you want to see me?'

'Yes, thank you, Maya.' Kym pushed her glasses on top of her head and gestured for Maya to sit down. 'DI Mitton and I are concerned to hear you've provided an alibi for a suspect connected to Operation Chrysalis.'

'I've just given my statement to DS Turner.'

'Would you mind giving us a precis?' Kym said. The expression on her face did not match her attempt at a pleasant tone.

Maya repeated what she had told DS Turner, speaking as confidently as she could despite how intimidated she felt in the presence of the two women.

DI Mitton laced her fingers together and placed them under her chin as she appraised Maya. An uncomfortable silence followed until she eventually spoke. 'Just so it's crystal clear. For my own benefit if you don't mind. You spent the evening drinking and socialising with a suspect involved in Operation Chrysalis. Yes or no?'

'Yes. I mean, no... It wasn't like that. You're making it sound like something it wasn't.' She was aware her voice had risen and how guilty she sounded. 'We recognised each other and started chatting. He joined me and my friends for a few drinks and then we all went our separate ways. That's all that happened.'

'You recognised each other how?' Maya shrugged nonchalantly. 'Where did you recognise him from?'

Maya faltered. She glanced pleadingly at Kym but was met with a blank expression. 'From... the warrant. At The Farmhouse. He'd been arrested and was waiting for the van to take him to custody when I arrived.' Maya let out a sigh, aware of how bad it sounded. 'We got talking...'

'And you just thought it would be a good idea to start socialising with a suspect you'd met during a warrant.' DI Mitton let out an incredulous laugh before shaking her head in Kym's direction. She glared at Maya acerbically. 'Have you any idea how compromised that could make you, let alone the potential risk? Anything could have happened to you or your friends. These nominals involved in Operation Chrysalis are extremely dangerous people.'

'But he's not. He was released without charge. He had nothing to do with it. He has nothing to do with *them*.' The words sounded puerile even to her own ears.

Mitton shook her head gravely. 'I suggest you think very carefully about who you associate with in future, Maya. You can't be a SOCO *and* spend your spare time associating with local criminals.'

'But I don't! I wasn't...'

Mitton silenced her with a stare before turning to Kym. 'I'll leave you to it. Thank you for your time.'

Both Maya and Kym sighed with relief as the DI left. 'Jesus, Maya,' Kym said as she raked a hand through her hair. 'If it isn't one thing with you it's another.'

Maya sat mutely. She did not have the energy to apologise or even begin to explain herself anymore. 'I really do take a very dim view of this latest event. You've put yourself in a very embarrassing situation. Yet again.'

'But, I...'

Kym raised a hand. 'For the remainder of your probation period, I'll be watching you like a hawk. I strongly suggest you keep your nose clean and keep your head down for the foreseeable. Both in and out of work.'

'Understood.' Maya bristled at being chastised like a child, frustrated at not being able to articulate her innocence.

'Are you still in touch with this... this... suspect?'

'No.' Maya could sense by the expression on Kym's face that she didn't believe her. But how could she plead Spence's innocence without sounding even more naïve and untrustworthy. The situation was too complicated.

'Anyway, what's done is done. Moving forward, how was the job?'

'Seemingly straightforward.'

'Seemingly?'

'There's no obvious signs of violence to the body. But we still can't account for how a renowned former drug dealer ended up in the canal.' Maya shrugged nonchalantly. 'He could have jumped. He may have been pushed. We deal with scientific facts not my supposition.'

'I don't appreciate your tone...'

'We'll see what the post-mortem shows up...'

The friction in the room was electric. Maya was at the end of her tether.

'I think you should go.'

'So do I.' Maya gave a double-clap and pointedly shut the door behind her as she left. Her head was spinning. If the bosses were so concerned with the fact she'd had a few drinks with Spence, then it certainly wasn't the time to speak up about the fact that Marcus Naylor had arranged for somebody to break into her apartment overnight.

60

Nowak was raging. He had just had a meeting with his solicitor, and it had not gone to plan. He had expected to be told when he could pack up and get shipped out of this shithole. What he had been told instead was the suspect who was supposed to take the blame for the McCluskey stabbing had three cast-iron alibis and potentially the added support of CCTV coverage showing him in a crowded pub at the time of the McCluskey stabbing.

As if that wasn't bad enough, when he found out exactly who the alibi was, the red mist had descended. His solicitor had been escorted out pronto while Nowak took his frustration out on the fixed table and chairs in the meeting room. His fists were swollen and bloodied where he had punched at walls and furniture. He was only marginally calmer now as he arrived back to his cell where Naylor was waiting for news of his friend's release.

'So, is this goodbye?' Naylor said jovially, unaware of Nowak's simmering rage.

'Is it fuck!' Nowak roared as he swept the contents of the table across the cell with one sweep of his meaty hand.

'Woah, mate, keep it calm. What's happened?' Naylor said placatingly, his palms held up toward Nowak to show he was on his side.

Shaking with rage, Nowak plonked himself down on the bottom bunk and snatched at the roll-up Naylor offered him. When he eventually spoke, his voice dripped with venom. 'That *bitch* of a daughter of yours. She's only given a fucking alibi to that prick we'd set up for the stabbing.'

Naylor lit his own roll-up as he processed this new information. 'Seems like my little girl just hasn't learnt how to stop causing trouble for people, has she?' he said eventually. His face was twisted in disgust and his rage was slowly building to mirror Nowak's. 'She just doesn't know when to leave things alone.'

Nowak eyed him thoughtfully. 'Aiden is already on it. Her mother should be getting a calling card anytime now and he's got something very special in mind for your Princess Maya. She's going to learn what it feels like to be locked up. That all right with you?'

Naylor nodded. 'Yeah, do what you need to do and make sure she knows I'm behind it too. It's payback time for her.'

'Oh, it certainly is,' Nowak said sinisterly. 'By the time we've finished with her, she's going to wish she'd never been born.'

'Well, that makes two of us, I wish she'd never been fuckin' born. I'd have rammed a knitting needle up her mother myself if I knew what trouble she was going to cause.'

Even Nowak was shocked with the look of pure hatred on his cellmate's face.

61

'Lurch, where the fuck are you? You're late. Don't piss me off today, mate, I'm not in the mood.' Donnelly swore to himself as he left yet another voicemail message for Lurch. He wasn't used to the great big lump not coming running when he clicked his fingers. It was early and he was tired, which was adding to his mounting irritation. He'd already done a little favour for Nowak and was now preparing for the second stage of their plan.

He sighed as he hauled the last few items of scrap metal out of the shipping container, so it was completely empty. This was Lurch's job. He shouldn't have to get his hands dirty. He had used this container for years; it had proved useful for storing stolen goods, including cars. It was situated at the back of an associate's scrapyard on the edge of a large, dilapidated industrial park outside town. The location ensured he and Nowak could come and go without arousing suspicion. Their privacy was guaranteed.

Now the container was empty, Donnelly could set about preparing it for his guest. He had secured a large metal chain to the back wall of the container along with some cable ties, a gym mat and bottles of water. It may not be five-star luxury, but it was going to provide several nights' accommodation for a special visitor very soon.

As he bent forward to unfurl the gym mat which would be used as a makeshift bed, Donnelly heard a sound. Just as he turned to see what it was, he felt a huge blow to the back of his head that sent him sprawling across the floor of the container. Crying out in shock, he scrambled to his feet, ready to turn and face his attacker, when yet another blow sent him reeling. The ground raced up to meet him and everything dissolved into blackness.

62

Dominique Barton stretched and yawned as she walked into her kitchen. She hadn't slept well because of the continuing heatwave and needed a strong coffee. She poured herself some cereal and decided she'd eat breakfast on the patio. She reached for the cat's bowl and poured out some food before setting it back on the kitchen floor. Jet was a creature of habit and would come careening through the cat flap for her breakfast anytime now. She was surprised the animal wasn't already posturing along the worktops, impatient for food.

Outside, she flopped into the garden chair. She lifted her face to the sun, revelling in its buttery warmth. She rested for several moments before taking a large sip of coffee and eating her cereal. Sated, she sat back and surveyed her garden. The geraniums were doing well, and her petunias looked stunning in the hanging baskets.

Her attention was drawn to the far corner of the garden. Jet was curled up on her side, sleeping in the shade. Although it was early, it was already hot. She smiled to herself. This weather was obviously too much for the poor furball.

'Jet, tchh, tchh, tchh,' Dominique called as she strode down the garden. 'Come on, puss, breakfast.'

The smile on her face faded as she got closer to the cat. She wasn't just still, she was rigid. She was curled unnaturally on her side, her back to Dominique.

'Jet,' she called again, her voice faltering. She sank to her knees and extended her hand to her precious pet. Beneath the velvet-soft fur, the body was like stone. She gently rolled her onto her back and then jumped back in sheer horror.

The cat's mouth was open unnaturally wide. Some sick fuck had wrenched the poor animal's jaws apart so violently it hinged like a crocodile. Its eyes were bulging, and a trail of blood tainted her shining fur. Dominique cried out in distress, unable to tear her eyes from the horrific sight.

As she stared down, numb with shock, she noticed something else. Something was protruding from the animal's throat. She knelt tentatively to look closer. It looked like some kind of paper tube. Keening, she slowly extended her hand and reached carefully into Jet's mouth. With a small tug, she removed the object from her throat. Bewildered, she sat back on her heels as she studied it. She unfurled it slowly. The paper was thick and strangely waxen.

As she unrolled it, she realised it was a photograph. She opened it up and smoothed the creases out. The picture was more terrifying than the sight of her beloved cat. She threw it from her as if it might explode, then let out a scream that brought the neighbours running.

A summer breeze tickled the photograph, causing it to skip across the dew-covered grass. The yellowing print saw a young couple beaming at the camera arm in arm. Back then, Dominique Barton and Marcus Naylor had been very much in love.

63

Maya lay in bed wide awake but reluctant to get up. Getting up meant facing the world and she really didn't want to. She still felt uncomfortable being alone in the flat. She was becoming increasingly unpopular at work and she was now screening her calls, reluctant to speak to Spence. Once released from custody he had rang her to plead his innocence. And he had sounded genuine. But she was unsure as to whether she could really trust him.

DI Mitton was right, on paper he was an Operation Chrysalis nominal. He had also been arrested for a Section 18 assault. A stabbing for God's sake. Yes, she had been with him at the time of the assault, but the facts were that the knife had been found in his room. Surely, he must have had some involvement. Instinctively, she believed he was a decent man. But perhaps that was a façade he had put on to convince her. Hadn't Naylor done a similar thing when he met Dominique – and look how that ended.

As for her instincts, how reliable were they? Her thoughts on the sudden deaths, for example. She was more convinced than ever after seeing Posner that there was a link, but nobody else believed her. What made her right and her more experienced colleagues wrong, other than an extraordinarily strong hunch. But she *knew* she was right, and the body count was rising. Why could nobody else see it?

Maya's reverie was broken by her ring tone. She checked the caller ID hoping it wasn't Spence again. She smiled when she saw it was Dominique.

'Morning, Mama.' The reply was a strangled sobbing sound. She sat up, panicked. 'Mama? Mama, what's wrong? What's happened?'

There was a rattling as the phone was passed to someone else.

'Maya? Hi, it's Jean from next door. It's Jet... Dominique has just found her in the garden, and... well, I'm afraid she's dead. Somebody has killed her... I think you should come.'

Jean continued to explain the horror of what Dominique had discovered. Maya could barely believe what she was hearing.

'I'm on my way.' Tears filled her eyes at the thought of poor Jet. She'd been the family pet for fifteen years. This was horrific. It had to be another message from Naylor. If she thought she felt scared after the break-in, it was nothing to the sheer panic she felt now. Things had gone too far. Jet had been killed for fuck's sake. Who would be next?

I know who is going to be next. I'm surprised it took me so long to decide when it's alarmingly obvious. This is going to be the hardest one yet though. I know I'm taking a real risk, but it will be worth it. Shouldn't every show end with a dazzling finale? Plus, this one really,

really deserves to die. I'll be doing a favour for so many people. Louisa my darling, this last one is for you. A symbol of my eternal love.

And then, I'm coming home.

64

Donnelly gradually came round. The pain in his head was excruciating and the dizziness and nausea left him in no doubt he was suffering with concussion. He had no idea how long he'd been unconscious for, but the bulging of his bladder suggested at least a couple of hours. He was lying on the floor of the shipping container. The metal chain he had brought had been padlocked tightly around his chest and his hands and feet were bound by the cable ties. He was trussed up like a Christmas turkey, and despite being in a level of pain he had never experienced before, he was raging.

It was hot in the container. The summer sun had turned it into a giant oven. He hadn't noticed the uncomfortable temperature when he had been emptying it, but now the door was shut, the heat was intensifying. He steadied his breathing and willed himself to stay calm while he gathered his thoughts.

Who the hell could have dared to do this to him? Surely it had to be opportunists, nobody who knew of him and his reputation would have risked doing something so stupid. When he found out who was responsible, he would kill them. Slowly and painfully. But first he had to get out. He suddenly thought of Lurch. He was supposed to be meeting the big man here. He would be along any minute now and then he could let him out.

Then a surge of apprehension rushed him like a giant wave. Lurch was late. Lurch was never, ever late and he hadn't picked up any of Aiden's calls for a while now. What if something had happened to him? What if whoever had had the audacity to tie him up in his own lock-up had got to Lurch first? Without Lurch, how the hell was he going to get out of here? He was trapped. A sitting duck for whoever had targeted him, and there was absolutely nothing he could do about it. Aiden Donnelly began to experience an unfamiliar prickle of fear, which he quickly smothered with his mounting rage.

'Arghhhh, get me out of here,' he screamed as he tugged frantically against the chain and thrashed his body against the restraint of the cable ties.

His desperate voice echoed around the empty container. He managed to manoeuvre his body enough so he could raise his feet and bang them against the walls. The result was a pitiful, desolate thumping sound. It was certainly not loud enough to attract attention.

He wrestled his hands round to the side of his body in a desperate attempt to check his pockets for his mobile phone, but it was gone. Panting with the exertion, he curled on his side while he caught his breath. His mouth was dry, and he was desperate for a drink. The bottles of water he had brought were lying agonisingly out of reach.

Eventually, once his heart rate had resumed to normal, he attempted to shuffle himself up onto his knees, attempting to stand. The exertion was far too much for him as the gravity caused his stomach to turn. He dropped back to the floor and vomited violently, spraying himself and his clothing in the process. Eventually, the nausea subsided. The pain in his head intensified and he started to see stars, before once again being swallowed into unconsciousness.

65

Maya and Dominique had been sat on the couch, holding on to each other for what seemed like an age. Despite the heat, they were ensconced under a blanket, both cold with shock. Their eyes were swollen with crying; their throats raw with talking and arguing.

Maya had been gobsmacked when Dominique had shown her the photograph. It left her with no other choice than to tell her about the break-in and the message from Naylor. Dominique switched from heartbroken to incensed. Maya had to wrestle the phone from her mother and beg her not to call the police. She had explained how she had not revealed her relationship to Naylor on her application form, and that if the truth came out, it could jeopardise the job she loved.

Maya had argued that even if she still managed to keep her job, she would be judged by her association with him. People would be different around her and the relationships she had worked so hard to build with her colleagues would be broken. She would be talked about and judged by other SOCOs and cops who didn't know her. Even if they didn't sack her, her reputation would be in tatters and the stigma would ruin her career anyway.

Dominique suddenly broke the silence. 'I refuse to live in fear again because of that man. And neither should you,' she added defiantly.

'What are you going to do? What *can* you do?'

'Phone the prison and find out who I need to speak to about this. Surely it counts as witness intimidation or something. He can't be allowed to get away with it. I'm going to make sure we don't hear anything else from him again. Ever.'

Maya pulled away, horrified at the suggestion. Fresh tears streamed down her face. The thought of Dominique phoning the prison would be like re-establishing contact with him. It was bound to anger him even more. Surely if they just ignored the situation, Naylor would get bored and disappear back out of their lives as quickly as he'd returned. Maya choked back sobs as she clutched Dominique's arm. 'Mama, no. Please. You can't do that. It'll make things even worse.'

Dominique smiled sadly at her daughter. 'Darling, things can't get any worse. We need to make him stop. Trust me.' She wrapped Maya in her arms, rocking her like she did when she was a little girl as she kissed the top of her head and shushed her tears away. 'Mama's going to make it all go away. And for good this time. I promise.'

Maya pulled away from Dominique and looked her mother in the eye. She nodded slowly. She had no choice but to agree. Whatever else was going on in her life this was the one thing she knew she couldn't fix but implicitly trusted that Dominique could. Despite Maya's age, Dominique's determination set the boundaries of parent and child. As far as this situation went, Dominique was going to do things her own way even if it went against Maya's wishes.

Maya understood how much Naylor had nearly broken

Dominique years ago. Her mother would find motivation and strength in not allowing him to control their lives a moment longer.

He had caused enough trouble for them both in the past and it was Dominique who bore the physical and emotional scars. Maya had no doubt Dominique was capable of putting Naylor back under the stone he had crawled out of.

66

The earlier unfamiliar feeling of fear which Aiden Donnelly had felt was beginning to grow into a full-blown panic. He had lost count of how long he had been tied up in the container. Whoever had him chained up had returned, but it had been during one of his many periods of unconsciousness. The only reason he knew someone had been, was because a couple of the water bottles had had their caps removed and placed within easy reach of him alongside a pre-packaged sandwich.

He took the food and drink as a positive sign that whoever was responsible, didn't intend to kill him otherwise why would they do that? Unless the intention *was* to kill him, but just not right now. The smell of his own body disgusted him. Not only had he soiled himself, he also reeked of sweat and vomit. The pain from his head injury was as intense as ever and his eyesight was blurred. The oppressive heat was also adding to his discomfort. The suffocating air inflamed his mounting panic.

Donnelly had never been a religious man, but right now he was praying with a religious fervour which any self-respecting priest would be proud of. He had long since stopped plotting revenge on whoever was responsible for his incarceration and was instead promising a God he had never before believed in that he would atone for all his past sins if only he would get out of this situation alive. For equal measure, he also prayed to the devil. He would sell his soul as long as it meant he didn't die here like this, coated in his own mess, alone and with no hope of a reprieve.

67

Nowak and Naylor were in their cell. Naylor was concentrating avidly on the news as usual, while Nowak lay brooding on his bunk. He'd not had any word from Donnelly all day, which was unusual. He had even tried to contact Lurch to find out what was going on, but even he hadn't replied to his texts or calls. Frustrated, he had returned the mobile to its hiding place. He had a sense of unease and was concerned that something had gone very wrong.

Suddenly the viewing hatch was slid back prior to the cell door being wrenched open. Four prison officers were braced expectantly in the corridor.

'You two, on your feet for a cell and body search,' said McGreevy, the eldest and largest of the wardens.

'What the fuck for?' Nowak snarled.

'Because I said so,' replied McGreevy as he pushed his way into the cell and began searching their bunks. Tutting and sighing, Nowak and Naylor got to their feet and stood back as McGreevy conducted his search. Two of the other wardens approached them and began patting down their clothing.

'How's that little granddaughter of yours, McGreevy?' Nowak

said pleasantly despite the sinister glint in his eye. 'She must be nearly walking by now.' McGreevy spun round, face flushed with anger and Nowak's mobile phone in his hand.

He shoved his face into Nowak's, visibly seething. 'Don't you fucking threaten me, you piece of shit.' He held the phone aloft for the other wardens to see. 'Get this bastard out of here and in solitary ready for a cavity search. I want a torch shone so far up his arse, his eyes and ears light up. Naylor too.'

Nowak laughed and smiled as he passed McGreevy. Davis, the youngest of the wardens, led Nowak away from the cell as his colleague followed with Naylor. Lowering his voice so only Davis could hear him, Nowak said, 'Don't you forget who pays your fucking wages. Make that phone disappear, okay?'

Davis nodded mutely, his face growing as pale as his shirt. Although McGreevy couldn't hear the exchange, he knew exactly what was going on, and was in no doubt whatsoever that Nowak had just passed some instructions or other. Well, he might have other screws on his corrupt payroll, but McGreevy's morality was without question. Especially now Nowak had had the nerve to mention his granddaughter. He would bend over backwards to ensure he and Naylor were held to account for the mobile phone, *and* for the witness intimidation which Dominique Barton had just reported.

68

Maya's peace of mind was almost restored. The prison had acted promptly following Dominique's complaint against Naylor. Whilst she was still very shaken up at the thought of her break-in and what had happened to poor Jet, Dominique had continued to reassure her that everything would be okay now. She had to put all thoughts of Naylor to the back of her mind and carry on as normal.

Ever the optimist, Maya was confident that it would be only a matter of time before things settled back down and she started to feel safe again. Even Spence had stopped calling her but if she was honest, she didn't know if she was happy about that or not. She was determined not to think about him either. It was easier that way. She decided the sensible thing to do for now was to follow Kym's advice about keeping her head down at work and home.

She arrived at work and parked up at the same time as Jack Dwyer. Perhaps now was the right time to start building bridges.

'Morning, Jack. Listen, I'm glad I've seen you. Thanks for giving me the heads-up about Spence being in the traps the other day. I'd have been mortified if DS Turner had marched me out of the office in front of everyone to give that statement.'

Jack nodded. 'I thought I owed you one. I recognised him as being the barman from The Eagle. He was there the night we went in. I didn't realise he was such a good friend of yours. You gave the impression you didn't like him.'

Maya shrugged. 'It's complicated.'

'Well, Turner reckons your alibi has got him off the hook for now, but that still doesn't explain the knife and bloodstained items they found in his house.'

Jack was frowning at her as he spoke, and Maya suddenly saw the situation through his eyes. He was judging her for her association with a suspect the same way DI Mitton and Kym had. For a moment, Maya wondered yet again if she was wrong about Spence being a good guy. Had she made another misjudgement in character? Was he as innocent as he claimed or was he playing her for a fool? She had spent all this time worrying about her association to Naylor being made common knowledge, yet she had associated with another potential criminal, and now everyone at work seemed to know about it.

'I don't know how those items ended up in his house, but what I do know is that he was with me and my friends at the time of the assault. That's all I can say. It's got nothing else to do with me,' Maya stated adamantly.

'Well, just be careful. If he is found culpable, it'll bring your reputation into disrepute.'

'I'm well aware of that, Jack, thank you,' she said through gritted teeth.

'Don't take offence. I'm just trying to look out for you as a friend, that's all,' said Jack.

'I'm perfectly capable of looking after myself, but I appreciate the sentiment,' she replied curtly. They headed into the station and both went their separate ways. There was something about Jack that riled her, and she didn't believe for one minute that he was looking out for her as a 'friend'. He was the type of person who always had an ulterior motive and only ever looked out for number one.

As Maya walked into the office, she was greeted by Chris, Elaine and Connor who were cackling away, clearly discussing something smutty. Generally, the office chat centred around food or sex, so she wasn't surprised. She grinned wryly as she caught up on the conversation.

'So,' said Chris. 'I'd only been seeing her a few months. Suddenly her dad dropped dead on the same day she found out he *wasn't* her biological father after all. She'd been drowning her sorrows and next thing I know she's as frisky as hell. Must have been the grief. Well, I wasn't going to say no.' He gave a sheepish grin as he scratched his stubble. 'Although with hindsight screaming "who's the daddy" as I shagged her wasn't very tactful.'

Connor groaned and Elaine let out a peal of raucous laughter as the phone rang. Shaking her head at Chris, Maya recognised the internal number as being the lab and she reached across to answer it.

'Is that SOCO's answer to Scooby Doo?' said Ewan.

Maya laughed. 'It certainly is. Hi, Ewan, take it you've got news about the suicide note?'

'Yes, I treated it with ninhydrin, which enhanced several fingerprints. I photographed them and passed them on to Sue in the fingerprint unit. She's loaded them onto the fingerprint database and has just let me know that one of the marks has been identified as Celeste Warren. No joy with the other set though.'

'But there's definitely two sets of prints on the note?'

'Yep, which is what we were hoping for. Unfortunately, though, we're no further to knowing who the other set belongs to, I'm afraid. Whoever it is, we've not got their prints on the database, so I can't identify them. Sorry, mate.'

'Bugger. Oh well, never mind. Thanks for trying anyway, Ewan. I really, really appreciate it.'

Maya hung up feeling deflated but curious that there was a second set of prints on the note. Her instincts had been right. Elaine, who appeared to have heard Maya's side of the conversation, looked at her inquisitively. 'What are you up to?' she asked with a wry smile.

'Nothing,' Maya replied a little too quickly, aware that she had a defensive edge to her voice.

'Really?' Elaine leaned towards her conspiratorially and lowered her voice. 'Spill.'

Maya sighed. She had hoped that examining Celeste Warren's suicide note would be something that would stay between her and Ewan, but Elaine's interest was clearly piqued, and she wasn't going to give up on finding out what the conversation had been about. Maya quickly and quietly explained, hoping no one else would overhear the conversation. If Kym found out, she was sure there would be hell to pay.

'Well, don't dismiss your sudden death theory too quickly,' said Elaine. 'According to the rumour mill, Aiden Donnelly is on the missing list. If you're right that there's someone going around bumping off our most notorious criminals, then I expect Donnelly's body to pop up somewhere very, very soon.'

Maya didn't have a chance to reply or question Elaine about Donnelly's disappearance as Kym swept into the office.

'Everyone well?' she asked rhetorically. 'I've just had Andy on the phone, he's going to be off for a few days. Nothing you all need to concern yourself with, he has just cited personal problems. Amanda, could you update the rota please to show him absent and let me know if anyone is interested in overtime to cover his shifts.'

Kym headed into her office as the others looked at each other questioningly.

'Personal problems, eh? More like a fucking personality problem,' said Elaine.

'Oh well, I could do with the overtime. Put me down for his weekend shift please, Amanda,' called Chris, 'That's unless anyone else wants it?'

Elaine leant across the desk towards Maya. 'You should put your name down too, make sure you're on duty for when Donnelly's body turns up, then you can say "I told you so", and be as smug as you like.'

Maya rolled her eyes at Elaine, refusing to engage in the conversation any further. She was curious though. Donnelly was the prime target of Operation Chrysalis. From what she knew of the investigation, she was under the impression a surveillance unit had been tailing him. So where was he and how could he have just disappeared?

69

Spence was getting ready for the late shift at The Eagle. He should have been covering the lunchtime shift but had asked Lisa for a swap so he could see his solicitor. He had been assured that his alibi would leave him with no case to answer, yet the fly in the ointment was still the knife and bloodstained clothing that had been removed from Spence's room.

He gave his niece a cuddle and headed out of the house for work. He had texted Maya earlier to see if she wanted to come and join him for an hour in the pub later. He desperately hoped she would. He was longing to see her, as just the thought of her made him smile. He instinctively reached for his phone to see if she had replied when a sudden movement caught his eye.

A figure was crouching down behind the thick rhododendron bushes which lined the border of the quiet avenue. Although the bushes were well adapted and quite overgrown, they were not large enough to disguise Lurch's huge bulk. Knowing he had been spotted, the man quickly got up, brushed himself down and began to stride hurriedly away through the estate.

Spence was temporarily stunned at the sight of the giant man emerging and then disappearing off. What on earth was he doing skulking outside his sister's house? They lived nowhere near The Eagle so he couldn't just have been passing. It was one hell of a coincidence that he should see him here. Spence didn't believe in coincidence. Could this man have something to do with the arrest?

'Oi, hey, mate, come here a minute. I want a word.'

Lurch glanced slightly over his shoulder before picking up his stride and disappearing out of sight. He moved surprisingly quickly for such a giant of a man.

'Hey, come back!' Spence called again. He must have heard him. He started to chase after the man and rounded the corner of the estate in no time, but there was no sign. The estate was like a maze, there was no way of knowing which direction the man had gone. And if he was in a car then it would be near impossible to spot him. Spence jogged forward, wondering which of the avenues to take his chance at searching first. Choosing the nearest one, he rounded the corner but again, there was no sign.

He quickly doubled back and chose the second closest avenue. He picked up speed, determined to catch up with him and get some answers. He had to find him. There was no way he had just been passing. He had clearly been hiding in the garden. He recalled Bella's nightmares and claims that a man had been looking through the window. Clearly Spence was being watched or followed, but why?

He frantically scoured the quiet street. Nothing. His desperation mounting, he turned to retrace his steps when he encountered a flurry of movement in front of him. Lurch appeared from the middle of nowhere. His huge fist smashed into Spence's face with such ferocity, he felt his neck crack. He dropped to the ground like a stone. Lurch leant over him, blocking out the sun. The big man's face swam in Spence's vision.

'Maya's number. Is it in your phone?'

Spence was in too much pain to comprehend the question. He nodded mutely as he clutched his face. Lurch held his hand out without further comment and without question Spence handed him his phone.

'Code?' Lurch demanded.

Spence reeled off the six numbers without protest as he tried to stand. A kick to his stomach winded him and sent him sprawling back onto the pavement. Accepting that he was no match in a fight against the big man, Spence instinctively curled into the foetal position. He hoped this would be enough to protect him from the vicious kicks Lurch continued to rain on his body.

As Spence lay lifeless at Lurch's feet, he pocketed the phone before running towards his parked car. Tears streamed down Lurch's face as he pulled away and caught a final glimpse of Spence in the rear-view mirror. There was no sign of him moving.

70

Maya's day had been incredibly busy. She'd spent all her shift at the local high school following an arson there. She arrived back at Beech Field tired, hot and stinking of the fire. She also unwittingly walked a trail of ash from the grooves of her work boots along the corridors of the police station.

It was only once she was sat at the computer with a cold drink, updating her exhibits, that she had a chance to check her phone. She had received a text message from Spence letting her know he had seen his solicitor and that things were looking positive. He had invited her for a drink so they could have a proper catch-up. Her heart had lurched at the sight of his name although she was still uncertain about whether she could trust him. She replied non-committally that she was pleased for him but couldn't meet for a drink as she was on call, which was a lie. She felt guilty that she was not more engaging.

Dismissing any further thoughts of him, she concentrated on updating her paperwork. She decided to go and see if she could get access to the cleaner's cupboard, so she could vacuum the mess up off the carpet.

'I can smell you a mile off and I'm guessing it's you that's walked the charred remains of St Patrick's High School throughout the nick?' said Jack.

'Afraid so,' Maya said with a sheepish grin. 'Don't worry, I'm going to clean it up. I'm just going for the vac.'

'You'll be lucky. The cleaning cupboard is kept under lock and key. The only way you're getting in there is with a wham-ram.'

'Hmm, maybe I'll just slip a note of apology under the door instead. Hey, I'm glad I've seen you. Is it true that Aiden Donnelly is on the missing list?'

Jack frowned. 'Where did you hear that?'

'Elaine mentioned it this morning. I assumed it was common knowledge. I thought he was under surveillance.'

'Well, the budget doesn't always stretch to twenty-four-hour surveillance. We do the best we can with the resources we've got. I'd rather not discuss it,' he said quite sharply, avoiding eye contact as he spoke.

'Have I said something out of turn,' Maya asked, confused by Jack's guarded reaction.

'No offence, Maya, but I'd rather not discuss a person of interest with you.'

'Oh really? And can I ask why?'

'Let's just say it's the company you keep. Like I said, no offence.' He still wouldn't look her in the eye.

'Oh, I see. Like that, is it? Fine. In future I can see no need for us to communicate with each other unless it's on a strictly professional basis. And personally, I'd rather keep *that* to a minimum.' She sniffed derisively before turning away from Jack and storming back to the office. To say she was fuming would be an understatement. There really was no end to the man's sheer arrogance.

She was suddenly struck yet again with the sickening thought that maybe Spence wasn't as innocent as he seemed.

She could be completely compromising herself by associating with him. She was even more relieved now that she had been vague with him on the phone. Although part of her was desperate to meet him and discuss the situation face to face. How had life suddenly got so complicated?

She found the whole situation so confusing. She was torn between someone who she liked and believed was a genuinely decent person, and a seasoned detective who was clearly good at his job but was renowned for being duplicitous and arrogant. But what if it was Jack who had something to hide? It was common knowledge that someone from within the force was leaking information relating to Operation Chrysalis.

It had to be someone who was close enough to the investigation or who had access to the police computer. And who fit that bill better than Jack Dwyer? He had been late to meet her at Celeste Warren's because of an urgent phone call. Could he have tipped Wainwright off? Was it coincidental that his transfer to Beech Field occurred around the same time that the latest information was seemingly being leaked to the likes of Donnelly and Nowak? Perhaps he was even responsible for Spence being set up for the McCluskey stabbing.

After all, the exhibits seized from his house had to have been planted by *someone* in the know. Maya racked her brains to recall the conversations between her and Jack. Had she at any point inadvertently hinted towards her relationship to Naylor? Was he responsible for setting up her early morning wake-up call? He'd been to her flat after all and knew the layout. At that moment, Maya knew she had no facts to support her theories, but one thing she did know was that Jack Dwyer was a loose cannon. He couldn't be trusted.

Maya grabbed her bag and car keys ready to leave when she collided in the corridor with DI Redford.

'Sorry, boss. I wasn't looking where I was going.'

'No harm done. Funny I've seen you actually, I've just sent one of my lot down to custody to interview a shoplifter who was brought in earlier.'

'CID for a shoplifter? I don't understand.'

'When the cops started interviewing him, he had a meltdown and started to talk about Posner.'

'Our Posner. The floater we dealt with?'

'Yup. He reckons he saw someone push Posner into the water while he was out of it. He was too scared and too smacked up on heroin to know what to do about it at the time, but clearly wants to talk to us now.'

Maya's heart was racing. She'd been right all along. Surely this meant the deaths were connected. 'So, he *was* murdered?'

'We'll see what our witness has to say before we get too excited. Are you in tomorrow?'

'Yes.'

'Right, I'll let you know the outcome of the interview in the morning. Goodnight.'

Maya was gobsmacked as she processed what Redford had just told her. If someone had rolled the intoxicated Posner into the water, then no wonder there was no sign of foul play. And if Posner *had* been murdered, then that surely meant that the others could have been too. But who by? And why?

71

Maya had barely slept. She had been so consumed by what DI Redford had told her. Every instinct in her body reinforced that she had been right all along. She was confident that something had been amiss at Gorman's house, although she still couldn't think what it was. Likewise, the note at Celeste's. Ewan had confirmed there was a second set of fingerprints on the note, so someone else must have been there at the time. Plus, they still had no justification for why a narcissist like Celeste would commit suicide.

She had examined that scene with Jack. Now she knew his true colours, could she really trust his judgement? He had been so quick to persuade her it was a suicide. Perhaps he had been covering his own tracks. And then there were the others – an infamous rapist, armed robber, con man, drug dealer... They had all died suddenly, within a matter of weeks. The same few weeks since Jack had transferred to Beech Field. It was all too much of a coincidence.

Maya arrived at Beech Field early that morning and practically sprinted to DI Redford's office. She was relieved to find him in. She couldn't stand another moment of not knowing.

'Boss, how did the interview with the shoplifter go? What did he say?'

'Good morning, Maya,' Redford replied pointedly.

'Sorry, boss. Good morning.' She hopped from foot to foot waiting eagerly.

'In a nutshell, not only was he charged for shoplifting, but we've also considered charging him for wasting police time.'

'I'm sorry?'

'Yes, perhaps you should be. Once we got around to interviewing him, it was a different story. He didn't want to talk to us. Just wanted to be charged and released. No mention of Posner or the alleged individual he had previously stated had pushed him in the water.'

'Well, you said yourself he was a heroin addict. Perhaps he was rattling and just wanted to get out of here so he could get a fix. Or maybe he didn't think he'd be taken seriously...'

Redford eyed her stonily. 'The bottom line is, he told us that it was all a joke. He thought it would be a good idea to wind us up after your sudden death conspiracy hit the local gutter press. Told us he and his associates had read the article and had a bloody good laugh about it.'

Maya felt her face burning with shame and embarrassment. Her earlier elation and conviction faded quicker than the glow emitted by luminol. 'Oh,' was all she could manage.

'"Oh" indeed. We can only hope that none of our other detainees make similar accusations. God knows the force is strapped enough without having to deploy a detective to every detainee who takes pleasure in winding us up.'

'Boss, I...'

'Maya, whatever you're about to say, please don't. I've got enough of a headache as it is. Now, I haven't mentioned anything about this latest incident to Kym, but can I suggest you just keep your head down and get on with the job you're paid to do.' He waved his hand towards the door to indicate she was dismissed.

Thoroughly chastised and deflated, Maya made a huge effort to plaster a smile on her face as she said good morning to everyone. Kym was already in and complaining about the state of the vans. She had used one the previous evening and was raging about the fact she had discovered a half-eaten chicken burger in the driver's door pocket. Chris and Connor were the most likely suspects, but both were denying any knowledge.

'Well, as nobody has had the decency to confess, you can both make sure those vans are spotless by the end of the day. I also want full stock checks done. If you're going to act like children, I will treat you like children.'

With Kym clearly in a bad mood, Maya decided to follow Redford's advice and keep her head down and get on with her work.

'If you two sort the vans out, I'll go to the garage. There's a few stolen cars waiting to be examined, so leave them with me.'

She gathered up the paperwork for the vehicles and was about to head out until curiosity got the better of her. Despite what Redford had said, she couldn't overlook the fact someone had claimed they'd seen Posner being pushed into the canal. What if the shoplifter had been right, but his urge for a fix had been stronger than telling the truth?

Maya began to search the force's database to research Posner's background in more detail. She knew she was overstepping the mark, but with everything that was going on she was left with no choice. Knowing her luck, the truth about Naylor could still come out at any time, so she had nothing to lose. She was going to prove the deaths were suspicious before they had a chance to throw her off the force.

The database held details of intelligence pertaining to each suspect as well as their criminal history, lists of associates, aliases, addresses and even details of any vehicles they were associated to. Maya could also read the physical descriptions, which included any identifying features such as scars or tattoos and warning markers. The warning markers included details such as whether the individual was violent, had access to firearms or if they had any contagious diseases.

Photographs of suspects were also taken every time the individual was admitted to custody. Maya had always found it alarming to see how drink and drugs took a toll on someone's appearance over the years. The earlier photographs of someone beginning their criminal career usually displayed subdued and teary-looking youngsters. As the years progressed and addiction and poor lifestyle choices took their toll, the images displayed gaunt, hardened-looking, toothless individuals who had aged well before their time. Mark Posner was a typical case in point, and he hadn't been on the gear half as long as most.

Maya sighed. It was a fruitless task, none of the information she had read about Posner provided her with any answers. She decided to review the photographs taken at Karl Gorman's house. After all, that first scene was where her suspicion had been initially aroused. Perhaps whatever she had overlooked on the day would be revealed in the photographs.

She took a moment to recall everything of that scene, including her interaction with Chris before she even entered the house. She recalled how impatient he had been with her until he had found out Gorman was her first death. Then she slowly studied each of the photographs Chris had taken before she'd even got there.

She scrolled through the external house shots and the ones leading from the hall and the living room. Each picture had been taken before a stepping plate had been placed down so the floor could be viewed. Eventually, she clicked onto the images of the kitchen. Just seeing the photographs triggered her olfactory memory. Once again, she could smell the rotting stench with a top note of body odour. She was reminded of the state of disarray the kitchen had been in, from the overflowing bin to the sink which was piled high with rubbish.

Then she spotted it. There it was. On the table close to Karl Gorman's head and the overflowing ashtray – a tea towel. Suddenly, she realised what had left her with the niggling feeling of uncertainty as she was about to leave the scene.

Why would someone who lived in as much squalor as Karl Gorman, a man who clearly didn't even bother with the washing up, have a clean tea towel out on his dirty kitchen table? Fair enough if he had a couple tucked away in a drawer somewhere, but why was it out on the table next to his dead body? The sink was overflowing with detritus and being used as a bin. It just didn't make sense.

Maya was now adamant there had to be a link between each of the deaths. There was a common denominator somewhere. She just needed to find it. She typed in Gorman's details. One by one she scanned through each of the crimes he had been linked to and reread the circumstances. She made a note of the crime numbers. Then she logged into Socrates, the SOCO database.

She searched for the crime numbers and got a match. There had been a rape scene, which Gorman had been sentenced for. According to the system, Chris had examined the scene and Andy had dealt with Gorman. Interesting. She did another frantic crime search, this time against Posner. The last time he had been arrested for possession and supply of a controlled substance, officers had searched his house. Once again, Andy Carr had been the SOCO who had attended the scene.

The hairs on Maya's neck began to stand. This was it – she was getting close. She just knew it. She felt breathless as she reached for the phone and called Ewan. He answered straight away.

'Ewan, it's Maya again. Listen, I need to ask you a huge favour and it's quite urgent.'

'Fire away.'

'When we provide our fingerprints and DNA for elimination purposes, are those samples input onto the main database?'

'No. There's an additional system just for elimination purposes.'

'How often are eliminations checked?'

'It's not something that's routinely done. Usually just on request.'

'Is there any chance you can compare the other fingerprints found on Celeste's suicide note to the fingerprints on the elimination database.'

'Yeah, I can ask. You sound excited – care to share?'

'Not yet. If you don't mind. I'm learning not to open my mouth until my assumptions are proven to be fact.'

'Fair enough. Leave it with me. I'll let you know if we get an ident.'

'Thanks so much, Ewan.'

As Maya hung up, she pondered. The answer was so obvious it was staring her in the face. Andy Carr had to be the link between them all. She just needed to wait for the results of the fingerprint ident to be confirmed before she voiced her concerns. Even then there was still one huge question to answer: if Andy *was* responsible for all the sudden deaths, then why?

Today is the day.

72

Maya had hoped that examining the stolen cars at the garage would be a welcome distraction. Unfortunately, she still found herself checking her phone every few minutes in case Ewan contacted her. She was consumed with the link between Andy and the deaths and was finding it hard to think about anything else. She didn't even know how long it would take to check the elimination database. It might be an hour or a week. Would she be told the results straight away or would a fingerprint expert have to double-check the fingerprint like they did with crime-scene marks and suspects? She would phone Ewan again as soon as she got back to Beech Field and ask.

Finally, just as she was about to leave the garage, she received a text. It wasn't from Ewan, but Spence. She frowned as she read the message.

Need to meet. Urgent.

Maya was concerned, what was so urgent? What could possibly have happened now? She quickly typed a reply.

What's wrong? Come around after I've finished work.

His reply was instant.

No. Now. I'm at a mate's, 11a Bentcliffe Street, Wardley. I need your help.

Maya felt her stomach churn with unease. Whatever Spence needed to see her about so urgently surely wouldn't be good news. As much as she wanted to get back to Beech Field and speak to Ewan, she couldn't just ignore Spence. Despite her reservations, she cared about him and perhaps he had answers for her that would prove he was completely innocent of the McCluskey stabbing and all other wrongdoing. She was determined that today would be a day for answers.

She knew Bentcliffe Street. It wasn't too far from Ryan Johnson's flat and she would pretty much be driving past it on her way back to the police station. Maya replied to let him know she was on her way. Surely whatever it was wouldn't take too long. Perhaps it was even good news for a change. Either way, she was looking forward to seeing him again even though she knew she probably shouldn't.

73

Bentcliffe Street was rough. Even the summer sun, which always made the dourest of places look brighter, did nothing but accentuate the grubbiness of the street. Shards of broken glass glistened menacingly in the gutter and even the weeds looked spiky and intimidating. Most of the terraces were tinned up with council curtains – huge metal shutters which were covered in graffiti-sprayed phalluses and bad spelling.

The few remaining houses that weren't unoccupied appeared run-down and unloved. Broken gates swung forlornly from hinges. Number 11 Bentcliffe Street looked equally shabby with newspaper glued to the inside of the front window instead of curtains to afford the occupants some privacy. The number 11a and an arrow had been crudely spray-painted in white along the side of the house, indicating the rear of the property.

Maya wondered what on earth Spence was doing in a dump like this. She could only conclude that his sister had kicked him out and he had no choice but to sofa surf. Surely, he could do better than this? She carefully stepped over a pile of dog muck and dodged a piece of corrugated iron that was propped along the wall of the house. She made her way to the rear of the property. 11a had been sprayed with the same paint across the front door which swung open, revealing a cheap linoleum-covered stairway. Music was playing loudly inside. The throbbing of the bass line frayed her nerves and made her feel disorientated.

'Spence? It's Maya, are you in?' she shouted above the music.

She paused hesitantly at the door. Her senses were heightened, and she felt decidedly uncomfortable. She heard a shout of acknowledgement and shook her head. Of course, he was in. He'd asked her to come, hadn't he? She was being a snob. The only reason she felt uncomfortable was because the place was a dump. She knew better than anyone how down on his luck Spence was right now. Whatever was going on must be important for him to drag her round here. He had asked for her help after all.

She headed up the stairs, avoiding the mould-coated walls, and followed the sound of the raucous music. She stepped into the lounge. Despite the glorious weather outside, the room appeared dim, thick brown curtains pulled against the window to block out the light. The room was filled with a giant corner sofa, a TV and a dated hi-fi unit in the corner which was blaring out the music.

The air in the room was thick with cigarette smoke. It added to the Stygian gloom. In the few seconds it took her eyes to adjust to the darkness, she heard the lounge door bang shut. She jumped and turned towards the noise. Her eyes widened with sheer terror; her mouth dropped open with shock. Lurch was blocking the door, grinning at her.

74

'Is Maya back from the garage yet?' Chris had the office phone tucked under his chin.

'No,' Amanda glanced at the clock, 'she didn't leave until late so I'm not expecting her back just yet.'

'Ewan? She's still out doing jobs. Can I take a message? Oh, okay mate, she'll be pleased about that. Ta-ra then.' Chris put the phone down and turned to Amanda. 'It was only Ewan letting her know about a fingerprint ident. He's going to try her on her work mobile.'

Chris sat back in his chair, rubbing his stubble as he gazed across the room, seemingly lost in his own thoughts.

'What are you daydreaming about?' Amanda threw a pen at him to get his attention.

He shook his head. 'Nothing. I'm hungry, that's all.' He stretched noisily, scratching at his stomach. 'Fancy nipping out for lunch while Cruella isn't here?' He nodded towards Kym's office door. 'My treat,' he added.

Amanda raised an eyebrow suspiciously. 'You're actually offering to release the moths from your wallet. What's got into you?'

Chris pulled a mock-surprised face. 'Nothing! Can't I treat me old mate to lunch without having an ulterior motive? Come on, get yer coat, you've pulled!'

He scrawled a note announcing they'd gone for lunch and stuck it on the office door before locking it. Jovially, he linked Amanda's arm and the two of them strolled down the corridor laughing like a couple of school kids. Not a care in the world.

75

Aiden Donnelly's fear had been replaced by a renewed anger. The last time he had succumbed to the pain in his bursting bladder and once again felt the snaking warmth of his own piss creep down his trouser leg, had been the moment his trepidation had turned into a white-hot rage. His humiliation masked the pain and discomfort he was in. Who had the fucking audacity to keep him like this?

He had long since given up on banging his feet against the container wall to gather attention. He knew there was no chance of anybody being nearby. That was the reason he and Nowak had chosen this location in the first place. And that was exactly why he had intended to bring Maya here. It should have been her hog-tied like this and coated in her own fear and excrement, not him. She needed to learn her lesson. Whereas he had no idea why he was being kept like this. But when he did, that person would pay, and he would enjoy every second of pain he could inflict upon him.

His bouts of unconsciousness had thankfully eased off, and although he was far from well, the intensity of the pain in his head had lessened. He was also beginning to feel the benefits of having consumed the food and water left out for him. He had even managed several times to successfully get back on his feet, as much as his constraints would allow. Now he was sat with his aching back resting along the wall of the container, when he heard a noise. He held his breath as he strained to listen more closely. He had definitely heard a car door slamming.

Then he heard the sure and certain sound of footsteps. The scraping of the metal bolts being drawn back. He was on his feet quicker than a prize fighter, senses primed and raring to attack. He was shocked to register the face of the person, but the relief of being saved was all encompassing. He didn't even care about asking questions. He just wanted to be untied and let out.

'Well, I never thought I'd be pleased to see you.' He let out an uncharacteristic high-pitched laugh. 'What are you waiting for? Come and untie me,' he demanded angrily. Then he stopped. He was stunned at the sight in front of him. 'What's going on? Wh... wh... what the fuck do you think you're doing?'

His earlier relief was replaced with fresh fear and his bowels turned to soup. The figure strolled towards him with all the confidence of someone who had the upper hand.

And a loaded handgun.

76

Maya's legs were shaking so violently with fear she could barely stand. She had never been more terrified in her life. Every instinct in her body was screaming at her to get out, but there was nowhere for her to run. Lurch filled the door with his massive bulk, his head skimming the top of the door frame. Gasping, Maya staggered backwards until she felt the edge of the couch dig into her calves. She sank down wordlessly, without once breaking eye contact with him.

She flinched as he walked towards her, but he merely reached over to switch the hi-fi off before returning to stand in front of the door.

'Wh... wh... where's Spence?'

'He's not here. It's just us.'

'What do you want?' The words were barely audible, more than a whisper. She sank back into the couch, wrapping her arms around her shins, trying to shrink away from him.

'To talk to you. That Spence? I took his phone. It was the only thing I could think of to get you here.'

'Is this to do with Marcus Naylor?' Maya gulped back tears, sickened by the sound of his name in her mouth.

'Who? No.' Lurch was clenching his fists in frustration. 'I TOLD you. I just need to talk.'

'Okay, sorry.' Maya raised her hands placatingly. 'I'm listening.'

'I need your help...'

Maya was stunned to see the big man stifle a sob as he searched for the next words.

'I've done something bad. Because of you. For you. And now I don't know what to do.' Lurch groaned like a wounded animal. Maya was horrified to see him raise his fists and begin to hit his head.

She leant forward, pleading soothingly despite her own fear. 'Hey, please don't do that. You'll hurt yourself.'

This was obviously the right reaction, as Lurch stopped straight away. He dropped his fists to his sides, but his face remained lowered, unable to look Maya in the eye.

Maya became aware how volatile the man clearly was. She knew she would have to choose her words and actions carefully if she was going to get out of this situation unharmed.

'I can see something is upsetting you. I bet it's not easy to talk about.' She paused, letting the words sink in. 'But you've got me here to help you. You said you've done something bad. Do you want to talk about that first?'

Lurch swiped at his eyes before nodding glumly. He still couldn't make eye contact and instinctively she knew, if she was going to be able to communicate with him effectively, that that would have to change.

'Listen to me,' she managed a soft laugh, 'I'm asking you to talk to me and I don't even know your name. I guess you know I'm Maya. Who are you?'

This did the trick as he raised his head. 'Lurch.' He drooled slightly. 'My real name is Sydney. But everyone calls me Lurch.'

A cold chill ran through Maya. It ran down her spine to her

legs and almost paralysed her with shock. She recognised the name from the briefing at Ryan Johnson's murder. Lurch aka Sydney Barber. She recalled it being read out and how Elaine had snorted with laughter at the name.

This was Donnelly and Nowak's henchman. The monster who was believed responsible for the violent murder of Ryan Johnson. She recalled the haunting images of Ryan's shattered skull and her eyes widened with fear. This was the same monster who had terrorised her in her own bed. She flinched uncontrollably, inching towards the back of the couch as her eyes frantically scanned the room for an escape route. Should she scream? From what she had seen of the estate, even if the neighbours were in, it was highly unlikely they would be the type to come running to the sounds of a potential domestic.

Then her thoughts turned to Spence. Lurch had taken his phone so he could lure her here. She was sure Spence wouldn't just hand it over, which means it had probably been taken by force. Was Spence lying in water somewhere, his dead body wrapped in tarpaulin with his skull smashed open? Maya fought back a sob and took another deep breath. Fighting back the panic attack that was mounting in her chest, she frantically thought about what she could say or do next. Instinctively she knew that it could mean the difference between life and death.

77

The moment Spence opened his eyes, he regretted it. The light was a laser beam of pain, which burnt into his retina. His mouth was dry and woolly, every part of his body ached.

'Spencer, darling, you're awake. It's okay, sweetheart, I'm here.'

Spence was surprised to hear the familiar sound of his mum's voice and took a chance with the light, squinting carefully in her direction. He smiled weakly at the sight of her sat by the side of his bed. She looked to have aged overnight, the concern on her face was palpable.

He shut his eyes again and felt his body sink into the bed. 'I'll go and get a nurse,' he heard his sister say. He sighed as he felt his mother fussing with the bedcovers around him, before gently placing a cooling kiss on his forehead. He heard a sudden strangled sob before he felt her warm tears falling on his face.

'Please don't cry, Mum, I'm okay,' he said in a voice he barely recognised as his own. His mouth was swollen and worryingly, his teeth felt loose. He reached for his mum's hand and squeezed it carefully as he attempted to open his eyes again.

This time the light seemed more forgiving and he could take in more detail of the hospital room he was lying in.

'How long have I been here?' he asked, disorientated.

'Since yesterday. Tania said she thought she'd heard some shouting not long after you left the house but thought nothing of it at the time. When she realised your car was still there, she went to look for you. She found you out for the count in the middle of the estate.

'The doctors have kept you sedated since as they were concerned about a possible head injury although, thank God, everything seems fine. You've got a broken nose, fractured cheekbone, four broken ribs *and* a broken collarbone. Oh, darling, we've been so worried.' Janine James broke into a fresh peal of tears as she clutched Spence's hand for dear life, as if she was never going to let him go again.

Well, with all those injuries, at least it explained why he felt as if he'd been hit by a bus. He had a fleeting memory of chasing after Lurch through the estate and then suddenly, all the events of the last few weeks came flooding back to him. There was only one person he could think of.

'Maya,' he said as he made a futile attempt to sit up. 'I need to speak to Maya. I need to check she's okay.'

'You were mugged, love, your phone has been stolen. Who's Maya anyway?'

'I need to speak to her, Mum. Please get me a phone or something.' Spence attempted to sit up again, just as Tania returned to the room accompanied by a doctor.

'You're going nowhere, son, lie back down,' the doctor commanded in a no-nonsense, authoritarian manner.

Consumed with pain and frustration, Spence sank back down onto the bed as the doctor began to examine him, poking and prodding and asking all sorts of questions. All he could think about was Maya. He didn't have all the pieces to the jigsaw, but he knew Maya was central to it all. Tears began to fill his eyes and they had nothing to do with the amount of pain he was in.

If Lurch had done this to him, what would he do to Maya?

78

Taking deep breaths, Maya fought to stay calm. It was easier said than done in the presence of someone as intimidating and unstable as Lurch. She decided to chance flattery and distraction. 'Sydney is a nice name. Can I call you Sydney instead of Lurch?'

Her gamble paid off as he gave her a shy, toothless smile. 'I'd like that. I don't want to be Lurch anymore. I want to be Sydney.'

Maya smiled with more reassurance than she felt. 'Okay, Sydney. Can you tell me what you've done? Then we can work out how I can help you.'

He grimaced. 'It's my friend, Aiden...'

'Aiden Donnelly?' Maya gasped.

Lurch nodded as he swiped his sleeve across his nose. 'He's gonna be so mad with me...'

'Why?'

'I knocked him out and chained him up in our lock-up. He's still there. It's been days now. I don't know what to do. Usually, him or Nowak tell me what's what. I've never been in a situation like this before. My friends have always helped me.'

'You said you'd done this because of me but I don't understand why. I don't even know Donnelly...'

'Because it was supposed to be you in the lock-up. Aiden said we were going to follow you and kidnap you and tie you up in there to teach you a lesson. As a favour for Nowak's cellmate.' He sighed as he struggled to think. 'And because they were all mad at you for giving Spence an alibi for the McCluskey stabbing. Aiden had fixed it that Spence got sent to prison so Nowak could come home.'

As shocked as she was, things gradually began to fall into place. She didn't know what was worse – the thought that someone had planned to kidnap her or the fact that Naylor was behind it. It was almost too incomprehensible.

Lurch's lower lip began to tremble with emotion. He couldn't look Maya in the eye as he continued. 'I couldn't do it though. I've always done what they've told me to do before, but not this time. I can't stop thinking about you since I saw you in bed. That was wrong. I'm really sorry if I scared you.' He started to hit his head again, more violently this time.

'Sydney, stop, please.' Like last time, he dropped his hands immediately. He was clearly used to acting on instructions. He stared solemnly at the floor.

'I didn't know how to say no to Aiden. Even if I had, I knew he'd do it anyway and I couldn't stand the thought of you being hurt. But I can't keep him in there for ever. And I know I hit him too hard because he was knocked out for ages.' Lurch let out a sob. 'He's going to kill me. Worse, he's never going to speak to me again. What am I going to do, Maya?'

Wretchedly, Lurch sunk to his haunches and wrapped his arms around himself. He buried his face between his legs and sobbed noisily. He looked so pitiful; Maya couldn't help but feel sorry for him. Whatever Lurch may have done in the past, Maya was confident he had not acted with any deliberate criminal intent. He had clearly been following orders.

She strongly suspected he didn't have the mental capacity to know the difference between right and wrong. He had been used and manipulated by Donnelly and Nowak. He had spent his whole life being told what to do by other people. He was lost now he had no one ordering him about. He had come to her in the hope she would tell him what to do.

'Sydney,' she said carefully. 'What's upsetting you the most?'

He wiped a hand across his face, smearing tears and snot like a child. 'The fact I've hurt Aiden. I don't want to hurt anyone anymore. I've done some bad things over the years, Maya. Really bad. I don't like it. I want to be a good person. I want to be the type of person that someone like you would want to be with.' He blushed again and gave her a shy smile. 'I know I scare people. I know I scare you.'

Maya stood carefully and walked towards Lurch, then, sinking to the floor, she sat cross-legged facing him. 'I'm not scared now I've got to know you.' She smiled reassuringly. 'You've asked me to help you and I will. First of all...'

Her mobile rang, cutting her off mid-sentence. She glanced at Lurch who nodded at her to answer it. It was Ewan. Her eyes widened with shock as she listened to him. Her hands shook as she ended the call and her mouth hung open in disbelief.

Lurch frowned with concern. 'Are you okay, Maya?'

She shook her head imperceptibly before pulling herself together. 'Sydney, I need you to tell me where Aiden Donnelly is. I need to get to him.'

Lurch shook his head frantically. 'No, you can't go. If he gets out, he'll hurt you. Really hurt you.'

'I need to go. He's not safe there. I think somebody else might know where he is. And they're going to kill him.'

79

Aiden's eyes widened with incredulity at the sight of the gun. 'What the fuck do you think you're doing?'

'Something someone should have done a long time ago. Putting you down like the rabid animal you are.'

'Have you forgotten who you're talking too? You've not got the balls. Fair enough, you've got this far. Let me go now and I might be prepared to forget about it.' His bluster was starting to wane now. As incredulous as the sight in front of him was, even he couldn't help feeling anxious when a gun was pointing in his direction.

'I'd like to take the credit for chaining you up like that, but it wasn't me, I'm afraid. I'd have left you to starve.'

'Then who?'

'Your good friend Lurch.'

'Lurch? Fuck off. He's as loyal as a dog.'

'Seems you misjudged him. I've been watching. He's been coming and going, bringing you your little food parcels.'

'Bollocks,' Aiden spat with contempt at the floor. 'Why would Lurch do this?' He indicated his head to the squalor he was in.

'I've not worked that out yet. It looks like you'll have to die not knowing. Lurch is going to have a nasty shock next time he visits.'

'Tell me what this is really about. It's money, isn't it?' He sat up eagerly. 'That's what you want. It's what you lot always want.'

'And if I say yes, how much will you give me?'

'Whatever you want.' He was aware of the desperation in his voice and tried to shrug it off. 'Within reason. Obviously. Just fucking untie me, okay?'

'Manners?'

'Please,' he said through gritted teeth. 'Look, just tell me what it is you want. How much?'

'I don't want your fucking money. I want you dead.'

'So, what? You're just going to shoot me? Just like that? You?' He shook his head incredulously. As unbelievable as the situation was, he was scared now. Very scared.

'Yes, Mr Donnelly, I am. But it's not going to be quick. And it's certainly not going to be painless...'

80

Despite Lurch's concern for Maya, the thought of Donnelly being in danger was all the persuasion he needed to give her the location of the lock-up. She looked the address up on Google Maps and was relieved to discover it wasn't too far away. She could make it there in fifteen minutes.

Lurch was hovering in the middle of the room looking more vacant and lost than ever. 'Will Aiden be okay?'

'I hope so. I'm going to go now and do whatever I can to help him.'

Lurch nodded his thanks. Maya chose her next words carefully. 'Sydney, whatever happens with Aiden, you know the police are going to come. Because of... things that he and Nowak have done. Because of the things they've asked you to do.'

Lurch nodded solemnly, his face a mask of pain and contrition.

'I probably shouldn't even say this. But you asked me to help you.' She took a deep breath. 'You need to go. Now. Get as far away from here as you can. Start a new life somewhere new. Be a good person. Be Sydney.'

They stood for a moment staring at each other. A thousand

words passed unspoken between them. Maya tenderly squeezed Lurch's arm as she left. She couldn't waste another moment. The thought that Andy Carr was behind the deaths had been disturbing. Knowing who was really responsible for all the killings, was terrifying.

81

Maya pulled over on the dirt track which surrounded the back of the industrial unit. Parking carefully to make sure the van stayed out of sight; she could see the green shipping container through the trees. She was chilled by the sight of the white car parked alongside it, which she recognised immediately. Maya shook her head at her own naivety. She had been so convinced that Andy Carr was behind everything that she had overlooked the truth. She almost wished it had been Andy. That would have been easier to deal with. She had never trusted or liked him. She felt sickened that someone so allegedly respectable could be behind this. Someone she could once almost have considered a friend.

Straining towards the windscreen to consider the lay of the land, Maya's mind was whirling with how to proceed. Every moment she faltered could mean the difference between Donnelly coming out of that lock-up alive. She couldn't cope with having his death on her conscience. She needed to get in there. But what could she do alone and unarmed?

Maya grabbed her phone and began to dial the office number. She hesitated as the call began to connect and hung up quickly. She no longer knew who she could trust. God knows how many people were involved. She urgently needed police backup but how could she ask for it if she didn't know who the good guys were. Shouting up on the police radio would get her the help she needed but could also compromise her safety. And what would she even say? How could she explain the situation without sounding like a complete fantasist?

Looking at the radio in its vehicle holder she knew what to do. She pressed the emergency button. She knew this was one way of communicating with comms. It had worked when officers at The Farmhouse had used it when arresting Donnelly. They would be able to use GPS to track her location, and when she didn't respond to a welfare call, patrols would be allocated to her. She pressed the button and heard the alarm chirrup into life. On wobbly legs, she left the safety of the van and walked stealthily towards the shipping container. She passed the familiar vehicle before quietly and hesitantly pushing her way through the open door.

The heat was oppressive and the stench unbearable. Aiden Donnelly spotted her first, the figure clutching the gun totally unaware of her presence until Maya spoke.

'What's going on?'

The killer turned and smiled at Maya, seemingly unsurprised by her arrival, as the gun was turned in Maya's direction.

82

Amanda arrived back at the office at the same time as Elaine. Chris had dropped her off, stating he needed to do something before he returned to work. She was just settling her things down on the desk when the police radio chirruped with the recognisable tone of the emergency activation button.

Amanda frowned. 'You've not pressed yours by mistake have you, Elaine?'

'No.' Elaine picked it up to check. She could see on the display the collar number of the officer who had activated it. 'Hey, isn't that Maya's collar number?' She hurriedly passed the radio to Amanda. She squinted through her reading glasses. 'Yes, it is. Shit, I hope she's okay.'

'She was only going to the garage, wasn't she?'

'As far as I know, yes,' replied Amanda. 'Unless she's been allocated another job while we've been out. It might be an accidental activation. I'll ring the garage and check if she's still there.'

The comms officer was responding to the activation over the air, calling Maya's collar number and asking if everything was okay, but getting no reply. Amanda suddenly put the phone down, looking pale. 'Elaine, shout up and let comms know, Maya left the garage ages ago. She should be back here by now. I'll phone Chris. Out of all of us, if there was a problem, she'd have rung him first.'

'Shit,' breathed Elaine as she attempted to stay calm and relay the information to comms. She informed them that the emergency activation was by a SOCO officer, but they didn't know her current whereabouts.

Comms replied that they were currently accessing her location by using the Northgate mapping system. Amanda shook her head as she put the phone down. 'Chris isn't picking up.'

After what seemed like an age, the comms officer shouted up with a location. 'Confirm emergency activation is coming from Weir Industrial Estate. Any patrols free on an immediate response please?'

Several officers acknowledged that they were en route. A couple of sirens began to scream from the rear yard as they made their way. All Amanda and Elaine could do was sit huddled around the radio and wait for an update. They were both frantically hoping and praying that Maya was okay.

83

Maya thought the state of Aiden Donnelly was almost as shocking as the sight of the gun that was pointing in her direction. Alison Mitton smiled at Maya. She appeared completely unconcerned, as if Maya had walked in on a team briefing. 'Aiden here has had a rough few day,' she explained nonchalantly. 'I was just about to put him out of his misery.'

'Really? Like you did with the others?'

Alison smiled at her, nodding slowly. 'Oh, Maya, I knew you were smart enough to work it out. What gave me away?'

'I sent Celeste Warren's suicide note off to the lab for chemical treatment. The ident has just come through. I thought there was something unusual about the note. The way the wording was crossed out.' Maya heard the shakiness in her own voice which was mirrored by the trembling in her legs.

'Very good, I'm impressed. Obviously, I couldn't wear gloves while I was with her, it would have looked too suspicious, but it didn't matter as in view of the fact it was a suicide, I knew there wouldn't be any need for a fingerprint exam. The stupid bitch thought it was all a big joke. I told her I wanted her to write a note to say sorry to one of the many victims she had damaged over the years. I told her what to say, but she couldn't spell. My inner pedant couldn't allow her to not correct it.'

'What the fuck is all this about?' Aiden's voice lacked the bravado he intended. 'Where's Lurch?'

'Shut up,' the two women replied in unison. Alison laughed. 'I like you, Maya. You've got the same drive and ambition I had when I joined the job.' She turned the gun back in Aiden's direction, but didn't take her eyes off Maya.

'I'm nothing like you,' Maya spat. 'I'm doing this job because I want to help people, not kill them. It doesn't matter who they are or what they've done in the past, there is no excusing you...'

'Really? Your morality is commendable. Or at least it nearly is. Why didn't you tell anyone that Marcus Naylor is your biological father?'

'You knew?'

'Yes. I make it my business to know everything. That's what a good cop does. I also know that for the last twelve months, Andy Carr has been taking bribes off this piece of shit to provide him with Operation Chrysalis information. I hadn't done anything about it earlier, as I find it's always best to bide your time and wait for the perfect moment. I'd quite like to put a bullet in our Andy, but I'm running out of time. Donnelly will be my last.'

Maya stepped carefully around Alison and positioned herself in front of Donnelly. 'I'm afraid I can't just stand here and let you do that. I know I'm not perfect and I've made mistakes, but murder? Why? What you've done makes you just as bad as the likes of him,' she said, indicating her head towards Donnelly.

'Because I've given my whole life to this job, that's why. I've sacrificed so much to put the likes of him and Gorman and Jim Baron and Geoffrey Doran away and for what? They get released in the end and carry on with their lives, completely unaffected.

They don't *deserve* to live. Good, decent people die every day while scum like that remain untouchable.'

Alison gave a bitter laugh. 'His type never learns. The more we put away the more come crawling out of the woodwork to fill their boots. Right now, there's a wannabe Aiden Donnelly, Piotr Nowak or Celeste Warren about to embark on their criminal careers with the intention of gaining the next big reputation.

'And it's people like us, Maya,' said Alison, poking herself in the chest, 'people like *us* who will put our own lives on hold and work every hour God sends to catch them. We'll sacrifice all those precious moments, all that special time we can never get back. Think of all those missed weekends, nights out, Christmases, birthdays, weddings...'

She choked on her words and Maya could detect a tremble in her voice as she continued. 'Family celebrations that should be spent with the people you love. And it's not even the big moments. It's the everyday we take for granted. The meals that go uneaten because you're working a shift that never ends. Those cosy early nights that you promised your partner, but by the time you do crawl into bed at 3am, the reception is as frosty as the weather outside.

'I didn't realise how much time I'd wasted until it was too late. My partner, Louisa, she died of cancer last year.' She closed her eyes briefly. Clearly even the mention of the name brought her immense pain. 'The only saving grace,' she continued, 'was that it was quick, and she didn't suffer too much. But God knows I've suffered since.' She jabbed herself in the chest again.

'I took time off work, didn't divulge why, it had nothing to do with anyone else. Then when I came back it was as if the scales had fallen from my eyes. I saw things so clearly for the first time ever. I realised how futile the job was. That it meant nothing. All the time I spent trying to make a difference and furthering my career should have been spent with *her*.'

Alison was clearly wracked with grief. She had paled despite the situation and sweltering heat.

'I... I'm so sorry. I don't know what to say. But...'

'NO! Listen to me. You need to understand why I've done all this. For Louisa.' She shuddered with emotion. 'Have you ever been in love? I mean real love. Ever found your soulmate?'

Maya shook her head. Alison was showing an intensity and passion that was visceral. 'Then you don't know how wonderful and how fucking painful it can be. We were a cliché. You could say we met at work. Louisa used to work for Celeste. The first time I saw her when we raided the brothel... It was love at first sight. I did everything I could to help and support her. I got her away from that bitch. That woman ruined so many lives.'

'So, she didn't jump, you pushed her,' said Maya.

'Correct. I made her write that note and then she took me for a tour of her home. Couldn't wait to show it off. She was smacked off her tits, she'd been drinking and snorting coke like it was going out of fashion. She thought I was there because I wanted to sleep with her. Once we were outside on the roof terrace, all it took was one little push. Perfect.'

'And the others?'

'Not as satisfying as Celeste. I regret that Karl Gorman didn't suffer more. I persuaded him to let me in as I told him I was interested in taking him on as an informer against Donnelly and Nowak. He bit my hand off at the thought of getting a steady payout from the cops rather than actually having to work to earn the crumbs Donnelly was throwing his way.'

'Cheeky fuckin' grass,' mumbled Aiden. The other two ignored him as if he wasn't even there.

'Anyway, I talked my way in with a bottle of vodka, and, when he wasn't looking I slipped some GHB into his drink. It's amazing what you can acquire from the property store, you know? He sat at the kitchen table while I offered to start cleaning the kitchen up for him. I was surprised when he told me he had a tea towel in his drawer, but once he'd passed out, I used it to cover his nose and mouth until he stopped breathing. It was surprisingly easy. Disappointingly so. As he was so out of it, he didn't put up a struggle so there was no sign of trauma at the PM.'

'The tea towel gave you away. I *knew* there was something wrong. What about Jim Baron?'

Alison snorted with disgust. 'That silly fat bastard finished himself off in the end. He got himself so wound up when he saw me; he dropped dead with a bloody heart attack. Can you imagine? At least I knew Geoffrey Doran suffered, so that's some compensation.'

'The hit and run?'

'Yeah, I was a bit reckless with hindsight, but it got the job done.'

'You were reckless with Posner too. Did you know you'd been seen?'

'Only when I came in on nights and DI Redford did the handover. They hadn't started interviewing the shoplifter because he was rattling, and they were waiting for him to see the nurse. I managed to convince him he'd be out quicker if he retracted his comments. Fortunately, he didn't recognise me because I had my hood up at the time. But you're right. I was sloppy.'

'Surely you knew you weren't going to get away with it?' Maya said. 'It was only going to be a matter of time before someone else realised all these deaths weren't just coincidence. How were you planning on explaining it?'

She thought she could detect the sound of a siren approaching in the distance. If only she could keep Alison talking and distracted, then perhaps she and Donnelly had a chance of getting out of this situation alive.

84

Lurch had left his flat straight after Maya. He had hurriedly packed a bag before heading over to Aiden's place. Once inside, he accessed the safe, which he knew held a substantial amount of cash. The safe also housed fake passports and other documents for himself, Aiden and Piotr. Despite his many faults, Aiden had always been prudent. Although he had never had any materialistic needs or a desire for cash in the past, Lurch knew money meant freedom. He squirrelled away the sizeable nest egg and new documentation.

Finally, Lurch carefully placed the bloodstained hammer and towel, which he had used during the murder of Ryan Johnson, into the loft where he knew the police would find it. Mimicking Aiden, he tapped the side of his nose with his forefinger as he muttered the words 'forensic insurance'. Lurch knew Aiden and Piotr mocked him for his stupidity, but he liked to think he had picked up a couple of tricks in the time he had worked with them both.

The thought of being incarcerated for the murder of Ryan Johnson terrified him. The thought of a lengthy prison sentence would be like returning to his formative years in the children's home. He had been institutionalised enough to last him a lifetime and he knew that a prison stretch would be worse than a death sentence.

All the years of doing the following without being seen, had paid off. He left Aiden's house without being spotted. He was ready to do what Maya had suggested. He was going to disappear and start a new life where no one would know him. He was going to live the rest of his life being the best person he could be and helping others. He would repent. And preferably somewhere warm, where every evening, the sunset would turn the sky the colour of salmon.

85

Maya was sure the sirens were getting closer, although Alison showed no signs of having heard them. Yet.

'I never expected to get away with all this,' answered Alison, waving her arm in Donnelly's direction. 'I'm neither stupid nor naïve.'

'So, what did you think was going to happen? Did you think you could just kill one last piece of shit and then carry on as normal?'

'Hey!' said Donnelly defensively.

'I've done what I needed to do. I had to compensate for all the wasted time I should have had with Louisa.' She paused for a moment, deep in thought. 'It hasn't all just been for her. It was for the others too. For all the victims and their families. I've been delivering real justice. I've been giving a death sentence to all those offenders who have stolen precious time off me and *never* served enough of their own.

'They never suffered enough for their victims and I couldn't go to my grave carrying that knowledge. Life comes with a price, Maya. I appointed myself the job of Grim Reaper. Interesting career change, don't you think? But still very fitting and well deserved.'

The sirens were noticeable now, growing closer. Alison smiled and nodded her head, indicating that she had heard them too.

'You're going to be hugely successful in your career, Maya. Just learn from my mistakes and make sure you also spend time with your loved ones. You need to make sure you...'

Alison stopped mid-sentence as she grimaced. She swooned slightly, the hand she was clutching the gun in dropped heavily to her side. She squeezed her eyes shut as she appeared to wince in pain.

'Ma'am? Alison...' Concerned, Maya stepped away from Donnelly and reached for her other hand as Alison opened her eyes. A ghost of a smile lingered on her lips. Her ashen face caused Maya real cause for concern, and she was glad to hear the sirens growing ever closer.

Suddenly, Alison gripped hold of Maya's hand tightly. She twisted Maya's arm in such a way that she was pinned in a hold against the side of Alison's body. Stunned by the sudden movement and unexpected display of strength, Maya was unable to relinquish the hold on her and she could only watch in horror as Alison raised the gun and shot Aiden Donnelly in the chest.

Within a split second, Alison shoved Maya away from her.

Maya fell to the floor, sickened by the red mist which filled her vision. She felt Donnelly's blood moisten her skin. She turned towards Alison and her mouth opened in a perfect O.

'I'm going to be with Louisa.' Smiling almost apologetically at Maya, Alison shoved the gun into her own mouth. Maya screamed as she squeezed the trigger again. The second deafening bang was accompanied by another cloud of fine red mist which joined the dancing dust motes drifting through the air of the fetid container.

Alison's body dropped to the floor like a stone. Maya screamed in horror as the container doors burst open.

86

Maya peered through the keyhole before opening the door. It was a futile effort as she couldn't even see Kym and Chris because of the huge bouquets of flowers he was carrying. Smiling, she removed the safety chains and beckoned them both in.

'Here,' Chris sneezed as he handed her his bunch, 'take them, me eyes are bloody streaming. Kettle on?'

Maya laughed. 'Obviously, and there's biscuits. Go on through, make yourself at home as usual.' He stooped to kiss her on the way past and headed for the kitchen. Chris had been true to his word on the day he had offered his friendship to Maya after Gorman's post-mortem. There'd hardly been a day since Alison Mitton's death that he hadn't been in touch with Maya. He had told her about the journal they had found at Alison's house. In it, she had kept a detailed record of all the killings. Chris was a good friend and a frequent, welcome guest.

'It's good to see you,' said Kym as she, too, kissed her on the cheek. Maya raised an eyebrow as she admired the flowers.

'Have you been to Kew Gardens?'

Kym laughed before whispering conspiratorially, 'Chris

bought them but insists they're off all of us. You know he doesn't like to confess to being too much of a softy.' Maya smiled at Kym and led her into the lounge where she sank into the sofa.

'So, please put me out of my misery. What did top office say?'

Kym sat up seriously. 'You've been given an official warning for not disclosing your relationship with Naylor...'

Maya slumped forwards, her head in her hands and gave a little scream.

'But...' Kym was smiling now, 'they have recognised the mitigating circumstances and also thoroughly commended you for working out and pursuing a link into the chain of sudden deaths that subsequently would have gone undetected.'

Kym sighed. 'Despite the fact you broke countless rules in the process, they're happy you've completed your probation period and you're officially stuck with us.'

'Oh, thank God.' The relief was palpable, and Maya sank back into the chair.

'I for one am very, very glad you're staying. And that you're in one piece... I can't imagine...' Maya was shocked to see Kym's eyes brim with tears as she choked back the words she couldn't bring herself to speak.

The moment was broken as Chris bumbled into the room haphazardly carrying brews and biscuits on a tray. He slopped the offerings onto the coffee table before grabbing a biscuit and sinking down next to Maya.

'So, how's counselling going then? All that touchy-feely bollocks helping, is it?'

Kym opened her mouth to chastise Chris, but Maya belly laughed. It was so good to see him and be in the presence of his brusque normality. She would rather that than have people tiptoeing around her, scared to say or do the wrong thing.

'Yeah, it's helping a lot actually. The counsellor is great.'

'Good stuff. So, when are you planning to come back to

work? I mean the overtime's handy, but I'm bloody knackered. I'm covering Andy's shifts as well as yours.'

Maya leant forward eagerly. 'Has there been any news on Andy?'

Kym tried unsuccessfully to suppress a grin. 'Yes, actually. He's been charged with perverting the course of justice amongst other offences. It's looking highly likely he'll be serving a custodial sentence. I believe he's not contesting anything and is pleading guilty.'

Chris opened his mouth to begin his usual foul-mouthed tirade as to what he thought of Andy, but Maya was quick to silence him with a biscuit. It was nothing she'd not heard dozens of times before. She wanted to concentrate on her good news, not have it tainted by thoughts of Andy.

A couple of hours later, as she waved Kym and Chris off, Maya was pleasantly surprised to realise she felt the most relaxed and normal than she had in ages. Things would never be quite the same again. They couldn't possibly be after what she had witnessed, but she had her job, her family and friends. And with the continued support from her counsellor, she had her sanity.

Maya reached for her phone so she could ring Dominique and let her know the outcome from top office. Mama would be as overjoyed as she was to know that her job was safe. To hear that she could keep the career that meant so much to her. As she glanced at the display, she noticed a missed call and a text from Spence. She smiled to herself. Just the sight of his name gave her a warm, tingling sensation in the pit of her stomach. Her instincts were telling her that everything was going to be okay. Life was good. And it was all ahead of her, ready for living.

THE END

ACKNOWLEDGEMENTS

Firstly, huge thanks to all the team at Bloodhound Books for accepting Maya and I into the kennels. It was a proud moment when I held a published version of my non-fiction book, The Real CSI: A Forensic Handbook for Crime Writers for the first time, but I always said I wouldn't feel like a real author until I published my first work of fiction. This is a childhood dream come true, so thanks to Betsy for taking on the Maya Barton trilogy.

Thank you to friends and family who continue to support me. Especially my early readers for their time and constructive criticism. To Lindsy Slamon for her endless support and for crime-scene-managing my murder scenes. It's a different challenge writing a fictional murder scene than it is to investigate a real one! To Graham Bartlett, author and police advisor, for his SIO expertise and keen eye. To Eve Seymour for her editorial skills on an early draft of *Definitely Dead*, and her invaluable writing advice. To CJ Skuse, an author whose work I hugely admire, who was kind enough to take the time to read and comment on an early draft.

Much love to my writing friends who I've met along the way,

either on courses or at festivals, for your friendship, encouragement and social media shares. Also, to my workmates and colleagues whose hilarious banter and anecdotes provides me with an endless source of inspiration, none of which, unfortunately, is suitable for publication.

Special thanks go to Alice for taking the time to share her experience of being a mixed-race female with me. Her experiences and insight have not only been educational but invaluable in shaping Maya's character.

And finally, my eternal thanks to Gary, Sophie and Elissa for all your love and support. It would have been easier to write at times without the constant percussion of dropped iPads, Roblox and Tik Tok dances, but I consider it character building. Seriously, I could never have achieved any of this without the three of you helping and supporting me, especially Gary, my very own Annie Wilkes. I love you.

A NOTE FROM THE PUBLISHER

Thank you for reading this book. If you enjoyed it please do consider leaving a review on Amazon to help others find it too.

We hate typos. All of our books have been rigorously edited and proofread, but sometimes mistakes do slip through. If you have spotted a typo, please do let us know and we can get it amended within hours.

info@bloodhoundbooks.com

Printed in Great Britain
by Amazon

63626863R00215